What once was

Prophet Motive

is now

FREEBURG

By **Dan Harkins**

(with Saul McGinty Jr.)

BALBOA.
PRESS
A DIVISION OF HAY HOUSE

Balboa Press books may be ordered through booksellers or by contacting:

Balboa Press
A Division of Hay House
1663 Liberty Drive
Bloomington, IN 47403
www.balboapress.com
1 (877) 407-4847

Print information available on the last page.

ISBN: 978-1-5043-9198-6 (sc)
ISBN: 978-1-5043-9200-6 (hc)
ISBN: 978-1-5043-9199-3 (e)

Library of Congress Control Number: 2018902247

Balboa Press rev. date: 10/19/2018

For my babies – Derek, Banyan, and Isabel – and theirs...

"Finally, the official historical account of the very first attempt at bringing true equality and freedom to the American people through the mandate to vote."

-The Freeburg Eagle editorial board

"Be a lamp unto them who walk in darkness, a joy to the sorrowful, a sea for the thirsty, a haven for the distressed, an upholder and defender of the victim of oppression."
— *Bahá'u'lláh*, *Messenger of Baha'i*

"Money is the barometer of a society's virtue."
— *Ayn Rand*, *Messenger of Money*

"It would be transformative if everybody voted. That would counteract money more than anything."
— *Barack Obama*, *Cleveland City Club, March 18, 2015*

Chapter 1

WHEREAS, on this [25ᵗʰ day of May, REDACTED], Freeburg's voters will be called to ease their clutch on reins that have for too long steered our liberty toward apathy and fear. By doing so, we hope to forge a truly democratic path that aims us closer to society of, by and for all people, for which (almost; see Addendum A) every voice will be accounted, inclined to speak, and finally heard.

E veryone besides the corpse was voting suicide. Even those who'd only caught the gist on backyard breezes — him lying there all zapped on standard-issue VA meds, the wrists cut deep and sure, the frozen grin that spoke of sinful, painless satisfaction — even they just had to share their truth of how these things will often go: "Oh son, sometimes the end comes long before the heart is ready to believe." *Of course.* Of course, those privy to particulars, the little things that scream and stink, had no better explanation. All that loony talk of being watched just sealed their shame and his disgrace. *Silly to think,* the stares all said. *Look at the facts, the smile.* I did. The facts can lie or hide and do. For knowing that, at least remembering I'd known it once and should again, I'll take with pride not just the credit but the blame. My father can't.

Investigators press-released the news a few weeks into knowing all along: The coroner, with work to do and news to make that had to do with lives that didn't want to end, could see no other way. The paper was respectful, "his" paper; he "sadly took his life at home," the new obituary writer wrote of his/her/its veteran predecessor in the notice buried deep and gray without a mugshot in the mass grave of the day's departed. The slip into subjective might have earned him/her/it a dismissive rebuke by red-penning ("SAYS WHO IT WAS SAD?!"), but it's just as likely no one even bothered to notice. Until now. Who could have known the mistake would become almost prophetic, a blind pass by a soul mate we're not ready yet to meet? I speak now, of course, in the presence of future angels, but at the time even I had no choice but to nod in agreement with every round of clichéd condolences, every histrionic gaze down at the floor, that, without peer, without question, my old man was, above anything else, one illuminating idiot of a know-it-all whack-job, one who'd grown so untrusting that he couldn't even trust himself. I should know. I'd lived there, too.

Seven years had passed. That much dust. But still he hadn't thought in that dismantled brain of his to leave the house where all his living kin – just me, my Mom, and now-famous sister — had left him to stew in the rou of his (out)rage, which, with equal parts failure and hygienic neglect, in no time had steeped to reek like all those corpses he'd buried in unreadable words. How couldn't he have killed himself? That's all anyone was trying to say. Oh, *fine*: I'd thought it, too: He must have done it: It's what I would have done: It's what I almost did: The hero-wuss had left behind a testament without a will: He'd die a mystery that stank of myth. I'd never loathed him more completely or blamed him for more. Such was the bleakness of my own expectations.

I even volunteered to throw the rest of him away.

My mother wouldn't do it, though I suspect she'd really wanted to and still was living close, a town away in creepy-cozy Cassadaga. It's a haven there made just so to suit her demon-swirling ilk, its portent quaint yet concentrated, supermarket-style. In nearly every creaky house can still be found a psychic with a blog and Twitter feed who's stirring souls and selling dreams. My mother's built a healthy living there. She put two children through college with the proceeds and now is sought for counsel by her peers, some barrel-bellied detectives, the occasional cold-case cable show, and a growing number of Botox experiments from my sister's set. (You'd know them if I named them, but you shouldn't, so I won't.)

Though few who know her would deny that my mother has evolved beyond the mere side-show mindfuckery of her occupation's roots, and while her aims may in fact be wholly empathetic and often eerily insightful, these types of accolades will never apply to this type of historical endeavor, not even for the yellowist of unofficial biographies. Nevertheless, with my father's unplanned-for posthumous acclaim, which she'd prefer to call his "infamy", it's been my mother's word and none other's on his "cracked egg of a rotten life" (December 2017, www. accidentalfame.com).

No historian, much less one with feelings for the subject like myself, could ever swallow a story that steeped in sour grapes; in fact, among the 64.7 percent of U.S. adults (+-0.02 percent) who recently voiced their wish to send my father off with something more than the middle finger, a mere 0.23 percent (+-0.0079 percent) have ever had anything to do with chronicling, teaching or even predicting official history. That means my family gets to make it.

Excuse the poetics of my writer-for-hire, but it's clear enough by now to be conventional wisdom and thereby subject to whimsy that the base of my father's life grew to become much broader than only his basest of ways, sprouting from notice in a cloud of fecund stank to become more aware of the weight of the world than most. My mother, who prefers to describe this metamorphosis as "bacterial," has one theory as to its origin: "the lucky fucker factor" (http://mediumlegends.com).

Maybe; maybe not. She frames the world in light or darkness, rarely both, and certainly not both at once, and I suspect it cuts for her the profile that her clients keep coming with their checkbooks to expect, but the gray between is really where we live our lives and die. And so with awe I hold the People's gift to shed a more revealing light across both sides and deep within the gnarly roots of this long-beleaguered family tree. How else to fertilize and bring to bloom the only seed my father ever planted as a man outside my mother, the one he left for me to find? But smile, you cliff-hung legions only hungry for escape. The bulk of this true tale is muddied up by silly, tragic, sad mistakes, from which my father never thought a weed much less this whole new breed of tree would grow and grow to shade us all.

* * *

It was about time. About time standing still. As it flew by too fast. I hadn't visited Cassadaga in two years, Freeburg, as I've said, in seven, but it'd started to feel more like yesterday or eons ago, neither of which felt right. Then the phone rang. I launched with the power of cat physics from the couch.

I knew it was my Mom — who else was it ever anymore? — but not with the usual why. She always waits at least a week between calls, allegedly so "we can live some life worth talking 'bout," and it's always close to midnight when she does it, purportedly so "maybe we can dream about each other's lives and shit." I picked up the cordless from the coffee table and looked at my watch. Another ring, which made me flinch despite the first ring's warning. What made me knot my brow? She'd say I had a premonition; I'd say she had some life to share that couldn't wait. It was eight-forty-something on a Monday, no more than a few days after we'd just bored each other to sleep, and no one I'd know was celebrating a birthday, childbirth, divorce, or anything but an astrologically humdrum alignment of constellations. I let it ring four times, unliving more life, before I let her tell me what it was I felt was maybe dread or finally the gift she'd given.

"Mom?" She waited, not like her. "Mom. I smell your breath." No giggle either. "Mom?"

"Honey, your father, he..." She cut herself off, also not her way, but I'd heard enough to sit back down and smile, relieved.

"My who?"

"Your father, son ... he's finally done it." In her voice was concern, no doubt for me, all those unanswered questions, but there was mostly inconvenience and not a flicker of the shock I felt. I didn't ask her how. I didn't want to know. Not yet. She knew as much, so I let her fill the space with time, so many meaningless details that I could sense that she was stalling not just for me but for both of us. She'd taken an hour to call me, ending first a "big séance" with two hardy Saskatchewan women who'd flown in to Orlando, rented a Continental, and ignored all the amusement parks in a beeline for the place I think of as my childhood home, where they hoped to speak once more with their father, who'd recently died of old age without telling them how much he loved them for the millionth time. Lost in kid-listening, her shoptalk made me think to smile, which is when I realized I hadn't stopped since learning only he was gone. I started feeling as unburdened as my mother sounded. And painfully guilty. Then she told me the rest, enough.

"...and wouldn't you know that fucker was grinning ... grinning right out the window at all that world he never gave more than two squirts about." Saved for last, this seemed to be the image she most wanted and dreaded to share. A quiver in the space between the words she'd repeated that painted on his dying smile to let me pretend to hear the rasp of someone who'd been crying and stopped, or who'd stopped herself from crying, but since I haven't heard or seen or heard about my mother crying since leaving Freeburg, it's far more likely she'd just paused to swallow another bite of hoagie or gulp of smoke.

Then that gulf emerged through a clearing of quiet that's always made one of us smirk when the other was serious. As is her job, she was quick to mark her connection to the event: "I know what you're gonna say, but I just knew what that old bitch Arbuckle was gonna say as soon as I picked up the phone. I knew something sinister was coming. With him. From there." As is my job, I was resistant to the whiff of hobunk: "Sinister, you say?" I was the morgue attendant innocently making fun of all the corpses in my care just to survive another day surrounded by death. "Huh. Of course you have to consider the interference out there in the world, all that EMF effing up the ether. I mean, really:

You got screams of bloody murder coming out of every shadow day and night, right? Shit. What ends up warbling down your feelers might just be what's in the neighborhood. You ever think..."

"Don't yank my chains like that, boy. I know some things, some things you don't."

"Sorry," I told her. "I know." I did and didn't. She sniggered but didn't speak. I could think of nothing better than to keep trying to prove my point. I ruffled a nearby stack of unreturned student journals, a yearly trick I'd been taught to keep an elite few of them guessing about why I hadn't returned theirs when everyone else got theirs back before summer started. I pretended to scan the daily headlines like a newscaster getting makeup on. "Let's see here above the fold: Well, it's another bumper crop for Freeburg first-responders. Any of these get through, Mom?" She let me go. "Here's a kid got Kimbo-Sliced into the coroner's office for lampin' as an independent apothecary on the wrong corner. No? Let's see ... oh, here's some: murder-suicide ruled incest cover-up. Robbery-gone-rape still murder-one cold-case. Trailer-park cuckold turns prison-bitch snitch. Wait..."

"Saul." Under ordinary circumstances this would be when she would have given up with enough of a laugh to concede a middle ground and I would have said something respectful to show that her mysteries, though lacking in underlying attribution, could still excite me, but we both had demons to deal with, me to suppress and her to release.

"Mom, I just don't think..."

"Boy." This time some teacher in the tone. "Nobody's buying tickets today. I'm sorry, son. It's gonna feel better when it's all behind us."

"I'm just saying it'd be nearsighted, Mom, to..." I told myself not to even think about trying not to cry.

"Saul. Please. It's okay. I'm not asking you to believe me and I can't tell you how I know it, but believe this: I hadn't thought of that turd for years before today. Guess I'm just a quack that managed to pinch enough pennies to set both her kids up with *lives*."

I listened to her breathing. It didn't sound right to be hearing it force her to stop praddling on. Had she been pacing the floors or was she just blobbed into a chair? I felt guilty for picking on her. Who did I sound like? And still I couldn't help but form the same clichéd picture in my head that was far too outlandish to be fair but was oddly comforting in times of adolescent desolation. After all she'd done to keep me loving her, all I could do was paint her into a gypsy's wagon down under a bridge by the riverside, using those fat linebacker's hands in the glinty drag of costume jewelry to tug at a sail's worth of shawl and coax another batch of minutiae from a faux-crystal ball, to point at flecks of light in ghost-tour photographs as proof of what my knowledge would never let me know for sure, beckon with the whorls of her hypnotist fingers every sideshow spectator with a gambling heart into the fold of her wandering wagon. It was only for a few formative years that she'd been talked into plying her trade in a carnival setting, but I could still hear the barker's words: *"Witness Broomhilda! Our Seer of Seeecrets! Behold her third eye from its perch on the table! Fear only the unknown, your own! Leave the kids at the Fun House and your demons right here! For ten little tickets, ten monumental minutes! Your future unmasked! You, young man! Oh, it's you Saul. Would you get the hell out of here, kid!?"*

"Saul!" She was back and so was I, on a level that forced me to listen as a son and not a skeptic. I wiped at my eyes and didn't feel any tears.

"Present."

"True to form, huh? Selfish to the very end."

"Worst brain-damaged father ever."

"Couldn't think of anything past that chipped skull of his. *Somebody else'll clean up all this shit. Fuck it all!* But ain't no Oxy cleaning up that mess. That's dickwad's for all eternity."

"Mom."

"No."

"It's okay."

"No."

7

"Yes, Mom. I'm cleaning up that mess. I think I left some T-shirts over there I gotta grab anyway."

"Wait. But. Well, I don't..." I still am inclined to presume that all this was part of some larger plot that had finally reached its zenith and was leaving her speechless out of pure joy that it'd gone off so well. I knew, at the very least, that she'd stopped to smile, perhaps stymied by what some would guess was a welling of pride if not the tears she'd long ago emptied out.

"Tomorrow. I love you, okay?" As if she didn't know she was at that point all I had left to love. I was proud of myself, and I didn't want to ruin it by staying on the phone and potentially breaking down. As quickly as each new thought arrived, I delivered it: "I actually gotta run. I got a tennis, game. With a neighbor, a neighbor-*friend*. She's a she. I'm, ah, starting to actually not hate her." This kept her quiet long enough for me to hang up with a "... love ya!"

I tallied up the day's accounts, pulled my shoulders back, manufactured a chest with a painful dollop of air and looked around a living room that felt like someone else's, maybe even a guy brining people parts for head cheese in the hallway closet. I sunk back to slumping on the couch. It wasn't just the string of lies I'd just told the psychic who knew better or the unlived life they tried to gussy up. It was everything I felt before the call now sharing space with everything after. The leaning towers of overread books, mocking the order and color of bookshelves and knick-knacks, cast longer shadows now. The space around the television, already too small for its slot in the entertainment center, now gaped with darker shadows. I closed my eyes, but it didn't help. The seconds on the plastibrass wall clock left behind by the last tenant were ticking too loudly, too quickly, so I willed them quieter, slower, but then they were silent, unmoving. You play a tennis *match*, I told myself, hurling the cordless into pieces against the living room wall, which I had to note didn't even scratch much less dent with the contact. I lolled deeper on the couch and swooned into the same haphazard position I found myself the next afternoon when I awoke feeling overly rested and uncommonly resolute. I actually smiled then grimaced at how sinister that must have made me look to my own set of ghosts. I sat up with what was undoubtedly a purpose.

Though I don't pretend to have sunk to as lowly a state as our subject, I'd never felt such loneliness for so long a stretch. I hadn't refilled any of my meds for months; not even the good ones felt effective. The summer was almost over, and I'd be returning in less than a month to greet a fresh red tide of students with the same disconsolate lesson plan and wintry pallor more blue than pink. But still, somehow, wading through the nostalgia of my mother's interminable shoptalk, I'd come to grips with some resolve that some may be inclined to call hope: No better place existed, no better memories needed purging, than there and those to remind me that at least I'd gone somewhere in life and might again. That's all I had to work with then. It would last me long enough to get me out the door.

I didn't even flinch this time when my newfangled "flip-phone" rang from the bedroom with the promise of what I thought I needed most: escape. On the way to answer it, I stepped out of the basketball shorts I'd been wearing, potentially for weeks, without interrupting my stride, which some might have playfully described as a gait. Who *was* I?

"I'mpackingI'mpacking," I said, pulling open the bedroom closet and scanning the carpet for shoes that matched. I flung the smallest piece of my half of the wedding luggage onto the bed I rarely slept in and flipped it open. A few grade-schoolers bouncing a basketball past the window peered over and let me know by their sudden burst into a jog that I should probably close the blinds. I sunk into the shadows and pulled a new pair of shorts out of the pile of laundry in the corner of the room.

"That man gave me the willies, Boog, and they're still in there like a cancer," said the new-age witch through my head, machine-gun blasts of empty air. "Soul cancer is what. Stage, what? Six or some shit?"

"I'm a man now, Mom. It's Goob."

"I try to shake the shivers, honey, really I do. But there they are. Rar." A shiver. "See that? Saul, see?" She giggled but really meant for me to know she'd shivered.

"No, Mom. I didn't. But I'll take your account as proof." I emptied a drawer of holey socks into the suitcase, not one of them paired, then poured them out of the suitcase onto the floor, deciding not to wear any for the rest of the summer. Live a little. "You gonna be alright?"

"The place still haunts me is all. Stink an'all that misery in there. Skunky funk is all. Day in and out, baby: Thousands of them little nothing stories a'his, and every last one's got some little sliver of soul clinging on for some kind of dignity you know ain't never comin'. They're some angry little fuckers up in there, Goob, and not for shagiggles."

"Uh-huh." Metaphorically at least, she had a point.

"Your Daddy was a demon factory, boy, churning out them stories every day so frackin' boring even the survivors wouldn't even wanna read 'em through. Who's clipping out that shit for the scrapbook? Ugh. So effing sad." Another shiver (which I somehow saw this time). "How you fold your arms over your chest and let old formaldehyde fingers over here press your face into some fake Chicklet smile with that kind of truth left out there with the living? John Somebody was born there and died here. He was too old. Jane Nobody was born here and died there. She was too young. He belonged to clubs, and a whole bunch of people in his family are still alive. She didn't seem to do shit and didn't have much in the way of anybody to visit for the holidays. Who can read a life story, their own life story, being told via fill-in-the-fargin'-blanks? Right? So that's the send off. And then what? The fuckers scream, Saul. Or try to scream, and when they find out they can't, they start looking for folks to do all the screaming for 'em."

The explanation, though colorful, was nevertheless lacking for my tastes. "So things are gonna stink," I said, wadding up every pair of shorts I could find into a ball and three-pointing it into the suitcase. "And then of course what can only be described as poltergeists, but poltergeists who've been silenced by fate and crushed by an avalanche of regret, are gonna be pooling every scrap of hoodoo at their formless disposal to try and scare me into screaming the screams they can't scream themselves? Check and check."

I heard the laugh she fought to keep down. "Shmuck it up all you like, Goob, but I can smell every room as we speak. I can taste it, how sour that place is by now. So shit, put out a good scream as soon as you get in there. The fuck not?"

"Should come natural," I said. "Whatever it takes, I'm getting that fucking security deposit."

(This was how most of us all cursed back then.)

I finished packing with one hand, bit at spare fingernail on the other, and somehow managed to keep the phone wedged between my shoulder and cheek as my mother kept feeding me my briefing in little staccato bursts. I came to a thought of the long stale strands of popcorn garland that my father would unwind meticulously from the brittle-browned pine tree on the first day of every February, never a day before, after which he'd devour every tasteless rubbery morsel with a thankful grin and the same verbatim excuse that our dumbfounded glares would solicit for as long as our Christmases there lasted: "We gotta kill a tree *and* all this fucking corn every year, too?" Sound retard logic there, from the maker of each year's new string of popcorn garland.

"...it's, it's purgatory in a box, boy. Dreadful things. And lookey now: Can't even *fathom* what now, baby, you ... you better ... baby, well, you...."

"I'm perfect for this, Mom," I said, sort of believing it, as I looked in drawers I'd never opened for underwear I'd stopped wearing a few years before. Who would know? "He's dead, Ma. Always has been, really." I sighed a real sigh, then she did.

"Right? But Saul, now..."

"You'd think you two'd get along now, though. You could prove you were always right about, all the, you know. And maybe he'd find a way to fess up to how utterly vapid he always was about just about everything that ever mattered. I mean..."

"You take that know-it-all tongue off auto-pilot and *shut*. You don't even know what you're dealing with here, boy." She could handle me disparaging him all I wanted, but I'd eased right back into yesterday's line. It was time to pretend to listen again, to defer to the master. "That's way too flip a tone to be bringin' down here. Hear? *Here?* Fuuuuh..."

"Fuuuuuh..."

"Listen, boy: You open up them windows, turn on all the fans, if that's what's still there. Might be some kind of rotating tin-foil shields by now. And crank some music up. Don't need to be analyzing every rat turd hits the floor. And, oh. *Oh!* Don't you just start clearing out the place all willy-nilly from the dark corners on up and out the door and all that."

"Um. I'm not really sure I..."

"Just don't. And don't ask." I didn't. "And it's been my experience, if you wanna know, Boog, that ... Goob?"

"That..." Gone was much of the resolve I'd felt just minutes before. I couldn't help but ponder the inevitable: how cluttered with my mother's ministrations every step of this trip for meaning would be. By then, I'd taken on more than my share of our culture of stories, day in and out like the rest of us. I knew the arc my journey would have to take if, in the end, it could ever be considered a hero's. At some point, perhaps to lessen the morosity of the situation, I even started thinking of the trip in more archaic and prosaic terms, which, though only in my head, I'll admit sounded less like Chaucer and more like Benny Hill. As my mother droned on, I perked up to the sound of my own Parzival: *Ye of the protagonists* (me talking to me), *I beseech thy return to whence thou comest so thine foolhardy father, he of the liverish and besmirched disposition, may be interred and forsworn, burnishing for all due progeny the sacrosanctity of the McGinty crest and securing for the paupery of Freeburgertown its woebegotten Grail. At haste!*

"Saul. Saul, this is important."

"That's why I can't do anything but wonder what you're going to say next. I'm fascinated over here."

"Hardyhar, ghoul. All I'm trying to say here is that whatever you think is gonna happen's gonna be the last thing that will.

Hear? And whatever it is you least expect's gonna be what ends up drawing you into finally knowing what the hell..."

"Slow down. I'm trying to get all this down."

"You little stain. Now zip and ..."

I figured that my mother would be inexhaustible. The frequency of her calls would go from predictable and nonchalant to incessant and urgent. I knew she'd soon find a way to start in about her Aunt Susan, how she'd killed herself back in the 1960s, "and at least took that cheating-ass boyfriend of hers along." She'd bring it up for the same reason she always had — to flash the badge. Before despair had soiled her otherwise insouciant disposition, Aunt Susan purportedly bestowed upon my mother the wherewithal needed not only to speak with the dead but to prosper from it. To diversify her portfolio, after Aunt Susan died, my mother picked up Tarot, crystals, astronomy reading. She read books about soothsaying. She memorized the *I Ching* and learned how to cast its divining stalks and make those faces that portend unfathomable mysteries. I don't know how she had time, since by then it's claimed she'd begun hearing all manner of voices all day, at random ... voices with whom she'd share hard questions and celebratory answers. With all that ammunition, you'd think she could have reached Aunt Susan on the other side, or at least have agreed to tag along with me on this final trip to Dad's, a hand on my collar to keep me from running scared. In any case, she'd be bouncing all this off her son, hoping, as has always been her wont, that some would stick and make me one of her believers. (No matter how much I love that woman, I'll probably have to die first.)

"With this kind of ... thing, son, well, your father's made a creep's house haunted too, or he could have ... at least ... well ... I know you don't believe in much, Saul, but can you at least understand how he might still be, well..."

I kept packing. I'd thought of that but only in terms of how I'd disprove the possibility. What was belief to me by then? I still lived, if that's what dying's called, on the other side of a country I'd grown to loathe, already through with a career teaching history that felt too much like school again. I was finished with Ohio chills that never left my bones, snuffed by Rebecca, two seasons before, at a New Year's Eve party no less, to something less than ash. To nothing. All my friendships had morphed into passing niceties, lies about being too busy for a drink after work. No wonder all our friends were really just her friends now. I'd become paralyzed, obsessed with thinking about what my life would end up looking like at middle age, there with the crest of all I'd learned at my back and so much teaching left ahead. I wasn't prepared for all this starting over.

I'd once thought coming down was when the breezes came, the legs could rest, but coming down from where I'd gone up until that point in my life felt more like the slide of trash down the chute. Launched as a boy from such tenuous myth-laden coordinates, it should come as no surprise that, with military exactitude, the early stirrings of a liberal arts education would quickly ease me into pursuing a profession that seemed grounded in the holiness of Fact, one in which I at least could pretend to be an atom bomb of rage for Truth and Hope. Only this projectile was aimed like many of my classmates at an all-together eviler axis of American targets — those in the business of business-as-usual juggling Peace and Freedom and Equality with greed and war and pit-bull patriotic pride. For a time, all that power hadn't intimidated me. I and ours would stoke the embers of a bygone era back to life, and we wouldn't need a single stick from Woodstock's nest to do it. I left my black rooms at home behind seeking light that seemed to find me in blinding waves. I'd hid behind a hippie's mask. In months, I'd grown an unruly beard, a patchy orange scruff I'd yank and stroke as I pored through Howard Zinn's *A People's History*... like an angry rebel soldier learning how to strip my weapon down, pushing manifestoes on my college squad from Majors General Socrates and Chomsky, Sergeants Major Engels and Marx. We weren't socialist or freedom-fighters or anarchist or any of that, though. We were better defined by what we were against: anti-fascist; anti-war; anti-greed; anti-lie; anti-asshole. By sophomore year, I'd lost my virginity to several girls and let my hair clump into egg-yolked dreads that fell like orange daggers to my shoulders, while I memorized *On Liberty* and sometimes even felt drawn to recite it like a for-credit monologue to seas of soulless faces in the food court, in the commons. I lost some friends that way but gained a few who never left. (Until they did, of course. Where are all of you now?)

The more I learned, the more I saw the battle lines that had been drawn, the more it hurt to learn. But the glare of it all was blinding, too bright, I thought, for so many not to see it, to despise it. So many channels now, I guessed, so much more to discuss instead of what was dying to be said. It isn't hyperbole to say that my hunger for a better world, a true and lasting peace that too many professors still seem to dote upon as nothing less than utopian dreaming, became a warlike drive, devoid of numb vicissitudes, drilled into place. I trained my gut for how they fought to keep all peaceful movements down: canteen brimming with viscous chow from the vegetarian tradition and a dog-eared chemistry book that twice had been confiscated by my dorm's RA and twice had been stolen back by stealthier means, but in the process I'd learned to build purportedly mind-enobling compounds that I'd hoped could perhaps defuse the bomb inside my brain about to blow. It worked in some very concrete, educational ways, until, of course, it didn't at all (reference Wolfe's *Electric Kool-Aid Acid Test*). It all earned me like-minded legions to the cause, though. An army grew as molecules compounded into mystic manna. My letters home — what letters home? I kept my pen aimed at those who would *Abuse Your Illusions* of societal order, took a torch to the pigs in thee olde *Animal Farm* and pierced holes all through Paine's white-bread *Common Sense*. I inhaled AND exhaled and I kept my dharma flame from flickering out for seasons on end. We yelled the talk and ran the walk. So many slogans on so many poster boards. Mine was an armory crammed with useful thoughts on God and god and them and Us that click-click-clicked their way like bullets into magazines I stockpiled, cached and camouflaged under the artful scrim of nature-boy wanderlust and psychedelic wallpaper. I never felt alone and was rarely anything but high. I was one among millions, which felt huge compared to a spec of scared nothing in a dark room in Freeburg. And then, what felt like a decade later, from a dark room in Marion, Ohio, it seemed like a life someone else had lived.

"...is all anybody's trying to say over here. Are you gonna pretend to be fine with all this? Saul?"

"All what, Mom? I mourned the man's death back before my pubes were growing in right. You were there. You took a picture of me in the bathtub and both my hands couldn't cover all that orange. You probably have that shot framed somewhere for all your clients to giggle about, don't you?" (her laughing) "But it's okay, see? It's everything else that's a bit fucked, but this, this is fine."

I'd learned to bullshit from masters. I looked around my still-undecorated bedroom and it felt less like home than a cheap motel, where at least there'd be a pastel-mad painting bolted over the bed, maybe a bedspread to match the curtains, cleaned-brittle towels and tidy soaps to clean just so much dirt and no more.

"I know you aren't exactly, well..." (Cough.) It sounded fake, to hide a snicker?

"I'm well enough aware."

"Huh. Say whatever sounds right, honeybun."

Such routine nonchalance, like a vet will sound before ramming a finger up your cat's ass. It didn't feel as bad as I'd thought it would to be pitied. I was used to it, so I tuned her out again to look for wearable t-shirts, and my thoughts soon turned back to a time when that type of tone could still offend me. By the time I'd read so much that I could finally say with confidence not only what I knew but didn't know and didn't care to ever know, my penmanship honed like a poisoned arrow, I had at shotgun my main-man Che (Gutierrez, who nonetheless was rarely seen without a beret) when I steered my immortal Jeep (Cherokee Eddie Bauer Edition, primer gray to match our resolve) into the dawn of a union with two women who somehow made us both feel like we could finally start calling ourselves men. We fell without thinking too much about it, four months after meeting these girls in a free weekly yoga class that convened atop a small nation of fire-ant fiefdoms outside the Student Center, into the confidence of a drive-through Vegas wedding for four, followed by a honeymoon in two tiny tents at an Appalachian folk festival, where, surrounded by strangers who acted like old friends and a craggy second horizon from the hovering mountaintops that folks from places like Florida and Ohio find more exotic than most anything, we assumed a communal lifestyle for three days and nights. We shared and took turns preparing all the food we bought at the nearest gas station. We traveled to the stage as one neon-shackled orb of laughing light and danced to Parliament Funkadelic like it was just us as our parents in some Chitlin' Circuit dive, and even inched our way with no objections onto a luxury bus where George Clinton and a small coterie of his traveling armada held court in the center of a room filled with pillows and unctuous fog. He passed around a water bong taller than the average fifth-grader that carried a whiff of every place he'd ever been and sizzled with every cloud he'd ever ridden. He gave out his contact information (which we summarily misplaced) like he'd just met another clutch of his love children. We left when George fell asleep on the lap of one of his dancers, who was young enough to be his great-granddaughter and very well could have been. The night was still young for us, though. Our legs were sore and rubberized by the time we returned to camp, our voices rasped to suit the crackling fire, our heads so free of clutter that we all seemed scared to talk, wide awake in the quiet splendor.

So Rebecca, like some gypsy in flowing skirts and braided hair stepping gingerly around the site without a noise, macerated every wildflower she'd collected throughout the day, and threw the pulpy mass into a pot of water nestled in the coals, then dumped in a tiny sack of something in iridescent shades of green and blue. In ten minutes, the pot was a steamy cauldron. Rebecca squeezed in a full teddy bear of honey. Fifteen minutes more, and we'd all been reduced to silent tears, neither happy nor sad. Both at once.

It was a honeymoon on its own, without any planning. I turned to Rebecca and, seeing her crying too, told her below the distant campfire songs what I could have said in the McChapel had it felt less flourescent and Elvis-inspired, that I was sure "the right things will always change just when and how they should for us, and the rest will stay the way they are because the world, it needs way more of that." (So deluded the newlyweds.)

Her: "...because earnest and worldly Ju-Ju-Be lovers..."

Me (impressed by her spontaneous use of "earnest"): "...with Ju-Ju-Be teeth that make us smile rainbows..."

Her (loving Ju-Ju-Bes): "...with honest eyes and Dumbo ears..."

Me (who's been known to cry watching *Dumbo*): "...who love their work and work at love..."

Her (who loves both of those things): "...who claim titles like Soul Mates and BFF and Wonder Twins..."

Me: "...with Wonder Twin powers..." She butted her fist on mine and I felt our matching bands give a little with the stress, just enough to feel changeable and breakable: "...*Shape of* a case of that Fireball Whiskey..."

Me: "...*Form of* a condor to fly you around the world to apologize, with excellent buzz and breath, for all the conquest of our forebears..."

She: "...These heroes you've made us, they're human, you know, and they strike a wise balance between saying what they mean and lying to be nice..."

Me: "...They breathe the same air, too, so they stray from the pack only when lost..."

Her (without pause): "...or when straying's deserved..."

Me (aroused by a reasonable woman): "I will never deserve that and neither will you..."

Her: "So we'll stay, Ju-Ju-Be, and we'll always try hard to be sure about everything. But not here, okay, baby? I need plumbing. And no spiders in my bubble."

The others were watching but you could hear the whimpers in their crying now. Che told me he loved me, he loved us, and then he walked off with his first of three new brides, whose name to this day sadly eludes me, and it was years before I saw him again, in the kind of way that felt like fate. The man isn't the type to want to be framed into something as limiting as a Facebook page, so it was impossible to hunt him down. What time was left then for extra friends, anyway? We locked eyes, Rebecca and me, and we stayed that way for several months. Rebecca wiped away my tears when they came unexpectedly and licked her fingers: "Cotton candy." I swiped at hers and tasted nothing like that; I tasted ripe compost, the grit of foundation, cigarette tar, but I said, "Cotton ... candy ... too," and that made her stop crying and fill out her smile into laughing at her husband's first of too many lies to be nice.

"You stink, too," she whispered to let me know we both had shared another first. Such is the telepathy of campfire romance. Sorry: I won't linger much longer on Rebecca, since this isn't my story but my father's, but you must know enough to understand my state of mind as I mustered the necessary will to go tear through a past I'd hoped to leave buried. Quite simply, I was unmoored and afraid. I wasn't living well alone. Just look at the science for proof of how utterly disfigured would be my ability to see cups as half-full for months to come. I was chemically changed, physically altered. Understand (here I go again): Biology and chemistry, Rebecca's dueling fortes, are unmistakably objective, verifiably conclusive, and chemistry is what our biologies so clearly shared. It made sense when it was working and no sense at all when it failed. We were made for each other. She'd say it. I'd say it. And it didn't feel unfounded. Ask anyone who knew us when first we met, as we were before our lives started changing apart. We looked and felt too right together, felt too in sync about so many things, to ever chance a try at starting over again.

LOOK. AT. US! Tall but not too gangly, serious but still prone to silliness, loners with friends, dreamers with time to kill, driven but not to drivel, smart enough to know better than to think inside a Hallmark poem. Her, with the big brown eyes that demanded honesty, a long nose that twitched at signs of change, long straight hair that alternated between its natural rust and any number of store-bought primary colors but always advertised whimsy and adventure. I was driven to distraction just by smelling her skip a morning shower or seeing her pantyline peek above her bony hip. She felt what she saw in me, too. Me, with the blue eyes, but mine, she said, channeling the intensity of everything I learn. They glow neon in bouts of discovery, darken to gray when what I learn is hard to file away. She used to claim she could taste trifles on my skin when I was feeling especially ferocious (beef jerky) or nervous (butterscotch) or testy (Twizzlers). My tight line of a mouth still purses into little pillows when I can't think of anything to say. She'd talk about the children we'd have and describe them with my constellations of freckles and red hair that she said could probably be seen from space. We made ourselves the center of our own universe. It worked, time and again. When everyone we knew started calling the weed of Reagan grass again, we argued playfully, vainly, about which of us should claim primary responsibility. We both had done it, we'd decided, a successful propaganda sortie. What couldn't we do? Together. It was ridiculous. We even mailed a little gift-wrapped box of our obese friend Gupta's feces one bored Saturday to the Ayn Rand Institute, right after torching all her insidiously well-written books that we'd forced ourselves to read so that someday we might avoid getting trickled down upon and into something like an adjustable-rate mortgage. We made the papers. Gupta's feces made the papers.

Can anyone relate to this? Every day for what felt like years carried some magnitude of consequence, every outing reeking of uncovered meaning and memory-making. We carried ourselves like secular missionaries, feeling for all those who'd forgotten how or who'd never been taught, giving change to people who looked as though they were about to ask for it. We ate ramen by candlelight, read passages of poetry aloud, took walks because the moon was full, made love because we finally could. We did so much for doing nothing but turning on, tuning in and dropping out without having to actually drop out or go crazy, and then, in the time it took for me to tie a proper tie and trim away four years of hair and for her to dye her hair back to rust and pull something serious from her closet, we stumbled out of the humanities bubble into classrooms in her hometown of Marion, where my cadets were all lined up and spit-shined for their proper dose of "his-tory." I even wrote it that way on the board on Day One and sized up their expressions for a few seconds of uncomfortable silence. These boys and girls would be my answer to America's hypnotic dazzle, the People's Knights Templar, secular warriors aligned against the oligarchy.

(I tell you all of this to approximate the heights from which I was soon to plummet. We'll get back to my father shortly. Am I not his son?)

"Does anybody know what I'm trying to say by writing history this way?" I remember asking. I'd been itching to get moving with this kind of progressive introduction. "Not everybody at once now."

I felt alone in a room of future app programmers, bloggers all with bangs agog, the eyes overpainted, pupils Adderalled out and so bored through by digital marvels that no mere human in khakis could ever hope to elicit a glint of recognition there. "His-story?"

"We get it," cracked a puberty-plagued voice from the back corner, a hoodie-capped youth who gratefully bleated out a solid "Baaaaa" to cap off his introduction. I felt something like encouragement.

I pointed to my only fan in thanks and scanned the room with a smile just as some hidden frequency caused pretty much the whole assemblage of woebegones to roll their eyes at once and look askance in a show of fabricated exasperation. My warriors. I look back now and can count at most a dozen every year with the fire to maybe someday kindle something like an interest in cultural (r)evolution. Until then I suppose I'd imagined I would somehow come under the tutelage of not so much a principal as a mother-goddess with the same disregard for orthodoxy as myself, whose continual advances would never annoy and only cement the firmament of my marriage vows. Here in this world that never would be, I wouldn't have to use the same old books and rules and standardized tests and politically correct answers to mold these babies into shape. I could be the founder of my own little Dead Poets Society, pour through pivotal essays and folk lyrics. Yet by the end of Day One I was left with the paralysis of reality: I would be regurgitating the same lesson plans and churning out more of the same toy soldiers for the Army to play war, more pawns for the Monopoly game. It wasn't long before I felt cold inside where I once imagined a candle burning. I walked around feeling like I wanted to punch somebody, but I hadn't picked out the recipient yet. How couldn't Rebecca have hated to see that?

"...and don't think a minute you won't see at least some of that danky-stank residue up in..."

My mother's voice snatched me back from staring a hole through the bare bedroom wall. I started rummaging through a drawer of clothes Rebecca'd bought a few years ago, the polo shirts and cargo pants perpetually in vogue that I never would have chosen over the faded sloganed T-shirts, worn jeans and pea coats that she'd made me cast aside a few years before when we began securing rank. Since I didn't have anything like that anymore, it's clear she'd thrown it all away behind my back. I closed the drawer, zipped up the suitcase and carried it to the front door with nothing of the rooster left in my stride. My mother still a gnat inside my ear, I stared with no thoughts at my tiny apartment, the one I'd made Rebecca find me to fill with all the leftovers she'd had no use for in her tony downtown flat, which instead was stuffed with light from giant windows and her measure of our Facebook friends and coffee table books used to spark conversation with new lovers. I just knew she was having parties to celebrate her newfound freedom, and the thought always made me forget to keep breathing. I exhaled but didn't have anything inhaled. Time was standing still those days because that's what I was doing. I inhaled her name, *Rebecca*. Exhaled it, *Rebecca*. She was still stuck there, or was it me?

"...best just to pretend not to hear anything you might actually be hearing, which'll hopefully send the signal that they're not getting through and might as well stop trying. And..."

I leaned back against the front door and weighed my indifference against my urge to escape. Keys in hand, I felt as trapped in place as ever. Flashback to Rebecca's grand escape.

Several days had passed – a week? – after she'd told me we were through in as many words, and I was still on the couch, our couch, waiting to wake up and find her there smiling and cooing, "C'mon, baby. Come and get it." I just sat there, pretending to laugh or to gasp at the shows that were once somehow ours.

"Why don't you go back and live with your father?" was what she'd really been saying by way of insulting command. "You can stare all day at the wall together and obsess over dead people's lives like your own. The happy couple, living the dream!" How could she hate me that much to dig that deep in just the right place?

And I'd sat. Another half-laugh, not at her, at the screen, at it all. She'd looked, too. "A goddamn infomercial. You fucktwat. You ... *nothing!* I HATE THIS YOU! *I hate it.* The fuck aren't you listening, Saul? I. HATE. THIS. YOU!" The last one came across as a calm statement of fact. Then she'd left, looking vindicated, even wise, perhaps happy, and found me a new hole to dig for myself. That hole.

My mother droned, "...and it's crucial you don't..."

"Uh-huh..."

"That you *don't*..."

I crossed the room and there I was on the couch again, all mine now, sulking and stalling. Never had I felt so much gravity. For months on end, this had been my perch. My silence was shock when she'd left and still was, a half-year later. No desultory healing of tears could escape it, no words. It'd started so warm and substantial, so aware of itself, as you've been made to learn and probably question why. But then what? Ask anyone and they'll know. I blamed her for the shift. She blamed me. Problem was: I could remember too well how it felt when we'd started. I still can. I couldn't imagine romance that real, a central impetus in our lives for much longer than for most, could just evaporate without a trace like August dew. I mean, we gave gifts for no reason, left little notes here and there just because we could write: "I love's me some you" on a mirror in toothpaste; "You're amazing and mine!" back from her in red lipstick... I'd keep wanting more answers to questions about her. She'd never stop writing those rambling notes, which she'll fold into squares with the juvenile tabs. We'll be wrinkled and slow and still taking our walks at the sunset. We'll always be waiting at dawn.

"...and promise, boy. You see or hear anything, a roach fart, two mice getting it on, you call. I can guide you through what's...."

"Guide. Me. Master."

I sank back into the couch. Back when. It was hard not to try and find heat in how we'd kept glowing for so long, beaming, through festival fires and love-ins-and-outs on in to all-nighters and internships, from flip-flops and landlines and beepers to loafers and desktops and smartphones. We earned real bona fides that led us up north to land jobs at the same rural high school of 500 kids whose most prestigious alumni was some guy who'd invented a cleaner way of chopping off a chicken's neck. It was the middle of Middle America, and I couldn't have felt more at home away from home for at least a few years. We had plans that were really just a Plan, and who could take that away from us but us? I would teach history and she would teach science and these children would come back and thank us for everything, for giving the world just a little more light. We'd remark, until the joke was cliché, that we'd never once have to spend days apart either, even lunches in the teacher's lounge corner, agog. In a few years, we knew, the whole town would be waving and smiling and calling our name, "Hey, McGinty!" Our path was the same, so we'd both look up, beaming.

She'd wanted our home, a cream, brass-tacks Colonial, to be close to her folks. I did too, since I wanted mine far from my own and for hers to be something mine weren't. And they had been. For three years. Then they died on the Farm to Market Road. A semi had won. For weeks, I watched as my wife died beside them; and for months, we let something bleed out of us, too.

"...Saul? I know. This just sucks, son, so just in and out quick, and then over to Mama's. Saul? Baby, you..."

"Quick and cool and out the door," I droned.

Same-y days and same-y nights. The bored faces in rows

finally had their effect. I still can't recall exactly when we'd reached that plateau, when hand-holding and spooning and talks about nothing and hurried sex in weird places and dinners that couldn't be started without candles had receded to make room for frustration and boredom, into dinners in silence and meaningless sitcoms and the fights without context for hidden frustrations, over colleagues that one of us liked, not the other, who "just had to want *something* to be *that fucking nice*," over sex in the dark, for reward, or in pity, over drinking alone, over drinking all night, over drugs that I'd skipped over sadly in college, over nothing to say, not a question unanswered. Overall, overdone, dried to bone. Ju-Ju-Bee boxes empty out before long.

Around the time I'd made the couch my bed downstairs, so my once-cute sleep apnea wouldn't drive her insane, I'd suggested a baby, "maybe end us, as newlyweds, hee-hee, hardi-har." And she'd agreed, perhaps guiltily conjuring up the talks we'd shared in college about our little orange-headed progeny. I'd been shocked. I was back in the bed. We were trying again. Then months later – a year? – a doctor delivered the news that she'd passed on to me with a different touch: "I'm just barren, a hole," she'd told me while walking upstairs. "Please sleep on the couch. I'm so tired. And sore..." She was only half-right, I'd informed the closed door. "Guess we're both barren then! Guess that's it!" Guess I knew even then. The silence that followed was still with me later, despite all the ghost talk spilling into my ear:

"...It was really a miracle, son, really something I tell you. So she's leaving, this woman, and just laughing and crying and it's nothing but 'thank you' for setting him free. And I'm crying then, too, of course. How couldn't I? I'm like, 'Your soul's free now, too, let it be, let it be.' And then here comes the waterworks. I tell you, boy. My work? Stones to flowers. I got this. I'll be there, you need me. Saul?"

"I'll be there tomorrow, in the afternoon, maybe. I'll let you know if Dad wants to talk."

"You know, we can hire a crew if..."

"No, I got this. I've been waiting to clean up this shit my whole life."

"That's my..."

I hung up.

At the door with the suitcase feeling lighter than nothing, I turned and surveyed the bare walls of my warren. I stepped out in the sun, closed the door, thought to lock it but didn't. Perhaps, on return, I would find the slate clean.

For twenty-five hours, I felt my will drain, as I watched the rote scroll of a highway drag by like the background in old cartoons that barely changes as everything else keeps rushing past: green exits all drawn up from templates, each one rubber-stamped, with the same smattering of drive-thrus, gas stations, motels, the same dejected homeless man at the on ramp, the same beady eyes imploring, needing rides to the same sick old mother in the same ICU, in a town called "As Far As You're Going." I'd left at such a time that even the stunning Appalachian mountains were only a craggy line across the darkness. The states rolled past like wallpaper.

I was lucky to be moving and not bored to comatose. My Regal's stock stereo, worn down like the rest, had been useless for months, the antenna snapped off at the hood, so the Swiss-cheesed exhaust pipe filled the silence with rattling and dizzied my thoughts about what was to come. I'd also put off an alignment for months, so the smallest of bumps caused life-threatening tremors; my fingers grew sore from white-knuckling the wheel. A younger Rebecca would have never allowed this, for me to be suffering in such dangerous ways, to be endangering the other half of her whole. For no Cause, with no Sign?

New Rebecca would top off the tank while I waited.

I know she suspected I'd slowly become him, a crude reproduction of a reprobate scorned, but the truth is, I knew just how different I was from the man she knew only from my nightmarish stories. As I've said: I wasn't afraid to be there where he'd died, in that house I still hated for the memories it held. I fancied myself, in fact, morbidly eager to see a decline more dramatic than mine. I'd rummage through his things with a casual air. I'd be a stern judge, put each item on trial, then I'd sentence it all to the trash and be gone.

*   *   *

Mrs. Arbuckle found him, the old skank.

"His head's sticking out from the bathroom, oh Lord," she tells a dispatcher on the tape I've requested for due diligence. What else? "Well, his eyes are still open and he's staring back at me all blue and bloated and smiling, my God, my poor ..." Is she there? "I'm right here in the living room window and..." How could she be sure? "He's just there in the blood. Jesus Christ! Am I *sure!* He's been in there for days, not a peep or a light..." And why was she there? "He stopped paying the rent, so I came to come get some and he..." So why was he dead? "Don't ask me. Ask the Lord. I don't know. Wacka-doodles, for one..." Could she stay on the line? "Wud'ya think I been doing, fercrissakes you..."

I was stretching and moaning outside my fed-up, hissing car, acting even more exhausted than I was. The sky was the dusky orange of bug-bloated citrus. Mrs. Arbuckle started to relay the details and I told her I had them, as many as stuck in my head from my mother, so she shifted, as always, to comforting fundamentalist memes.

"The Lord is here with us; he's our rock in these times," she said, in lulling tones that sounded too rehearsed for spontaneity. "These things aren't meant to be easy, but, sweet Jesus, hold on, Saul. Even when we just wanna be left on our own, there it is..."

My first shudder of the trip. "Our rock," I said.

"That's right. Just know that, okay? God is with you. And Jesus. They're working a plan and you're a part of it, Saul."

I stared at my feet, pretending to yawn until a real one came out. "Try and proselytize this," the yawn said, then I said, "How long do I have?"

She heard the yawn's bite. "It all has to be out in a week, will that work?"

"I don't plan on being here any longer than necessary. Maybe

27

two days or three? It's all trash, for the most part, I'm guessing. I just know there's some things that I left here, from way back, things I kept putting off getting, until, you know, I could get here. To visit."

"Well, you're here now, in God's hands," she said. She pointed the spare key at the house and somehow followed it with just one eye to leave the other on me. "It's not like you'll remember. In there. Not a bit."

Everything else was. I swept road-weary eyes all around me, took a sip of cold coffee and tossed the Styrofoam cup to a mound of brush at the curb. Lizards of every shade of brown scurried for better cover. I felt young and uncertain all over again. I landed my gaze on the house facing his, right across Walnut Circle, Mrs. Arbuckle's identical rectangle in contrasting colors: hers beige and brown trim with neat bushes and perennials, his the turquoise and peach that can only fly here, fronted by the sandy, sand-spurred yard and the deadest-looking live oak around. My upper lip quivered to hold back what could have been another yawn or something deeper-rooted, a melancholy moan, a wail of terror. I inched closer to the door. She followed in silence, my stooped future shadow.

Wasp cities the size of softballs stood like crude rooks at both corners of the house, smaller versions in each upper corner of three facing windows. The living room's vertical blinds were missing a few slats and open a little in the middle, just right of the door, but all I could see from this distance were books. In the two smaller windows on each edge of the house, from my bedroom at right and Katie's at left, the blinds were closed and still mangled by my father's once-proud menagerie of stray pits and rotties. I assumed they all were gone by then, since nothing was snarling or fogging up the glass anywhere.

Motionless for long enough to lose the only breeze, I felt the heat of my childhood for the first time again, that boggy liquid air that steals some of the soul from every breath and seeps into the pores to suck the sweat from inside out. Such humidity can make a trip to the mailbox a reason for a shirt change if not handled calmly. A uniform sheen welled up and rolled from the tiny bald spot atop my head as a single ringlet in seconds was dripping from my chin and tapping rhythmically on the rubber toe of my tennis shoe. Tap-tap-tap. I imagined somebody cracking a fake egg on my head with delicate fingers and feeling them make the yolk run down slow. I swiped my hand across my face, wiped it on my shorts and immediately needed to do it again.

"I just ... I don't know if I really ... if I could just ..." I wasn't sure what I wanted, so I really wasn't sure what I wanted to say. There was always something unsaid there between us.

"Take your time, sweetness. We've got all the time you need." She rubbed an abacus that was her knobby hand up and down my spine, left it there hanging from the belt loop, and I felt something deeper, darker welling up. I'd barely had time to forget.

To illustrate the depths of my dismay for being here (not to mention the poetic dissonance of would-be pubescent poets the world over) I provide this prose description of my deepest hovel that I'd torn from a childhood journal to turn in for an English assignment in the beginning of ninth grade, long after we'd moved in when I was eight and just months before I'd gotten to leave at fourteen. My mother found it in a fat folder of have-to-keep-its she'd labeled "SHIT" and thought it would be useful in my research. I know why she really earmarked it for inclusion here. I must admit: The funereal imagery I note today is nothing short of the family fortune-teller's (or, it can't be denied, just uncannily coincidental):

> *"The house changes daily,*
> *Becoming a coffin,*
> *The cinderblock model.*
> *On sale now! Don't miss out!*
> *Rustic chic: The sandy paint peeling,*
> *Like skin at the seams.*
> *Authentic: Original windows,*
> *Clouded finely with time,*
> *Just four at the corners,*

Two big ones at center,
All letting the bugs in,
The fat and the flat bugs,
All fighting to gobble
Live corpses inside.
"We'll need all those holes,"
Some old ghost at night sighs,
"For the handles."
"The handles?" I whisper.
"All coffins need handles."
"Not coffins with people
Who no one would carry."
The ghost shuts his mouth.

In violet ink, scrawled across the top of the page and onto the back, are the words of a man I remember as a good teacher, a stoic mentor who did his best coaching in private, whose face I can vaguely recall as being pox-scarred and whose last name started with an N or maybe it was a silent K:

"B+(for Barely) ... Vivid imagery and clever dialogue got you that far, as usual. The slapdash organization and disregard for directions kept you short of the A. Maybe we'll get to see the Deluxe model next time, huh? Some grave mistakes here ... hi-he-ha-ho-hu [how he wrote his laughter] ... but not unforgivable: 1) We're a few hundred words short; 2) You turned in a poem that was supposed to be an essay; 3) You didn't give your piece a title and placed your name and period flush-right (can you read the board from that nest of yours in the back corner of the room?); and 4) Where have all my line break slashes gone, my sullen Mr. Poe? Couldn't see them through the rain of tears and raven droppings? I'd love to hear your smile when reading your next assignment. Who knows: Maybe your pen can pull you out of that quicksand you insist on sinking into. (But really, Saul: If you ever need to talk, you know where half my half-baked life's been lived. At least keep writing out all those hobgoblins inside you.)"

I made a habit of looking at the papers of the students around me, mostly out of envy, and rarely did their notes contain anything beyond curt praises or terse reprobations. It didn't make me feel special. I was a Special Case. My teachers soon learned that the black cloud over my every move hadn't come from spending too much time on that rickety haunted house on the midway on my way from the Bouncy House and Bumper Cars to the Hall of Endless Mirrors and Sideshow Freaks. This was the undertone lurking below much of my upbringing, forming the pitch of every sound, determining when and if any harmony would ever be felt much less heard or appreciated. What I heard: truth that sounded a little like lies, lies that sounded a lot like truth and the constant prattling of parental types trying to keep everybody quiet or full of spirit or in line and in their seats with peace signs and whistles and harumphy hands on hips and curse words heard by reading lips and the fanning of empty referral slips and the stealthy language of infantry squads: *See my eyes? See 'em? Yeah? Means I see yours too, fucktard. Back of the line.*

I could keep my mouth shut, made a habit of it, but I had a hard time censoring what I knew my teachers would end up reading and sharing later in the teacher's lounge. Some seemed to treat my mandatory journaling as if it were the early stirrings of a landmark case history; others kneaded it like dough or coaxed it along like the golden thread of a true-crime novel they might someday write in the first person about the school massacre they *should have seen coming,* back when those types of tragedies were pinned on death metal or so-so coming-of-age novellas with ambiguous endings or that catch-all demon inside us all named evil with a capital D, just before the Goths and grunge bands and immortal-shooter videogames started getting all the press. What damnation would have been loosed upon the world of pubescence then had we all been comparing our junk and random witticisms on the Internet with only our thumbs and a bank of emoticons? What a relief when everybody started blaming all the weapons doing all the dirty work. To think of it now, my paltry contribution to my little world's worries wasn't much at all by comparison. All told, seven childhood journals were darkened edge to edge with the stink of zit blood and Doritos dust and dried-dead half-lives that could easily have been mistaken for tears or toilet dribbles. I'm not sure when I stopped thinking of them as something I'd like to show my grandchildren someday, but I burned them all in the fireplace of a grand foreclosed home in my first semester of college in Tallahassee, lest they be discovered by someone, anyone, with whom I'd hoped to develop at a minimum a relationship of mutual respect. Nothing in them was the me I'd quickly become. Lyrics to songs about nothing ever happening when it should that I'd never write because my sense of melody was as much of a laughing stock as my singing voice, even at family gatherings, where I was prompted to sing anything that came to mind to add some comic relief. Sketches of swamp monsters and bridge trolls with faces so undefined and unfeeling, limbs so asymmetrical that my sixth-grade art teacher, my first and last ever, had to muster a histrionic breath before instructing me with a straight face to maybe ply my creative impulses with something more along the lines of music or literature. Poems to girls who really were fairies or cartoon characters or both made a sad showing at odd intervals, half-hearted pleas for future lovers blending every girl I'd ever pictured topless to take care not to break my heart in two. But mostly: run-on sentences for pages of me being metaphysical without meaning, wounded without wounds, coy with no audience, punchy with a chin and a heart made of glass. Fill in all the rest of the spaces with cheery admonitions of teachers with no shortage of pen colors who rarely met me eye to eye but nonetheless knew me well enough to commend every step I made away from being labeled autistic and understanding how very shallow being sulky in the shadows actually amounted to. Whatever it was, the emo lifestyle matched the unifying mood of my early life. And while my attitude slowly brightened in proportion to my time away from Walnut Circle, for a time anyway, I must admit that my poetry never progressed very far past these types of clever conversations with myself, who I called a ghost. Picture a darkness so dense that not a single pimple or pubic head hair the color of a basketball can be seen inside it.

Picture a boy comfortable there, still a few decades shy of being lulled like a bug toward the light of a standard-issue cellphone and laptop. Picture the boy as a junior, when his father reluctantly bought him several cans of black spraypaint as a birthday present, just so his occasional weekend visits could be to a room that was as dark as the other half of his life. Picture everyone waiting for the boy to grow the fuck up.

Especially my mother. I could blame her for why it took me so long. She'd been witching around with stray ghouls and exaggerated murder mysteries since my birth in a quest not to creep out her kids, but just to sort out the voices she couldn't explain. That was her darkness, never mine. My real darkness came out of this place, through my father. Even after he was gone, that foreboding remained. In fairness: He never laid a finger on any of us, on anyone for that matter, but how was anyone to tell when he'd take that next step?

I felt my body leaning back, inching a half-step away from the door.

"He was bragging on working up some real stories again," said Arbuckle, vainly masking the pity with her best stolid stab, "and not just the usual death notice stuff from the homes. Was a time I'd have seen this thing coming for days, but I'll tell you, Saul Jr., this set me swooning a little. Guess he had some big stuff going down, for a time."

"Some big stuff, eh?" Eyelids half-mast. *Council split on new sidewalk plan.*

She was standing too close, the smell on this lady: that sex-with-the-neighborhood stank still remained. *Octogenarian claims own 'Immaculate conception!'* She'd been widowed a decade by then, so I put what I knew back inside the black box. "Guess we know better now, huh? Just another obit's all."

"No, Saul. He had actual people in there, time to time. Never thought I'd see that again. But that was only when he was there. Months now, he spent most of the time away somewheres. Probably getting the scoops before deadline or something. Is that right? Getting some scoops?"

"Yeah: getting scoops," I said flatly. "Is the ... did they, like ... you know...?"

"They didn't want me in there," she said, then bit her lip fast in what would look, to the untrained eye, as the stifling of misery. "Not until they were done, with their blottering and gumshoe stuff and such. They had a crew in, a'course, cleaned it up good enough. It's been, what? Two, three days? What's today? I don't want you to have the wrong ..."

"I know when he died, ma'am." I leaned my shoulder against the tree, right where, at a time before us, someone had spray-painted a red crown for protection against some ganged-up neighborhood menace. It was maroon now but still visible from the road. I hugged myself and let my eyes roll free in my head.

"God bless your poor heart, Saul. I'll keep praying on this. Chin up, little man! Your mother, I called her as soon as I could. So she knows all the..."

"Right." My feet were in concrete, my mind still back on the road catching up. I wanted her gone but I didn't want to be left here alone yet. I just kept standing there, staring at the door, so she let me and preached: "... 'One set of footprints? God, how could you leave me?' 'My son,' this is Jesus now, 'Don't be a silly man, that's when I had your big patootie up in my arms!'..." I closed my eyes, so she must have thought it was hitting my heart.

Ambivalent memories weighed me down deeper. His presence was undeniable then, for the first time in so long. Once, in her droning, I thought I'd seen him in the window, scowling and pointing behind him like he did when I'd done something wrong. I tried to hone in on the good points, like him teaching me chess, but the bad clung like barnacles, like us never once playing again once I'd learned. I could see him pull out his infirm ice cream maker – "Ice cream?! No, *she* screams!" – but only when hearing the ice cream man's music. He's telling us war stories, then "Shut your mouth when I'm talking!" He's singing old songs we'd never heard on the way to the park, then he's sitting there quiet the whole time we're there, then he's helping with homework, then drilling the walls through when I didn't seem to be listening, then holding my hand, then brushing her hair and spitting out murderous threats but only in jest. He's teaching me this and teaching me that, but then staring at a wall for days on end. Almost everything verging on treasured my father would neutralize quickly to empty and worthless. You call a man like this less and less through the years because you've run out of original ways to engage him. You're too busy and tired of hunting for words to make him believe you aren't still disappointed. "I love you" meant nothing from my father's lips. He called maybe twice and both times I'd been shocked. I'd stopped calling years before.

"...and then he's gone," said Mrs. Arbuckle, snapping me back from old stupor to new. I looked away from the front door where we stood side-by-side by the tree and gazed blankly at her with the shameful reproach I could hold back no longer.

I moved toward the door. It was that or let the no-see-'ums snacking at my sweaty neck make a permanent home in my nose and ears. I stopped just shy of the mat, which only said "Welcome" to those, like myself, who'd seen it say that before the word was worn down to nothing but the shit-stained blur of a dirty lie. It was dark out by then. Five or six types of insects bopped around the bare yellow bulb beside the door that somebody felt it best to leave on: mostly moths and daddy longlegs but also gnats and their blood-lusting cousins the midges, and some flying ants as plump as those iridescent horse flies and some other unidentifiable specimen that looked like chunks of tan bark from the oak tree behind me. I held out my right hand, palm up, and she put the key in it like a scalpel. I breathed a cramped, wheezy, chain-smoking breath, inserted the key into the deadbolt and turned.

Someone braver than me twisted the handle and pushed, and the door swung open to an immediate slap of bleach, iodine, tar, ammonia, and the copper of what had been blood, none of which would submit to the sage bundle Mrs. Arbuckle had lit surreptitiously and was waving around like a torch in a cave. She flipped the switch by the door and the light on the fan illuminated in stark outline the big shoebox of one man's nothing. Every inch of wall, floor to ceiling, was covered in books and two couches. I couldn't even remember myself ever being there.

"Jesus," I said, stepping back toward the door.

"That's right, honey," she said. "You pray on things."

I moved forward again and heard scratching, from the attic. I froze. I was rooting for a cute raccoon family and not an army of rats to be living up there and especially not what was there when, as a boy, I'd sent my sister up a ladder in the closet of my single-car-garage-turned-bedroom to find nothing more than waterlogged insulation, rivers of coaxial cable, castaway holiday paraphernalia, and a nation of arrogant, unafraid roaches. The noises, which I pretended to have the quality of comfort and belonging, petered out as my listening intensified – listening back. Mrs. Arbuckle hadn't heard anything, of course.

"It was right there," she said, pointing, left of the front door, to the stubby hallway outside the tiny bathroom, which led from the claustrophobic living room to two of the home's three equally cramped bedrooms: his and what used to be Katie's. "Ugh. I'm sorry. I suppose you've heard all about how he was smiling, right through the window there where he knew somebody'd finally come to see him."

I felt numb.

All I saw, out the corner of my eye, was more books on both walls of the hallway, making it no wider than a wiry man's shoulders. I leered at Arbuckle hard but finally creaked my neck to see full on what seemed to still be there but wasn't. I forced myself to study the scene. Despite what appeared to be a slapdash cleanup, the grout was still darker where Lake Dad had been and some red stained the bottom shelf of books opposite the bathroom door, apparently where some had pooled deeper than elsewhere. The visual brought a stale dead stink into my nose to match the tang of pennies in my mouth. I closed my eyes deliberately and waited, then opened them again and turned my head in a semi-circle to take it all in: the same drabby-sad nowhere. Only now it was filled with books that I figured he'd used as wallpaper to cover all the damage he'd done. Suddenly, I was Junior again.

"Junior, get that ass outside and show that fuck what yelling at a McGinty's gonna get him," still echoed back across the years. I shivered and looked at Arbuckle intently to come back and see only, hear only the now of him being gone.

"Been keeping the fans on a few days," she said, drifting into the kitchen, opening and closing some cupboards, the fridge. I followed with stooped shoulders, then turned back toward the front door, contemplating escape. "Got a few people calling about the place. Like I says, it's a different house now, right? Mostly books is what you'll find, and all them candles melting over all the tabletops and papers. Surprised he didn't die in fla..." She shot me a look but I didn't register alarm. "He's got his shelves in the bathroom, the hallway, the kitchen. Quite the wordworm, your Daddy. I never saw the need myself; Bible's the only book I ever had a mind to find an end to."

"They should have stopped right there," I say quietly, studying her expression in her reflection in the opening of the front window. I should have known: an empty slate.

"Don't you know it?" she amened. A ripple of fervor flattened her smile lines. "That damn apple of knowledge. See all these books did for your Daddy?" She looked up, held a weak veiny fist to the ceiling. "Eeeeeve!? Could it be a coincidence the name's one step shy of 'Evil'?"

"Couldn't be," I said, shaking my head. I didn't think my father had read any of these books, and I believed Arbuckle when she claimed to disavow the practice, wondering about what unknowable hardships must have befallen this old hag to have led a life so far afield from ever learning about less mythical women named Eve. Eve Ensler came to mind. Then her "Vagina Monologues." Then Arbuckle's vagina. Then shivering and the woozy type of feeling that causes one to rush for a place to lie down or throw up.

Shivering despite the summer, I forced my mind to change the subject. I took a deep breath through my mouth to avoid the stench and turned my gaze again to marvel at how a once-modest collection of crackpot books in a few towers beside my father's bed

37

had morphed insanely into a library branch run by an Alzheimer's patient. What was an embarrassingly small home in my youth was now an isolation chamber of unspoken words. Arbuckle turned off the kitchen light. More shivering, only this time it came from memories flitting in like bats through the front window that was no longer a mirror but a black hole.

"Can I see your phone? I really just have to go home." Some pubescent croak, a former friend whose name was lost to time. "It's no offense or anything," which by adding that made it obviously an offense. "I just don't feel good."

"I understand. I don't feel good either."

Another voice then, recognizable but faceless: "Atari, huh? Huh. Wanna go outside?"

"Not out there, man. Believe me. It's not just a jungle out back."

"Wanna just sleep over my place?"

"Duh. Should I bring my trunks?" I'd always bring two sets of clothes and as much candy as I could muster up, hoping my sleepovers could last full weekends on the sheer value of the sugar buzz I could provide.

To someone with a more comfortable soul, it wouldn't have been an embarrassment to bring over my contemporaries, who lived in all the other-sized houses, full of pillowy seating and feng shui and videogames worth playing, in neighborhoods with sidewalks and architectural forethought. But to me, every crack, every fault was my own. Standing there as a man, I still felt the inferiority. The floors: still supercenter tile, worn shag in the bedrooms. The ceiling: still popcorned and stained, but now with rings of gray dust around the fans and uniformly tarred a sickly yellow. The blinds: still grimed over and missing slats, only now they were mangled by a rotation of dogs my father liked to pin with names like Cat or Tits or Whoreface. He never kept any animals when I had to live here, and I was glad for selfish reasons; I know the smell would have been just another reason to be ashamed. As a boy, I sensed it was the kind of house that made people from other streets draw up their noses, either in pity or disgust, when made to visit for an underling coworker's barbecue or to surveill a garage sale. As a man, I knew that it was likely equal parts pity, disgust, and superiority.

I'd never seen the place more disheveled. Any place. At least when I had to be here, my mother had kept the place fairly tidy. My father had never cared about those types of things, and the long sweep of neglect, both his and perhaps that of those like myself who'd left and never returned, now gave the place the feel of a hoarder's den: matted furniture spilling stuffing and smelling of long-ago dog piss and drool; burger wrappers and empty soda cans topping tables cluttered deep with local newspapers and unopened mail; the formerly white walls not covered by books now a study in tans. I wanted fewer shadows so I returned to the kitchen and turned the overhead light back on, kept wandering about. A tall pile of dishes, food crusted to glue, filled both sides of a sink that was stagnant with a gray bilious water reeking of infection; more plates with leftover food, now magically miniaturized, cluttered the dining room table, the floor; and scattered about, the roaches, legs up, fat as beetles, fed to death. I moved to the books along the dining room wall and started scanning the spines. I could recognize the authors, and it made me something like curious for the first time that day. I also marveled at how they were alphabetized. Camus. Chomsky. Defoe. Descartes. Dick. Dos Passos. Dostoevsky.

"The police were actually over here a few times," Arbuckle finally said from right behind me, startling me as I scanned, with an ear to my shoulder, a bottom shelf. Kafka. Keats. I kept scanning as something Keats once wrote and I'd once read and then forgot miraculously came out of my head from where it'd been lodged since probably college and escaped my lips.

"Here lies one whose name was writ in water," I said, which made sense for a second, fit the scene, but not to Arbuckle, who very well might not have heard a word.

"No note, I guess," she said, since I was talking again.

Not like him, I couldn't help thinking. *Wouldn't he have had something to scream out first and break?* "I know," I said, leading her back into the front room. "It probably sounds weird but I'd kind of like to sleep. It's been a long haul, and I still have to sort out where I'm actually going to do that."

"Got a hotel now out by the highway," she said. "Maybe you saw. A Burger King, too, if you can believe it."

"We'll see. I hadn't given it much thought." In fact: I'd already considered it several times and by then was actually visualizing the check-in and wondering whether continental breakfast meant do-it-yourself waffles in an iron or just the regular plasti-wrapped danishes and coffee.

"You need something, honey, you know where I'm at," she said, and there was no mistaking the flurried pointing motion she flashed between still youngish me and old-as-dirt her, despite, or perhaps even highlighted by, the elderly quiver that accompanied her every move. I stepped back to make my bubble larger as she came around the coffee table, which was really just a gray filing cabinet, tipped on its side. "Bless your heart for doing this, baby. Don't slap yourself around in here. Not everybody's ready for the pearly gates, that's all. Don't mean he didn't love on you. Not a'tall. He'd be talking sometimes about you and him yuckin' it up on the phone, all them letters you'd be sending about your travels and such. All these years later, just proud as can be. Got one picture up, in all this mess, in there," pointing past the sullied grout to my father's room, "that one of all of you? Still up behind the bed. Nothing else but books, but not where he laid his head. Left your room over there just like you had it. Miss Emmy Award's too. Guess he knew least a few things he done right."

"And what was that, Mrs. Arbuckle?" I was at the door, holding it open. "He never called me, not once in all these years. Not once. He didn't even come to my wedding. Not even a present or anything. He never even met my wife, never even wanted to know the first thing about her. She's pretty much my ex-wife now, but he didn't know that either, did he? I had to be drunk to call him. And what letters? He never had shit to say and I guess I just kinda found other people who did. I don't even remember what him laughing even sounds like. Do you?" She looked down as if thinking or avoiding the sting of my eyes. "And then this: the big family reunion. *Come on in, son. What's mine is yours!* So, Mrs. Arbuckle, you were saying? What did he get right? Who's fucking plan am I a part of here?"

"My heavens, well..." Her head warbled like a bobble-head doll as her eyes searched for words that her mind couldn't find. She tugged at her blond wig where bobby pins and bald scalp were showing at the temples, looked for a watch on her wrist that wasn't there. Along her slouched route out the door, her head perked. "You're here aren't you?"

"Praise the Lord," I said and closed the lid.

I was alone. I listened for something and could only wonder how and why Mrs. Arbuckle could find such kind words to describe him. I thought to scream as my mother had advised but worried about the neighbors hearing and calling the police. I could only wonder to myself: How had he changed and why and for whom? Or had he just run out of walls to put holes in? Easy answer, I answered myself: *Do the math, Junior.*

I remember well our introduction to the place. A few days after moving in, Mr. Arbuckle had filled us in on why the place had "a few pockmarks," that this couple, who for months had seemed all smiles, had morphed into feral cats that wailed and clawed and hissed all night, until all you would hear were the three kids crying, then their mother along with them. In any kind of lighting, even the flame of a candle or the setting sun, smooth drywall patches in crude circles shaped more like fists could be seen, reflecting how, I'd often imagine, the man would become like a sock thrown into the ceiling fan. The man left first, Mr. Arbuckle had said, obeying a restraining order. The rest packed up and moved a few weeks later, presumably to somewhere the angry man wasn't. My mother had been authentically shocked: "Those poor babies..." My father stuck to the facts: "It's a sad world for some..." Then our own drama began.

I used to lay in bed and wonder what those kids would hear their parents screaming, what it was that finally made them cry or if they'd plead or hide and where, and then I'd wonder how those fights would measure up to those I'd always hear my parents having from underneath stuffed animals and shoes that lined my closet floor.

How would my father measure up in death? In the silence interrupted only by occasional scratching from above, I started counting holes, one by one. There were three when we'd moved in, all bored through two walls for what looked like someone's attempt to get at something or someone hiding in the bathroom – two that entered from the hall, with exits by the bathroom sink, the third above the stove, whose exit I would study every time I took a dump. When we'd moved out, the count was up to twelve. We all felt it was only a matter of time before it was us with the holes. I shoved the books aside and found each one of them quickly, the smooth swipes of putty. But I didn't find thirteen.

"Where's the rest, you fuck?" I said to silence in a voice that was both a whisper and a scream. I went outside, stood in the yard and called my mother. "I'm here," I told her voicemail in a blur. "Same old dump, different day. 'Night."

I tried to breathe but felt as if I'd run somewhere. I scanned the street and felt the same repulsion here as inside.

Though dark, I saw it clearly as I had when I was just a boy. The weed-choked yards and shine-dead cars were still parked in skinny driveways, all leading up to boxy garages crammed with junk or, like mine, an extra room that still felt like a garage only with cinderblocks and a window where the levered door used to be. Still, the norm was cars parked side-by-side – one in the driveway, the other digging rivets into beach sand in the yard. I squinted my eyes, as I did when young, and watched the neighborhood morph into something more affluent, the houses with two-car garages and porches with swings and second floors, just like the ones I saw in all my friends' developments that sported little pocket parks and tennis courts and unarmed cops in shorts on bikes or, later, Segways, with nothing better to do all day than give the old thumb's up to the old ladies on the front stoops and the mailman everybody knew by name, who'd never complain about having to deliver on foot at every door because that's where he'd get bloated from all the lemonade and gossip and Christmas gifts that, once a year, would fill his bag as full as when the days began. These delusions can only last so long. In the time it took for a truck to circle the cul-de-sac with a boy of no more than fourteen at the wheel tugging at a joint and roll out of sight again, I was back to feeling as deprived as my childhood neighborhood still looked. I hated this place so much as a boy that I still hated it as a man. That breed of loathing doesn't really die; it only waits.

My exhaustion brought me back. I yawned and couldn't stop, out there in front of all the faces I knew were staring at me from the curtain cracks. Escape was a viable option. I thought of fast food and hotel rooms – immaculately clean, uncluttered, hydrant-strength showers – but the thought of driving anywhere and spending money I was fast running out of was worse than going back inside. I was used to being alone. I turned around and shut the door. I cranked up the air-conditioning, lit a Camel Wide and turned off the living room fan. It kept delivering new scents and I didn't want to guess at their origin any longer. What I wanted to do was peek into the bedrooms, perhaps to remember something I'd forgotten.

Sure enough, they were just as we'd left them at eighteen and never returned. My sister's was as pink and white as ever, and still dominated on every wall by collages of posters and magazine pages that featured bronzed statues of men with obsessively cultivated abs and surgically white smiles. Her bed was made with the same purple comforter she got for Christmas one year that featured a life-size image of a *Purple Rain*-era, pompadoured Prince stroking his guitar like a mystical penis. Her white dresser was completely coated in retro, markered song lyrics scrawled by the friends she was never too ashamed to invite over. I scanned the front and couldn't help but miss her, though I could still feel that pit in the gut that started growing when I realized she was never going to let me be friends with any of hers. A year or two my senior, not one of these girls was allowed to show anything but disdain for me. After a night listening to my parents' music from the Reagan era, they inscribed my sister's dresser in kind. Get a taste for what had passed me by: "Might as well face it, you're a dick with a glooooove!" "J.B.Jovi ... I've been doing sex scenes for living. Trying to seduce an audience is the basis of rock, and if I may say so, I'm pretty good at it. (Um, duh.)" "LIKE A VIRGIN. HEE! TOUCHED FOR THE 94TH TIIIIME!" *"No sin but stupidity, suckafoooo!"* **"Fuck Simon Le Bon. Marry Andy Taylor."** **"Dog in heat, freak without warning, got an appetite for sex, 'cause ME SO HORNY!"**

I'd mourn all those missed opportunities for years.

A smile planted on my face, I hopped over the hallway crime scene and drifted to the other side of the living room. I slid open my old pocket door. I saw nothing, as usual, since it was still a mass of black from ceiling on down each wall. I'd even painted the dresser and desk to match, wrapped my bed in electrician's tape and used the vampire's cape I'd worn one Halloween as my blanket. It all was still there. The matted brown carpet was the only thing that spoiled the effect. It was just as dingy now as the day we moved in.

I went in, shut the door and flipped on the ceiling lamp that amazingly still glowed purple from the black light I'd installed years before I'd left for good. It used to illuminate the only touches of color I'd ever allowed here, besides my blood-red lava lamp and tiny hand-me-down television: the neon posters of my favorite bands, which tended toward the mopey stuff that spoke to my gothic ethos. It was a wonder, from all the songs I sighed through by The Smiths and Echo and the Bunnymen and The Cure and Joy Division (which perhaps committed the biggest lie in band-name history), that I never felt the need for anti-depressants or contemplated suicide. The only posters left now shone from the ceiling, the Dead Milkmen and Sugarcubes, which had been too tattered and grimed over by the fan to bother taking with me. Still, the sight of that glow light still living bemused me enough to bend over and grin into the tiny mirror atop the dresser just to see my teeth aglow.

I could have stopped there, curled up on the twin bed and fallen deep into slumber, but a second wind blew through me that left me feeling more alive than I'd felt in a year. I could have been skipping when I crossed the house again to the only other bedroom. When I hopped again over the site of my father's final fall, it was as if his limp form were still there in the same way I imagined all his smoky-funky breaths made up a part of every inhale I took. I stopped at the end of the hall. The skittering from above was loudest here and I slammed the side of my fist against the door jamb to his room to make it stop. I dropped my third cigarette in ten minutes onto the last square of tile outside his room and stomped out the cherry just as it rolled to the edge of the same traffic-rutted, burnt-orange shag that once (and forever after) made me think of the post-Woodstock orgy scene I'd seen in a porno at a friend's house in middle school, a spectacle that would make me wonder for several years thereafter how a woman's vagina could ever be entered through such an impenetrable bramble of pubes. I could smell him now, his rank presence, here more than anywhere else in the house, and I'm not embarrassed to admit that I half-expected, my mother's half, for him to be sitting there, in the very last place I looked, picking his nose or pretending to read another book, just to mess with his only son one last time for posterity's sake.

But he was only where he'd always been: suspended in two-dimensional form. At the foot of my father's bed, I stared into his eyes staring back from a place called Olan Mills, frozen in time among the forced smiles of his family and sort of looking proud. I snickered to erase the thought and felt a wave of exhaustion pour over me. I did what I still can't understand. I yanked the drab yellowed blanket and sheet to the floor, both of which were worn through with butt burns and sweaty socks, then I collapsed, consigned, into a baby ball on top of gray sheets that used to be white. My teeth were grinding, so I opened my mouth. My eyes were windswept and dry, so I let them close. The theatrical smile I'd brought into the room was flattened into a quivering grimace. I couldn't keep one word out of my mind: hate.

I hated him for everything, for how Canoe cologne and tar

and Cheetos drool befouled the pillow. I hated how the books that lined all the walls in here too concealed more holes I'd yet to find but knew I would. I hated how he wasn't there but left a stink of waste for me to handle. I hated him, I hated this, I hated here. It's hard to say how such a hate could let me shrivel up into a fetus, to hug that funky pillow while I cried myself to sleep.

Chapter 2

WHEREAS, the Freeburg City Council, duly elected and sincere, have pondered with resolve this quandary of just how wide to cast tomorrow's net. Tireless research and debate, with public discourse from all sides, have led us surely to endorse this higher path of liberty: Even (most of the; see Addendum A) free riders, vagabonds and cogs, all those averse to evolution's ways, must have a hand to pull these curtains back so even they can see the light.

Another sunset filled the window that at first I thought was just the dawn. Alert, I felt the clutter pressing in. I told myself to move but didn't recognize my inner voice. Ready for action, I swung my shoes, still on, to the floor and darted from the room before adjusting for my lack of any real coordination; so I stubbed a big toe on the nightstand, jarred my shoulder on the door jamb, but still was able to jump the hurdle of his imaginary body in the hallway before yanking on new clothes by the front door. Escape. Deep, hot breaths that weren't fogged with grime and death.

At least some curiosity remained. Though I'd merely passed from one nightmare to another with some better air, I somehow felt reset if not rested. It would last as long as it took to move halfway up the block and ask for the time from this wereman in a wife-beater and boxers bent over the engine of his corpse of a car and humming something melodic that made him seem marginally approachable: "Almost 6, I'm guessing." "Thanks ...

wait, p.m.?" He laughed. I didn't. (At the time, I didn't think I'd ever laugh again.)

I trotted up the street, calculating the hours I'd lost in my head, but then I suddenly felt weak and went back to walking. My gut moaned for the food it knew I was headed for at the convenient store. It was just four blocks away, but still I got there out of breath, in a gloss of sweat that reeked of poor dietary choices. I swallowed air like a gulp of soda and belched out the exhale.

The store was the same as how I'd left it with a static but Technicolor bounty of stale necessities equally unappetizing and reaffirming. I knew where everything would be, since the aisles and inventory were arranged like all the aisles and inventory in all the other convenience stores I'd ever frequented. I could have closed my eyes and nosed my way right over to the hot dogs spinning in the corner, the aisle-ending selection of rawhide jerky. I could have let the heat of my neck draw me toward the coldest reaches of the beer cooler in the back, but instead I watched my feet and walked right to where I'd have the chance to pay double for a generic can of instant coffee and a tube of powdered doughnuts. It still felt like morning, so I acted it out.

At the counter, the man in front of me, a big gory polyp commanding my view of his throat, was getting in his numbers and picking out some scratch-offs with an exuberance that screamed of fruitless toil. Big Gory Polyp, in fact, was the first of two people that day who, in quick succession, would make me question whether any of my father's secrets should ever have been shared.

"Jackpot's something like 1.2, 1.3," he told me conspiratorially, as if it weren't posted there in the front window. By framing his mouth with a grimed-up hand, his lone front tooth, tarred to dirt, assumed the polyp's place, replaced it entirely. I pretended to welcome his words.

"Wow," I said, backing up a little to avoid the spittle that had to have been coming next, "they must be raking in the dough. Hey: for the kids, right?"

An ornery nod from Gushing Polyp Tooth, all smiles with a

35-dollar accordion of scratch-offs in his hand, and he's out the door with no less than a skip in his step. What right did *he* have? I remember wondering.

The cashier asked if I needed tickets or anything else I hadn't asked for. "No thanks," I told her, "I don't play taxes. I pay them," giving a little orchestrated grin to the lady behind me, who raised her brow dispassionately to ask if there was something else I just had to share with a stranger-for-life. I turned back dejected and stared into the cashier's poker face then asked for some Camel Wides before the silence dinned. The floor keened beneath me.

Not one single giggle. I rarely got to use my only other go-to witticism – "This is how I try to see it: You just add an 'o' to 'God' ... 'Good,' right? ... Now take the 'D' from 'Devil'." (punctuated by a spaced-out look) – and although I'd come to expect a few bemused frowns in that one's wake, it could always be counted on to elicit at least one true look of discovery, especially when I launched it on a klatch of students caught talking metaphysically. "I am, indeed, a teacher," I'd sometimes think. You can't break that one out every day, though. But "Playing Taxes"? It had *never failed*, Circle K to 7-11. That some pride remained to be squashed is what had shocked me the most. Mercifully, with the cash changing hands, Can't Read the Nametag gave me the little giggle I'd come to expect, the tiniest glimmer of shared connection, albeit belated, then she said, "Not in the mood to play, huh?" Then I might as well have vanished as she directed her gaze to the next customer, who announced her scratch-off numbers with such emphasis that I could hear each syllable stab into my back as I walked toward the door.

Still, in the parking lot, I managed to leer in judgment at Hungry Polyp Head, sitting in a rusty Olds and just scratching and searching for some kind of a life without want, while absently shushing the elementary-age boy too big to be strapped into that booster seat in back and mourning the gummy bears he must have been promised. "I told you maybe,'" said Neck Tooth through the pus, without looking up from his lap. The boy slammed his back into the seat and the car rocked and groaned. I shuffled on, blatantly staring while trying to bite open my package of doughnuts. Then I turned to look in my path and saw him, dropping the doughnuts into the dirt. I stooped to pick them up, but couldn't peel my gaze from a stupor of staring directly into a past that had long been buried under a mountain of books and a nation of miles. It was him. I knew it.

He was picking up a lit cigarette at the corner of the store and struggling not to blow a gasket in his head. He held his breath and his face grew redder and redder. His rusty beard had a dull threading of silver, but all the rest of his hair fell just shy of his shoulders as it always had, that same pubic protest of tabby orange. It was my hair, only mangier, and it's how I knew for sure it was him, despite him morphing by then from menacingly angular and peaked into someone just a few value meals shy of obese. A vintage Mountain Dew shirt that I'd seen him wear in childhood now failed to cover the trip over his belly, which had the same tangle of rusty hair as the rest of him and threatened to blow out his blue jeans with the dip rings on both back pockets. The child still inside me then shuddered. Finishing the look were Doc Marten boots and a silver chain linking his front belt loop to something no doubt menacing in his back pocket. I should have been moving on, away, but I was frozen. He stood up and turned to face me as I lingered, still avoiding his eyes, which I knew would have that same wry look of felonious plotting, the same too-piercing pair of blue eyes, and I struggled to swallow old fears that, until then, had felt long-replaced by new ones.

"Serge?" I couldn't believe it myself, that I was speaking. To him.

His ears perked up of their own volition, separately but in quick succession, a dog's ears. I noticed the lobes drooping almost to his shoulders from being stretched by an ambitious piercing regimen that apparently had been abandoned in favor of paying rent and utilities. I begged the god of my own personal universe to keep him from recognizing me and still I stared, frozen, like prey into a predator's mouth.

"Oh no," I said, looking forcefully down and moving into a

purposeful walk away, only I was headed in a direction that no one would think coherent, straight toward an overflowing Dumpster. "You're definitely not the Serge I thought you would be. That's for sure." I turned to look at where I was walking just in time to avoid a concussion. "Have a nice day, young man." (Maybe he'd think I was as old as my students always thought I was.)

"I might be," he said. "I mean..." He paused for too long, seemingly considering the odds of there being another red-headed Serge like him somewhere else in the cloistered world of Freeburg. "I mean, Serge. I'm Serge. Ma ... Magumfrey?" He was walking in my wake of dust now, apprehension in his nostrils.

"Ma-wha?" I said, casting what felt like a sincere grin and giving a quick 360 twirl to appear calm, only the twirl happened when I stepped onto a piece of cardboard next to the Dumpster that sent me into more like a 450 that had to be corrected for by adding an awkward extra 270 to point me back toward Walnut Circle and away from this maladroit who still wore his t-shirts from high school. Over my shoulder: "Ma-who? No. No, I'm sorry, but that's definitely never been my name."

I turned the back corner of the store and went into a double-time trot for the few seconds I had alone before he was at the corner too. I was on Pistachio Drive, panting and red-faced.

I felt him there, sniffing the air like old times: Sergio Arredondo.

As dusk fell, a flood of memories poured into my head as I moved toward a home that never felt like one and still held no such promise. Two years my senior but only one grade, Serge was and presumably still was the menace of this neighborhood and many others for miles around. He'd been born for it. The regular thrashings he endured at home were public displays, since his parents were the kind to eschew air-conditioning in favor of keeping the fridge stocked with beer, which meant the windows were always as open as their mouths. Me and what few friends I had then assumed things would end bad not only for Serge someday but for everyone we knew named Arredondo, that their lives would be one long cascade of bad endings. Serge was even molding his little brother, Renaldo, into a sidekick.

Renaldo was two years younger than me and at least five years shorter, but with that Happy Meal thickness and the same family curse, I'd fully expected to be trampled to tears by him too, most likely in as humiliating a fashion as possible. Waiting for it was my life for several formative years. On cheap bikes they would circle our cul-de-sac, cartoon yammering sharks in captivity with dead eyes to match, never smiling or waving, just those sneers of disdain or, when prey wandered by, random insults that marked the Arrendondos as dangerously stupid and marked all of us for a pounding that we'd never see coming. And the taunting insults were so macabre that many would work their way into your nightmares. My nightmares:

From the randomly misguided ... "Nice day, huh Sally-boy? A fine day for sucking my DICK!" from Serge, lunging from his bike to pose menacingly from my tree lawn. "Yeah, you dick-snugglin' faggot," confirmed Renaldo supportively from the second rank.

To the cannibalistic... "That goofy haircut's got me thinking it's time to take that stupid head of yours off, Mafagfrey, see how you taste with some hot sauce." "Do it, Serge. Eat the pussy faggot's fucking face right the fuck off his faggoty corpse!"

To the criminally perverted... "So I stop raping your Mom, Macockfrey, and she can't stop calling for me. I'm like, 'Bitch, I told you, you whale of a who-er! No more rape for you! You like that shit too much!'" "Yeah. No more rape for mama! Hey, what's rape, Serge? C'mon, Serge, what's rape?!"

Petrified, the kids in this neighborhood typically chose to play indoors, but we never lost a sense of pity about the Arredondo line. We knew it was Peter Arredondo (referred to in private as Dick) to blame for giving his sons such twisted comedic instincts. Let the record show, for instance, that not one but two of countless police interventions I'd been on Walnut Circle to witness ended in mirror image with Papa Arredondo being escorted off in cuffs, mace streaming tears down his face and the pine bat he kept by their front door leaning up against the cruiser that would whisk him away. All I could wonder after that second incident, bathed in the afterglow of community comeuppance: Had he gone out and bought a new bat or had someone thought it best to give this man his old bat back?

The man was never gone as long as it seemed his own children wanted him gone, but their mother, JudyJulieJune was how I remember her name, always seemed to welcome him back garrulously with a long weekend of pretend merriment, silly radio karaoke and frightened-sounding sex. Then normalcy would return: At least two or three times a week, from six houses away, at any time of day or night, you'd hear the moaning and screaming, the slamming of doors, all that ignorance in fear of a world that already despised them just roiling them all up like root vegetables in a pressure cooker. If all of them weren't yelling at once, it was one of them yelling and the rest of them crying. It all made my father's random nonsensical explosions, in retrospect, seem touched with restraint, since he only warred with drywall, complicated books and personal demons.

In our teens, nothing changed, only the circling in the cul-de-sac was done with a hood-less Civic coated in stickers stolen from other people's cars. Sometimes, Serge let a way-shy-of-teenage Renaldo drive while he chucked grapefruits at the tin garage doors of elderly people's houses, causing at least three heart attacks resulting in two deaths. By this time, thankfully, I got to spend most of my time in Cassadaga with my mother.

I'd never had to fight them, I must admit for the record, but I'd come close; in some ways, not fighting had inflicted more enduring wounds. "Why don't you come out here and say that shit, pussy!?" bellowed Renaldo into my window, just the once. "I heard what you said! Say that shit to my face..." First, I couldn't recall saying anything in particular to anyone of late, though we'd all had much to say about these two menaces on a regular basis. Second, it would have been much less emasculating if the taunt caused that pussy to burst out the front door and take out "the punkassbitch who dared scream shit like that at my house!" Those types of taunts will form a shaky foundation, however, for the pussy who stays in his room with the blinds drawn and cries loud enough for his tormenter to hear it from outside, a pussy who knew how the gossip would lead to an interminable gauntlet of rolled eyes at school the very next day, only to be elucidated by a girl I didn't even know, who would point out while passing, in as populated a hallway as possible, that "... Renaldo is, like, still in elementary school or something, isn't he?" But all of it's even worse when the crying draws the interest of the pussy's father, who'd set the whole chain of events in order by asking plaintively at his pussy son's door, "You gonna fuck that kid up, call the cops, or snitch at school? Just choose now. 'Cause whatever you do, it's coming, son."

"I don't want to fight anybody," I wailed from under my black shroud of pillow, sheet and blanket, which was the truth and a lie, and so it went that I both cherished and loathed my father when he took that as his cue to sidle to the front door, open it wide and use the sheepish voice of a serial killer to tell the little fat kid in his driveway that I, his son, was "not a lover or a fighter at the moment," but that I was "gonna figure that out someday," and when I did I was "gonna come looking for your fat ass to either fuck you up bad or fuck your wife good, hear? But he ain't gonna find you. Know why?" His voice hushed. I threw off the covers and strained at the window to hear. "'Cause I'm gonna already'a fed your fat ass to that gator over here so nobody but some archeologist of the future's gonna find you. Now go eat something before you faint."

Renaldo must have left because the door closed and the house went as quiet as the street outside. My mother was working her night job at the Dollar General and my sister was headphoned away in her room, so you could call this something like a moment my father and I had shared, one of our few. Later, I managed to slide to the blinds again to survey the street, where I saw through the Arredondo's dining room window a wildly gesturing shirtless Peter screaming something at somebody for something. Normalcy had returned enough for me to sleep, but not well, for I knew what humiliations were to come.

Passing by the Arrendondo house again, reflexively speeding up as I did as a kid, I noticed the same aura of despair and lurking danger, though it no longer had the tall sandspurs, the strewn car parts, the torn window screens. Then as before, however, the place was a symbol of tormented ignorance and misbegotten confidence. I could still see it as it was, the blinds always yanked open in every room, like a cadaver dissected, to a bare-bones collection of chipped pressed-board furniture and raggedy swapmeet quilts that no one had the knitting skills to repair or surplus income to replace. Along the biggest wall in the front room of the house, which was laid out in exact reverse as my father's, family photos and school pictures in faux-brass frames used to show the evolution of the family's slowly darkening smirk, but nothing remained on that wall as I passed as a man. It was painted dark blue and had a single framed portrait of someone I couldn't recognize from afar. I wondered if they all were still in there, though, brooding and scheming and licking their wounds. Sure, the whole place looked tidied up now, but not in my head.

"Hey Magumfrey!" I peeked, startled, over my shoulder in a quick snap. He was shouting from deep in the distance, still pursuing but looking too round now to break into anything but a slightly faster walk. *He'd seen me leering at his house.* I hurried up, into a speed walker's effeminate gait, elbows tucked, arms barely swinging, legs working from the knees down only, in a dead giveaway for fear. I rounded the bend, three doors shy of the circle's end, and was out of sight again but not earshot. "Magumfrey!?" His final confirmation must have come from seeing the manboy up there shifting into speed-walk. I could hear him or remember hearing him laughing, the same hoarse whinny that haunted so much of my formative REM sleep.

I got back to the house and locked the deadbolt, drew the blinds in front and back, then I peered stealthily back up the street from a barely touched slat in the front room. Through the tangerine dusk turning as I peered to a gaudy-gray mauve, I spotted light from the dining room window of Serge's house that hadn't been on a minute before. I turned around. I'd thought the days of watching my back were over; that I'd be the only one watching my back from then on.

Don't be misled. Life did grow to feel a little safer in my later teens. Not all of my youth was marked by torment. My circle of local friends slowly widened to include a few scrappy heads who could have easily taken Serge in a fight without any weapons, while Serge's crew seemed to remain just Renaldo and that lithe, twentyish girl everyone knew was a caseworker, who'd visit every other Sunday to throw a football with him in the street. One weekend in my freshman year, I darted past on my bike and Serge made sure I knew the lady was actually his "cousin with benefits." I feigned a look of admiration to placate his animal instincts, but later made a point of bringing his name up in the company of rowdier friends, insinuating this or that minor downfall. Brash with the deepening of voices, the hardening of will and wit, we brainstormed a slew of misfortunes aimed at upending the Arrendondo scourge.

Around the time that Serge turned seventeen, just as I was entering my sophomore year and he was starting his second junior year, the rumor mill was churning out a local journalism based entirely on the hearsay of fabrications. It was(n't) Serge, by then sporting a full orange beard shaved into lightning bolts at the burns, who was infecting all the water fountains with herpes, something the Freeburg Health Department had to warn against during a special morning assembly. And it had to have been Serge (even though it wasn't) who put a used tampon in Dean Leavenworth's pencil drawer too, an offense for which he was suspended on the basis of seemingly separate anonymous tips and had to repeat his junior year. An older kid I barely knew, M. Smithorjones, had lost a very public fight to Serge at a party where no grownups were around to break it up, and he nurtured some hard feelings for so long that, just before graduating, he thought of pushing word that Serge had even gone so far as to rape Margaret Fisher behind the tennis courts and that this had been the crushing blow to cause her family to move back up north for her to finish high school in hushed disgrace. The words "Serge" and "rape" found their way into a whirlwind of whispers. Since Margaret never had that many friends in Freeburg, the story of why she'd moved so suddenly stuck much better than the boring useless truth we'd learned a few months later: that her father had gotten a job in a Minnetonka rebar mill that paid way better than unemployment insurance. The rumor got so unruly, so loaded with corroborative lies and descriptive adjectives, that one day Serge just stopped coming to school. I feel both liberated and ashamed to admit this.

I also regret to acknowledge that the memory brought a sinister grin to my face all those years later, a guilty calm, as I moved from the front window to the kitchen and turned on the radio above the microwave, both crud-dusted and out of date. I rolled the dial to a Carpenters song that, for the first time up until then or forever after, somehow sounded appropriate, then I crept onto the back porch, sat down in a creaky vinyl-strapped chair and stared into the darkening woods as I always had on those few occasions when I had the place to myself. I should have known the song would change in seconds to the brooding lament of a dying anorexic:

"We've ooonly just beguuuuuuun to
DIIIIIEEEEEEEEEEEEEE..."

I couldn't stop thinking of Serge and Renaldo over there still, probably plotting a new chapter of my downfall. I tried to recall, as bats flitted in and out of the darkest shadows, what had happened to truly break the last shred of tension back then, hoping that wave would carry me forward enough to get something done inside. Then, finally peeling open my package of doughnuts and eating one after the other in quick succession, I remembered. Another sinister grin formed, this one coated in powdered sugar. I must have looked like the asylum patient whose wrists always have to be tethered during group activities and visiting hours.

Serge had always been chief antagonist in my childhood dramedy. Had we ever been given another choice? But by the time I'd turned sixteen, Serge was officially a man in terms of whether he could kill or die in an instant for his country or in the long, slow strangle of the cigarette manufacturers, and perhaps that's what had turned his attentions away from the meaningless torture of others toward something more self-destructive. According to several threads of uncorroborated gossip that Serge himself has never denied with anything like a straight face, he'd started buying with every spare dollar a faux marijuana known in the very early 21st century as spice. These chemical-laden lawn clippings were typically popular among: crackheads too poor or afraid to buy crack; dealers looking to dupe their most scared and naive customers; diehard potheads trying to pass urinalysis screenings; and all the many legions in between who'd lost contact with their drug dealers and college friends. On first drag, this drug gave the user the same sunny feeling of pot, but over the course of a bowl-full, it was more like huffing on paint from a paper bag. The throat burned, the spine coursed with uncontrollable fury. It's hard to believe today that something like this would be legal while legitimate marijuana remained officially taboo, but these were the types of decisions made by politicians beholden not to the populous but their most generous donors. In the fabricated freedom of our nation's not-so-distant past, you got deadly chemicals sprayed on lawn trimmings and marketed "NOT FOR HUMAN CONSUMPTION" as "EXOTIC INCENSE" but branded playfully and artfully with obvious suggestions like "Mr. Happy," "WTF?" and "Jazz," most with a picture of an iconic cartoon figure like Scooby Doo staring out red-eyed from the label with a look of utter ecstasy. But since it smelled like nothing more damaging than stale potpourri and smoked enough at first like the now state-regulated marijuana, spice hooked its tweakers from the back end, when many had no choice but to keep on smoking it until they could do nothing but. Millions suffered.

(I know one of them well enough. My father, a spice survivor, described the drug's magnetism faithfully in an audio "cassette" recording that I found in a closet drawer during my cleanup but didn't listen to for several years, since that's how long it took to come across an adequate "cassette player" on which to play it. Allegedly, he'd chronicled the experience as part of some aborted class-action lawsuit he'd envisioned spearheading in a rare moment of lucidity. It's fairly obvious that he'd still been in its clutches:

"...*Nine times in, you got that breezy walk to the edge, you know? Nice and numb. Neat. But then the tenth, it's 'Holy Batfuck, Robin, I'm over the edge. My heart's punching my ribs, old buddy, and some kind of rat poison is running all through my spine or something. And then it's 'thisiswhatdeathislike, thisiswhatdeathislike...' – we're talking maybe a fifteen-, twenty-minute panic attack, no shit. Just sliding down a razor and throwing your three or four hidden stashes away, and not just in the trash but shoving it up to your shoulder to the bottom with the coffee grounds and cigarette butts. And then there's this WHEW: another fifteen, twenty-five minutes of graciousness, digging all your stashes out of the garbage, rinsing off the gunk and smoking up some more and just celebrating with yourself, you know? All 'I made it! I'm NOT dying! To LIFE!' And of course, the bills aren't paying themselves and the old lady, the EX-old lady's always asking the wrong questions so you gotta find a way to keep Spice your bitch on the sly, see? My ONLY bitch on the sly thankyouverymuch, but still... You're wondering how you're gonna find the four or five bucks to get another batch, figuring out what shit you can pawn that nobody's gonna miss, and you end up looking around one day and you might as well be on an unlivable island that's got all the bridges burned down to what. But you're no quitter. I'm. No. Quitter. So you keep buying and buying it, see? But you might start flicking off the random olive-skinned cashier too on the way out of their store, telling 'em 'Thanks, Mohammed! Jihad! Lalalalala...' It's that kind a love/ hate relationship, see? Only heroin or some shit could kick this bitch out the door, and believe me ...* [recording in its entirety.]")

Clearly, this drug could drive the crazy even crazier. Perhaps it was heroin that finally ended my father's devotion to spice, or maybe it was local governments for miles around that eventually banned its sale. In any case, I kept clear, but only after smoking too much one time with some friends in a dirty garage and feeling all as one, all at once, like our spines were bored through with gun powder and our lungs were going to pop like balloons. All five members of that huddled group of teen thrill-seekers actually drew up and signed a document that night (burned in a bonfire the following night) that stated, "If you find us dead, this was NOT a mass suicide. Spice is a monkey whore."

That was goodbye for me. Others were more fearless. Take Serge, who already had experience calling police for help by the time spice made him call for it. Around this time, a few months after disappearing from Freeburg High for good, Serge ended up on the phone with a dispatcher who learned that 1) he'd been having dreams foretelling that he was going to be in jail that night, and 2) that he needed to get the call officially on the record to prove to his parents and everyone else unaware of his special gifts that, despite not having much in the way of social or academic ambitions, he might at least be able to scrape away a living in a place like Cassadaga someday. Thereby, he said and I paraphrase, he would have proof of his mystical prowess and the wherewithal to finally form the beginnings of a fledgling flock of devotees.

The newspaper ran a story about the whole thing, of course, and a local DJ and his sidekicks read through the transcript like it was a big Hollywood script, background music and sound effects and all. For weeks at the end of my sophomore year, for much of that summer, the transcript of this 9-1-1 call was all my paltry group of sort-of-friends could think about. Eventually we could act the scene out from memory to fill every gap in any conversation. This is the part (recorded in my journal for posterity) that always killed us:

Dispatcher: *"What's happening?*

Arredondo: *Everything that happened today is actually in my dream, and I want to prove it to everybody.*

Dispatcher: *What did you dream about that's happening?*

Arredondo: *It's all on paper. I wrote it down.*

Dispatcher: *What did you write, Mr. Arredondo?*

Arredondo: *(long pause) Well, it's not in my dream that I told you on the phone what was in my dream. You'll have to read* *it later, maybe tomorrow. Gimme your name and I'll make you a copy later tonight. You're gonna wanna read this.*

Dispatcher: *Well, I'm already in the middle of a really good book, so I'm not sure if I'll have the time, but you can give me your name. Guess you already knew I was gonna ask for that, huh? Weird."*

Even now, all these years later as I read this passage to my writer-for-hire, I'm ashamed to admit it still brings a bloom of rapture into my chest, the sincerest grin to my face, even a little tear of hysterical triumph to my eye, but it no longer comes from amused condescension like before; now it comes with a forced kind of empathy attached, like the look I give to students who'll "just never learn," followed by a terrible sorrow for having rejoiced in the misfortune of the misfortunate.

Serge, who you'll see did learn some things through the years, wasn't sent that time to the juvie hall that was starting to feel safer than home. He went to an institution with jail-like security measures and then down yet another smirking coterie of cops, court audiences, bailiffs, DAs, PDs, judges, psychiatrists, psychologists, nurses, preachers, outreach volunteers, church missionaries and family therapy coaches, all of whom did a lot of shrugging and harrumphing.

By the looks of him years later, I imagined (incorrectly) that it probably wasn't his last stretch in orange jumper and shower shoes. What did I know? With no fanfare, he'd vanished to me and I'd vanished to him. But really, it was only me. I'd vanished. He'd never left.

Silencing my breaths, I stared over my left shoulder, sitting on the porch, and remembered eavesdropping at eighteen from this very chair, the last time I'd heard a cop try to scream over a screaming-louder Serge, whose dad had just been put back in for spinning like a Tasmanian devil right down the center of the burrow again. These arrests always left Serge as head devil, a role he was well-trained to assume, so every time this uniformed voice in the dark started touching something deep, making any sense at all, Serge would invariably interject with logic that varied in sequence from idiotic to militant to publishable and usually right back to utterly imbecilic for the next loop. It was the family line, and, though depressing, it was riveting entertainment.

"You might not have a choice now, Serge, what house you gotta live in, what's for dinner tonight, what clothes you gotta wear, but soon..."

"You got room at your place, Ponch? Gonna get me a job down at the mill until I get me a turn through the Academy? Let me wear your jammies?"

"I don't allow that kind of disrespect in my house, so no."

"I don't allow that kind of disrespect in..."

"Break the cycle, Serge. This doesn't have to be you."

"No? Who else can I be?"

No matter the dumbfounded route, it was good police work, leading him to that question. That brought the first wave I'd heard others try so many times before, the join-the-Army-or-go-to-jail kind of pleas about *man*ufacturing some maturity. Bigger, stronger, faster, tougher, leaner, meaner – all that. I shuddered to think of Serge becoming any of those things, being issued a semi-automatic rifle, being taught to use it well.

"Have you even talked to the guy? You get your GED and you're in, man."

"Killer or cook. Those are my choices, right oskifer? You mean I can go and get blowed up somewheres and I get paid to do it? Where's a motherfucker sign!? I'm leaving to-NIGHT, bit-CHES!"

"Sergio, I'm just..."

"Man, Uncle Stan can suck my cock, see?"

"It's Uncle Sam, Serge, and watch your f...., watch your mouth."

"It's Suncle Tam, Urge. Burga-burga. Mmm, donuts!"

Maniacal laughter, alone on a long breeze of dumbfounded silence. Then: "Either you show some respect or you end up where your Daddy goes all the time, Serge. You want that? I was just like you, man. Out in DEELand, running me a corner. Had Stetson U. all lit up like Sparkler City, right? Sellin' and smokin' and hustlin' my life away, but where's that taking me, who's that making me? Huh? Serge? Are you getting the message here? Mrs., Mrs., um...?"

"Are you listening to this man and his fucking message, Sergio? Does he have to smack you in the fucking head to get the nice words out of that fat empty fucking melon of a head of yours, Sergio? Hello? Sergio!? Do you see what I'm..."

"Ma'am, you're not helping with..."

"There's your message right fucking there." Five houses away and across the street, out of view, I could hear it all and see Serge in my mind pointing a middle finger at everyone, everywhere – past, present, and future.

"Please, son. Try to use your brain for a second here. I felt the same way. And then I went and found out for myself what was true and what wasn't. You'd be paying your way, seeing some of the world besides this old tired-ass town. You'd be defending our country, defending our freedom. Our way of life."

"Who's life we talking about here, Sarge? This way of life? Defend this dump? Freedom to what? Suck dick for crack? Stamp pans in a factory like the old man? Drink Save-a-Lot beer for the wife to get pretty? Huh? That the life you're meaning?"

"You little...!"

I hated Serge then, but felt gooseflesh from the chill of sincerity in those words. The feeling wouldn't last for long. It was always about this far up Serge's wall that the cop would start to sound stymied and look for other ways around. This particular cop must have had special training in empathy or knew things about the Arredondo household that only private glimpses can afford because he tried harder than any before to get through.

"Look. Fine. The uniform, it's not for everybody. But get yourself a trade, son, something you're proud to say you do. Please. Go every day and get something going, Serge. For your country, just try and be a better man, okay? It's in you. I believe that. Do you believe that, Serge? Serge? Son..."

"Listen to this man!" screamed his mother between sobs. "You act like a fucking animal. You little...!"

"Ma'am, please. Serge? Serge, look at me. See? See? You're not an animal. See that? Serge? Look at me. Serge!"

Had Serge shed a tear? He can't recall and most incident reports don't record those kinds of things.

"I'm not a fucking animal, you bitch!" The words were definitely delivered in something like a whimper.

"Serge, you gotta stop disrespecting people like that. You gotta stop teaching your little brother it's okay to shoot BBs through the fence at cars, right? At the neighbors? At people's cats? Because it's not. It's five to ten. Hear that? Five. To ten. Don't start shaking your head all over the place. We've been getting calls, Serge. You know what I'm talking about. Wipe that smirk off your face."

(The first shots were at squirrels, cats and then me. I felt it was my civic duty to call.)

"Your poor Mom, she got..."

"My *poor Mommy* gets what's comin' for pickin' convicts to fuck for a living and then letting the motherfucker *keep comin' home* after all this bullshit up in here. You're damn right she's poor. She ain't never had no job."

"I can't do this!" she screamed. "He's just like his father. You see what I'm saying? He's just like Peter! Doyouseedoyouseedoyousee...?"

"I'll kill a bitch say I'm anything like that mother..."

"Please, sir. See? Take him. Just tonight. Just for tonight? He's going to kill me. One of these nights, he's going to..."

"Ma'am. Can we just take it down a few notches here? Sergio, do you want to go with us tonight?"

Silence. Then: "But what will I wear? And, uh! Look at my hair! I mean, if there's room, then sure, but I wouldn't want to impose, you know? It's..."

Then more exasperated tears, then wild sobbing, then the noisy woods and my noisier thoughts. It always ended like that, with the cops in their cruisers, searching for words to fill up another report, two well-paid law-enforcement professionals writing a story about Serge instead of policing Freeburg. As always, I had to imagine the rest: Serge returning to his cave within the cave, the family dunce cap on, leering out from the one broken edge of vertical blind and making a list of all the people who'd seen his latest humiliation. I always used to crane my neck in hopes of seeing him in the backseat of a cruiser. I can only remember one time he was riding along, a few years before this final episode, and it's memorable because he was wearing the kind of aw-shucks smile a kid will wear on the way to somewhere exciting like an amusement park. Until then, I'd never seen him smile like that, at no one's expense.

I don't know why I was looking again. All those years later, I still expected him to join the nightly racket at any second, drowning out the whooing and croaking and crickety whining and slithery crackling that heralded the nightly primordial orgy of pleas and moans in my childhood backyard. I turned away from old torment and tuned into this cacophonous roar as it pulsed as urgently as ever, throbbing away and aghast and as afraid as I was and ever was. That incongruous music of the trees came through, and even though Serge's perpetually quavering voice, always tipping into mania or daredevil theatrics, didn't come through, it might as well have. He was there in my head and in the way I saw and heard and felt the night.

* * *

I kept glued to inaction, then as always before. I felt like nothing, going nowhere, so that's where I went, the nowhere nothing inside, which I'm inclined to note, much further removed, at least was somewhere and something in one way or another. I only knew so much about the way to get there, a meditative state, but had gleaned from my time in the company of wanderers and other assorted humanists that the key to the door was the air that I breathed. I yelled at the monkeys in my head to zip it. I focused on my breathing, my breathing's breathing, but grew bored in seconds. The monkeys rattled the bars and screamed for more complexity, so I shifted focus to coax my faithless consciousness into a constructive meditation I'd learned from Amy, a ("Saul, you know I have a boy) friend in college. So there I was, remembering how to relax, still avoiding what I'd gone there to do.

I allowed myself to swing in as oxygen through the rote forest of nostrils and trachea and lungs and bronchial trees and alveoli leaves, then back as carbon dioxide down the same remembered trail, in and out, until I'd logged every stupid detail and could no longer forestall my approach to the next station, imagining the scarred-over shrapnel of self-loathing dislodge with the force of each inhalation and spewing forth into the smog of night. *This with that, that for this, this is that, that is this, this is ridiculous, ridiculous is this...* I screamed inside so only I could hear it. Too much reason remained, too much faithlessness, too much that was real that had hurt too much to forget, and all of it muddying up the waters that were meant to be made still and clear just by breathing and breathing and... But it was useless. I tried another tack. I talked myself into actually leaving my body here in the chair with an exhale and going where it carried me, ride a breeze away and above all the chatter in my head. Advanced reading stuff. I opened my eyes. It was dark.

So there I was, doing nothing and leaving a metaphorical nothing behind for the anything of something more. It was my way through the clutter, and it was no way at all. Everything returned to the voices in my head, so I just sat there and stared at the darkening night. I watched with what I knew was there as the scrubby flatwoods to the south merged in minutes with a starless sky, jaundiced by the torch of the coal-burning power plant into the same gray slate. All I heard were the monkeys, screaming "Sergio is still here!" or "Get this place packed up, you bum-to-be!" or "Go inside, you fool, and lock the door or die!" or "Do something, stupid! Anything! Only the certifieds just sit there and stare into the dark all night!"

So I scanned A1 of the *Eagle*, the history teacher catching up on history's first draft. Isn't that what was right? The paper was still being delivered daily, as indicated by the small pile accumulated by the front door, but this one was a few weeks stale. I couldn't get below the fold, either, because some neon-green lizards as fat as sausage links were copulating on the screen and watching me watch them watching me... And wouldn't you know they were taking their time and under no circumstances going to stop to find a more private setting. Seemingly unashamed, they might even have been reveling in their voyeur, and that temerity held more sway than whatever envy I felt; I stifled the urge to kick them off into the night. Fuck on, lizard friends.

I dropped the paper to my lap, leaned back and propped my bare feet on the edge of a small round table spray-painted black and littered with dying plants, empty Big Gulp cups, bottle-cap ashtrays, spent candles. I saw it all as future labor, time I had to spend doing things I wouldn't be paid for. I tipped over an empty can of OFF! that clanged against the Astroturf floor and the whole tree-line orchestra halted its music at once, but only for a few tentative seconds. I focused on more of the work left ahead of me, scanning what I knew I'd have to haul from stacks that hadn't budged since when I'd lived there. I didn't want to think about it, so I drifted back to ogling the lizard couple then off I went again into the night beyond the screen.

Think: Don't think. *Think harder not to think*, one of my wiser monkeys scolded, so I did that by thinking of things I had no questions about. I tried to raise the sun again with what I heard and knew was there, attaching names to things to prove I had a mind for something useful. I started where I'd stopped, the long spare sweep of sandy tangle unrolling toward the west down a slope of ferns, pennyroyal, beautyberry, and tarflower, which wove in a few dozen paces into a thorn-thick marshland of cypress and gum trees and, in their shade, a slithering, impenetrable sea of saw palmetto, poison ivy, and morning-glory, with deceptive flashes of blue, white and violet merely cover for stalks that can turn machetes into butter knives, clothes to rags and skin to supper for a hundred species of blood-loving bugs. I drifted and kept drifting, surprising myself by how deftly I could escape what needed to be done. I hadn't thought of Rebecca all day! Until then. This was the backdrop I'd hoped to conjure in the dark, the one that held the sway to depose, if you pointed your chair just right toward the west and tuned in the nocturnal clamor, any hint of humanity's rein. My mind raced for enlightenment, labeling this, situating that. In a daze, I filled in the blanks, top to bottom:

the falcons and turkey vultures, high in threadbare slash pines half-garlanded in catbriar or skunk vines, peering down past the screech owls and mockingbirds, the crows and nightjars and grackles, nestling in garrulous cliques on the sagging branches of moss-polluted oaks, to gaze, all as one, on the buffet of choices further below in the mire, at the nerve-wracked squirrels and fun-sized chipmunks sprinting to anything anywhere from something somewhere, one shadow to the next, wherein lurked this black racer or that cottonmouth skulking through vines and roots that felt more like family, in search of little snacks, these littlest of hearts, these lizards and frogs and caterpillars and grasshoppers not fucking but screaming, shrill voices to match their alarm, all in concert – "Pleeeeeeeeeeeeeeeeeeeeeeeeeaaase. Leeeeeeeeeeeeeeeeeaaave. Noooooooooooot. Meeeeeeeeeeee..." Their torment was my calm because at least giant serpents weren't trying to eat me. Not at the moment.

It had worked, for a spell. Finally enjoined to a regal state of calm, I started judging all this prey too foolish not to deserve such tragicomic ends. Who hasn't found themselves imagining all the eyes staring back at them from the woods at night, those hungry, jealous eyes, all of those creatures undulating in a sticky breeze in wait of being eaten alive from the head down or another chance to go eat something alive from the head down? They must know, all these millions of creatures, in observing human life, how very hopeless their own lives are in comparison. I know this is such a cheap way for someone to feel better about their station, but back then it worked for me. To each their own medicine. My writer warned me about straying this far from the subject, but you will see that these woods hold great importance to this story, which I acknowledge isn't mine but only mine to tell. Incidentally, speaking of creatures:

I could see it as soon as I heard how it moved. The crunching of pine cones, a beer can, the snap of frond stalks, the crackling of leaf matter, started just beyond the edge of the backyard, in the first mounding of wild verbena blanketed in milkweed, then the sound growing louder, more conspicuous, as it trudged away through the deepening thicket and slid back into the county-owned retention pond due west of the house. I felt my shoulders slack after a full minute of flexing toward my ears. Amid the randomness of all the other sounds, the steady drag of tail made me certain that my stalker was none other than the dinosaur mastermind of the most premeditated and frighteningly sporadic spree of alligator attacks against a single family in recorded history, a rampage that started just months after we moved in with the disappearance of my childhood cat, a ginger freedom fighter like me named Dharma, and wouldn't end until, decades later, someone took a stand and made the carnage stop.

A light patter of rain began to fall, erasing any color in my thoughts. Suddenly, I'd returned to the mute gray of dread from before. I followed the water. Down. After storms of any consequence, it would stream down Walnut Circle, slurrying shit pipe and road slick into a big pool at the end of our driveway, where, after mixing with the bilious seepings from all the leaky septic tanks for several miles around, it would pour down a hill and into nothing less than a monster's mouth. I hated that creature before it hated us, not all alligators, just that one. I'd never gotten close enough to see the pond itself, but I knew it well from nightmares.

Encircled by cattails, shrouded in duck grass and hydrilla and several potentially uncharted subspecies of vines and weeds, this loner reptile no doubt stewed as an orphan in a utopia of ignorance through its early years, slurping and inhaling the stench of a thousand toilets, until one day it awoke without the reason to fathom why vengeance was its central purpose. I couldn't help but feel this way. Maybe it didn't eat my cat, but surely it would have. I understand today it just as well could have been the taste of freedom or an obsessive craving to torture lizards that carried Dharma off and away to higher climes. Or a pack of dogs or the venom of a snake or a kindly neighbor unaware of her lactose-intolerance. I've even entertained the idea that Dharma may well have magically sensed her own looming death, as some lore purports that cats can do. In any case, the gator wasn't a suspect in the beginning because I didn't know it existed.

For so many months that it might have been years after Dharma was gone, on days I was wistful or taunted to hide, I'd find myself looking for her, even for snatches of her tabby offspring, who would finally find themselves at the end of adventures that had led them back home. I'd run all this supposition by my parents to mute shrugs of the shoulder, until the day my father knew better – "that prehistoric monster is what ate that cat. What else?" His certainty, as you'll learn soon enough, was not to be discounted. Not in that matter, anyway.

As quickly as it had started, the rain petered out to near-perfect quiet, the prey still silent in the soggy darkness. The lizard lovers on the screen were gone now, off to eat or be eaten. I tried scanning the paper again, a sentence here or there about this terrorist front or that political backbiting, headlines about this threat to market confidence or that bound in joblessness or this murder or that house fire, then a curt knock at the door was all it took to shoot me to standing. The paper flew into the air and fell like a kite on a windless day.

I ran to peer nervously through the peephole and exhaled away the thought of Serge standing there. A lanky woman, with a thin gray box held like a basket for grandma, was lackadaisically tucking a buttoned-to-the-neck sky-blue blouse into the waist of a dowdy navy-blue skirt, which hung well past the knees and, with the dull black flats, gave her the all-business profile of a pre-clear Scientologist. Her face followed suit: eyes green and prominent like an owl's but with no trace of makeup and brown bangs cut straight across the brows, the rest flat-ironed to her shoulders.

I opened the door with an inquisitive twitch of the forehead and only then did her embarrassed-looking smile fold back to show a mouth full of braces with pink brackets. I looked for a wedding ring and registered ambivalence when I didn't find one. My lizard friends flashed to mind and were gone. A desperate state.

"Please, come in." I looked at the card in my face but not for long enough to know her purpose. "...Mrs. Nettle. So you're, what? Detective? Probate court? Reporter for *Hustler*?"

"Precisely, Mr. Um.... Saul? Saul Jr., sorry. The probate part, yes."

"Next in line to the throne malady!" I bowed, sweeping an arm down and back to reveal the feeble kingdom. She stepped past me into the living room with a seasoned prism of pity and gloom in her eyes. It was my look. I felt drawn to her, to the security inherent in her position. I scanned her ass as she passed and, not finding one, closed the door. It wasn't a deal-breaker.

"I'm sorry it's this late, Mr. McGinty. Last stop of the night and all. Had some paperwork to wrap up before I headed out. Your mother said you'd be here."

I'd never so hated the sound of my own name. She had to have sensed this. She proceeded with fastidiousness. She put the safe-deposit box on the table, said it was delivered to her office by Wells Fargo after the police and then the coroner had a chance to inspect it.

"They wanted to get a whiff of all that money my old man left his only son, huh?"

"Apparently just some writings he wanted you to have, sorry." She wouldn't look at me, probably not knowing whether I'd be smiling or crying or, the creepiest, both.

"Me?"

"Family."

"Right."

She pulled a tiny voice recorder from the purse still strapped to her shoulder, pressed a button and set it on a knee, quick-draw. "Still no note. Apparently. Nothing about..." Her eyes flashed in several directions, then returned to stare at mine. "Perhaps you'll find something during your... Well, let us know if you learn anything helpful about his final days. As you probably already know, the coroner has made her ruling official based on the police investigation. And toxicology tests. He'd been showing signs of distress again, your father."

"Yes," I said nonchalantly. "Again. Day in and out with the distress that one."

"These recurring feelings of being watched, through the sockets and fans and such." Her look again. I couldn't act over my first genuine look of disbelief. "I'm sorry," she continued with all the apologies. "And his medicines, well, they were as would be expected."

"Lightweight."

A sad look now from Nettle, this one for me. "Police found empty bottles in the medicine cabinet, too, his antidepressants, pain, anxiety meds, presumably, ect. ect.... But it doesn't appear they would have been enough to kill him, judging from how much he should have had left and how much he had in his ... That's what the final, um ... It was just enough to, well ... maybe a way to ... I don't know ..."

"To feel no pain," I said flatly. "Numb enough to do it."

"Speculation, Mr. McGinty, is limited, as a rule, especially when the deceased is, well, he's..."

"When he's also the perpetrator, you mean."

"We can't pretend to mark the final steps he made or state with certainty how a person can sink to making such tragic decisions, Mr., um..."

"Saul."

"Saul. I'm terribly sorry."

"Please. Stop saying that."

"This just must be so difficult. The court has, it..." Her head cocked to the left a little. I was watching her lips to see if the tape player wasn't speaking for her. "Maybe this will help you, at least, I don't know, help you understand his state of mind." She slid a print-out of a newspaper clipping, a brief item, from her file. "The coroner found this online. I'd never heard of it. It's fascinating, really, the phenomena involved, not, well... Very rare. Police observed on separate occasions your father suffering from these ... these delusions."

"Finally on the record," I said. "In all honestly, I can't remember when he wasn't suffering from something."

"I'm so ... I'm just out of words to describe..."

"How sorry he was. Yes. You said that."

Shaking her head weakly, as if to tsk-tsk my flippancy, she extended the clipping across the room, flashing a pale, freckled arm unusual for summer in Florida. I took it and she started opening the safe-deposit box. I read the little headline aloud, barely: "*The Truman Show* Delusion?"

"Yeah, um..." She slid the box, lid open, across the coffee table, which was, again, really just a filing cabinet on its side that was covered in a foot-high stack of clutter to bring it to proper coffee table height. From my father's torn brown suede couch to her matching love seat by the door, you could almost shake hands. The walls felt closer than ever before.

Inside the box were a black-and-white marbled journal, the same as I used to take notes in college, and a smaller journal on top that was really just a wire-bound reporter's notebook. It even said "REPORTER'S NOTEBOOK" right there on the front, right above a few lines on which my father had written in blue block letters, "THE WHY AND THE WHAT."

"That's it? Where's the savings bonds, the treasure map?"

"Just read through a little after I'm gone," she said, forcing the grimmest of grins, the tersest of chuckles. "You'll see. The police, as I've said, they're pretty convinced, after looking through everything, Mr. McGinty, that..."

"They didn't look through everything. All of *this* might have been his suicide note. The *why* and *what*?" I said it like I was delivering a punch line, darting my hands and eyes about me to indicate the clutter I hadn't made a dent in. But she could tell I wasn't joking.

"Perhaps." She stood with her belongings already gathered, emptied out the bank box and held it by the handle. "If you could just read through everything a bit. We're not aware of any will. I'm sorry. He went bankrupt a year ago, so there's really not much in the way of an inheritance. Nothing, in fact. Other than the contribution he's made to this community for so many years, of course. And to the nation. He was a hero, as I'm sure you know, and not just because of his service and the Purple Heart. You'd have a hard time finding somebody who doesn't have one of his obituaries tucked away inside a photo album or someplace. I know I do. I mean, he must have written the notice when my father died in the mill a few years ago, but who knows? Never have a byline, the obits. Kind of a selfless job if you think about it. Must take a quiet kind of dignity, huh, to do that every day and never get any thanks?"

I didn't answer, just stood up to stare into those eyes with a similar type of gloom. "Well," she said in a way that meant, "Goodbye." She made to leave on tip-toes, tiny steps that spoke of repulsion. I'd picked up most of the dead roaches by then, but I'd missed two. When she opened the door, she popped one of them with her foot. In an instant, the room filled with the smell of rotten nectarines. Gracefully, she pretended it hadn't happened. On the front mat she turned coyly and smiled, probably glad to be breathing something other than a dead man's air.

"And the police, they might be able to help you sort out some of the details, Saul. Them being the police and all. They can show you the reports and all that. They really spent more time than usual going over everything."

"No doubt, all the thises and the thats. And hey, I've got all the whys and whats I'll need now, too!" I ran my hand up the edge of the door. "Thanks again. I didn't have anything to read."

She smiled a real-looking smile that time, but it was probably just to fight off the impulse to start crying. I closed the door, locked not just the deadbolt but the handle, set the chain. As soon as her silver Taurus chirped away, the embarrassment, the shame, I felt for being there – for being his – overtook me. *I know, I know,* I thought, red-faced: *You think I sleep where I shit too, but I'm not like him. I'm nothing like that!*

Nevertheless, hole number thirteen is mine, there beside the couch opposite the front door, in the open space between two books. Kerouac and Kesey.

*   *   *

The *Truman Show* Delusion?
By Frances Li-Gonzalez
URL: [DEFUNCT HTML]

A tiny segment of the population currently suffer from what has become dubbed "The Truman Show delusion," reported a team of psychologists from the United States, Great Britain and Japan this week in several scholarly journals.

Named for the popular movie of the same name, in which a man discovers that his whole life and community have been the fabricated setting of his own reality show, the condition appears to be isolated to those suffering from drug detoxification, deep-rooted addiction, or long-term psychosis for which prescription medications have had no lasting effect. Some appear to have been suffering from all three conditions to varying degrees.

"Maybe a few make it up to get attention or got the idea from the movie," said Nigel McIntyre, professor of interpretational psychology at Cambridge University, "but a vast majority of this very tiny minority appear convinced that they're the stars in their own movie or some show that scores of others are somehow in on for their own enjoyment at the sufferer's expense. It's quite remarkable."

Scientists at Rutgers University and the University of Tokyo sampled case records from a dozen patients in three countries and found the phenomena, in general, to reflect "wisps of inculcation to the Communication Age," McIntyre said, but more specifically "a grandiosity that's somehow formed by sociopaths so full of themselves that they always feel like they're living life at center stage...."

75

As is their duty, the experts kept fishing in polluted ponds; it's not worth a full rehashing. I couldn't help but notice, however, the lack of speculation about people who really were being watched, as if espionage weren't a respected career choice, as if surveillance only happened as a plot device in cop dramas, always involving two fed-up gumshoes near retirement, trading back-stories for binos for one-liners for doughnuts. *Either a person is being watched or not,* I thought, letting the clipping fall theatrically from my hand. But him? What was to gain from that?

I just stood there and stared at what else she'd left for long enough to realize what I was going to do next. I lifted the cover of the reporter's notebook, and there was the suicide note that supposedly wasn't found, a long strip crisply trimmed from the edge of a soft and yellowed piece of paper. Terse, neatly rendered sentences, all caps in red, coated both sides with no room for a single letter more. Fleetingly, I wondered which he'd done first – write me something and cut out the paper on which he'd written it or cut out a length of paper he felt could adequately contain all of what he had to say – then I concluded that neither mattered. I dropped back onto the couch on the kitchen side of the living room and started reading:

"SON, IF YOU'RE READING THIS, SOMEONE UP HIGH, SOMEONE WHO THINKS THEY ARE ANYWAY, HAS KICKED THIS PAWN OFF THE BOARD. PRECISELY WHO, I CAN'T SAY. PERHAPS YOU ARE MORE QUALIFIED TO GUESS. PLEASE, SON, DON'T SET THIS ON FIRE YET! PLEASE KEEP READING AND DON'T STOP. ..."

"It's you!" I yelled. "You did it! Case closed!"

I tried to stop a laugh that came from somewhere deep inside, and I never laugh alone; there's no point if no one's there to hear it. But I filled that shoebox with cackling until I noticed something macabre in it, familial too. I leaned back and my tailbone sank painfully to the frame of the couch, so I collapsed onto my side, pulled my feet up and read the rest with the grimace of someone guiltily enjoying an uneven fight or dividing the very bloodiest center of chateaubriand into two equal portions, the last bite and the second to last. I rolled my lighter around in my jeans pocket, flicked it to feel the burn on my thumb, my thigh.

"*...I KNEW YOU WOULD COME AND THAT YOU'D BE EQUIPPED TO UNDERSTAND ALL THIS. BUT I CAN'T JUST START THERE, CAN I? IT HAS TO BE SOMETHING MORE LIKE: WHAT A FLACCID TWAT OF A FATHER I'VE BEEN, ABOUT AS GOOD AS A BIG HUNK OF MEAT AGING ON A HOOK IN THE MIDDLE OF YOUR LIFE THAT YOU NEVER EVEN GOT TO EAT. HOW FUCKED IS THAT? I COULD USE ALL THE INK IN ALL THE PENS IN THIS HOUSE AND EVEN START TAPPING MY ARTERIES AND STILL ONLY SKIRT THE TRUTH OF HOW CRIMINALLY SPINELESS I HAVE ALWAYS FELT ABOUT LETTING THE GAP BETWEEN ALL OF US GET SO DEEP AND WIDE SO FAST. SEEMS THE LONGER I WAITED, THE MORE IT STARTED FEELING LIKE THE MOST CHARITABLE THING TO DO WAS JUST LET YOU KEEP FORGETTING ALL THE WAYS I NEVER WAS AND ALL THE OTHER WAYS I WAS BUT NEVER SHOULD HAVE BEEN. WHAT CAN YOU SCREAM ACROSS ALL THAT SPACE EXCEPT MORE SHIT THAT MAKES EVEN LESS SENSE THAN ALL THE EARLIER SCREAMS? I THINK I'VE THOUGHT ENOUGH TO KNOW THAT, REALLY, THE IRREFUTABLE TRUTH WOULD ALWAYS BE THERE IN ANYTHING I EVER SAID OR DID, MORE AND MORE OF IT THE MORE AND MORE OF IT I LEARNED. I EVEN PUSHED AROUND THE IDEA OF CRAFTING A MORE LAYERED, ETERNALLY MISUNDERSTOOD ME. I GAVE SERIOUS THOUGHT TO THIS, ACTUALLY. SUCH THINGS, YOU KNOW, WERE MY FORTE, IF I COULD BE SAID TO HAVE EVER POSSESSED SUCH A THING. YOU'RE PROBABLY WONDERING: WHAT DO YOU KNOW ABOUT ME? AND I WILL SAY: WHAT I COULD KNOW FROM HERE, FROM THIS NEW INTERNET THING. WHAT MORE DO I DESERVE TO KNOW? THAT SAID, I DO KNOW THIS: YOU KNOW YOUR HISTORY, SON, AND HOW IT'S WRITTEN BY THE WINNERS, BUT DID YOU KNOW IT DOESN'T HAVE TO BE THAT WAY? SILLY, TO THINK, YOU'RE THINKING. I*

USED TO SAY THAT ALL THE TIME, AND NOW YOU DO TOO! DON'T YOU? I KNOW IT'S ON THE TIP OF YOUR TONGUE RIGHT NOW. SO, YES, IT'S SILLY. TO THINK. BUT THINK. LOOK INTO THINGS – INSIDE THE RAINBOW, SAUL, NOT WHERE IT STARTS OR ENDS. STUDY OUR HISTORY. START TODAY! THAT'S THE KEY! I WISH I COULD BE THERE TO DO THIS, BUT THIS, I SUPPOSE, REQUIRES SACRIFICE. I'M PROUD OF WHO YOU HAVE BECOME. I HOPE SOMEDAY YOU CAN BE JUST A LITTLE PROUD OF ME. YOU'VE BECOME A CAPABLE MAN, SO BE CAREFUL OF HOW YOU GIVE UP AND WHAT YOU GIVE UP ON. AND DON'T GET BURNED! BE YOURSELF: LOVER/FIGHTER. LOVE, DAD"

I crammed my eyes shut and together with my fingers so forcefully that stars, colors, kaleidoscopes in random patter, filled my periphery. I closed my eyes until all of it was gone and nothing but darkness returned. Open or closed, the view was bleak. "Fuck is all," I whispered to the room. "The dead man finally speaks."

A giggle sputtered out, this one uncomfortable from the start. Exasperated, buried alive by so many dead words, I gazed all around me at the books: a myriad of colors dulled by time, inside them millions of ideas, most of them lies to suit the story, stories to suit the lies. *A riddle from a crazy man*, I thought, *will have nothing but a crazy solution.* Still, I was certain that the riddle's rainbow was there. I asked the room, full voice, "Which book, you dick? What rainbow?" As if the asking would summon my answer.

Don't ask me why I stood up. Don't ask me why I started with the As, behind the front door, where a hole gaped in the wall. I only know that I'd finally found a way to make what I'd come to do finally seem worthwhile. I fanned through each book in haste, tossing them in the trash beside me without even registering the titles, then, minutes later, with just two shelves cleared, don't ask me why I felt that something foreign yet chromosomally identical had just swept through me with the power to erase my reason like a chalkboard and replace it with the chicken-scratch of a creepy substitute. More sane, I (don't know why I) thought – or instructive and interesting, at least – would be to postpone the shelf-gutting until such time that I could better strip the meat from the bones and instead leaf through the notebooks to get a better idea of what was to be found. Don't even ask me why I thought it might let me finally look behind all the doors my father never let me open.

I grabbed the reporter's notebook and flopped on the couch again, this time falling stiffly to keep from ramming my spine on the frame, only to slice my left butt cheek on a spring. I ground my teeth until the pain subsided then started skimming through, not really even reading but cramming too late for a test. The only time I ever read that fast is after I've written something that still needs to be swept for typos. I barely registered what I was reading. I was too busy separating the arguing monkeys in my head.

By now, I've read the words a hundred times, and I'm loathe to bore or confound the reading mainstream with a full transcription; the hows and whys are nowhere near as conclusive as my father's cover page teased. Suffice to say, its stream-of-consciousness tone must have made the coroner's job a snap, especially in light of an overriding theme that reads simultaneously screamed and muffled, like wailing from a padded cell. Flitting through, about halfway deep into the hole, I found by accident more proof of the alleged delusions mentioned by the probate lawyer:

"...Inside the sockets, sticking out just far enough to monitor the room. In the attic, leading to the fans. Those are the types of places where they've hidden things. Who knows where else? Who are you?! What toys did you bring??!! Nano-transceivers, penlight cameras, wireless listening devices – I don't even know what money can buy these days, but my guess is whatever it takes. Who can properly imagine what we're dealing with here? They can shoot an [REDACTED] beam to make people crazy or hungry for pancakes or even horny for whatever pussy's available, any old ugly crack. Just read what's there on the Internet. It's all there. And now this: three cables..."

I feel foolish to admit it, but I looked, right then, in the place I'd always feared to go. Don't keep asking yourself why I'd follow such a shit-strewn path. Maybe the motive was self-serving, to prove I could finally go up there myself, instead of sending in my overachieving sister with an Oscar the Grouch flashlight and strict instructions to report back her findings in detail with every new discovery. No way was I going up there as a boy, especially after what my sister described was something like a holiday-junkyard-turned-insect-carnival. But I was somehow driven now to finally see all of this through, to clean up this mess from the top corners down, every inch. Perhaps I was hoping to find some real treasure up there on the way to discrediting my whack-a-doo father. At the time, I was acting too quickly to even think of my reasoning, which wasn't like me at all. "You sweep steps from the very top," I (listened while I) told myself aloud, "so that's where to start."

I folded up the bottom corner of the notebook page I was reading, found a barely working flashlight in a kitchen drawer, providentially the first one I looked in, and took a dining room chair into my old bedroom closet. On the chair, which I noticed only fleetingly was just as wobbly as when I lived here, I stood up and slid over a warped rectangle of plywood then pulled myself up, surprised by my agility and failure to talk myself out of it. Easy enough. There was even a light I could turn on with the pull of some green 5-50 cord. But the light was red, which matched the reticence I suddenly felt for the task at hand. I turned on the flashlight to make the light pink. Something had changed. The air-conditioning shuddered and wheezed to a stop outside, and I froze.

What should have been a fade to quiet wasn't quiet at all. I was greeted in the silence by rustling sounds, more frenzied and rapacious than those from before, and it didn't help that the air was even fustier up here than below; it felt and smelled alive and dead at once. It was alive, crawling at every nook and corner. I asked myself, *What are you doing up here?* At last I could identify a thought as my own, but then I repeated it aloud more emphatically – "What the fuck are you doing up here?" – not at all out of fear but instead the knowledge of human frailty, the blindness of territorial disputes, the deleteriousness of rabies, the varying gauges of needles and incisors, the understanding of insect defense mechanisms under intensely cloistered conditions of natural selection ...

Fine. I could have pissed my pants, but I had valid reasons: Insectophobia aside, the loudest of the noises were coming from the far end of the attic and seemed to be caused by something larger and more organized than mere bugs. I sat there a minute, then stood up, bumped my head, crouched, winced, rubbed at my head, pointed my light and took my first step. Across bare rolling hills of pink insulation, plank by plank, I crept closer away from defeat. The noise had stopped, but all around me the rafters and ducts and sheathing swirled with motion. I wouldn't look at anything but where my feet would have to fall, but still I saw what I knew was everywhere. Twenty paces, one for each two-by-four, took what felt like minutes to traverse. When I could walk no further, I forced myself to stoop down and discover, snug between a bent-up corner of the corroded ventilation grate and the naked, reposed corpse of a Mrs. Claus doll who could only be identified by her reading glasses, that I'd conquered my fears to evict the occupants of a bird nest that had been craftily fashioned out of dead pine needles, silver tinsel, pastel strands of Easter grass and the exoskeletons of so many little roach meals.

I let out a little chortle of victory, inhaled a moldy gulp of dust full of fiberglass, and then focused nervously on all the other roaches that were still very much alive and unhinged. I waved the flashlight around and saw even more than estimated by my imagination, which was busy anthropomorphizing them into as great a threat as possible. I couldn't discredit the regimentation on display. Some were so bold as to run at my feet, the dimwits and man-babies recruited for suicide bombings and daylight food runs. Others kept prominent posts but stayed frozen in awe, the grunts awaiting orders, the intelligence detachments reading scraps of ancient newspapers detachedly, the sentinels radioing back my coordinates to unseen commanders, which I could only assume were lurking within the safest caches, maybe even downstairs, in the hollowed-out bunker of a hardened jelly donut or box of Frosted Flakes, with just their antennae protruding for regular updates from the front lines on the invader's latest position, apparent disposition, available weaponry and political leanings. The rest – *how many of them could there be?* – were undoubtedly the civilians, frozen in dumb silence among and under all the junk I was hastily inspecting and crushing with my awkward footfalls. Every movement would send them flittering further into shadow with a scratch of sounds that sent shivers up and rivers of sweat back down my spine. I had no feeling about roaches until that day but have loathed them ever since with a dread approaching mania, and for what? A giant, broke-necked Rudolph with his red nose chewed off and his bangle of sleigh bells riddled with holes? A box full of Christmas lights tangled to obsolescence? A few bags of broken, oven-baked ornaments coated in tinsel and old popcorn that obviously the roaches didn't even want? Certainly not the fat plastic Santa with the caved-in face and missing arms, or the pumpkin light made in the image of Mickey Mouse, which clearly lost favor after losing one of its ears, or the frayed and fading Easter baskets cemented into a statuesque stack by what appeared to be a glue made of ancient Peeps and castaway jelly beans. This was my treasure.

I was hastened more than deterred. I hurriedly tried to find something, even the other types of bugs my father suspected to have been planted there. But the fans were fans, with no suspect cables leading in, except the ones the fans needed if they were to be called fans. Okay, I checked the first three of the house's five fans, with a rudimentary tug with just my pinky on the cables attached. What was I supposed to even be looking for? I needed an electronics wizard for a sidekick. I'll admit to seeing a stray coaxial cable sticking out of the fan assembly to my father's room, but it was just lying there, connected to nothing, and it led back to the attic entrance, where it ended with another connector that wasn't attached to anything either. If someone was watching something here, they weren't anymore. I envisioned my father being the last person who stood here, stretching this very cable out to lend credence to his paranoia. By then, I'd seen enough, was sure enough, by scanning the first and last chapters of this sadly overwrought tale, that the butler had been killed (pause for quiet) ... by himself!

I came down a sweaty mess of dejection. I was itching from the fiberglass and the thought of all the roaches getting antsy for sustenance. I felt gypped but proud of having conquered an ancient fear. I thought of how wonderful it would have been to explore other family's attics and their glimpses of a past preserved, with full armoires of flapper dresses, creaky chests with grandpa's suits and desperate letters from the war. After playing dress-up, you'd find some vintage toys or long-lost Picassos, maybe proof you were adopted – things to bring downstairs besides the heebie-jeebies.

I stripped naked and took a shower. Wincing, shuddering, I used the thin bar of soap on the corner of the tub, even though it had a few of his hairs still clinging to it. It was maybe nine o'clock, but I didn't feel like going through anything but the deluded thoughts of a man I'd always loathed but still hoped to know better. I laid on the other couch by the front window and started reading the notebook again, from the beginning. It had the same effect as Ambien.

*   *   *

The next morning, I woke up inexplicably wedged under the couch cushions, a decision I'd apparently made while sleepily searching for covers. I immediately decided to shower again after noticing my whole left side dusted a deep gray from something inside the couch and my mouth full of grit and a hair that wasn't mine. I stripped naked but paused this time at the mirror in the bathroom, examining my exposed ribs, the paunch to spite the ribs, the sad downward gaze of my long-sequestered penis. I imagined him taking a final self-assessment here, thinking thoughts like this. I felt his feet under mine, his eyes boring into my own, his breath bouncing off my reflection. What could he have seen besides this same ginger-topped, horn-nosed monstrosity of a specimen, only one with even less to live for? Were there any last words?

I tried, "Dead Beat Down," then decided that he hadn't said

anything, or if he had, no one would have been here to hear it, which is the same as not having said a thing anyway. Every question I had was impossible to answer now. And so, yeah: Staring right at myself, in a deliberate motion that carried the force of all my regrets, I jabbed the mirror right between my green eyes and followed through so effortlessly that a blood-smudged dent was left in the drywall where the mirror used to be.

I don't even remember feeling anger; I just wanted to break the mirror, okay? And the lackadaisical manner with which the job was performed sent coursing something like pride through my spine. The shards had cascaded into the sink in a crashing racket but had all ended up in a tidy pile for cleanup, which made the whole tantrum seem even more destined than before. The nicks on my knuckles didn't hurt, either. I scrubbed them with the bar of soap in the shower, which finally dislodged the last of his hairs. I watched it drift all the way to the drain.

I felt strong. I brushed my teeth in the kitchen sink while studying the ancient putty job in the wall that accentuated more than disguised the holes that were here before we'd even moved in. I threw on basketball shorts and Chucks, made a conscious decision to let my beard grow in not just another day but for the rest of the year; see how the school board likes that. Okay, I felt strong but also weary. I wasn't tired, just loathe as before to dig through all this garbage. I turned on the floor-model television in the living room for company. I looked for a cable box or satellite receiver until I realized there wasn't one. No remote in sight. Stooped over the clumsy rotary dial, I flipped through the five available channels the antenna on the roof could summon.

My first stop had me staring into the void at a rotund local politician, the waistband of his slacks riding too high on his navel in the style of anyone trying to appear less obese, who looked an awful lot like someone I knew but not that well or for all that long. The interviewer was priming the politician's pump with such lobs for questions that his lust for this leader's favor shined as glaringly as those too-white teeth of his. I tried to count the lies this man tried to pass as truth but quickly lost count...

"...nothing other than a proven fact, Kip: Socialized medicine has failed. Look at any country that's ever instituted it. Look at Mexico. You think they're healthier there? [Host pretends a shrug with the perk of a brow.] So why do they all seem to be itching to get over the fence and take our jobs? Look at the lines people are waiting in just to get some aspirin, a flu shot – and I mean every place that's got this system. That's what I hear, anyway. I got friends all over the world, and America's still the beacon. Believe it, Kip. You wanna play on Michael Moore's team, huh? [Host feigns disgust.] Man's worried about everybody's health care and he's feeding his face day in and out with enough cholesterol to drop an elephant. He wants the taxpayers to foot the bill for that? [Host chuckles with no sound.] Why you think we got all these sheikhs and princes from Thisastan and Thatslovakia coming over here so the Mayo Clinics and the Cleveland Clinics can do all their angioplasties and, and liver transplants and all that? Ask yourself that, Kip. [Host is fawning silently.] I can hear all the whiners out there from here: 'But what about Canada,' they're all crying. 'What about England and Sweden? They seem to like how they get their meds in the mail.' Yeah, well maybe if we had somebody fighting all our wars for us and policing all our borders, Kip, maybe we'd have enough left over to give free health care outside the emergency room. [Host, shifting chin from left hand pedestal to right, nods and beams a grin of assent.] What's that? Oh, that's crickets chirping. Nobody's got nothin' to say when you put 'em to it that way, do they? And now we got this Adorable Care Act. I tell you, it makes me sick to think of all the free rides we're..."

After realizing no one was on deck to disagree, I stooped to twist the knob and came through a few stations of snow to by-then-exhausted footage on public broadcasting of a would-be Mormon president caught decrying those with nothing left of their bare minimum household wages to pay federal taxes: *"... and this banquet-hall bartender thought he was just recording a little slice of history for his Facebook friends and ended up with something a little more warts-and-all, didn't he? ... 'There are 47 percent who are with him, who are dependent upon government, who believe that they are victims, who believe that government has a responsibility to care for them, who believe that they are entitled to health care, to food, to housing, to you-name-it. That that's an entitlement and government should give it to them. And they will vote for this president no matter what. I mean, the president starts off with 48, 49 – I mean, he starts off with a huge number. These are people who pay no income tax; 47 percent of Americans pay no income tax! So our message of low taxes doesn't connect. He'll be out there talking about tax cuts for the rich. I mean, that's what they sell every four years. And so my job is not to worry about those people. I'll never convince them they should take personal responsibility and care for their lives.' Indeed, it was a serious blow to the candidate to have such a candid exhibition of his innermost fangs, but does the weight of his words carry forward in the hearts of those who ascribe to his beliefs? With us tonight are political insiders Ted Kowtouwar and Marjorie Subordinado for a discussion at the bottom line of just how many of our nation's citizens really don't pay any federal taxes in a given..."*

Another bend and twist, to more blather – "*...you vote for Mayor Freeley and you vote for Freeburg's future, no questions asked!*" – which spilled into my first sighting of a once-mutable cub before her time as a lion: "*We're back with more coverage of Electiooooooon Standoffoffoffoff... I'm Don Adular and joining us this evening is a former Harvard law professor turned left-of-center senator from the great state of Massachusetts, Elizabeth Warren, who by most accounts has met great resistance from lobbyists and pundits on The Hill, and even from some of the more moderate members of her own caucus from outside true-blue New England, for what has been dubbed as her take-no-prisoners disdain for those most interested in preserving the American way of life. Senator ... hmph. [Host pretends to ponder his next question.] How do you respond to all these detractors who say your views are nothing but Kucinichesque smokescreens deployed strategically at election time just to*

secure your now-form-fitting seat of power? Is your stance...?'
'My stance, Don, doesn't change. It's pretty uncomplicated: If
we started in 1960 and we said that as productivity goes up –
that is, as workers are producing more – then the minimum
wage is going to go up the same, then the minimum wage today
would be about 22 bucks an hour, Pat. So my question's: with a
minimum wage of $7.25 an hour, what happened to the other
$14.75? It sure didn't go to the working...' 'Well, that comes across
as a well-meaning platform, Ms. Warren, but how would you
suggest...' 'I'm saying, Dick...' 'It's Don.' 'I'm saying, Don, that
the people of this burgeoning democracy should have leaders
who worry less about helping the big banks and more about
helping regular people being cheated on their mortgages, on
credit cards, on student loans, on credit reports, on...' 'Senator
Warren, pleaseplease. [Host flinch-laughs, as if on the receiving
end of a squirt gun.] 'Dick, I just talked with one of your viewers
earlier today and she shared with me an intimate glimpse into
her personal finances, but they're really what's happening to so
many of our neighbors. Your viewer gave me three numbers:
She and her husband have paid over $200,000 for a house that's
now worth less than half that, and now their bank wants the
house back because they don't have the other $125,000 they
still owe. Is this your...?' 'Our other guest tonight, conservative
blogger Randy Peonim, has been waiting patiently to throw his
hat into the ring here. Surely...' 'DON, I CAN'T BELIEVE THE
SHELL GAME YOUR SO-CALLED DISTINKGUISHED GUEST
IS PLAYING TONIGHT WITH THE FACTS. FRANKLY, I'M...!'"

Click. Click-click-click. A deep breath for *The Jerk*, a loosening
of the jaw to ready for a grin that couldn't take shape: "...*I don't
need this or this. Just this ashtray. And this paddle game. The
ashtray and the paddle game and that's all I need. And this
remote control....*"

Click. Click. "...*Kip, this is the same...*"

Simpering to trap the simmering inside, rolling my neck in
the clammy face of such jovial impasse-making, I bent one last
time to turn the TV off, wondered for a second how anyone could

ever enjoy the television without a remote control, then, in the premeditated motion that had become my way, put the soulful sole of Chuck Taylor through the screen with a single front kick that seemed entirely too practiced to have come from me. Not only was I able to retain a detached smile throughout, but I let it blossom into a toothy grin that felt downright deserved. I'd always wanted to do that and never thought I'd get the chance. This television was going to the curb anyway. I pulled my foot out of the hole and shook the glass fragments from the laces. I considered the hole for a minute, its perfect contours, until it started to assume the stretched shape and serious import of Rebecca's face when nothing I said or did could make her smile. I made her become the hole. Then I turned to focus on other things.

This cavalier trajectory allowed me to move again with, if not purpose, at least perspicuity. I didn't start to pack a thing, though. I started reading the notebook again from where I'd last left off while perched upright on the couch by the window with an air of eloquence I'd hoped would march me quickly through the pages. But the path of my father's words were pat and laden with clichéd devices, telegraphed arguments that, as a whole, read like the script of a Perry Mason cross-examination: "... *So a man lives his life devoted to writing about all these strangers who just died, the same old story every time, just different names plugged in or different branches of the service or spaghetti dinners. Consider this: Is that the kind of man who would ever want to die without tacking on some other shit to his resume besides Nameless Form-Filler? Here he was, gets blasted in the Gulf War, writes about dead people for 30 years, his family doesn't know him, the end. Does that add up, Saul? I'm not the type of man to go out with a whimper like that. I had a memoir to write, ferchrissakes...*" This generically addressed deposition had shifted focus in the middle somewhere to a jury of one, just me; he addressed our shared name in every other sentence as if he'd originally planned to deliver it over the phone as a monologue before remembering that his every move was being weighed against the greater good. Near the end of the notebook, his ideas veered too wildly to ever be taken at face value, even to someone used to grading high school essays. My final grade for Dad on the notebook: G for Gibberish. But for import, it held tremendous sway.

Still, he was trying to accomplish too much too late in way too many words: It was the suicide note that – out of respect and/or pity? – police had claimed they hadn't seen; my father's indictment of the nefarious forces that killed him and the American Dream; the longest riddle ever written in recorded history; and The Key to The Code that The Man lacked The Power to solve. The ending rant is all one needs to grasp why the authorities, who'd never been treated to my father's farcical sense of humor, tasted this fruit and found it sour:

"...They're good at this, Saul. They wrote the rules. You tried to teach me that, but I wasn't listening then. Not to anybody. And I'm sorry for that. Watch them fix me up nice and tidy, though, just clutching my dead father's shotgun that just blew the back of my head out to match the front. No. Too loud. Who knows how I'll go? Maybe they'll just make me drink something they came up with in MKULTRA to make me spill all my beans before I pass out and sleep through the cover-up. I don't pay a gas bill here, so it can't be something grand like an explosion either. I can only hope for something dignified. Whatever the method, all this madness will be on their hands now. It always has been, really. Unfortunately, I can't even say who those hands belong to. Take your pick, son. It could be anybody with the mind that paying $100 in taxes equals 100 votes in the ballot box. Reach in the grab-bag, but DON'T GET BURNED: Illuminati? Masons? Shit, Illuminati Masons? Fundamentalist Republicans? Gun-making warmongerers? Maybe a few of them ReublaDemocrat brothers from Skull and Bones rubbing weiners with some local cardinal on orders from the Pope? IMF?? Daddy Warbucks?! Mr. Smithers?! ... Hell, even the college snoots and some of them walnuts out in the woods on the dole would find a way to be scared of what something like this would do. Aaaaaaaaaand (sigh) still you're wondering: something like WHAT would do, you old bastard? I'm sorry, Saul. If I'd told you about all this

sooner, about everything, you wouldn't have to search for this
THIS *in the dark. But how do I come back after all these years*
with just an apology and then this? I hate putting you in this
kind of danger, son, but I have no other choice. It's their fault, not
mine. Study the history. Start today!"

I wanted to nod in agreement at some of my father's madcap
truths, which sounded an awful lot like mine, but they shot by
too quickly down their slippery slope to deserve that kind of
treatment. Really: I was embarrassed for his memory then. But
still so protective of it. My eyes floated free of my brain to dart
and dance about the room in a frenzy of transient freedom. This
is one of my standard responses to moments of crippling self-
doubt or special-needs confusion, and though it's not a graceful
maneuver, and can actually become painful once the eyes float
free of sensible motion and press for extremely peripheral views,
I think it helps me think. But not that time. I tried humming an
impromptu melody but couldn't silence his voice in my head,
speaking this litany of final words that I'd only guessed at in the
bathroom mirror. I closed my eyes for a reset but instead felt the
sharp sting of an imagined hook through my cheek as I rifled
through my thoughts for something reasonable to explain why
I'd let all this insanity pour into my mind with no drain to flush
it away. The pain was gone when I opened my eyes again, but not
the confusion.

I'm grateful now to have been lulled into his trap – if I hadn't
labored through these words, no one else ever would have – but I still
can't explain how I'd been snagged and led along so meticulously. I
could pretend that I'd been trying to pay my respects, but it's clear
I had none at the time that I knew of to offer. I could even allege
that my hunt began as a quest to discover something redeemable
in a man who'd always been an open book that no one wanted to
read. Of course, the only emotions I could summon in his wake
were the same loathing and pity I held for this dump he tried to
pass off as a home. I had no answers. For instance: Why was I
on my feet, methodically scanning every grungy shelf again for
the one book of pages with the same coarsened patina and sandy

color of the note he'd written, apparently in haste in what were probably his last hours alive? I spent an hour looking for this unspeakable *this* of his, breathing dust and air sullied by a few decades of kicked-up detritus and tobacco smoke, but then my stomach groaned in protest and turned me to face the kitchen.

Clearly delusional, I took my first peek into the fridge. What I found: a few to-go boxes, a flat two-liter of Bubba Cola, some condiments sealed by a gluey decay, a plastic sandwich container crammed with what appeared to be a solid mass of limey mold, and four fish sticks on a paper plate. I wondered perversely which supper had been his last. In the freezer, on the other hand, a full bottle of Smirnoff brought a wave of relief then a guilty sense of renewal. I was still rational when I called for the pizza, with the ham and pineapple that *he'd* always shunned as "fairy toppings," but then I was something else entirely when I was eating the whole thing in between shot after shot from a Solo cup, while taking the rest of the afternoon to read the second journal, the big one, propped comfortably against his headboard in the bedroom, in the very spot where he used to pore over my old *Mad* magazines like they held the alchemical wisdom of *Scientific American.*

Before I could think to start thinking on my own again, a few hours had passed. The windows were blackening mirrors. Dizzy with vodka, I teetered on my haunches between two equally haunting extremes: in this tilt, emptied to hopelessness; in that whirl, engorged with fresh hatred for yet another dickhead McGinty. I tried to steady my torso by finding my reflection. The face I saw in the dresser mirror, the windows, was ours, not mine alone, but the expression there had yet to match the way I felt. It was just a rictus bearing mild disdain and a zombie's droll bemusement. I knew that was the crack through which this added rage would spew. I waited patiently for it to happen, so it wouldn't startle me. I still was shocked by what came.

"Two piles of shit!" I bellowed, the rictus reamed apart into a gaping hole of foaming roaring rabies. "So fucking ... you ... one big, one small! So fucking what? You both reek. Like pig shit! Puked up by a pig! Both of you can DIE!"

It didn't calm me when I realized in a quick flash of clarity that both piles of shit already had, indeed, died. I was lost in a rage that he'd planted and I'd been containing all those years. That's the only way I can explain it. My lungs were heaving down to the diaphragm, churning the contents of my gut into a sickening pizza liqueur that pressed caustically back into an overworked epiglottis on the verge of surrender. My arms flailed at the dead air around me. I may have been drunk and ranting from a padded cell of my own making, but I was still sober enough to fight against letting my father, even in death, push the blame up and away through a fog of pity.

"Smoke and mirrors, asshole!" I screamed. I'm certain something diagnosable was happening, a panic attack or a nervous breakdown or, at the least, the venting of some seriously pent-up demons. Whatever it was, I couldn't keep it from making me feel helpless and small in the dent on that side of his bed, his side, childish for the tantrums that I knew the boy left inside had yet to purge. I tried to throw up, forced my finger down into my throat, but nothing came up, so with what few waning threads of reason remained, I savagely appraised the room for something, anything, to make light of and keep me from erupting again or breaking down any further. But all that came was how ridiculous it seemed for this decidedly un-regal man of all men to ever think he could qualify for a king-sized bed, and this thought led me to ponder more closely the other, flat side of the bed, where my mother would sometimes sleep all day or cry all night or, I imagine, try to love an emptied-out man; no light can be made out of something dark about your mother.

I tried to move, to rock myself away from the hole of his side, but all I could do was roll back into the deepest part, a baby bird stymied by what it saw at the edge of the nest. Before all this reading, I'd tried her side, but kept rolling over into his dank hole. Eventually, I gave up trying to get out. That dent had become a crater. I'd never escape. My breath was fire, a noxious fuel enflamed by the words I boiled in yearning to spit into the air of every human's next inhale. The rage erupted from my mouth again like something timeless, but this time, somehow, all the words I screamed were his.

"ASSHAT!" I heard him scream over and over, not just at his own father, a man I'd never heard about because that's what the man deserved, but at a world full of deserving targets I could see in the haze of vodka vision but would never have thought to single out myself: at all those ghosts undeserving of rest whose obituaries were laced with the accolades of a community's pretend appreciation but were known assholes to everyone they knew; at the elusive figure/s who'd been deployed yet again and again to keep the people of this country, every one of them, blissfully ignorant of how free they could someday be; at mysterious figures everywhere who do things like plant bombs to kill people just to earn celestial favors; even at that dick who sold graying steaks from the trunk of his Celica on Walnut Circle one time and was long gone before the whole family started puking from both ends; but especially every nabob plutocrat behind all those heavy doors at every country club that ever was. They got an "ASSHAT FUCKNUTS!"

Mind you: Neither asshat nor fucknuts has ever been a part of my vocabulary. Those were his words, never mine. So I knew that he'd been the one doing all the screaming that night. Somehow. Don't ask me how. My mother's tried to explain it to me, but the explanation doesn't mesh with anything I know to be possible. Still I recognize that it was his voice, his pain, even his visions, never mine, that I could hear and feel and see that night. I couldn't leave him on the page. He just went on railing: "You money-grubbin' slavetrains! You greedy pubebrushin' suckadicks! You, you...! You think you won? Sure, a cog like me's gonna go down nice and quiet. No questions asked. But just try and bury us all! You, you..." until something louder than our screaming, a crash, returned me to something more like me – that, and the silence of inebriated confusion. Keening to and fro, I started to feel my own sick feelings again. I could breathe my own breaths, feel my own throat sting from spitting all that dragon fire, and I could think my thoughts enough at least to point my eyes and words where they belonged. I stumbled to my father's half-bathroom and vomited all over the sink and toilet, then, after noticing the giant hole in the bedroom window, stumbled back to the bed and rolled back into the hole.

I wasn't ready to forgive the man for anything. The word "hate" came into my head again, spinning its way in right alongside his good buddy "blame." I lolled back against the headboard and focused those words on my own targets then. I blamed him for the crash, for the journal's misguided trajectory, how it sailed through the window and not to the wall, and not just that but for the way I'm sure the throw looked awkward, like when somebody who knows how to throw will use their weak arm to throw something just to parody all the people like me who throw like gimps because their fathers never taught them how to throw. I hated him for the loneliness that sunk into me long before Rebecca ever left, a desolation I thought I was destined to carry for life because he'd never shown me how to make a woman feel special. I blamed him for Serge and Renaldo because no father should tolerate his children living so close to potential serial killers. And after reading his second journal, I blamed him for even more, like for never even speaking of this whole other family I could have known if only I'd known they even existed. Losing consciousness, my head throbbing with every heartbeat, my last thoughts were of my father's head and hands captured in an old colonial pillory, to which he'd been sentenced for innumerable wrongs. *On all counts, we find the suspect guilty of complicity, your honor. Ride him out on a rail to the crotch!* The darkness that was light, when last I looked, before he made me break that window: *The chair!* The hot wind and hungry bugs gushing through the hole: *You can watch the phone all day for a pardon, boy. The governor, he knows zackly what you done did!* Me giving up and passing out, my face finally slackened by sleep into the very spot that reeked most like my father's drool, the monkeys still chattering away: *So who's this one? ... It's Raul! ... No. Is it Paul? ... No, but something like that ... Is it Saul? ... That's it! Saul! ... But which one? ... Wait, there's two? ... No, there's one ... Just one now ... Yes, the boy ... Has a temper, this one ... As the father, so the son ...*

Chapter 3

WHEREAS, the free voters of Freeburg will be wise to respond to some long-unanswered calls, like the one from President Thomas Jefferson that he managed to make from a slave-owner's porch, when they only let white people vote, and then just the men, only those who owned land: "We shall crush in its birth the aristocracy of our monied corporations, which date already to challenge our government to a trial by strength, and bid defiance to the laws of our country." That cry had no echo, nor this one made on his deathbed: "The issue today is the same as it has been throughout all history: whether man shall be allowed to govern himself or be ruled by a small elite."

"E, eggs," said my father from the vinyl backseat. "On that barn. Way out by itself!"

"I seened it," said my grammar-averse grandfather Paul at the wheel of the Suburban he'd kept running through 300,000 miles, mostly with parts he fashioned with a blowtorch and an obsessive brand of frugality. "But yain't ready for this kind of shit, kid: C on that-there plate. D cause what's that say? Uh-huh: Denny's. And E, on that exit sign we done just passed. Badda and boom." A good sweep, Saul remembered thinking, though the car was all over the road.

His father might have been drunk, but those seemed to be among the only times Paul McGinty ever felt like playing games

95

with anybody, much less his son, who'd made his disdain for his father's favorite sport of baseball known early in life. He'd even turned down a few of his father's attempts just to throw the ball around. It started out early, when the ball stubbed his knuckle when he was young, so he grew averse. He didn't much like going eye to eye with the man, really. And clearly: It wasn't so much that he didn't like the sport but only how magnetic a sway it held on so many in his world. That last time, when my father was in the fifth grade, he claims to have heard my grandfather mutter "pussy" as he walked back to the barn, at a volume that made it clear he meant for his only child to hear him say it.

Paul McGinty rarely asked his son to do much else after that but get his chores done right or else.

"F, fine dining," said Ann Abrams McGinty, my grandfather's wife and temporary teammate, then she whispered with a hand to shield her left cheek, "F, fuck the game, big boy, and stay on the road, kay?" My father's impromptu memoirs, which hog the big journal he left behind with pedantic detail, note that he'd heard what she'd said quite clearly that night, despite the lack of lips to read, and that he'd been alarmed at the hint of command in the tone. My grandfather turned a graven face at his wife and held her gaze for long enough for her to turn away, then he found his son's eyes in the rearview to do the same, before looking back at the road and turning up the radio. Message sent.

"F, food – and they're all tied up, folks!" announced my father, attempting to usher some levity back, something, anything. "It's anyone's game here at the Jake! Hey, speaking of food..."

The road hummed and crackled under the tires. Nothing came in response.

"G, gas," managed my grandfather, who is described as one who hated to lose anything, from power trips to games played with children. My father mentioning the Jake was deft maneuvering. The Cleveland Indians were my grandfather's team, since that's what was ordained by his birth. "An' t'ain't no signs left on this here road. Guess that means this trophy here's all mine. Lemme see how'ma gon' carry it."

My father, then 12, didn't need to see where that hand was trying to get to figure out his father was talking about snatching up my grandmother like some kind of a six-pack of sex toys. All he needed was to see his mother's face go deeper into red through every stage of her resistance: exasperated to embarrassed to mortified to giving in for a few seconds to furious to "C'mon, Paul. Ow!" What's to see?

"G, gas," my father said just seconds later as they passed another exit's offerings. "Guess some signs was left. Hm. Hear that, Mom?" Winning the game now was the only way he could think of to piss off my grandfather without getting his ass beat.

"G, guess so," she said, staring at the road. "You sure can spot 'em. Make a fine farmer, you. Spot every weevil 'fore it lands."

He looked to see his father's eyes, just waiting for him in the mirror. Just as soon at their eyes locked, my grandfather looked away and said, "H, Herr's Bakery."

Ann shot Paul a look that asked him curtly to please, just this one time, let my father win, or that's what my father took her pleading stare to mean. But Paul never seemed to notice little looks like that. She stared back at the road.

"I, Indians season tickets," Paul said with something like a grin. Then he lowered his voice, but not enough, to say, "You know, that game? With the balls and bats and such?"

"Where?" my father asked, ignoring the barb and searching the dark slopes leading up to farm country on both sides of the highway.

"What'a you care, boy? Back where you want lookin', Mr. Green Jeans. Maybe you'da seen it if'n you want back there staring holes into all that space in your drawers where a pecker's sposa be. Go on'n tell your journal bout all that."

He let out a real laugh, a car-swerving belly roar, that had nothing but evil in it, my father recalled, since it had been one of the few sincere-sounding laughs my father had heard out of my grandfather and it had come at his own son's expense. Ann shot him a stern look that dissipated as soon as her husband saw it.

"Boy's gonna have just what his Daddy's got, no less anyway," she said, avoiding eye contact.

My father knew he'd have plenty of pecker someday, he made sure to note, because he heard his mother call his father "the biggest dick in four counties" one Friday afternoon right after Paul had left in a huff and didn't come back until Sunday night. My father kept searching for letters, but he was distracted by his stomach groaning. They'd just passed billboards for Waffle House, IHOP and Wendy's, and the man-sized waffles, pancakes, and beef patties on display were enough to make my father miss his chance for an "H" and an "I."

My grandfather hadn't seen them either. Finally, with home still an unknowable distance away for a child unaccustomed to knowing such things, my father braved the tension enough to say, "I'm starving. Mom, can you please ask Dad to stop?"

She faced my father, pouted, then toward Paul with something more like dread and paused, waiting for the inevitable rebuke.

"Just passed Avon," said Paul, "so we an hour out, tops. Eat something when we get in. Hey, maybe next time we can stop for something when you ain't too wussy to ask me ya'damnself."

The game ended, Paul the victor.

They passed another exit lit up with signs, but only Ann looked for letters. My father didn't really care or at least that was the signal he felt like sending to the front seat. He just sniffed at his upper lip, which smelled like all that chargrilled meat they'd had earlier, and smiled. It was just a small barley farm in Solon, long boring rows of little mounds leading right into a towering wall of pines and maples that glowed amber when the bonfire took over for the sun. Behind the barn was a small flock of sheep that my father noted were more sociable than his father's flock. At the road was the tiniest of one-story houses, painted bright yellow and overflowing with flowers and herbs on every windowsill. My grandmother marveled at the sight and learned that just before his wife made him a widower the year before, after a long bout with some sort of cancer, the man of the house had to promise that he'd keep the window gardens growing, so that's what he'd done.

As simple as that, he'd said with nothing but a shrug. "Never thought I'd get to feel a woman's touch again," he told my grandparents, breaking into a laugh. "Now, I can just touch myself and there it is."

Ann had pouted and nearly cried, then laughed along, reported my father, who was inspecting the soil in the garden nearby and watching for the man's son; Paul had acted like he hadn't heard what the man had said.

The man, whose name my father could only recall had started with a J. or maybe an L., had met my grandfather at a bar in Brunswick, another rural type of town outside of Cleveland that some locals still like to call Brunstucky. The bar was filled for an Indians game, so my grandfather's obsession was at its least conspicuous. The man invited a few of his new friends that night to an impromptu gathering at his farm, and Paul and Ann were the only ones to show. But they weren't alone, something Ann seemed to appreciate and Paul seemed to worry over.

A few younger men who looked and sounded like brothers, with the same blond tendrils of curly hair hanging over their thin, bristly faces, the same cozy get-ups of faded overalls over baggy flannel, and the same type of singing voices that made their harmonies sound like they were coming out of the same mouth, had set up their tents inside the woodline and seemed to be playing their homesick campfire songs to keep the farmer happy enough to let them keep camping there for free. Maybe they were just buddies of his. Or workers. It seemed to be working. But not on my grandfather.

For reasons both known and unknown, my grandfather had only wanted to talk baseball with his friend and what trades would finally give his beloved Tribe the upper-hand. The man was either too polite, gracious for the company, or knew my grandfather well enough to change the subject too abruptly. After feeling out the other two's interests, which were worldly and rebelliously lacking in superficiality, my grandfather'd stopped talking to either one of them for the rest of the visit, even shooting lasers into my grandmother whenever she'd tried to offer even the slightest glimpse of appreciation for their merriment-making. Though he couldn't recall their names, my father was glad they were there, if only for how they'd made my grandfather feel uneasy and inadequate. They'd swap banjo and fiddle from song to song, melody and harmony from verse to verse, like that's what they did for a living. My grandfather, on the other hand, had quit the guitar after learning a few chords in high school because practicing made his fingers hurt. This fact made the day even more festive for my father.

The rest of the drive home, Paul grumbled and his family pretended to listen: about picking up his guitar again, something he hadn't done since Ann came along; about the cruddy song selection on the radio; something derogatory about every driver who sped past in a blur toward Toledo. Ann nodded and smiled, even tried to sing Paul back to the living: "That's the way, uh-huh, uh-huh, I liiiiike it, uh-huh, uh-huh..."

The seats were sticky with sweat. My father doodled in his journal and sniffed at the skin on his arms, which smelled like coal and spilt beer. He caught his father watching him in the mirror and stopped.

Then, not twenty miles past two scrappy factory towns called Elyria and Lorain, in an odd patch of rolling hills that punctuated wide swaths of freshly sown and rowed crops, something popped under the paneled Suburban and the McGintys warbled to the side of the road.

"Piece a shit, mudda..." Paul McGinty declared in a monotone through clenched teeth, full-bore yelling without much noise. He fished around in back for the tire iron and spare, clanged the iron against the asphalt and my father could hear it bounce off into the pasture of orchard grass and bluestem to his right. A cow at the fence mooed in protest and ran back out of the headlights' view.

When a patch of quiet settled in, my grandmother got out and drifted up to the fence. "Right back," she told my father, who stayed buckled in the backseat. In seconds, his mother was squatting in a stand of prisoner-planted pine saplings on the side of People's Interstate 90, talking to Paul as if she were sitting in the car. He could see her through the ditch with every passing set of headlights, through sagging blooms of "hemlock, wild oats and goldenrod," so surely everyone else could see her, too. She met his eyes and looked away, embarrassed, then looked back giggling. Saul braced for the silence at the end of each car's slow whiny approach.

"Get these going, never have to plant grass again," she said, waving a hand through the wildflowers, taking her sweet-assed time with her pants down. "Course, the flock'd take 'em down to the quick."

Paul did what he usually did and ignored her, finally finding the wrench in some weeds by a fence. He started creaking lugs from the front driver's-side wheel. I still can't fathom what she ever saw in him; guess there are parts of a person only certain people get to see. Finished, Ann stood while stealthily slipping her panties high up on her hips, then moved forward some steps to give Paul an audience while yanking her jeans up, the occasional, "Look at the pit, folks! A blur is what..." She knew what drove such a man. He rewarded her with a lift of the eye and an unnecessary extra crank on the iron. And then that smile that my father hated to see. My father looked down at his legs in disgust.

That's when my grandfather, struggling to grab the last lug for the spare where it had rolled under the axle, let his leg dart out into the road for balance and let out a scream that Saul had heard only once before, a little girl's scream really, when the organ his mother wanted to learn tipped over onto the toe of the same foot that now, all those years later, ended up disassembled in a ditch right in front of my mother, her pants half-cocked around her lower parts. It was a dangerous sound when heard coming out of a tall, gangly man like my grandfather. Saul only saw a blur of motion and then he sealed his eyes shut and laid down on the seat.

Time collapsed into a succession of telling sounds. A screeching, then my grandfather sobbing in a field of quiet for miles around, wailing half-questions to the heavens in seek of unknowable knowledge, then just my grandmother crying, then some gruff-sounding man apologizing without punctuation, then him asking for divine assistance, then just my grandmother crying again, then a few seconds of silence. Within a minute, however, my grandmother had managed to throw a blanket over where my father lay on the floor of the backseat, a shadow of the thickest tree, and yelled, "Ain't nothing out here worth seeing, baby. Write me something there, and I'll be right back."

The dome light illuminated, he let his eyes work again but only to record what was down there on the backseat floor like a young Truman Capote – *"a dumb broken pair of sheep shears, some dumb-ass's Kit-Kat wrappers, half-eaten burger wedged under the driver's seat by some idiot, but it's magically preserved, and fire ants, red and angry, are trailing in and out of that patty and on to some universe of a colony deep inside that old sponge that was a backseat of a Suburban owned by an asshole and a..."* – until his mother pulled him from the backseat, wrapped the blanket over his head, put him into a police car and they drove away.

She helped the paramedics find Paul's foot in the field when they got there, as if walking again were the issue. He was already on the way to the morgue, and Saul didn't see any of it. He peeked once, near the end. The road was alive in red and blue and shining white off all that black, but mostly red, the shiny red of the slicks on the road. His father was already gone. He didn't know how to cry about it.

*   *   *

My father shut out most of the memories from my grandfather's funeral. He remembered a lot of empty seats, quiet declarations of his father's unassuming virtues – like how happy his sheep were, hard-working, a family man, all empty words to my rolling-eyed father, who described the event merely as a *"cultural necessity."* Only the local Presbyterian minister spoke, the fill-in-the-blanks eulogy for the Christmas Christians. Some things were clear, though: Saul swore he remembered his mother punching his dead father's face before the few dozen guests arrived, as a local vet from the VFW checked his medals for the funeral director. "I fucking hate you," was how she'd put it, so he didn't think it could have meant anything else. But she did, so everyone was just sad and quiet about it except the funeral director, who thought he was the Rodin of formaldehyde or something and used his shoulder to nudge my grandmother away to preserve his handiwork.

Heavy hands weighed on my father's shoulders all day, his mother shockingly unavailable.

"You're the man now, Saul," said his ancient neighbor, the frail, yellow-haired Virginia, of whom his father had never even spoken. Her husband had chores to do and couldn't make it, she'd explained.

"Fuck you, lady," my father remembered telling the kindly old hag in a tantrum at the curb. "You're the man now. How's that?"

He'd never spoken with or of her either, but only because she was the type who'd always spin around and retreat back indoors whenever anyone came within speaking distance. A few days later, he'd felt sorry enough to say so. "Bless your heart, little man," she'd told him. He never spoke to her again.

My father didn't know how to pretend mourning. He wasn't exactly happy about what had happened to his father; it was something more akin to relief. At least one person kind of seemed to understand. His Uncle Floyd had darted over from Buffalo, where he sold insurance, with a few leisure suits and a new wife, at the time his third of six in all, riding in the backseat of a new Cadillac so, he explained, "my little bean bag could stretch out on dat leather back der and tell me about the braless days at Penn State." Jean was a plump car saleswoman in her early 30s by then and my great uncle was a balding former U-Buffalo tight end pushing at 50 like it was a blocking dummy. Even then my father knew not to get too invested in Jean, but he had only fond moments with Uncle Floyd.

When my grandmother started screaming obscenities from the laundry room, something about hating my grandfather again but this time with more name-calling and nobody standing in her way of destroying things, the half-dozen grownups my father barely knew, who were sitting around the coffee table and staring at the bottle of scotch and cheese tray that amounted to my grandfather's wake, just looked morosely at their feet and tried to talk about things that had nothing to do with my grandfather, but Uncle Floyd had led my father away from all this cultural necessity, his scotch glass topped off with no room to spare, with a story about how my mother, his sister, was the one, the only one, who could ever talk my grandfather out of anything. Except he usually referred to my grandfather Paul as "that prick." She's the one, he told my father, who kept them from moving south to Florida, from where they'd grown up a few miles apart outside Ithaca, to start a family in the sun and raise a flock, have a kid, maybe two, but no more. That was my grandfather's dream, but my grandmother couldn't see that happening so far from anyone she'd grown to love. It didn't matter that he'd been offered a foreman's job, something like a real future – union-free! – at the phosphate mines outside Freeburg. For months, he'd been gearing her engines up for the trip, but she wasn't having it. "You know your Dad, that prick," his Uncle Floyd had said. "Who could talk to the fuck? Right? I never could see what..." He gulped some scotch and let out a guilty little laugh they both could share.

My father's recollection of Uncle Floyd's story was probably a bit too Rockwellian, kicking dirt on backyard swings, but the essence of it is that his uncle slowly eased into a crude imitation of his mother back then as he remembered her as a young bride, back when she used to speak her mind to everyone, *including* her husband. I've seen a few pictures of her back then, standing next to men who weren't Paul and smiling happier than my father had ever seen her be. Floyd recalled as best he could my young grandmother railing against everything having to do with a move down to Florida and how all my young grandfather would do is pretend to laugh along with everybody else in earshot. Nobody wanted to see Ann go either, none of these distant relatives of mine I've never met or even read about. "'Ya' got douchbaggery is what," Uncle Floyd squeaked. "Got NASCAR grease monkeys. Da Spring Break 'hooas, all slicked back in the cocoa butta', what? Leering out from them bug-eyed goonygoggles of the upper echelons there, the smut elite. Yeah, you want all that attention on all this back here, Paul? All dis up hea? I don't think as much. Not with the temper you got. Fucking Harleys everywhere. Hairy backs, the jiggly asses, leather vests. You know I'm gonna be all up in that 'cause them's our people here, right? The fucking chaps, Paul. You're gonna be asking for that shit for Christmas, Paul. And den what? Where does anybody go when the chaps come out? Paul? You know how this ass is gonna pop in some fucking chaps, Paul?"

Laughter from the gallery. I've never seen her wearing anything like that in any of those pictures.

"How old are you again, Saul?"

Floyd was having a hard time holding his drink and balancing still-formidable shoulders atop the kiddie swing.

"Old enough for that PG shit."

"Okay, so she had the man by the horns and I imagine I know exactly how and which one but can't say because that's gonna be some R shit right there."

My father stared blankly ahead to move them on, then gazed off worriedly at the side door to the laundry room.

"A month of that badgering and your father's putting a sign up and selling his Mom's place, Saul. You know that? Putting her up in a nice retirement village near her new ponytailed boyfriend, paid for with the proceeds – God rest dose souls – and he's putting your Ma in that old beater truck of his with a real hard-working smile, and he's got the bed and this trailer all piled up like Sanford and Son, and what are they doing? They're coming over to my place, your uncle's house, me. You didn't know that, I bet. You'd be sweating your nuts off right now down in that fucking swamp, and not up here where you belong by your Gramma Sally, Saul, and a long day's drive from your Uncle Floyd here, if your Ma didn't matter, if your Pa didn't give a shit what your Ma had to say never..."

"I never heard about none of this, Uncle Floyd. What kind of sad-sack family is this?"

"It's our kind a sad-sack family, boy. Hey. What I hear, the ladies are gonna love you, so it's in your hands to drop that sad-sack shit in the grave, know what I'm saying?"

"Word."

I hadn't known any of this either, until floating through my father's exegesis on a cold vodka cloud. I didn't know how I felt about feeling something like empathy for this twelve-year-old boy, this story's embattled protagonist. I decided to pretend that I was reading a fairy tale, fully investing my hopes that, at some point before becoming the dickish bane of my upbringing, he'd be rewarded with the dividends of at least one triumphant journey. I'd never felt this much for him before.

"Come to think, you was conceived on my couch in Buffalo, Saul." The scotch formed a dusky aura around his uncle, as their hands started getting sore on the chains and the sun dipped to a peach half-circle above the line of boxy houses in the way. "Most likely you was. Dat ratty-ass thing down in the basement now, you know? You slept der a few times, on some visits. By dat ping-pong table. That's why you're hea, Sal, Saul, dat's who you are. And you're one of mine now, you get dat, Saul? Saul?" My father wrote about looking at him with so much devotion that he almost cried for the first time since his father died. "I'm not your Daddy. No way! I'm different dan dat. I'm Uncle Floyd, but I got you, see? Your blood's my blood."

My father didn't say a word for several minutes, just pushing the rest of the sun out of sight with his mind. When it was gone, he said, "Is Mom going to be all right?" Uncle Floyd stood up, yanked my father from the swing and led them toward his cream and gold-trimmed Cadillac. "She's never been better," he told my father. "And you?"

"What about me?"

"C'mon, son." My father followed, not feeling the least bit creeped out that a man who wasn't his father was calling him son.

"So who are you?" his uncle cryptically asked minutes later, breaking the silence on their way for some Frosties at Wendy's. My father noted, with blind praise, that *he was weaving the Caddy from curb to curb wildly, but his face was a child's steering one in a videogame, unafraid for our lives or anyone else's, so I wasn't scared none either."* Rubbing his hands along the brain-tanned leather seats, letting the wind pull his bangs back from his face, he shot a crude approximation of his uncle's unworried gaze to the driver's seat and said, "I'm the man." And then, shifting his eyes to the road and assuming that wan smirk that all kids master by junior high, he gulped a fat swallow of air and just belched. "Wanna hear the whole alphabet? I'll do it."

"Take your time," he told my father, dragging a heavy arm over his shoulder and pressing a tape into the dashboard.

"You're Saul," he told him. "You're frickin' twelve." *Aaaaaall ... riiiiight ... now, baaaaaby it's a-aaaaaaaaaaalll right nooooooow...* This was his uncle's favorite, according to my father's journal, so that could be why it was cued up. Or, another of his theories, was that his uncle, with that oafish heart that would last him many great years, *"had practiced the whole spiel in the mirror back in Buffalo and maybe even with his wife in the backseat, so not even the scotch could keep it from happening just right. What I guess he was trying to get across is: Don't sweat the small stuff."*

What a man, this great uncle I wouldn't meet until much later in life. My father, the dead man, had never thought to visit, call or even mention him while both were still alive at once. We all have these people.

*   *   *

My grandmother skipped denial and went right for anger after her husband died. This is clear. Then, in a flash, the anger was gone, too. She retreated into the steamy bathroom for hours-long baths, several times a day for nearly a month. Saul could hear her singing along to the radio in there, the feather-haired "Yoooooouulightupmyliiiiiife..." kind of nonsense, or else she was talking to angels (or to herself through imaginary angels). He didn't hear many sad songs being sung, but he still couldn't be sure at what point in there she'd passed through bargaining and into acceptance; he was just thankful for the freedom to rummage for the first time ever through all his parents' things. He was sure his mother would be fine, just like Uncle Floyd had said.

Under the bed, in the closets, dressers and nightstands, through the basement and garage, his vision quest led to new discoveries that coincided providentially with his first shadow of pubes. Again, he wasn't sad so much as guilty for not feeling all that sad at all. By my grandfather driving his only son, his only offspring, to follow in his sheep-herding steps and by secreting his bevy of old *Playboy*'s in a box labeled "CHRISTMAS PRESENTS" on a high closet shelf, he'd managed to limit his only child's knowledge of sexuality to the barnyard. And so Saul had lost a judgmental father and replaced him immediately, in that closet, with masturbation. *"Not an even trade,"* my father wrote, *"since both ultimately amounted to empty promises and loneliness, but it was a trade I could live with at least."*

Emptily from the hole, I found myself glancing over at my own father's closet for those or other similar magazines, which my father used to keep in a box under a giant dusty heap of blue county and state fair ribbons. The box was gone. I figured they were buried somewhere under the mess I kept avoiding or tossed out, like so many other private stashes, with the advent of the Internet. I let my lazy-drunk eyes roll back onto the page.

Thankfully, for posterity's sake, there were many more savory discoveries to be found in his final writings. Though my father's early carnal proclivities are well-documented on more than five graphic and frankly inappropriate pages of his memoir, which somehow have been leaked to and unofficially published by a South Korean blogger by the name of Shank U, it must be stated that my father exhibited some early glints of scruples, no doubt embedded by my grandmother, and varied interests well beyond just his penis and where he might someday stick it. These traits reveal themselves as a congenital passion for digging into his past and perhaps emerging with something like a destiny.

"A boy can only whack off for so long before nothing at all can come out of it," he noted sagely.

Proof of scruples: He sorted through and neatly arranged

family photos during these quiet times, too – sepia dreams that included a long series my grandmother started when Saul was just a baby, with all three of them in and about a bevy of sheep somewhere near Sandusky, where they'd moved just before my birth to be near my grandmother's dying mother Sally – another family enigma. Sally and her corn farmer husband, whose name escaped even my father, came to the area when it was devoted to a small amusement park, some weekend crusaders to Put-in-Bay and Kelleys Island, and a thriving community of farmers, who'd come to town on weekends to roll their eyes at the outsiders and claim the downtown area as their own.

By the time my grandparents arrived, though, the city proper was devoted almost exclusively to the amusement park, hotels, restaurants and bars, as well as the half-assed homes of the service industry workers paid in paltry dividends to support the relaxing, expensive façade of well-earned-but-fleeting leisure. Still, Paul and Ann clung devotedly to a pasture and flock that would soon be surrounded by new subdivisions to the north and west, a crowded highway lined with bumper-to-bumper traffic to the south and my great-grandmother's claptrap farm to the east. When Great-Grandma Sally, who snorted snuff for much of her life, died of throat and mouth cancer just five months after my grandparents arrived, her late husband's family perfunctorily sold much of the homestead to the highest bidder, who perfunctorily erected a neon-yellow dollar store at the road and a neon-orange storage facility behind it. All my grandparents could do is plant as many trees as they could afford to make their view as bucolic as possible. Eventually, they just knew where to look, out which windows, to keep the encroaching city out of sight and mind.

Back to the photos: One year, when my father was about ten, Ann took four identical photos of her tiny family surrounded by their sheep, one for each season, at the same windbreak of ash and maple they loved for how effective it was at blocking not just the wind but also the outside world. The concept cast their familial mold in widely contrasting lights of white, green, pink and orange. Their body language in each added different-colored memories for my father, and for me, too: in winter, with Paul freezing and leering impetuously at the lens; in fall, it was his mother refusing to smile, since my grandfather had slept off a hangover until the middle of the afternoon; in summer, my father stood too far apart from my grandfather out of anger for being denied his request to rent a trumpet and start playing in the school band; but at least in spring, they all were smiling since they'd just sold two stud rams and were planning a trip to Hershey, Pennsylvania. But that plan got sacked when Paul decided that Indians season tickets were at cut-rate prices he just couldn't pass up. He always went with his bar friends and only asked my father to go once. By then, my father hated baseball, so he pretended to have a fever by rubbing his forehead raw when he heard his father walking toward his room. Ann put the pictures in simple oak frames that she hung in a square above the fireplace, and that's where they'd stay through eighteen successive moves. In homes without fireplaces, they were over her bed. In the nursing home: next to the droning TV.

My father said he couldn't afford to visit my grandmother up north. He called his mother sometimes. I don't know what they talked about. I visited her twice, despite her incoherence, the last time just a week before she died, but some relative I'd never met from Canada got to the photos first. I still don't know how she could have had any other living relatives. By then, she didn't even know who I was. "Who let you in here?" was the last thing she'd said to me. We were two strangers in a room. I left.

That was before time and circumstance scattered my family. At twelve, so much was at my father's fingertips. He found his father's shotgun in the back corner of the closet, and, with his mother still singing in the bathroom, went and sniffed at the barrel. I managed to get out of the hole just long enough to go over and do the same. I knew it was the same one. I only knew how to fire it from watching movies. Unlike the porn, the gun is still in the family.

"...A few times a year I'd hear my father rustling around in the closet, pulling a shell out of the nightstand, slamming the screen door open to go put this or that sheep down. I never

wanted to know which because they all had a name to me: Lucy, Brianna, Britainy, Ra, Scratch. I'd named all the ewes after the prettier girls at school, and all the rams were gods like Hercules or Krishna. The nutless ones called wethers, though, would get the names of dickheads like the Lorrie brothers or rich snobs like Doc Toth's only son, Phil. My father would cry (almost) every time he had to lay one down, get sullen and even angry for days like the Indians had lost too many straight at home. I knew that's why he didn't name them, only giving them numbers that weren't branded but hung from little earrings in the shape of hearts – my mother's idea. Mutton for weeks after that, though, and anything else we could trade for it. Killing a sheep was a sad endeavor for my father, but the rest of us had a dark desire for these times of plenty. I don't remember my Dad ever using his shotgun for anything but to put a sheep down. Not the hunting type. I knew that he loved those sheep more than any of us, though. Wasn't it clear? Maybe I'm wrong. He talked to them all in different tones, like maybe he had named them, but just hadn't shared the names with us. He was all talked out by dinner, that's for sure. I talked to my mother. She talked to me. He drank and watched sitcoms or baseball, sometimes grinning or shaking his head. I did my homework in the dining room, sneaking glances at what he was watching, but never found much funny there. I'd shower, she'd kiss me, then drift off to bed too, and we'd listen together to his laughs, now sincere and piss-drunk, through the walls...."

My father found lots of things in that closet that I'd hoped to find in his. In a later family picture, marked just two years before Paul's death, my attention was drawn to his corduroy jacket, the deep patchless blue with nothing but the name of the local 4-H center embroidered over my father's heart and a U.S. flag on the shoulder. It advertised an utter ignorance of farm know-how. He loved the sheep, but in those few years, he'd begun to lose interest in the flock, just to spite his father, I presume. Mother wore a distracted look, her green eyes gray, but I'm told that's how these early paper photographs would dull things like that prematurely.

Her eyes were definitely green, my father confirmed, but by then they most certainly didn't shine.

Like a stick that could have been shaped into anything, Saul Sr. was being whittled into a shepherd by not the sharpest of knives. His great-grandfather had tended a flock, so that's what he did, too. He couldn't understand why his son would want anything else but to carry on that way of life. In grade school, Saul planted a small kitchen garden for something to do besides tending sheep. It was a flop. Ann had beamed from the kitchen, but Paul had bitched about losing man hours from his farmhand, *"a lame-ass hand at that."* Still a novice at most everything, my father ended up frying his corn trying to keep grasshoppers off with tobacco water. He left his cucumbers on the vine to turn yellow and grow horny spines. The basil and cilantro were chomped to stubs by some errant sheep, which he blamed on his father. The tomatoes and broccoli were torn asunder by cutworms, and cabbage worms and cichlids had pockmarked every leaf worthy of a salad bowl in a single night. The carrots never grew longer than little yellow nubs. The pumpkin vines, his last hope in fall, had never even bloomed one promising orange blossom. His only consolation: serving Ann one of the few Roma tomatoes before the ants overran them.

"Think maybe you ain't got the patience for this, boy?" his father said, pointing at the wide swath of vegetable death encircled too late with rabbit fence to keep the sheep and invading deer out. "Or the know-how? What's that extension fella say? 'Mericans like the lamb is what, wool's warmer than ever, yadda-yadda. How'za 'bout Ma tries her hand at this pussy-ass shit? We need to get some shearing done right quick. Think we can get some of that done without fucking shit up? Think we can do that, boy?"

My father just kept plucking weeds from around all the dead stalks as his father toyed with his Pall Mall at the corner of his mouth. It was my great-grandfather's brand when he served and lost his hearing and four fingers to a grenade in the Marines during the Korean War. Those were among the few things his father ever told him about his own grandfather, who died at fifty-two from eating rotten mutton and eschewing formal medical care in favor of remedies culled from the *Farmer's Almanac*. Half of these 100 acres in Sandusky were going to be my father's, if he wanted them. By then, however, he was of the mind to just hoe up all that timothy, fescue, and canary-grass on his side and plant soybeans and a vineyard out of spite.

"Need a invite through the mails, kid? Off your ass and into the barn. C'mon, now. Need me some help with 24 first. Pussy's done swole up with twins." *Ariel*, my father thought. He went but turned back to see the end of his father's triumphant grin. His only ambition by then was to escape. He saw my grandfather as somebody who would have been Amish if he didn't like drinking beer, watching baseball and missing church, telling his wife, "Blame Jesus for all this damn work! Bahahahahahah!"

Saul Sr. suspected a cultural virus for turning his father into the sheep that they raised, how the team sports and beer and constant bleating had morphed my grandfather into something more useful for the nation than someone who thought for himself. My father had proved just as unpromising an athlete as me, dropping ball after ball with a glove that was more "I-don't-care!" than "almost-got-it!" This seemed to have been the last authentic thing they had shared: mindless rooting for the Indians and hating all other cities that dared to field teams. Ultimately, my father had to have been seen for the phony fan he always had been.

"...Always two teams, never more, with their legions of fans making slurry excuses for their absent drunkenness. Everyone dedicated to us vs. them, like we all aren't part of the same fighting force, country, planet, whatever. This succeeded, of course, in brainwashing enough of us to accept how America probably came to be ruled. "In this coooorna! A record of ten and just 2, the Repuuuublicaaaans!" Their half of the fans for blind freedom all standing in cheers just as angry as proud. "And in this coooorna! The contenda! Just three wins, one loss and a draaaaw. The Deeeeeeemocraaaats!" Then more of the same from the fans for equality. Freedom sucks! Fuck equality! Tastes great! Less filling! My father was inexplicably on the Republican* team since long before I came along, so those blasted Indians had an unexplained magnetism. If they won, which included him too, he was happy and we all could be happy along with him. If they lost, and the Indians sucked as a rule in my youth, he would carry this loss like a burden that we knew not to try and relieve with reason. 'You know anybody on that team?' my mother asked him only once. "Cause you're acting like your life depends on who wins or loses.' He turned at her, drunk, and said, 'How's 'bout you go and be a Yankee then and leave me here with the Indians...'."

You don't try again after getting that kind of nonsense, my father concluded, not when enough of that kind of talk came unsolicited anyway.

"With a horse, when times are tough in the cold and you're lost, or some shit, you can eat the meat and climb inside at least," my grandfather reportedly told my father one time, out of the blue, after the Indians had lost something like eight-straight. Blank-faced, Saul had just stared at the television, happy that his father had said that before heading out the door to go find a barroom in which to get drowned with like-hearted company. These were among the few times when he could watch some television with tidy endings, a real purpose. Even a *Love Boat/Fantasy Island* stretch would delight Saul and Ann to tears.

Saul Sr. had never met anyone who'd had to eat horse meat because there was nothing else to eat, much less have to climb inside one to keep from freezing, so he couldn't fathom what could have led his father to care about being a survivor like that or what, aside from fear tactics, could have possessed him to share this advice with a boy who had barely started puberty. I still have yet to meet anyone who's gutted a horse for a warm night's bed.

My father tacked off a few other sour memories, just to make sure the jury (me) would side with his client (him). There was the ram that ran off, when my father was in fifth grade, and was gone for a week, then returned to a shotgun blast with his father's nut reasoning pulling the trigger: "Couldn't let all the others start to planning vacations." That was one of the few times no tears were shed at the trigger. Even with a pennant in sight, three wins on the road, he could rail in a way that would scare his wife and child. "If they do it, if they make it, the Tribe, the World Series, I'll shoot all these fool sheep just because they don't give a shit. The money that'd bring? Ooooooeee, the feast. Then I go out and get us a new flock know what's *what*! You *know* that!"

It was meant to be funny, of course, but his family believed him, and so it was frightening instead. They silently wished for the Tribe to fall shy, though, not by too much, just enough. And they had. The sheep lived. And later that night, my grandfather apparently pushed so hard while taking a shit that he popped his own heart. ["The coroner's report confirms this version of my grandfather's demise. Apparently, Saul Sr. was not only disappointed with how Paul was alive, but also how Paul came to die.]

By that time, my father's 4-H jacket still matched his largely empty expression. Its lone patches were for county fair participation. A disgrace; it was all for Paul, anyway. But after Paul died, Saul Sr. found something resembling a reason to live. His flagging passion for the flock surged, now that it needed someone who wanted them all to have names. He found himself in all these things he'd been kept from finding in his parents' secret places. Day in and out, he'd hear the music die down in the bathroom, the gloop of the tub plug coming out, and he'd pack these family relics up until next time, when he'd somehow feel even more alive than the day before. In a month or so, his mother emerged from the bathroom one afternoon with the same relieved look on her face that my father had worn the whole time. She started taking quick showers after this, two minutes tops. "You okay?" she asked her son. "Uh-huh. You?" He grinned, she smiled. He giggled, she laughed.

When Tater, the workhorse, died weeks later, Saul talked his mother into using the money to plant corn, a few long frames of Chardonnay grapes and a tightly packed but diverse restaurant garden instead of just plowing forward with another horse and more sheep. Ann didn't put up a fight; what could she say? It's what her boy wanted; it's what Paul would never have allowed.

They supposedly taught each other how to cook like master chefs. This, judging from my diet growing up, was another mind-blowing revelation. Where did all this giveafuck go?

Uncle Floyd would fly everybody up to celebrate Christmases or mail down a box of presents every year. My father and Floyd were close, as close as a boy can be with a drunk uncle living a few thousand miles away. These were their first truly happy times as mother and son, with a full schedule of television to fill in all the quiet spaces, but the stain of Paul's abuse kept them mostly cooped up there and scared of a world they guessed was more like him than not. Whichever way they looked, there it was.

Before long, my father was sitting at his graduation ceremony and watching his mother play with her Instamatic camera, which made a sound that embarrassed her son, even more than the dull-gray, old Taurus she'd gotten, plus $3,000 cash, for the Suburban. He still hadn't found anywhere productive to stick his penis, but his blue corduroy jacket, back home in his closet, had run out of space for all the patches he'd ended up earning in that fatherless time.

"Your father'd be proud," his mother told him as they walked to the car after graduation. "If he even knew how." Just a few of his classmates waved curt goodbyes forever, while most just stared through him to others in the distance, as they always had.

"Wuzatma? Who?"

She stopped walking. He kept going.

* * *

Just two days later, after a bender on his own label, Ra Red, Saul Sr. had raked together enough concern for himself to join the Army, in "peace time," whatever that meant then. He walked into the recruiter's office, took some tests and got a job as a [REDACTED]. The recruiter reportedly asked, "You want the airborne option?" and my father thought that just meant he had the option to go earn a maroon beret if he wound up growing the balls. It was a costly assumption, as many are. A few weeks before graduating from basic training at Fort Leonard Wood, Missouri, my dad was among those a drill sergeant ordered outside to start doing PT in the morning *and* at night. He sheepishly told the beady eyes under the too-generous brim that he had "the Airborne *option*, drill sergeant," at which time he was informed of his only option, which was to: "Shut your fuckhole, McGinty! That numb ass full of sheep dick of yours is going ... to ... Airborne ... School!"

He went, of course, chiseling his physique to magnificent effect and letting out little girlish chirps with each of his five jumps as a paratrooper trainee. (Many more would come later, and the wussy yelps never subsided.) With his beret still fluffy and poorly shaped he wound up at [REDACTED] school all the way across the country in Monterey, California, and it's just a shame that, while most of his classmates were preparing for dress-green desk jobs in important-looking office buildings in places like Ft. Meade, Maryland, and MacDill Air Force Base, Tampa, my father, after excelling at all the same training, would be rewarded by wearing fatigues on his way to Ft. Bragg, North Carolina, which, just days before my father arrived, his unit had deserted to go fight for oil in the desert – peace time was over that quick.

He had a weekend to get drunk then was headed there, too. The mission for his elite light-infantry division: to be speed bumps for freedom against thousands of tanks stacked up by a puppet madman ruling over a nation of sheep way more scared than American sheep. Puppets need a good scouring every so often in toxic chemicals and hot ironing. To prepare his mind, my father was told to start imagining the face of someone he hated (his father) on that crazy mustachioed dictator's body. He would soon discover that this guy's portrait took a place of pride (read: fear) in every one of his subject's home above the couch. To be even more ready to kill or be killed, though, my father tried to make all the starving pawns they bumped into wear the same mug of his father Paul, King of Sheep, the Dead Shepherd. But he couldn't do it. None of them seemed to have the right temperament. They were happy for food, parched for water, overjoyed that our bombs had stopped falling, curious about our gadgets and watches, praying only that we'd whisk them away in air-conditioning to be well-fed prisoners of war. The folks the troops were allegedly sent to defend in Saudi Arabia and Kuwait, my father opined, seemed much better suited to wear the mask of Paul. Hate blazed from their eyes.

*　*　*

My father landed in Saudi Arabia to a fly-strewn sandstorm that carried in his mind the dead skin and bone dust of every Persian left behind or led astray through time immemorial, congealing and crackling and stinging with no-telling-what-else on its way up his nose, the piss and shit of a thousand generations, levitating to cloud, alighting to dune and back again to pestilential dust.

His rucksack was only half as heavy as it would be when a lieutenant led him to his four-person squad and the portion of batteries, food, ammunition, and antenna equipment it would be his responsibility to lug around, assemble, and disassemble at wildly random intervals, often on foot, other times crammed into a Hummer. "You need anything," the lieutenant advised with a laugh, "just get used to it." A torrid sun drilled through every day, soaking their clothes and making the nights feel like winter. Home sickness and camel spiders, which somehow married the treacherous qualities of the tarantula and scorpion, turned their dreams into nightmares, making the nights colder still. "*See the world*," my father recalled the recruiter's sign advertise, adding, "*Start at the bottom.*"

I was flabbergasted. He'd never spoken of any of this to any of us. I'd just reread his second journal on the porch, after cleaning up shards of the window and taping the hole, and that time through I'd caught his reference to a war diary that I would find in his closet, behind the butt of the shotgun, which was still loaded with buckshot and oiled for action. The diary rambles too madly for me to, in good conscience, not keep paraphrasing and highlighting just the main thrusts. You're welcome.

First off, a primer debriefing for the uninitiated, bless their untarnished hearts: Not until recent historical advancements did everyone officially understand and attempt to solve the dilemma of why society's dueling tribes fought all those wars for all those generations over trillions in assets and other natural resources, but everyone had a pretty good notion. Not nearly as much thought was given to such complicated machinations then. It was easier to explain with narrative illustrations like "big versus little": the hairy-backed Goliath (Iraq) wanting back more oil and a more expansive view of the Red Sea, versus the hairy-backed David (Kuwait), who we'd groomed very nicely, thankyouverymuch, to be another one of our greased-up pump monkeys. We get the oil, you get the army. Done. We'll even hold your hand while it's happening. Mmm. Propaganda like this is so easy to push on even those who loath sports and silly sitcoms; even peaceniks and news junkies with a nose for international policy abhor the needless suffering of an underdog; surely, they reason, Gandhi wasn't referring to big meanies when he said, "An eye for an eye makes the whole world blind."

This war in the desert, of course, would get harder and harder to sell down the road, as more Davids were found to be harboring rancor not so much for Goliath but the utopian western ideal of a mall at every highway exit and as much of the oil and poppy we'd need to get people shopping and filling up their SUVs there. In the next war, as we all are embarrassed to know, Big US sold the world a dozen lies to explain how they just *knew* this new Hussein had weapons of mass destruction. They could have just told the one truth for how they knew: "We" sold him the goods for his war with Iran. Oiloiloil... This we all now agree is the case, but for how long was it something we knew but ignored? It's so simple to say things are too far away to fathom. So much harder to fathom those evil complexities. Silly, to think.

My father, it must be noted, was one of the few completely under the sway of his first sergeant, an apparent pervert named Blinker, who was suspected of rifling through everyone's care packages to see all the homemade porn photos first. Follow-up letters from home mentioned salami or popcorn tins that oddly had made it overseas, but only to Blinker's cot. But all this suspect activity apparently hadn't tarnished my father's view of the old man. When their captain had his top NCO deliver the pitch, early in the campaign, that his troops needed to ingest over a series of evenings some tiny white pills that "might be effective protection in the event of ingestion of enemy chemical or biological agents," my father was among those who acquiesced to this Blinker, in hopes of staving off what the old man said was "a very distinct but unconfirmed enemy threat. KISS, people. Why be unprepared?"

"Baaaah!" bleated a few of my father's more independence-minded peers. "Keep it simple, sheeeeeep. Baaaah..." I drew an immediate comparison to my first experience in the classroom.

For several months they just ran around in circles and got used to the heat, riding here to there in long convoys that kicked up so much dust they had to clean their weapons twice a day. They went on long marches with all their equipment to get used to the stinging hot breaths and terrain that was more like what you'd find on Mars than anything they'd ever experienced. They sat in the saunas of their gas masks for hours on end, played soccer in full MOPP get-up, groaned about going home. They also apparently whacked off a lot, at least my father did, nursing his childhood obsession with unashamed abandon: *"...If you don't play the field and switch up to the left, you get bored with the right and start wiping your ass with it one day on accident, which they used to do here with the left or still do..."*

Meanwhile, the Air Force was dropping bombs all over the cradle of civilization, not just on the hundreds of thousands of armed-to-the-teeth armored and artillery divisions at the border, but all along their supply lines (read: car-strewn highways) and into the hearts of every city, where the enemy would sequester their Russian-made weapons and armor. It was a distantly echoed affirmation among my father's fellow foot soldiers that what needed to be done would be cosmetic, from the air; they'd get to go home heroes without ever having to actually be the killers of anybody, for the most part, not directly anyway. When any of my father's fellow troops showed signs of rebellion or remorse for what was happening to the enemy, Blinker was quick to pounce" *"You don't think Henry Kissinger knew what he was talking about? You got all the answers? Man said, 'You control oil and you control nations, control food and you control the people.' Last wise thing you said, Fangboner, was 'Hand me that lotion.' Now zip your flaps and do your crying on your phone calls home to Mommy, hear?"* My father admits to believing this type of propaganda then. *"I was raised on Reagan and Alex P. Keaton,"* he wrote in later journaling, by way of explaining everything. *"It was trickling down all over everybody. It felt nice. It even had us pegging our pants and wearing penny loafers again, argyle socks even. I didn't know enough then to know better. I only knew enough to want to stay alive."*

Nobody in charge of Iraq was giving up, though, so they sent my father and the other soldiers in to finish what couldn't antiseptically be handled from above; you can't stockpile prisoners and bury dead people from the clouds. With oil fires choking the sky from the time they crossed the imaginary line between Saudi Arabia and Iraq, making daytime dusk and nighttime black, my twenty-year-old father was brought to fire his M16 on just a few occasions in this, the first of the last great wars – at an invisible enemy on a ridgeline and, again days later, in darkness across a dried-up riverbed into the source of tracer fire. That was it. A few grunts he knew had bullets audibly whiz by them. They'd bragged up and down about it. They'd finally gotten to do what all their training had been for. Still, when anything that registered above a "skirmish" kicked off, it was quickly snuffed out by something mounted on a Hummer. It kept the apparent danger at a safe-enough distance. The most jarring part for everyone seemed to be the explosions at odd intervals, mostly the work of combat engineers removing trip wires and chemical weapons caches. They had the effect of making everybody jump for decades afterward, whenever anybody dropped anything unexpectedly, like a plate on the floor or even a fork in the sink. These casualties weren't registered until many years later, at VA hospitals and 12-step meetings. Some of his colleagues met a little more resistance in Kuwait, but not much. A few hundred Americans died in all, a few hundred limbs went flying, many from friendly fire. It was the Second and Final Gulf Wars that proved the most deadly and protracted to the People's Republic. Those wars, of course, were still much costlier for the "enemy," by far.

Anyway, as we all know, it worked out, through the grace of Google. We are One. Enough said.

My father reports (and newsmakers confirm) that regaining the little kumquat of Kuwait on the sea was all that was needed to successfully land-lock the enemy again and allow for the successful safeguarding of a much more expansive port position and fossil fuel hub between fundamentalist Saudi Arabia and fundamentalist Iran, an agreement subsequently tidied up by Presidents Bush and other lesser investors. Nevertheless, the battling was over for my father. It was the beginning of the cleanup, which he apparently never quite finished. Some of his worst memories (edited for charity and clarity) stand out as emotional landmines, not just for him but for all of the soldiers who have ever been made to suffer them:

"...We just arrived where the Tigris and Euphrates rivers get on, this dried-out and rocky wasteland that Capt. Reynolds says was the [mythical epicenter of] the Garden of Eden. It does seem like it'd be impossible to grow much of anything around here, so maybe they figured God willed it to be that way. CO told us to dig into this big circle of Russian T62s that the Iraqis were using to protect some SCUD missile launchers, which were in chunks all around these big, bloody craters by the time we rode up. It's like the Imperial Guard just ran as far away from their uniforms as they could as soon as they heard we were finally coming in. I can't imagine being so scared that I'd leave the Hummer and just run out into the desert in my underwear. Everywhere we go, it's hairy naked men giving up and begging for food, pointing at this hole or that hole the cluster bombs made. Better starving and surrendering, I guess, than shooting and dying. A pretty sad lot our strategy made. Little families here and there are dead in their cars, just too awful to want to get into, except to say, better them than us and better here than home. It's just rock and sand, sand and rock around here. And surrender. There's more prisoners

giving up than we have translators and guns with laser scopes to point at their heads and scare them into sitting cross-legged and doing what they're told. They're loading them up in long caravans of comfy bus rides to a temporary camp somewhere in the rear. We tell the Kuwaiti translators to let them know about their choices. They can get a bullet where the red dot is on this guy's forehead or get three squares and Geneva Convention interrogations. Their choice. They all seem to want the food. And some air-conditioning. I don't know. Maybe this will teach them to want to be more civilized. The flies are even wilder here, aggressive, like those bitchy monkeys I hear they got in Tibet. They get into my food, even with all the dead bodies around, so we start eating like first sergeant, inside our mosquito nets, but the flies get in anyway. After a while, you just start giving up and trying to see if they add anything to the taste, like cilantro or basil. (They don't.) We're scared about what got left behind for us to find. They said over the radio that the sappers went in first to make sure nothing was wired, but then they told us NOT to even THINK about going in any of the tanks. I wanted to know if there were dead bodies inside before we bedded down some hooches on top of and up under this one (that's where I am right now). If they're in there, they don't smell like the others in plain sight. Night. Got some grave-digging to do in the morning!..."

After a few days pining for a "*greasy-ass burger*" or television "*that ain't CNN*" or a "*sun that doesn't want to kill you,*" his entries returned to chronicling events worth full inclusion here:

"*...We buried some more stiffs today, just so they wouldn't be on the flies. The first night, the smoke from the oil fires* [and nerve gas stockpiles; see Google on history of vaguely quaint city of Kamisiya] *tasted thick and tangy like tomato soup. It makes you cough and keep coughing. During the day, it's like night with a full moon; during the night, it's nothing but nothing, but even colder than before when the sun worked. Me and Rivera make random noises to scare each other, like when we're pissing, just to get ready for something to go off but also, I think, to have little moments of relief for being alive. Then I nearly kill myself or fall* *into the hands of the enemy, which first sergeant says the enemy uses as toilet paper, the savages. Last night, when everybody but some grunts were sleeping, I left the perimeter to shit and got turned around when out of the nothing I hear the flapping wings of a million dung beetles coming to pray over and prey on my meal like it was Mecca or Medina or some shit. Then my red-lens, which was dying, barely spotted the first-place winners, and that sent me to spinning in circles away just trying to pull my pants back up. I was dizzy and scared, so I don't know which way was safe and which way was far from it. I could still smell my shit so I knew I was still near it, but I didn't know which way was back. My flashlight was pretty much kaput. It made just a pink light the size of a penny in my hand. So I walked in circles for what I know was miles, until I bumped into some wall of a house or a compound or a business. It was something made of a wall. It was dark there, too, even in all the cities, no electricity for months for miles. Only generators, during the daytime only. Then I bumped into what felt like a light post, a car, a street sign. I think I even stepped on a watermelon, since it felt hard at first but soft inside after I stepped down hard. I was too afraid to make a noise or see if God let my flashlight work again. I just sat down when my body was as tired as my head. It smelled like I'd stepped in shit. I listened for a long time, then I started to hear the wind, and it had another language on it and insect wings and the bouncing of my knee against the butt of my weapon. I waited and waited until something like light came up. When the sun got to around 10 a.m. in the sky, it was finally not completely dark, and I saw the perimeter way off away, hiding against a ridgeline to the south. Much closer was the family of four in the muddy Fiat I bumped into on the way back to the perimeter. I was so eager to get back, but they were smothered all over each other and the windows. I guessed a cluster bomb had done it. What were they driving on a major supply line like a highway for? I don't get it, but I figured they deserved some kind of a burial like all the others with all the flies on them, so I pulled them all out through the shattered windshield, after I stepped through it with my boot and wrapped my nose with my balaclava, then I rolled their brittle bodies into the low part of a ditch nearby, one by one, which was no kind of ditch that you see has some water in it sometimes, and I piled rocks up on top of them until I couldn't see any more red there. Then I ran back to my team, who were brushing their teeth and laughing about a joke that some passing grunt had told them. No one even knew I was gone until Hitch looked at my boot with his flashlight and asked me why it was all red. I told him I didn't know and ran off to wash all the red off my boot at the water bladder. It came out good enough with dish soap. When I got back to the tank where our Hummer was parked, I changed into a spare uniform and kicked sand over the old one. Whew! I could have gotten in TROUBLE!...*"

The diary wound down with my father registering no alarm or ailments, only elation that he was going home to maybe, finally, as he stated, "*get some of that classy-ass pussy.*" He knew what he wasn't going to do, too: "*Fuck that farm bullshit.*" His last entry reflected a soldier coming home to the rest of his life, with any number of paths yet ahead, and a wish to have made more of an impact on those he was tasked to protect with his life.

"*...If I could take one thing, just one, with me back to the United (and Beautiful) States of America, it's one of these ladies the towel-heads make ride in the backseat of their Beamers like little kids that they can fuck and boss around. They even keep them in the back corner of their mosques when they go to pray to Allah for guidance. Here's some advice: Don't be a dick to your women! I haven't even seen them, but I've seen their eyes. They're as big as almonds. Every time they speed by our Hummers, way over the posted speed limits, it's always the same. Hubby looking over, his gutra waving in the wind, red like his angry eyes. Those eyes tell me he'd rather be shooting us than thanking us. And there she is in the backseat, there's wifey, or wifeys, and those almonds are just pleading, begging us, please, please, get us out of here! I guess my mother had those eyes, too, but at least you could see her whole sad face. ...*"

He couldn't take any booty home, much less a burka-clad

woman with pretty eyes. He didn't need convincing; my father was a good soldier. No one doubts he could have done more with these loyal qualities as a civilian in peace time. At the coastal Saudi high-rise condos where he got to stay for his last few weeks overseas, they cleaned and treated, treated and cleaned their equipment and vehicles obsessively to remove, as Blinker told them in a rehearsed manner, any "known and/or unknown chemical or biological agents that wouldn't go over well back home. We keep this shit here!"

They were all starting to act a little nuts by then, apparently. My father mentioned how a teammate named Alan Hitch had sincerely started asking people to call him "Hawk" and before their return from the desert surreptitiously started throwing dead radio batteries in the daytime fires so they'd explode and scare the shit out of everybody. They didn't retaliate, though, other than to tell everyone else to watch their asses around Hitch, who they really should start calling "Hawk," at least until they got home. But it's not in my family or the People's interest to disclose every minute detail of my father's former acquaintances, only those details of his life that might best explain the effects of his injuries and the effects of ours.

Like this: Out of the blue, a day before his team was to come home, part of my father's head was hanging open after a bomb exploded on the ground floor of that Saudi high-rise, shooting concrete, glass, and shrapnel all the way up into the third-floor unit where he was taking a nap all alone, cuddling his rifle like a good boy. He was one of dozens spilling out of themselves, but the only one from his team, since the others were all at the makeshift Burger King ordering milkshakes and flirting with Air Force girls. It all just seemed so unfair. My father's secretary of defense, the now-deposed serial Wizard of Oz Dick Cheney, would go on in the coming years to secure that infamous fortune of his. My dad would lose an integral part of his mind. How do you do the math on that?

He told me only once, just before I'd left for college, about how it felt to get blown awake from a nap. He said he was just making random declarations in blasts, like, "Dream of the century!" or "Texas tea just gone blew out of my skull!" or "Who threw the first stone?! Who threw the first stone?! ..."

Crazy. The stuff I can hear him saying.

* * *

These from-nowhere verbal ambushes had no end. I came to see them resulting from a faulty dopamine dispenser, until I learned they'd likely been the outgrowths of real-world addiction and, of course, the well-documented brain damage he'd suffered at the hands of history. Innocuous, silly things like: Stubbing his toe, screaming, then switching to a mock angry voice to say, "I hate you toe! You're nothing like the other! I'll get you next time!" Or plain weird: in the middle of a sleepover, charging into my room right when the last of us had just gone to sleep – "They've done it! Under the bed! C'mon!! Them sneaky ambushing Amish! You! Wake up!! Get my shotgun out of the closet! Faster! It's a Mennonite Massacre!"

When my father came home and was all mended up, he "started drinking himself stupider," according to my mother. Still he managed to get a job writing obituaries and picking up police reports just by saying he used to be in the Army and liked to make sure everybody got a fair goodbye. He'd never thought to go to college, but I sure as hell had, just by knowing he hadn't. He was actually lucky to latch onto something in the way of a desk job. He was damaged in more ways than the one. His arteries and organs were caked in bismuth and titanium from the oil fires, [ect.] – confirmed by a hair analysis ordered by a doctor at a treatment center he later attended, documents I was fortunate enough to discover folded inside a box of crayons in his closet. So, apart from the brain damage and memories of getting used to eating flies and burying bodies for weeks on end, my father also had to contend with his ass bulging with hemorrhoids that pained him so much that he was forced into seclusion to write standing up at a tall corner table in the dining room for more than a decade-and-a-half, well into my teens, when I stopped wanting to come visit because of the conclusion I'd come to that we never would relate. Perversely, I'd once wished he could have just gotten really good at playing ping-pong in an Army hospital like Forrest Gump, then come home for a long run to sort out his place in the world. No such luck.

As a child, trapped by inescapable circumstances, you're forced to marvel at your father's edgy sensibility, play it off as the silly genius of a war hero when your friends are around. You come to find something like hope for inheriting your mother's sanity and bone structure, too, despite a lingering disdain for the red mop of hair, flubby nose and pale-blue skin that have always made me have to work twice as hard to make girls and, later, women friendly enough to say, "Aw, what the hell." You even find yourself coming around to an understanding that maybe some brilliance was left there behind his disability, particularly when you consider The Chair.

Still there at the dining room table, taunting me to pack it up in the trunk for the drive back to Ohio, The Chair still retained all those years later a glimmer of brilliance. My eyes kept coming back to it during the cleanup. Sometimes he was in it peripherally, then I'd look and it was empty.

As with many great inventions, The Chair had been born of painful necessity. After my father's legs were tree trunks from a generation of working from standing for the paper without a newsroom, in an office that really was just a dining room, he'd had enough of an ailment known to afflict the very best of us: external hemorrhoids. He'd soldered and sewed for weeks, things I'd never seen him do before that. When he was done, The Chair had hung down like a parrot's nest from a high, arching bend of steel to just the perfect height to reach his computer on the far side of the dining room table. The basket was a seat woven of parachute risers that held his back upright and level after securing straps around the thighs with seatbelt buckles he'd found in an old Chrysler at the landfill – the effect of which instantly relieved all the rest of the strain on his wildly troubled sphincter that his prescription-strength suppositories and pain killers couldn't handle. Problem, if only the one: solved.

He was back to work, though, at least not kept from working. At the various hand-me-down city meetings he got to cover, which were few and far between all the obit writing, he'd reportedly walk along the back of the chambers conspiratorially, framing every story in such a way as to avoid having to ask any confrontational questions after the gavel had sounded, any questions at all really except those editorially required; but at home, he could relax and sit again to write about this new batch of deaths or that rural barn fire or any such sewer plan that only writers like my father would ever want to wrap their heads around. He seemed happy, but maybe that was just the pain killers and mood stabilizers.

Hesitantly, I strapped into The Chair at the dining room table and swung in the seat like a parrot on a perch. I scanned the dark street outside. Then, in a dash, I fumbled my way out of the riser chair and fell to the floor. Someone had just dropped a slat on the living room blinds in Arredondo's house, way down the block, someone like a spy, only what kind of spy leaves the lights on in the room to show his silhouette to the world like an Amsterdam hooker? A hulking, pearish outline. *Serge? Renaldo? Peter? Who?*

I dead-bolted the door and twisted the blinds shut. Then some serious shit started getting thrown away.

Chapter 4

WHEREAS, by 1963, Jefferson's plea was unheeded, at which point President Eisenhower made his words a warning, just three days before his seat went to John Kennedy. Who better a messenger, he who served as a spoke in the strongest of wheels? From what better vantage to survey our flaws? From the front, Army general during World Wars I and II, to the first U.S. leader of Occupied Germany, pushing up to the Allied Commander of NATO, to finally ascend to our Nation's top post, after which he delivered a farewell address and the warning that, lacking safeguards to temper insatiable greed, our Nation's dependence on war would grow ravenous, feeding more and more children into all the fires that oligarchs set by and with their puppets on political and media perches: "In the councils of government, we must guard against the acquisition of unwarranted influence, whether sought or unsought, by the military-industrial complex. The potential for the disastrous rise of misplaced power exists and will persist. We must never let the weight of this combination endanger our liberties or democratic processes. We should take nothing for granted. Only an alert and knowledgeable citizenry can compel the proper meshing of the huge industrial and military

*machinery of defense with our peaceful methods
and goals, so that security and liberty may prosper
together." Heed that, Freeburg voters, then answer
at last.*

Sure, curiosity may have killed some cats, but it's also been a real boon for investigators, religious seekers, cuckolded spouses and academicians, even high school history teachers like me. So that's my on-the-record reason for setting up a time the next morning to meet the police detective later in the afternoon. *Silly to think,* I was thinking I'd say.

Before I left, I spent several hours hauling bags of my father's most overt garbage to the curb, each pregnant with empty cans, soiled underwear, more dead roaches and strewn-about clothes that I knew wouldn't even fly at Goodwill. On a shelf in the living room, I found my father's wind-up Timex. I slipped it on and it fit. I got in my car. It was parked, as per neighborhood protocol, in sand beside my father's dusty maroon Corolla in the driveway, which he'd parked snug against my old garage of a bedroom. I turned the key and heard the engine turn in exasperated shrieks that died to a few terminal chokes. I grabbed my father's keys from the hook in the kitchen, but his didn't start either. So I jogged.

I managed to reach the police station parking lot, which it shared with the McDonald's next door, just twenty minutes late. A uniformed receptionist under a teased-apart helmet of faux blond inspected my sweat-soaked I'M HUGE IN JAPAN t-shirt in judgment, then looked at the clock. I told her about my luck. She hadn't asked. Nodding in a way that was full of mistrust, she directed me with a frozen smile and a pointed pinky to an unmarked door, which buzzed mechanically to enhance the frigid invitation.

"Not silly," the salt-and-peppered Det. Pablo Escondido told me with a handshake at the door to his office, reading the question on my face. A little too muscular for a married guy, I thought, ogling the woman next to him in the picture on his desk. "Just a little sick. That's all, son. You've been paranoid some, right? So you can understand."

I sat across the gunmetal gray desk from the detective, who, after some mouse-work and screen-scanning, noted that I was looking good compared to the mug shot he'd found ahead of my arrival depicting my marijuana possession arrest several years before. It was the booze that brought me in, though, he ascertained to my astonishment.

"Alcohol'll kill you," he'd said before I'd even adjusted my ass in the chair.

"Make that shit illegal," I agreed, oddly prescient in my day.

"You Mormon or something?" Escondido didn't look up, just smiled.

"No way," I said. "Just observant."

The office was somehow cluttered and organized at the same time. File cabinets lined the walls, where real paper used to be. Dirty, hard-copy photographs were posted on every available surface, like the school picture of a poof-headed teenage girl taped over the light switch, the switch itself poking through her stomach, or the ethnically diverse collection of mug shots coating the blades of the unmoving ceiling fan. The wedding picture with his wife was the only one that got a frame. The desktops were stacked with file folders of varying thickness, yellow notes sticking out here and there to make even organized stacks seem unkempt. Escondido pushed rectangular reading glasses up his nose and puffed away at an e-cigar non-stop. I smelled cinnamon in the vapor, the coffee pot's final gurgle. I finally got the gumption to ask the question he'd already answered:

"What if he was right?"

"Son..." Eyes through my skull. Another puff of mouthwash.

He pulled a folder – not the fat of a murder, nor the thin of domestic dispute – out from under a bunch of others and slid it across the desk. A picture of my father's newspaper mug shot was paper-clipped to the front cover, about twenty years younger than he looked at the end – largely the norm, unnamed sources would later confirm. I flipped it open and Escondido dropped his sausages fast to conceal a few pictures on top. "If it wasn't the government," he said, "it was always somebody." Then his hand slid away with the pictures in tow.

Besides the report on the suicide and those few gory photos I'd never want haunting me, there were two other incidents, both tersely recorded by the reporting officers. The first was recorded right after I'd moved to Ohio. I could read in the officer's words some frustration with having his shifts bogged down by the crazies, who, before Reaganomics, had been neatly corralled into state institutions and coaxed by taxpayers and modern pharmaceuticals, six patients in ten, back to something like sane or at least quieter lunatics who understood boundaries.

DATE: REDACTED
TIME: 2214
ADDRESS: REDACTED

NARRATIVE: On this date and time, this officer responded to the above address after the report of menacing by stalking and/or illegal invasion of privacy. The occupant, Saul McGinty, was waiting upon my arrival at the curb. Mr. McGinty told this officer that he was having difficulties with the landlord at this address, the above-mentioned Rex Arbuckle, to wit: He suspected Mr. Arbuckle had been systematically observing his activities, "not stalking from outside, but with cameras inside." This officer asked Mr. McGinty what had led him to suspect said surveillance and, further, to suspect his landlord of perpetrating said surveillance, to which Mr. McGinty responded, "The man knows things about me, private things, that had to come from clandestine surveillance." When pressed for specifics to bolster the allegations, Mr. McGinty referenced an encounter at the door three days prior, during which Mr. Arbuckle had come to collect rent and had asked if Mr. McGinty thought it was hygienic to go a whole week without showering. This officer asked Mr. McGinty if he had, indeed, gone that long without taking a shower. Mr. McGinty alleged that most weeks he showers a handful of times, but hadn't once during the week in question, nor had he changed his clothing. "You see what I mean?" Mr. McGinty asked, to which this officer informed the complainant that such an exchange was hardly a solid foundation to support a charge of invasion of privacy. Mr. McGinty said there were other comments from Mr. Arbuckle that reflected an intimate knowledge of his activities, but he didn't want to offer specific details, prompting this officer to remind Mr. McGinty that only specifics would matter with such defamatory allegations.

Mr. Arbuckle was out of town on business, according to his wife, the above-listed Ursula Arbuckle. The couple lives directly across the cul-de-sac at REDACTED. She denied the allegations in her husband's stead, then asked, "Who in their right mind would be a fly on that man's wall?" Mr. McGinty answered what was clearly a rhetorical question with, "Your pervert husband's who."

Mr. McGinty informed this officer that he'd found some suspicious conditions inside. With Mrs. Arbuckle and Mr. McGinty escorting me, this officer proceeded to inspect the home for recording devices.

In the living room, Mr. McGinty had several electrical sockets hanging from the walls. On the socket closest to the dining room, he pointed to a few strands of what appeared to be copper wire tied to the end of each socket's adapter. This officer noticed only copper wire. Mrs. Arbuckle also reported seeing only copper wiring and that she was "under the impression that that was the kind of thing you'd expect to find in an electrical socket." This officer concurred.

In the master bedroom, Mr. McGinty had the ceiling fan disassembled for my inspection. Hanging beside the customary wiring bundles for the fan and light assembly was an unidentifiable cable that Mr. McGinty said led to the attic and what could be the recording device his landlord had been using to capture his most personal affairs. This allegation elicited laughter from Mrs. Arbuckle, who said, "The only personal affair you've got going is that torrid triangle between you, your left hand and right." I informed Mrs. Arbuckle of the seriousness of the allegations and not to goad the complainant through humiliation. She agreed to concur.

After conferring at length with shift supervisor Sgt. Pachenco, this officer was made to comply with a direct order to inspect the attic or face disciplinary action. The aforementioned cable had indeed been routed through the fan apparatus and was followed to where it lay severed, apparently by wire cutters, near a heap of badly damaged Christmas decorations that were coated by what was clearly the attic's heaviest concentration of cockroaches. A quick inspection revealed no surveillance wiring or equipment here or in any other area of the attic. Mr. McGinty, from his position on a step ladder at the attic entrance, noted, "So the cable goes through the fan and then just ends up cut over here? Hm." This officer informed Mr. McGinty that this would be an accurate appraisal of the facts but hardly proof of any wrongdoing.

This officer reminded Mr. McGinty that, though his training was that of a peace officer and not a certified electrician, it's possible that this cable had been up here since long before he even moved in. "So you think I should have somebody a bit more qualified come and look at all this?" he asked. I informed both Mr. McGinty and Mrs. Arbuckle that an exterminator would be a good person to start with, then ordered Mr. McGinty aside to let this officer exit his attic at once.

Upon leaving the home, Mr. McGinty told this officer that his car "had to have been" tapped too, since Mr. Arbuckle also seemed to have "uncanny knowledge" of his whereabouts outside the home, as well. Mr. McGinty was informed that not only was this officer not an electrician but also not a certified mechanic. Clear scene.

"Go on, son," said Escondido, who kept his eyes on the screen while flipping the first report over to reveal the second, dated a few months before my father's death. I felt foolish and self-absorbed for wasting any more of his time. Here was a man clearly pretending not to be overburdened by this village's inordinate load of deviant and/or greed- and jealousy-born acts of violent desperation, just for me to come unrushed to terms with my father's tragic life and death. I felt guilty of abetting all of Escondido's suspects still at large, who would have my shallow grasp of civic duty to thank for being free to strike again. I stood up.

"You want to just make me some copies of these?" I asked Escondido.

"If you want, later," he said, still enmeshed in the screen and puffing his e-cigar. "Go ahead. I'm just catching up on some things." I couldn't help but wonder what type of sleuthing had him so immersed, so I leaned over and saw what looked a lot like the website for Carnival Cruise Lines. He looked at me then, so I leaned back to let his eyes return.

"You teachers still get the summers off to get your heads straight, don't you?"

"Three weeks at Christmas and Easter break too." I saw his point.

"There you go."

DATE: REDACTED
TIME: 1744
ADDRESS: REDACTED

NARRATIVE: On this date and time, this officer responded to the above address and spoke with the resident, Saul McGenty Sr., who was acting erratically, to wit: repeatedly shoving his index fingers into his ears, then inspecting the tips both visually and nasally. Mr. McGenty told this officer that a "horrible ringing" would sound in his ears every time he tried to log into his computer, which he suspected had been implanted with some form of government bug that doubled for some "nefarious weapon of psychological warfare." Mr. McGenty also alleged that said bug would cause him to get sleepy, hungry, apathetic, lustful or angry at all the wrong times. I asked if he'd serviced the computer lately and whether he thought that might work to fix the problem. Mr. McGenty was certain that wouldn't work, adding, "You don't find government plants, they find you," then he resumed pushing his fingers into his ears and inspecting them again. This officer asked Mr. McGenty if perhaps psychiatry might help to remove this suspected bug, at which point he walked back inside, his middle finger raised, and slammed the door just after screaming, "Slave!" Clear scene.

I looked up at him with a weak, final *Aaaaand...*

"Son," he said, which was starting to annoy me since we were pretty much the same age. "We saw the note, the journals. The coroner read it all. I had to read that shit too. Well, I'll admit it: I only got through a few pages of the second journal; I've got other stuff picked out for my summer reading. But we did our due diligence. At the expense of all else." He circled his hand over his head like it held a twirling lasso. "We searched through all that junk in the house, too, and, just like when it all was the landlord's fault, we couldn't find anything to indicate any kind of tampering or wire-stalking. We even checked with the Feds, let them look inside his laptop. Aside from a deep history of porn, some of which I couldn't even fathom, they couldn't find anything to lend any credence to these ... sad delusions of his. These things happen, son. They do. Some people just get all wrapped up in..."

"Thanks for your time, detective. I understand. I don't need bereavement counseling." I was even more embarrassed than before, but it was spawned as much from latent suspicion as familial disgrace. I got up but didn't make for the door.

"I don't think you need counseling, son. I'm pretty sure your father did, though. That's all I'm saying here." Escondido stood and put his e-cigar down for the first time.

"Can't deny that," I said, offering him my hand, then dropping it when Escondido didn't take it.

"Colds. What's the government or anybody want looking into your father's life?" Escondido had to add. He seemed genuinely curious.

"You tell me," I said, not knowing where it came from. "Why don't you ask the government to fill you in? I'm sure they'd be willing to share."

Escondido's eyes widened at the gulf that widened between us. "We asked around at his work, talked with people he worked with before he started working at home, and as far as anyone knew, he worked and then he didn't. They didn't know all that much else about him. Did anybody?" I knew what he was asking: Did I?

"Mrs. Arbuckle." I said like an idea out of nowhere. "She told me people were coming around."

"Who's coming around?"

"People. I don't know. I'll ask her. She, well..."

"She's getting up there," Escondido jumped in. "Seems she's the only one cared what he was doing. We asked his editor why he didn't call us when he didn't return any calls and stopped turning in work, and he just figured your Dad was on a bender and had a reporter fill in until he came back around. Mrs. Arbuckle didn't come along, he might have been dead for years in there before anybody even cared to find out about it." He let that linger for what I thought was a little too long. "Son, they were..."

"Miserable," I said, then asked resignedly if I could take the folder, return it the next day. There was a computer disc, a few more papers I hadn't read. He obliged by making copies of everything, but not the disc, which he said, "had views no son should have of his father."

I waited quietly, perusing all the faces in the room's collage. The victims and suspects seemed to share an equal space here; it was hard to know how to feel about any of them; even the orange-clad convicts could have ended up on the losing end at last. I wondered how many of these pictures Escondido would ever get to take down with a sense of accomplishment. At least some cases get solved. This one sure seemed closed and filed away. As soon as I was gone, he'd probably rush to remove my father's ginger mug from a bathroom stall, where no doubt it had been adorned with the customary dripping dick next to his horsey, freckle-strewn face, maybe a thought bubble: "They killed myself." Or not.

"Don't be hard on yourself," he said, holding the door open and handing me a thin folder that held nothing like an answer. "These things happen, son. They're never easy on anybody. Just clean up and try to get home to your family."

I stifled a chuckle. "Look, detective: I've always had a hard time trusting anything that came out of his mouth. He was crazy. Everybody knew it. But what if somebody was watching him? I don't know why. I'll admit the government probably has a shit-ton of better things to do, but what if he was just blaming the wrong people? What if he was being watched but never found out who?"

"Watching him for what?" Escondido, clenching one side of his jaw, let that float out and dissipate like scorn into the hall, which was just as cold and unadorned as my shame. A lanky janitor with pink skin and dingy coveralls had just left a slug-trail of bleach on the linoleum. He was about to turn the corner, still sloshing back and forth, but shot me a look that asked the same question.

"I'm sorry, detective," I muttered, tiptoeing toward the buzzing door after too abrupt a turn that nearly sent my feet out from under me. "I'll let you get back to catching up on things. Have a nice cruise."

"I was thinking of taking my mother," Escondido added. I hadn't considered he had one of those.

"The wife's okay with that?"

"My wife was killed a few years ago," he said, letting go of the door, which slowly inched closed. "She ... goodbye."

"I'm sorry," I said, but the door was closed. Only the janitor heard me. He was shaking his head with contempt. "What?" I wanted to know.

I left the squat brick station, no taller or wider than the glassed-in McDonald's Playland on the other side of its parking lot, into an afternoon full of humidity and haze. Cars zipped by on Main Street, a once-thriving pedestrian hub that by then had been cratered by (mix and match!) suburbanization, consumerism, virtualization, big-box domination and the housing bubble bursting. What remained without soap-bar coating in the windows: a liquor store where the ice cream shop used to be; a Salvation Army instead of a family drugstore; watering holes where blue-collar shifts used to end and now began, spotted with sag-eyed regulars and twitchy-footed dealers. On every corner, a fat bucket of weeds sagged, hanging baskets of the same. Dandelions bloomed, though. I picked one from a crack at the roadside, then I crumpled and tossed it to the curb.

Unable to escape to anywhere, I walked west into the dying sun across the patchy grass of Freeburg Square, with its hoary laurel oaks, pallid sugar maples and long-deserted cabbage palms coating the usual assortment of the directionless masses with the gray pallor of suspicion and destitution. The shade offered no comfort. Past a crumbling, one-story City Hall, with the anticlimactic pillars at the entrance just four steps from the sidewalk and the tree lawn's tattered skirt of campaign placards, a ramshackle tenement building sporting a Soul Taco take-out dive at the corner – "¿Mexican Soul Food? ¡Si!" – cast a long shadow over Amberlane Way and a cluttered used car dealership farther east, its primary-colored promises to those with no credit or down payments to spare like little white lies on parade. A salesman with a malnourished expression watched me pass like a missed meal. I didn't know where I was leading myself until, a few blocks south on Amberlane, I came to Mission Avenue and looked sunward again at the dull yellow façade of the *Eagle*.

It was just past five, so the front lobby into the sales and advertising departments was closed. I circled the building and even entertained entering through a propped-open door by a smoking coffee can of cigarette butts in the empty loading bay, as a small cyclone of coupon inserts swirled around a grate. A few cars bunched in the lot closest to the back door to the editorial department. I didn't dare commit. I sniffed at the air like a dog and could only pick up a pungency that I thought was just ink. I skipped into a jog again. I had a feeling no one would have really known my father there anyway.

On the outskirts of downtown, nearing my father's neighborhood, I passed a country-style restaurant, Family Hearth, and that's when I saw her and knew it was her: Diamond Debbie, her boobs sagging now to a fat belly barely concealed by a ragged, blue sweatshirt, a big "M" on the front that maybe stood for Mickey Mouse. She'd changed.

The last time I'd seen her she was one of the hottest girls in my school, which no doubt had landed her the best dope connections. This is where all that had taken her. A gangly coffee-colored man with just a few teeth left just got out of the passenger side of the late-model white Aries that she'd just pressed into behind the wheel. Her once-golden hair was a confusion of tangles and colorful twisty-ties. Deep rivets of purple buried in under her eyes.

I watched as she pulled around the back of the restaurant then parked immediately on the other side, where another man, this one also a crack-riddled stick of the Anglo Saxon line, got in and said something Deb must have found funny because she cackled. They sat with the car idling for no more than a minute, then he got out and walked east through an alley. She pulled out of the spot again then, the white paint blinding in the sun where the clear-coat hadn't faded away yet to gray, and drove to another spot back on the other side of the restaurant.

Back and forth I watched her travel from the bus stop park bench at the street, through four customers in quick succession, until I decided to see if she was still slinging the lesser illicits, too.

"Deb! Diamond?" I pretended to be excited to see her and not at the prospect of getting high. (The Diamond was an inside joke that I'd never been let in on. Her real last name was Dennis.)

Her ears perked up, Serge-style.

"Other side," she said without looking, still moving, pulling into yet another spot beside an elderly couple in a cratered-out red Buick, who couldn't help but gawk disapprovingly as they hobbled off.

I got in fast, told her a cop had just passed, craning his neck. "Hold on," she said without flinching and pulled out onto Main Street with a chirp. I felt something kick the back of my seat, chalked it up to imagination.

When I knew her after high school, she was the full-bodied life of the party who either sold or knew who was selling the best grass in Freeburg. Today, hunched behind the tattered wheel of her Aries, she was a frail, saggy-breasted tweaker with bruises all up and down a set of legs that were so pale they came across as blue.

Another kick. I turned and finally noticed a pre-K girl with multicolored beads dangling from a yellowish mop of untended braids.

"Hello there..." The little girl stared at me and sniffled.

"You stupid," she said like a compliment.

"That's Charity," Deb said, rolling her bloodshot eyes, and then she shot her right arm into the backseat like a missile as a warning, her eyes still scanning the road in every direction. Deb started jitterbugging around even more when she noticed through her mirror that the girl had gotten out of her car seat. She yanked the car into a spot in front of an empty barber shop, its proprietor sitting in the first chair with the paper and only glancing up for a moment. Deb crammed the car in park and turned with laser beam eyes toward her daughter: "You keep it shut, little shit, and get that ass back up in that seat or I'm a slap it off." Then she turned to me with as businesslike an expression as a mattress saleswoman. The little girl strapped herself in with aplomb and her mother asked, "What you need?"

I asked for an eighth.

"Sure you ain't won something a little stronger?"

"Just the green," I said. "Never been much for losing everything." I regretted it instantly. "So ... how's it been?"

The now-tooth-deficient Deb gave me a fake grin with her lips sealed, fumbling in her purse between the seats. She was pretending that she hadn't heard. Probably sensing my discomfort over the third wheel, she explained how it could have been much worse, only in a wan tone that didn't match the memories: "...when I found out Charity's daddy molested all my kids, but no more. Got a number now, the bitchass, and a whole lotta dick in his mouth. Ain't that right, Charity? Fucked all 'a us up. Courts come and take all my babies away 'cept the one. Just me and Charity, now, ain't that right, baby?"

I didn't know how I'd recognized her. We were at a light and both of us turned back. Charity stared blankly ahead, sniffled a booger back up from view.

"Ain't that right, Charity?" She looked at her mother with the wisest eyes of any pre-schooler I've ever seen, or the most barren. In them, Deb had her answer.

"Some people..." I said, shaking my head. "At least he's locked up. Sucks you all had to go through that, though. Some people..."

"Oh, some people is right. Not me, tho'. Not a day inside the house. Not you, either, huh, Saul? We all proper now, huh? Just the green, huh?" She's putting something together for me between us on the seat with her right hand, steering back toward the Family Hearth with her left. She looked at me again, hard. "You won meet me back at Gus's 'round seven? Catch up?"

I giggled and shook my head, pretended not to be disgusted. "You're too much for me Deb. I'll make a mess and you'll never be able to get rid of me."

"You always been the smarty pants. Prally some doctor a some shit. What? A lawyer? You ain't 5-0, right?"

"I teach middle school, Deb, up in Ohio, so none of the above." I kept looking for cruisers pointed at the road that would surely know Deb much better than I ever had.

"You ain't a cop, right?"

"No. A teacher. History. I hate uniforms."

Either she hadn't heard me or she wanted to hear me answer twice. Her shoulders dropped back to slumping, eraser nipples pointing toward her lap. "Cops is some of my best customers, though."

She laughed. I pretended to. I handed her $40, and she slid a tight sack as thick as my ring finger into my pants in a quick, practiced motion. I pretended to ignore the tiny white rock she'd tucked into the corner of the bag. Her daughter started hacking up something croupy behind us.

"Gus's, huh?" I said, letting my eyes dart around through a windshield spidered with cracks, getting Deb's mind off the backseat and on the intersection we approached and the red light that she hadn't seen yet. Memories of bathroom deals, dodging barroom fists meant for other less-fortunates. "Gus's is still Gus's?"

"It's $60 now, honey."

"Oh."

I fiddled around for more cash in my pants and told her I was out. "You take Visa?" She didn't laugh. "I'll just pull out some," I said.

When she pulled back into the Country Hearth, she took a cleansing breath and rolled her head.

"Don't these people, you know..." I nodded toward the diner.

"Owner's a good friend," she said, "and his wife ain't gone find out how good 'less he stays that way."

"I see. Tidy little knot you've got there." I get out.

She harumphed, then immediately changed into old Deb in spirit. "Hey! Gus's! 'Round 6?"

"Will do," I lied, peering into the backseat. "Nice to meet you, sweety."

"You stupid," she said again. I looked at Deb one more time and she's staring at my jeans.

"It was great to see you Deb," I said, which was true but for all the wrong reasons. "Hang in there guys."

I made off toward my father's house at a trot. But before I could make it back to Main Street, Charity's screams yanked my attention back to the parking lot, where Deb's car was parked alongside the diner now. Charity was getting her legs smacked hard. "Call!" Smack. "A man!" Smack. "Stupid!" ... "I'mo...!" Again, again. I thought to yell something back, something distracting or silly to tranquilize her feral rage, but the customers were all looking – at me, at her, one on his cell, a waitress with her hand cupping her mouth. Nobody got up, though. The fussing didn't stop. The cops were surely on the way, I thought, as I hurried away. This is what people called the cops for, right?

Chapter 5

WHEREAS, voters of Freeburg must think of their children and then theirs and all those who will come when they've gone to the grave, and consider which wars they will fight and for what and for whom, to make whose world more free for the freedom to what? Will their hands be more bloodied or calloused with work that their leaders deem urgent to protect us from fear? While they hunt for new wars to export all this fear to? Will their monied investors be proud or ashamed, as they cash all the checks that, by then, will be printed in blood? Cast your vote accordingly.

The house was filled with smoke of my own making as the sun dipped low through the front blinds to give the room a muted pastel glow. The sad cloud of my exhales clung like smog to the floor and lowered my lids to slight Asian creases. But I was working! Euphoric with interest in even the mundane, I was making much better progress, even moreso after finding the yellow rubber gloves under the kitchen sink. I could see more of the walls now, but still hadn't found any more patched holes. Even some of the cabinets were bare.

Most the day had been spent poring through the books, shelf by shelf, with the kitchen radio set to classic rock in the Air Supply vein. When that would grow tiresome, I'd duck into the bathroom or a closet or the kitchen cabinets to cut the monotony, transform the spaces from cluttered to empty. But I kept easing my way back to the alphabetized wilderness of the bookshelves with the zeal of an addict, hoping to find the one book my idiot father willed me to read before I hit the floor, too.

I was fanning through every one of those bloated, dog-eared tomes now, growing more ashamed for a dead man every time I'd discover, camouflaged and out of order, this or that stupid stash of old people porn magazines, word-search compendiums or too many *Mad Libs* – too many even for a child. I found a few hundred of the latter, also well-worn and yellowed. I flipped through a few to find something to laugh at, but nothing seemed funny at all. Instinctively, I thought of finding a red pen and grading them with big Fs at the top: verbs where adjectives should be, pronouns for adverbs, a dirty kind of filth that took form all throughout. "The <u>PUSSY</u> put in for overtime, but his <u>PLUMBING</u> wouldn't allow it, so he found someone to <u>DIARRHEA</u> for him instead. He figured <u>TITTIES</u> could use the <u>BOUNCING</u> more than <u>WIENER</u> ever could." I grimaced in disgust at the thought of my father sitting somewhere – At the toilet? The kitchen counter? – filling the dirty holes in his head with more senseless grime. I threw one after the other into the big trash can in the middle of the room. I could never imagine him writing this filth. And then keeping it?

I got a clue as to their origin when, in one of the few *Mad Libs* I looked through, I found the name "<u>HAWK</u>" written into all the proper noun slots. *Hitch?* Into the trash they went, like so many batteries into the burn pit, only these never did explode.

Here and there, bag in hand, with the grass as my muse to enlighten the hunt, I decided to try a new round-about way. "Fuck this order," I said to the unhearing books. *Fuck whose books?* a voice asked, in the room, in my head. What good's righteous order to such unpardonable clutter?

For sport, I delved into the genres that had always enraged him – starting, of course, with the subject of Love, unrequited or not: *Orpheus and Eurydice,* and all future iterations*, Pride and Prejudice, Gone With the Wind* and *Jane Eyre,* waded through all those tears stored up by Emily Dickinson. I flipped through them all, then started packing the keepers in boxes. I was packing things now. Not just throwing them away. Even this one: *Jesse Bering on the Adaptive Value and Biochemistry of Heartbreak?* I flipped though that one deliberately, then tossed it in the KEEP box; it had clearly been written with just me in mind. By and by, the lot left me feeling that my father had tried but failed sadly to grasp even the core tenets of tenderness. But he'd loved, I could sense that. How well had he loved? And with what? We shall see. No one's immune: Everyone falls in love, with those who love back and with those who pretend it, with pets and toys and shows and songs that impart the most Quixotic notions, attesting "everyt'ing's gonna be all right..." and, to themselves, "What a woooonderful world..." Some fall deeply in love with themselves in the mirror and with money that keeps them securely entwined with the trappings of wealth on luxurious parade, like the finest of homes filled with imported furniture; shelves of autographed books; wall-sized paintings picked out not for impact but color scheme; ancient artifacts serving to make things look brand-new. What did my father love? Some things, I imagined. What didn't he love? A whole bunch, I could tell. Money was high on his THINGS TO LOATH list, below love. Why else would he wallow away in such squalor?

I moved on. Any books with ecclesiastical themes, whether masked or explicit, were surely devoid of the torn page I sought. I was dumbfounded how they'd materialized here, but I found nonetheless, dutifully fanning frayed corners, my father's rushed scribblings polluting the margins as proof that he'd pushed his way through this muck too. *Paradise Lost. Screwtape Letters. The Death of a Pope. Yuck,* I thought. In *The Hobbit,* in black Sharpie, someone who could have been him had circled and underlined, "There is more in you of god than you know, child of the kindly West. Some courage and some wisdom, blended in measure. If more of us valued food and cheer and song above hoarded gold, it would be a merrier world." Next to a giant smiley face, my father added, "Now pay your tithe of 10 percent and be on your hairy-footed way." Another genre we abhorred with equal scorn contained those books employing dead or should-be-dead Olde

English, pomposities from Chaucer, Joyce, ad nauseum. My father had a full oeuvre of Shakespeare. Impressed but also scornful to find them flimsy from use, I scanned them all to find what such an apparent imbecile could have gleaned there, only to find more common ground for us to share. An underlined quotation: "The man that hath no music in himself, nor is not moved with concord of sweet sounds, is fit for treasons, stratagems and spoils; the motions of his spirit are dull as night, and his affections dark as Erebus. Let no such man be trusted." In the margin, my father wrote, and I agreed, "Sure is a long-assed way to say, 'Never trust an asshole with a poor taste in tunes.' And who is this Erebus asshole?"

After several hours of tidying, I had three boxes full of classics and forward-thinking novels I'd thought would be worth reading or rereading, two boxes for charity, three garbage bags by the door containing nothing I'd ever want my fellow citizens to read, see, touch or smell, and more of the same in waist-high heaps at the curb. I looked around from the front door, inhaling dust I knew still carried remnants of my childhood, and I felt overburdened, not just by what was left to trash but also what I'd felt like keeping. The shelves still looked full.

It wasn't always like this, this hoarder's oasis. My father used to love some things and treat them well. I lay down on his bed when it was late enough to think of sleeping there, on the flat side, tucked myself under the covers and kept rereading his journaling. After a few minutes, I'd rolled into the hole to face sunlight slanting through the taped-up window. An ancient dust played on the house fan's breeze; it made me breath just through my mouth, not wanting the scent of my surroundings to sully my reading.

"...In high school, with my father gone, I shepherded a few flocks so proud that old coots would come calling from other counties, this one guy even as far away as Australia, just to watch me call and shear. I showed off the hand-signals I used mostly and called them out by name to bring them over, one after the other. The shepherds had these faces that showed their *wonder at how some boy could keep them all straight and quiet and waiting to get their winter coats off. 'Why no fence?' one man asked me. 'What for?' I replied, 'Got a barn for bedtime, all this grass to mow all day. A fence would only make them all scared about the grass that grew over there on the other side of it. They wanted to know why I never branded or ear-tagged any of them like my father did, like everybody did, asking, 'How do you tell them all apart?' I said, 'They come to me or don't in the same way that makes them unique, eat their feed or they don't, in a way all their own, have this patch or that scar or this bleat or that grunt that really is their way to ask me for a name that's only theirs. How couldn't I recognize them?' It didn't matter though. All the visitors at the 4H Center back behind the school barns always left looking just as dumbfounded as when they'd gotten there. 'Don't know how he's done done it!' They gave me the credit then, just as proudly, I'd give it all back to the flock. Just by calling their names later on, one by one, I'd give each sheep an apple or pear and say, 'Thanks.' And believe it: Before they would take it, they'd nuzzle their noses against me, and I knew it was them saying, 'I love you, too'."*

He'd stood out in husbandry, of course, but had also been anointed a local 4-H hero in ornamental horticulture, aquaculture, pest abatement and soil conservation. His own wine label, Ra Red, was named after the only ram they'd kept to stud a whittled flock of a dozen ewes to be lawn mowers, milk maidens and sweater fodder. This was back when the locals thought maybe my father really would turn out to do something respectable, like maybe run the university extension office or grow the farm into a famed source of gourmet produce or gold-medal wine. I glanced into my father's closet, scanned for that blue jacket, then returned to his journal, my hunt unsuccessful. (I did, however, find his senior yearbook, which anoints him Most Likely to Blow Up, whatever that means.)

With his father alive, Saul was aloof in his duties, forced to learn all he could and feign just enough interest. His passion, though, was just as barren as his 4-H coat. But when his father died, something more like devotion took hold. When his classmates were sleeping off hangovers or cornering girls with promises of carefree times and fake IDs, Saul was oiling sheers, bundling wool into categories of perfection, shoveling manure, pouring feed, trimming hooves and yanking lambs from their wombs. To the elbows and grinning in shit, piss and amniotic goo. He took the reins of the farm with something like the feeling of freedom.

For two hours every morning before school, on the outskirts of Sandusky, he'd toil behind the family barn, as the sun rose steady over a line of dead copper pine needles and a distant thinning wood line, he'd feed and cajole his own lazy herd into another day of life with songs, not taunts – songs of his own making, now dead to posterity – then move them a few houses down the county road to a neighbor's groaning, rusting homestead for them to graze inside a sagging row of ancient fences. There he'd slop more shit and feed around, send more welcomes to some cows, that horse, those chickens, before he'd bike two miles to where another flock grazed the life out of a little table of dandelions and switchgrass, this one maintained by the school board for the sole purpose of having Saul raise a perfect set of specimens for county fair supremacy. That's what he did. He pushed through every minute of it like a soldier just trying to get home, and he saw in the eyes of every animal a look of acceptance and, he imagined, even admiration as he pushed quietly past with a stroke to this coat or a nuzzle to this neck.

My father was already tired by the time his classmates were just making their way out of showers and sugary cereal to a brass-tacks school with just a few hundred students per grade, which by his third stop, was within sight of his prized flock. He'd get there a little stinky, but for the spritz of his grandfather's left-behind cologne, a fine sheen on his forehead, his armpits yellowed and dank. He got years' worth of straight Cs in the humanities, a few Ds in math and science, and always As in his forte, courses like The Diagnostic Application of Pesticides or Applied Aquaponics. His mother had a local man tend to the fields and kept the kitchen garden neat herself, but most everybody seemed to come to

Saul Jr. when questions needed answers to pivotal changes on a farmstead.

He was a good boy, too, at least in the sense that he kept his mouth shut; this was rewarded religiously with exceptional marks for conduct – to a fault, I figure. Stuffed at the bottom of a shoebox on a bookshelf, under some homemade cards and crayon art neither my sister nor I could recognize, was one of my father's freshman year report cards. His 4-H advisor's ominous remark inside: "A real serious boy, dedicated to his stock, though I'd like to schedule a conference as soon as you're free to discuss a lingering detachment from his peers."

What else about our dear King Ginger? I believe it's poignant to note how, according to a handful of uncorroborated eyewitness accounts, many of which can be found at Reunion.com, my father would amble around with the most strident gait of anyone, despite the loner image and incessant taunts from Alpha types, who'd invariably point out how much his sheep's vaginas resembled the real thing. "He knew something we didn't," was how one girl who used to ignore him chose to describe my teenage father's appeal, or lack thereof. Of course, that's cryptic; much the same might have been said about a young Ted Bundy or John Koresh. Another former classmate was a little more succinct, marveling at how such a "fatherless hermit could ever reflect such balls-out confidence." Several others were irresponsible enough to give my dead grandfather all the credit, in assertions that implied my father had been reared "so self-assured" that he'd accommodated my grandfather's untimely passing with a Zen-like acceptance of everyone's suffering and ultimate death. "How could he dwell with such a firm foundation in a now that was so sad and lonely?" one bookish classmate wondered in wonder. As is plain: No one had known him in the least. To their credit, a few former classmates were bitterly honest about their abbreviated associations with him. Their characterizations, in fact, were reflective of a deep-rooted loathing that had grown, with maturity, even more unwaveringly fearful, using terms like "sheep-fucker," "turd-scoop," "Jeff Dahmer Lite" and, most frequently, "The Nose."

My father never tried to pretend to have won any popularity contests, but he had to go so far as to grossly exaggerate the extent of his lone relationship with another person his age. He reported in Journal II that his "one true friend" as a kid was a round and studious boy of comfortable means named Ari Humphrey, whose father was the round and well-respected town pharmacist, not to mention the keeper of a full and verdant six acres of herb garden back home. My father reported that Humphrey was *"kind enough to suit me fine, always there at least to say 'hi' or 'bye' like he meant it, to trade some of his father's gardening know-how for my shepherding prowess, and he was a 4-H friend when and if I ever needed one, which was sometimes, not always. Also, I was his confidante in times when Ari felt the weight of his obesity threatening to crush him flat."*

Humphrey's memories had a different tenor. Years later, when reached by phone for a short-but-gregarious chat about the rotund days, Humphrey was eager to set the record straight. First of all, he said, "I'd only say 'hello' in the mornings to Saul, you see, since I took the bus home in the afternoons, so that's only half-true." Now a regionally famous architect in Kansas City, Kansas, whose latest project is an upgrade to an outlying water lift station, Humphrey didn't want any incorrect information on the record about his upbringing. "I didn't do 4-H in school" because "my mother didn't want me getting all shit-smelly," and, "To be frank, I'd rather pick my food out at the grocery store, not get to know it all by name. I don't remember my Dad ever keeping a garden, either. We always lived upstairs from the pharmacy downtown, so I don't see..." The best he could characterize my father: "a yearbook buddy." He could never figure out why my father chose to stand out with livestock in high school, other than to presume it had been the family line. "My thing was LEGOs; it's still my thing. His thing was sheep; it always was. But he hated sheep. He named them all but he hated all the people he named the sheep after." Would he count his old acquaintance as a confidant of sorts? Quietly, he chose his words, then concluded, "Not at all. I've always had this aunt I'm close to for things like that."

In my father's junior yearbook, the only other one I found in his house, Ari wrote the lone salutation: "Have a good summer. Ewe don't be baaaaaaaaaad now, hear? Ari"

Many seemed at least accepting of my young father's presence, though: unafraid, unconcerned, perhaps repulsed or perplexed, but not entirely disgusted or fed up. It'd take years for him to perfect those powers. What stood out for many back then was how my grandfather had died right in front of the guy and he was able to hold things together so well.

Then my bean-pole father met my pear-shaped mother, and her round face, frumpy style, telephone pole legs and lazy midsection would cancel out his bulbous nose, orange shock of bristly hair, translucent skin and collie-long face – the effect of which would be to balance out each of their way-too-high expectations.

This is the genesis story I was made to hear repeatedly throughout my youth:

She was hungry, and he was selling lamb kebobs from his grandparents' flock on the midway at the Erie County Fair. His egret neck was straining to support his head while bending his six-and-a-half-foot frame down through the food cart's window, just to hear her marveling about how lamb tasted a lot like pork and chicken at the same time. He considered that an astute observation and said so.

"I'd like to go to culinary school," she told him, "when high school's done. Can you imagine: eating all your homework and classwork on the spot? Maybe I'll be a massage therapist, though. I don't know. I got strong hands."

"Both of them sounds good," he said. "Both of them's got lots of good classwork and homework."

"Right? I'm into New Age-y stuff too." She took down half the kabob in a bite.

"Like what? Like what's your sign kind of stuff? How far do your hand wrinkles stretch?"

Chewing. "Sorta." Chewing. "Like that." Chewing. "But not really." Chewing. "It's a lot of things. I'm really into more of the less silly side, like psychic readings, crystal prescriptions, Ayurvedic herbs and all that."

"Wow," my father said, flipping strips of lamb on the flat top, shooting his eyes from the grill to her to the grill... "That New Age stuff sounds an awful lot like a science all its own," adding in a whisper, "You witches best watch out. I hear they're still burning y'all at the stake."

She laughed. "The nuns at my school are the only ones I'm scared of. They'd probably try to smack the devil out of me or something."

"Nuns?"

"St. Crispin? He's the patron saint of cobblers, so..." She pointed north, as if that would take him there.

My mother saw my father's eyes start darting around again. The line was now too long for her to linger.

"Nice to meet you," she said.

He handed her another kebob. "You, too."

"Oh, you don't..."

"I raised them up myself. No worries. Only the best, for the best. If you want to see his sisters, head over to the sheep barn. Got Nancy, Lady Love and Carolyn here this year. I'll give 'em word you're coming so they'll act like proper ladies."

She pointed at the stick in her hand. "His?"

He smiled. "That mutton there once had the name of Damon. A real asshole that one. In Damon's name we feast."

She took a big chomp and started walking away. "Tastes sweet to me."

He waved goodbye, and it felt too final.

They both were seniors, grew up there and never once had met. He'd blown it. Didn't other teens fumble for pens and write out names and numbers on the backs of each other's hands? The thought of losing touch with the only girl who'd ever been sweet to him innerved my father. It was enough to make him bump his head on the cart's awning, as he followed her frame through the crowd and into the rabbit exhibition. He asked his mother to come up from the truck behind the trailer. Frantically, he wrote his name, address and phone number on a crumpled napkin. He asked his mom to tend the cart.

"Just wear one of them condoms, hear?" Ann said. "We got enough lambs on our hands."

He ran into the rabbit barn, looked everywhere and couldn't find her. He stuck his finger into the cage beside him and stroked the gray fur of a mammoth hare, then scanned the barn more closely. He couldn't find her anywhere. The rabbit bit his finger. "Shit!" One sharp pain faded. "SHIT!" One dull ache festered.

*   *   *

Four years later, my father had changed in countless good and not-good ways. Besides the bronze tan, gangly muscle tone and world-weary disposition, the desert had left him languid and stoic, with a sand-swept demeanor that, in a flash, could turn him panicked and frenetic and ogling strangers who really were just loitering. The deep purple gouge of stitches stretched from just above his left ear to the crown of an already balding head, which now he kept shorn seriously close. His hazel eyes had changed as well: In tandem with the look in all men's eyes that said, "Please fuck me," was an undertone that added, "Please, just leave me be." He cut a gruesome profile, even with a hat to mask the scar. His forays into finding love were met with lies told like the truth: Even hard-to-marry girls were holding out for mythic suitors still fighting something somewhere, someone they *just could never hurt like that. Friends?* My father had enough brain left to know what that meant.

He wasn't without his attributes. Shamefully self-deprecating, he was always the first to admit his overall lack of luck in the lady department, as in Journal II, during which he makes mention of some other passing friend who fell away to never be heard from again: "*...We couldn't find a woman unless we went shopping for one, is how my buddy Burless would say it like a broken record every time it was me and him and everybody else paired up boy/girl. We'd be outside this bar/that bar at closing time, and we'd be thinking with our beer goggles on about where in this*

*godforsaken shithole of a town we could find a place of warmth
and comfort for our wieners. Except we was always poor at
closing time, so the hooker market was closed for business just
like the bars."*

Mercifully, my mother has always been the kind to accentuate
a person's strengths. Even something like a battle scar would
only make her reach out with more yearning to heal the pain
inside it. In those four years, she'd grown even more portly, with
more chins, and more pessimistic, with more points of view. She'd
stopped holding out for magic by the time she'd bumped into my
father for the second time. He'd been walking down the steps
of some township police station. After an awkward minute of
guessing about why they looked familiar to one another, he'd told
her about his job at the paper, how he'd just been flipping through
a stack of incident reports. She'd been impressed by the potential
for such a job. She couldn't help but notice a mature man standing
there, fully employed and filling out his shirt to magnificent
effect. The nose and horse's face were just the nose and face that
made her remember him; so those she graciously accepted with
the rest. She'd felt a stirring. He'd felt it too. He'd looked into
blue bulbs for eyes, their frame of golden hair. Her Jesus sandals
and homemade flowered dress, with too much frill to be called
fashionable, couldn't hide her bulging folds. How could they? Why
would they? These were what had made her recognizable as well.
Both thought it odd – no, fate – to have encountered each other
here and now, or rather there and then. The questions already had
answers: "How long's it been?" "What was Iraq like?" "What are
you doing now?" "How 'bout we get some cake?"

No matter what my mother says, in these pages or elsewhere:
According to the pictures of them lying around in this pile
of leaves or that pile of presents or those side-by-side beach
towels, they were happy for a while as obituary writer and stay-
at-home psychic hotline operator. She looked at her husband like
he deserved some kind of dignity, her style of adoration, despite
his shallow well of deep emotions that would only become clear
when it was too late to bow out too soon. He didn't seem the least

bit demented in any of the photos I saw, and she didn't seem the least bit unhappy. It was fairly clear that he'd fallen for her, too.

My trash collection had finally arrived at my parents' consummation as a couple. On one of the lower, dining room bookshelves, a small hand-sized photo album, resting inexplicably in the "G" section – "G" for good riddance or get-the-fuck-off-of-me?! – under at least an inch of greasy dust and a stickiness that my nose told me was cat pee, was their wedding photo album. I recognized it by the thin, blue ribbon tied where a metal clasp would normally be – homemade like all my mother's clothing and shelf kitsch. First shot, I see Gangle and Gobble McGinty, all grins and hidden sins, him swimming in a rented white tux with turquoise trimmings, her bulging against a dress her mother had made her before she'd even graduated to junior high. Second shot, I find his massive fingers actually dwarfed under her even larger talons in the cliché'd photo of their pawn shop rings. (The photographer, ever the rural pretender, had apparently busted out his special lens to make those fake gems shine sincerely.) It all seemed real and true in these pictures, though – his tall to her short, her fat to his skinny, his agnostic to her wiccan, his flurried yin to her centered yang. They seemed to be heading in the right direction, despite all the differences. He was towering so high above her that day she could only get so high as his necktie when it came time, in photo twelve, to smear cake on each other. He nailed her smack on the top of her head of fat baby-doll curls. Everybody was smiling. A drink in every hand. Half-lidded grins on a Saturday night, why not? Photo thirteen was the last: her sitting on his lap, red-faced and laughing; him cupping boobs, testing cantaloupes for ripeness, poking out from behind her a devilish grin.

I see people in these pictures I remember from this birthday party or that Easter egg hunt, a funeral, a few weddings, some drunken excursions. Some of their names are still fresh in my mind and cast under favorable light – Uncle Floyd, Gramma Ute – but most are just blank nameless stares through the ages. They could all be dead now, for all that I know. Still, I see every one of them in my worst dreams, to this day. They used to tell me things that I didn't know and hadn't learned to be true about my father. They'd call him "kind," "gentle," "courageous" and "bright." In my dreams, I'd argue back, angry: "Stupid!" "Druggie!" "Embarrassing!" and "Loser!"

My mother reports frequently that my father had her fooled from the start. How else to explain falling hard for such an "arse idiot." But she wanted to have sex with him enough to have me and my sister, Katie, eighteen months apart. And they wanted to be happy enough to be stars in a plethora of photographs, many of which had been bound and placed neatly on shelves to grow dusty with implied significance. They must have wanted to get somewhere at some point.

My mother was and still is a love addict, though. That's all the understanding one needs to know why she could fall in and out of love so decisively, for man after woman after man, none of whom could have ever lived up to the vision she had in her mind for their post-transformations. Sorry, Mom, but you know this to be true.

The next chapter, as she likes to say, is "herstory." I promised to let her tell her version, and the People's representatives [eagerly] agreed, because I was nothing when they'd met, as I was when they'd divorced, so, my mother wonders, "what in the fuck did you know?"

Fair enough.

Chapter 6

WHEREAS, the people of Freeburg are now and then and always one, as long as half-plus-one will say it's done.

P raise be to objectivity. After a lengthy legal rigamaroll and some heavy late-night phone conversations, I finally get a few shots at our (over)exulted target. Here's how I see the fool: Despite missing a gumball-size wad of brain gunk, my late husband, our flavor of the month I'm told, always seemed to struggle to carry around the weight of two swollen heads on his shoulders: One was a cranky ram's head that bounced off things, set limits, like he was trying to set his own boundaries more than he ever was really angry at anything; and the other was a lost sheep's head that just kind of lulled there, waiting, consigned to be chosen for someone else's greater needs. And it seems the part they blasted out of Saul Sr. was mostly from the limbic system – hypocampus, amygdala, all those things that make us give a shit, and scared or angry, but sweet and understanding, too. It's where we feel things with something we started calling our heart before we knew to call it a limbic system.

Anyway, that's what he came to be missing, a consistently working heart, and it was a big weight on all of our shoulders.

Maybe he did wear a hero's medals. Or invent The Chair (I want it back now, son). And it's not inconceivable that he might even have tripped accidentally over a defining historical landmark, then handed it off in the right direction. So what? The man is not a hero to me. [Someone else], as you'll see, deserves the credit here.

That man did nothing to adorn my home with anything but holes. He never did anything there that even remotely approached valor or mindfulness. He was always inside himself and because of it, rarely inside of his wife.

If he wasn't sitting somewhere staring like a brainless mannequin, some high-minded book in his lap just for show, he'd be pouring his herky-jerky heart into Solitaire or memorizing the Bible just to find all its lies or pumping more drugs into whatever holes remained in that war-jarred brain of his that weren't already corked tight with all the conspiracy theories he tried to make sound credible, which, of course, only made the credible ones ring hollow like the rest.

But really, whatever he was doing, he was just pretending to be doing something normal so he could get a chance to drift somewhere unobserved to blast another dose of numb into all those cracks. If my son mentioned any of this, I'd be surprised.

Please don't take either of us for fools, though. Everyone comes to terms with their own disappointments in a way, but the smart ones turn them into lessons. Saul Sr. turned his into a career.

So how was I sucked in?

Loathing isn't something you feel for someone until you know the smell of every type of their farts, I guess. I don't know, but I got out just in time. I had no reason not to trust Saul Sr. in the beginning. Things started, as a matter of fact, quite celestially. His views hadn't soured yet. They were still hidden under a mask that said he knew enough to know some things, and he kept that long scar under a tidy bowler hat or ball cap in case I was the type of person bothered by how you could tell no hair would ever grow along it again. He even pretended to understand how I might sometimes be able to hear people who've passed along, sometimes even talk with them where they went, but only when I know how and why and exactly when they died. With those guideposts, I can hear them more loudly than if they were screaming in my face by way of megaphone, echoing back the questions in my mind with blaring answers, loud and clear. I'm that good. Believe it, if you're so inclined.

I say he pretended to believe me because I now suspect he was just trying to get laid on a fairly regular basis, and nothing made me want to more than sharing what I heard and from whom with someone who didn't make me feel stupid for hearing it. He wasn't always such a naysayer. Just after we'd bought cheap rings at the first pawn shop we stopped at, mine with the noticeably thinner extension on the bottom and more of a cluster of tiny diamonds than anything singular and showy, we met this older lady at Huntington Beach in Bay Village. She was hunched on a bench overlooking the lake, just crying and wringing her wrinkly hands. I went and sat next to her and we talked for a spell. Saul sat behind us on the grass and pulled out food from a picnic basket I'd packed. Somehow I could tell that her husband had died and I told her that "He says he's fine."

"Rrr..."

"Raul."

A light went on in the old lady's eyes.

That was his name, I knew it, she told me with her eyes bulging out, and he'd just died of a heart attack close enough to where we were for me to hear him tell me to tell her that, only that. After the woman stopped crying, she couldn't stop thanking me, and she continued her walk with her shoulders held back and her eyes pointed straight up to look at the trees, like, maybe he's not out there somewhere but still in here, in there. I sat down with Saul and started crying myself. He told me he'd heard the whole thing.

"You're a diviner," he said, shaking his head in what looked like amazement. "A seer, right? What's it called? Clairvoyance?"

It was one of the sweetest, most sincere things he'd ever said to me, about me, it being so closely tied to the woman I believed myself to be. I really am and was, in so many ways. It melted my heart enough to feel it pulsing down in my pants. Then he says, "Can you see what I'm thinking?" That made me take his hand and find a quiet place in the woods to reward him for, at the least, being so sweet, and, at the most, believing in the fundamental me. The blanket, basket and food were gone by the time we got back, being so close to Cleveland proper. We weren't angry, we couldn't be. We just laughed all the way to Dairy Queen and were still laughing all the way home with chocolate ice cream dripping down our arms.

He actually taught me a few things that made me pretty angry at his world, too. The world of the conspiracy theorists. Like how the Rev. Martin Luther King was killed and officers all the way up the chain knew it was going to happen and the world never got to know about it. The media never said shit about that civil trial that the King family won all those years later. That beautiful man could really sling those words around, couldn't he? Saul was furious about how the man went down. I remember Saul quoting the man one time after we'd just started dating, like a human computer, saying, "Our lives begin to end the day we become silent about things that matter." Shit. I still haven't gotten over how that whole thing petered out in the world's mind. Saul never could either. (With that and so many other things.) Because really, in King's case, his life began to end the day people started listening to him speaking out against all the forces that have always seemed to keep the poor folks in their places and all the soldiers on the battlefield.

How sly a fool Saul was, to memorize something from somewhere that couldn't have been from that head or that heart. He told me that quote from MLK and I thought, "This white boy?" No matter: These tender moments, rehearsed or not, slowed to a trickle after Katie was born, then dried to a sallow frown by the time Saul Jr. came along. Something must have settled into that gap in his brain pan, or maybe nothing ever did.

That's when he started taking on something more like an icy demeanor, a too-sharp edge. He'd pass the bedroom as I was giving a phone reading and yell through the door, "The house, it's burning down! How could you have missed this?!" Or he'd be finished with me in bed and ask, "Bet you knew that was coming." Real charming line, that.

"Ha-ha," I'd laugh, in slow-motion sarcasm. When I'd learned this would pretty much become his signature line, I'd just stare back in silence, a geologist stumped by a strange-looking stone. Funny, how an asshole could grow on a rock.

Eventually I stopped even letting him inside me, as much as that hardened my own soul's direction and severed the only release valve he had. I know what I know: Quite early, he'd shattered every foolish vision I had of us turning that house on Walnut Circle into a home. He was too busy taking a dump all over everything there to let anything else happen that mattered. Our home was his prison; so, it was our prison, too.

Sure, a lot of people don't think I'm all there, either. It's a burden that comes right along with the gift. At the bottom of all of this is this: I'm a person who needs people in my life with a little belief in other people, and after a while, Saul didn't seem to believe in that much of anything. Not God. Not people. Not himself. Nothing. That's what he was really good at, actually: not believing in things. But those were his fields to hoe, and he neglected them like the government was cutting him a check to do it. I imagine him now as some gargantuan, ignoramus snake with a head full of poison that had to keep biting, releasing the venom, to keep all those toxins from poisoning himself. He kept biting and biting. I kept moving and moving. I saved us that way, me and the kids.

But this is my only husband's biography, not mine, so I will keep my loquaciousness at bay and stick with how I met Saul, was brainwashed into having two kids, and ended up thinking of him as no more than a phony with a sack of excuses for amounting to nothing.

To fathom how a man like my ex-husband might have ultimately stumbled upon an idea so earth-shattering, you should know a key trait that he shared with most of the men in my life. My father, Saul's father, Saul (and others) were all fiending addicts in one way or another. They could never find calm in the simplest of moments. They were always awaiting the next door to blow in. My theory: Perhaps in some altered state of clarity, Saul had happened across some idea from somewhere that would change the world, sure, but only by proxy. It could happen. Saul's apple fell onto Sir Newton's big head, but you don't hear of anyone praising the apple. So if anything grand came to be from Saul Sr., I'm guessing the drugs were what led him to find it.

All these men, not just them, all those drugs, all those things to forget: They'd supposedly earned all their cravings, in war after war. Not to say that it takes a war to make an addict, but it doesn't help. My father returned from Vietnam yearning the nod-out redemption of heroin's cradle, but he'd managed to stop, was gentle again, then dementia returned him to nasty. His name was Nathan. Paul, Saul's dad, used 'Nam as his reason for drinking his way to losing his mind as a sheep-herding sheep. Saul Sr., from my view, got hit worst of all. He didn't discriminate so much. Saul had so many drugs, probably more than I know. Smoke was all that he had when we met, got things started smooth enough, but Saul was just picking up steam as I was settling in. I understand that this is Saul's biography, so there's no point in being pedantic and dealing with all of his flaws. In fact, I'll delve into only the dourest of memories to illustrate how close to the edge he would trudge, just to lull his brain's barrel of monkeys to sleep. I leave these memories here with great hope that they'll stick to the page and be gone, like removing the rottenest of eggs from my basket.

On our wedding night, Saul was romantic, assured. He was boasting to a truly sad collection of friends and family about how he was going to make night cops reporter someday soon and be able to take care of any babies we might or might not be having somewhere down the road. Nudge, nudge. He actually used the word "lucid" to describe how he finally felt. I'd never heard him use this kind of word. I had visions of going to school for massage therapy at the time. He told everyone that he couldn't wait to be the homework. I actually laughed and believed him. Then the open bar closed down on Saul hard. Later that night, he vomited tequila sunrises all over my wedding dress and fucked me instead of making love. We didn't have a honeymoon, only a night stay at a Howard Johnson's that one of my distant cousins footed the bill for. That's where I woke up, sore and worried, to pancakes in bed – ordered from room service, I learned years later, by Saul's dying mother from home, as Saul kept vomiting in the toilet and marveling at how blood could even be coming out of there. These were loud retching hurls that actually startled the housekeepers into action: "Eddytingakay?" Saul: "Fi-ine, just dying of all this LOVE in the air." That quickly he'd smashed me into something lesser than the dead people he eulogized like a robot every weeknight from four to eleven, which soon enough had become my bedtime. I pretended to be sleeping when he came out of the bathroom, wiping the puke from his mouth. *Sure, I thought.*

A few years of distant banter later, on the night that my little Katie was conceived, Saul stayed inside me until he was soft and then told me like I was some other person that he wanted a baby girl so he could finally learn to be a gentleman. I warmed for an instant, like a quick pass by the campfire. I smiled into his eyes and told him I could teach him how, so he was ready for when she came. That's when that idiot glaze came over his eyes, and he got hard again inside me. He smirked like an atheist and shook his head when he started his lower motor going again, again. "Why haven't you turned me into a gentleman already with all those magic powers you got?" I closed my eyes until he was done again. I know this was the night Katie was conceived because I'd been withholding sex to maybe get some sense out of him in our conversations, some midway point where I could find level ground to happily let another baby into this world.

I always tried, still do in vain, to remind myself about how he suffered, pulling charred bodies into their graves, coming home with shards of metal inside his thinking, but I wanted to talk to my husband about something besides television shows or interesting dead people he filled the blanks in for as filler that night. I couldn't bear to hear him recite another passage from a book that deep down I knew [assumed] he couldn't have been reading as intently as he should have been, not to have been [or seemed] that ignorant of so many things. And to think, in another time, he used to rehearse passages and recite them just to make me think.

So he was calm that night, until he wasn't. I pretended to fall asleep, snorting and breathing all weird, to hear him in the front room acting like he was lonely again at last with his cravings. I could hear it every night by then it seemed. Still can. He'd go and do things like crunch and snort his anxiety medication, drink shots of vodka from the freezer, maybe go and smoke something to make the whole house reek of his hot, lying breath. I told myself over and over, night after night of hearing him drink, snort or smoke our lives into cinders that he and I were never going to have side-by-side gravestones. But this or that hope kept sucking me back in those early years, before I found the resolve to finally shit on him like it always seemed to feel he shit on me: He'd flash that eager smile I'd recognize from the midway, when we both were kids, or wipe away an actual tear that would form the 100th time he told me about that "haji" family and the car they all "had to die in because they were driving somewhere that was right near a place us liberators wanted flattened into a ghost town," I remember him saying. "Bad place to be just out and about," I remember agreeing. Saul and I both always wondered where that family was heading that day. "To meet something like an eternity of nothing," Saul said with certainty in his delivery. "Guess it's the beauty of having jack shit to do or know or socialize for ever again. Snap! Done." *Sigh*, right?

Another night, he brought a maroon, hardbound book to bed after his regular routine, and he stayed up all night leafing through it like a speed-reader. I know this because I saw him start, and when the birds started chirping and the stars fell away, I woke to find him pacing the bedroom with the same book opened to the end in his white-knuckled hand. I summoned the empathy to ask him what was wrong – always the soul floating free getting trapped in another person's net – and then my eyes adjusted enough to see the holes in the walls. Five of them, softball-sized and frayed from pulling the fist back out. How couldn't I have heard? "You wouldn't understand," he said flatly as I stared through my twilight, then he threw the book lazily through the bedroom window, like he'd rehearsed it all night just for me. "He was God's son, Ann, and they killed him! Just like MLK! Just like the Kennedys..." I knew exactly what he was talking about but all I could think of was, "Give me a fucking break!"

He came and laid down next to me then, all quiet chaos, and I was afraid to move until Saul Jr. stirred and gave me an excuse a few hours later. After he was fed and watching cartoons, I peered out the broken window and saw, nearly concealed by the neglected collection of weeds we called a yard, that the book Saul threw out there was the Bible, one of Our many prophet's collected biographies, and that a robin had been tearing out the pages for a nest to have more babies in. That made me think, for the first time ever and ever again [until recently perhaps], that he'd finally read something seriously, had taken it to heart. I taped up the window in the early afternoon from the outside, picked all the glass from the sandy soil. Saul slept in fits until dinner. I made our family favorite: beef wellington, with wild mushroom puree and extra-thin prosciutto the way he likes it. "That was the best dinner a sinner on the road to Hell's ever had the luck to eat," he'd deadpanned with the sense of humor that always had made me horny. He patched the holes with wire mesh, newspaper and spackle after licking his plate like a dog, while I did the dishes and the kids retreated to their corners of the house. Not another word, except a weakly whispered "sorry," left his lips that night, but I'd heard it enough times by then, for all manner of miscalculations, to just figure it was just another recording. He stuck to pot that night, though, like most people always seem to try to do nowadays, and I let him make love to me again because I thought that maybe he'd learned something new, something about being a gentleman. I'll go so far as to admit that I even got on top, my favorite position, to maybe show him I could take over from there, but he shoved me gently but surely off with a grin after I felt him finish, like that was exactly what I wanted him to do. Who does that? So, I kept yearning for that little fleck of brain that would make Saul and us whole.

I slept on the couch when I could, started listening even more intently for the voices my aunt claimed to commune with so well.

He took his nighttime rituals to our bedroom then, and it seems [might have seemed] like that's where it stayed until the end. One of those nights, I saw him fire up the backyard burn pit and throw that bird-gnarled Bible into the flames. When he came inside, I pretended to be sleeping, but still he said, "I'm not a sheep, I'm a shepherd. *Know* that." *Sure*, I thought, still afraid but not sure of what.

Saul Sr. was lucky to have a decent job but that was only because nobody else was ever clamoring for it. That's how the asshole idiots of the world have always gotten work. He went about it respectfully at least, and people must have respected him for it. He made a show of burning a candle every night he was still writing obituaries from a real newsroom, going through a half-dozen at least every year. That must have been all that anyone knew about him because that's all any of the Secret Santas ever got him. Any number of cloying scents: oatmeal raisin cookies, sandalwood, cinnamon bun, ect. Nice touch for a crazy dufus.

This must have kept everyone at work from noticing anything right away that was too weird about this brain-damaged war veteran who'd beg for barn fire stories that only he would pick out of the scanner traffic. Those would keep him there until well past midnight, so I was grateful for this early drive, but he stopped caring even about those after days upon days of finding them buried deep inside the rest of the paper. He could be as high as he wanted, all day, every day, and they just let him be the harmless fixture with a past that everyone agreed was due at least some form of honor.

And he was always high, for the record, on whatever he could secret from our funds. To glimpse just a day in that pisshole of a life, you need only imagine a man awakening to somehow sniff out the stash of weed I'd hidden the night before. He'd smoke some and shower, then sneak a few shots of something in his coffee, even cough medicine when payday approached and I'd make him pack his lunch for work. He'd see me off to this crap job or that in the early days, with a "Ptht" and a blown kiss to pretend he was joking, then see the kids off with actual hugs that I envied, even though they'd had to dress and feed themselves by an early age or probably go hungry and naked some days to the bus. That's when he'd started snorting things he could trade for on the street, from people he knew only as nicknames like "Bugs" or "Fink." Admittedly, he was honest to me about all of this. It's like he felt that he was owed this much inebriation, on account of the bomb and all that.

So by the time me and the kids were home, he was usually off on the rails to write about dead people when they were alive or whatever else nobody else wanted to write about. Then he'd drink and smoke and smoke and drink his way to bed, snorting this and that color up behind his eyes to make them glassy and pinpointed ... and always when he thought the kids weren't looking. On the weekends, it was more of the same, just with the kids around all the time and more time to build up a solid wall of make-believe bliss.

One weekend, at the pit of an especially deep bender, Saul's boss called. He'd [purportedly, since attribution is unattainable] needed a night cops reporter to cover a murder. (This, of course, was early in his time at the *Eagle*.) Apparently, the real one, who had down-pat all the crying people he'd need to find and interview, had called in sick. Did he want the shot? Saul managed to mumble nothing but uh-huhs into the phone/walkie-talkie thing they gave him to look important, then he hung up and got this fearful look in his eyes, the way he'd look when his hookups weren't answering his calls.

He finally left, but not until after an hour in front of the mirror adjusting his hair and tie. At the murder suspect's home, where I imagine the man's wife and small children moaned inconsolably from the driveway, Saul stayed in our only car, just up the road within sight, for an hour smoking crack he'd been hiding from everybody before a flashlight hit his face through the window and the assignment was over. A night in jail and a month in a rehab bubble later, Saul had his job back doing obituaries. He flashed me the Welcome Back card that night that everybody signed. Later I saw it had nothing but names and not a single word of support but what came printed on what was obviously the cheapest card at the store: "YOU WERE MISSED." *Sure*, I thought.

Saul came back from this time away an apparently changed man, though, full of all the right kind of drugs, talking all this mind, body, spirit jibe I could finally relate to. He actually said wise things that didn't seem rehearsed, that he planned to "do in the now what's best for my future," to "not die with my music still inside me," all of that, and I couldn't help but welcome him back into our bed. I'd enjoyed the break, was ready to see how long this new Saul would be like the very young Saul. He'd go to NA meetings and get a different color keychain as things went along – one month, two months, six months... The lingo was in his head – "clean and serene," he promised. "You couldn't make me cry with a shotgun blast now that I got my meds all straight." "Great," I said, with the sincerest smile I could muster. "I'm so proud of you, baby."

And I was. For months, we smoked pot occasionally, nothing else. I imagined us on a road to somewhere different. Instead, he'd just learned to hide things better, picking one drug back up at a time, doing them in the car, in the bathroom, at work. After a few months, he confessed everything after I'd caught him snorting something out of a pinky nail that looked like a fucking press-on. He made a big show of throwing it all away, though, then not five minutes later, I turn the corner into the bedroom to catch him snorting something yellow from the nightstand. This time, he promised to stop when the rest of what he had was gone. "This shit ain't cheap," he reasoned. He'd collected all the NA keychains there were, even the one that meant something to those who really got clean and stayed that way for more than just a year, but he was only getting better at looking that way. I took quiet pleasure at the thought of how he'd have to see this rainbow of a keychain every time he turned on our car to go score another break in the clouds that put the rest of us deeper into his own personal dark. Small pleasures. "Look here," he said. "Means multiple years clean and serene. Had a cake and everything. Wish you could have come." *Fuck off,* I thought.

I could keep going. Is it needed? I started at the end, our end, with these horrible tales, to color in as quickly as possible with objectivity what indubitably has been subjective thus far under my son's idealistic gaze. It wasn't too much longer before I had my bags packed and 47 Walnut Circle [in the area that is now The School], the haunted box we moved into when Saul Jr. was eight and Katie was finally a teen, became nothing but the launching pad of my real life. I promised my son not to avoid the high points, though. So I must include how this period is when my divining powers seemed to surge to true effectiveness and my destiny in stamp-sized Cassadaga, just a five-minute drive from crummy Freeburg, finally became as clear as the one soul We all aim to share.

There was just one other period before the end in which I held out just a small shred of hope for us. I can't exclude it from the record. After Saul was back to work but wriggling uncomfortably in The Chair, his editor suggested he start working from home to save everybody time and money. It's not like they needed him to pick up police reports anymore. So this gave Saul the run of the house and in no time he'd concocted this grand scheme to clear a twisted path of stones down into that county-owned floodplain behind the house. He'd gotten maybe twenty waist-wide feet in, paved with old bricks and landscaping stones, and I started to think it was going to happen, that we'd have a little garden oasis, a real reason to look up and out again.

"If I get another twenty, somebody owes me a backrub," he said, looking at me, but the kids both volunteered, always eager to form something like a bond. He got just another few feet one day before launching a squeal that was alone in the afternoon except for a loud rustling that slowly faded into the green nothing that was to be a path. Then it's mindless screaming: "Man down! Man down! Medicmedicmedic...! I need a fucking medic down here. Man. Down....!!!!!!!!!!!!!!!!!!!!!!!!!!!!!!!"

Never had a man needed me more than right then. Who has an alligator bite off his right foot? The same foot that got ripped off his father when he died? Nobody. It made me feel all metaphysical,

I guess. Like I used to feel when we were coming up in Ohio. It held me there a little longer.

Both of us were born to the same midwife, Sunny Silver, him in Sandusky and me in the tiny town of Litchburg, Ohio (population today: 4,007), which sounds too much like Lynchburg for it to have been some accident. A lot of people I used to know didn't even admit they were from there, just to avoid the inevitable suspicions of the town's nefarious beginnings. In 1977, the town fathers took the best stab they had to change the spelling, to honor an actual man, the suburban contractor Tim Litch, who served a few terms on Council and pushed through the construction of a new building for the two-truck streets department. I actually dated his son, Tommy Litch, for a few months in high school. But we fought "too much to want to talk about anything," he told me at the end, so we decided to go find our heart in somebody else's head. I always wonder what would have happened if I'd married somebody whose family had their name on a whole town like that.

I didn't meet Saul until my senior year. I was at the fair, waiting for a friend of mine. Not a special moment or anything. He gave me a free kebob, I think. Didn't even ask my name. Then he was gone to the war to spill his brains out and I was left to keep considering my future, which of course was tied to his, even if I didn't know it then. It took a lot to rip me from the past, though. Litchfield had a hold on me.

My mother's sister, my Aunt Susan, used to visit a lot. She told me that the whole town of Litchburg taught her how to sense the dead, since so many people had died in every house, which left so many of their souls behind to stir up dust. And I believed her. I'd never caught her in any lies. So I started listening for the voices too, asking the right kinds of questions. And there they were.

They didn't even have to die in a building. One time, Aunt Susan asked the mailman about one woman I didn't know from the other side of town, who was staying at the house of her widow's sister, who I didn't know either, and had died just a few days before. "Where did they find her, poor Ms., Mrs.... What was her last name? ... Withers. Yeah. ... Oh, no, hunched in the car, my dear Lord." She was the half-full kind of atheist called agnostic, and smart enough not to admit it. "You know where? Because, because ... Uh-huh ... Right out front the diner? Shame. That's how I'ma go, though: heading somewhere ordinary like poor, what's her name? ... uh-huh Mrs. Stout." Then she took me right away to sit in her car in the very same spot where Ms. Withers passed along, for me to watch her meditate behind the wheel with the car on for heat. Over an hour we just sat there, the windows cracked to keep the frost from forming. I was 12 or so, reading in my history book about what everyone agreed was real and glancing over at my visiting Aunt Susan, who eventually started whispering to someone, not me, about this gibberish or that. Then, she put the car in drive and took us home. "Kate," she told me. "Kate Withers. Her husband died a long time ago, and she was ready. Wish I could've met her. She used to be a nurse." She didn't know this woman or her husband. I knew that. And nobody told her a first name, either, or anything about Mr. Withers, who never even lived there. I hadn't heard a thing but the engine, so I started really listening after that, asking the kinds of questions that would maybe help me hear some voices, too.

Some of the local farmers, many of them recovering descendants of militia-style Klansmen or former Amish carried into the real world by Rumspringa, would pay for my aunt's divining spirit. They swore up and down that she could predict to the hour when rain would finally fall or the exact day pumpkin or cucumber flowers would break into bloom. I found her to be right about 70 percent of the time, which are pretty good odds in Vegas.

My father, one of those salesmen who kind of sold a little bit of everything somehow, including the right to be a salesman for him, moved us, when his daddy died, out toward Sandusky, just outside the reach of the steel mill tang of Lorain and closer to a quiet, hillier section called Birmingham. Saul was home from Iraq by then and we bumped into each other in the most unexpected of ways. He was wearing an Indians cap so you couldn't see the scar; I didn't notice it until he told me about it weeks later. I was visiting a friend in downtown Amherst and he was picking up something at the police station for his boss. I wanted to know what Iraq was like in person, so I told him I'd be glad to meet him later that night for a drink.

He was quiet that night, kept looking at the door, behind him toward the jukebox and bathrooms. He asked a lot of questions about where I was going, where I was coming from. I hadn't had any time to ask my own that night. I liked his solid demeanor, his history. His rounded chest, the sharp cut of his chin, the profile of a man. That man. As you know, that man was just my hopes. The drugs, the disbelief, the disrespect – that was the man I got. He may have puttied all the holes smooth, but I still knew where each one was. It wasn't long before I started wondering when it would be a hole through me or one of the kids.

Then my son did it one day, just a little boy shy of middle school punching right through a wall and cutting his hand on something metal inside and crying because that actually hurts and doesn't feel good to most people. I knew then that somewhere else, anywhere, would be better than feeling sorry for somebody all the time. The times I'd think he was going to do one thing, anything, different – better, I mean – got spaced further and further apart, until one day he went and strapped himself into that stupid chair and wrote about dead people, the house stinking of some dollar store deodorant, and I was packing a trailer. He didn't say a word to try and change my mind, didn't even look up.

Oh, fine: I love him; I'll always love him. But what the hell does that have to do with anything?

Chapter 7

*WHEREAS, the voters of Freeburg have elected
leaders forward-thinking enough to look outward
and upward, to a truer democracy paid for by all.
It is hoped, with this bold cultivation of trust, that
new flowers of wisdom will blossom to life where
before only weeds of distrust could survive.*

Full disclosure: Yes, my father had asshole-ish inclinations
and was addicted to a myriad of mind-altering or mood-
enhancing drugs, in many forms, at many times, for any number
of wrong reasons, to balm this pain or stomp that thought and
especially to smile a fake kind of happy we could always see right
through. But he wasn't tyrannical, I started thinking, deep inside
his half-cleaned nest. He certainly wasn't as alone as he seemed
to always feel in his addiction.

This much became clear when I got to the "I"s, way up at the
ceiling in the hallway where he died. That's where I found a Hav-
a-Tampa cigar box next to a falling-apart copy of *The Ingenious
Don Quixote, Man of La Mancha.* I grimaced to find it stuffed
full of browned syringes, strips of latex, bent serving spoons and
three unlabeled prescription bottles all about half-empty – or
half-full, depending on one's outlook. I wondered why he'd kept
it with the "I"s: *Illicit? Intoxication? Inebriation? Idiot loser in a
roach-infested cave with his needles full of joy juice?* So really:
How could I have left out my father's tragic cravings? Did I not
hastily include the swooning recount of his love/hate affair with
spice? Before the end, I knew it needed being said.

I stopped looking at the books, threw the cigar box on the coffee table. I had laundry to do. I'd packed with the intention of spending just a few days here, and the washing machine and dryer were both rusted over and fried. These are tell-tale signs of the addict: long-suffering appliances and vehicles, bought when already verging on death and now well past the point of resurrection. See? How could I have avoided all these pivotal details of my father's stinky life? Or my own.

I grabbed what was left of my father's detergent, the cheapskate powder kind, and a few dryer sheets. I rounded up my dirty clothes from where they lay strewn around the house and bundled them up in the sweated-up linens from my father's bed. I breathed through my mouth to ignore the dizzying cocktail of sweat, cologne, tar, and ass. It was my stink and his, blended into something toxic. I left, trying to ignore my dead car, afraid to have it diagnosed. If it was favorable, I could deal with it at the last minute; if not, I didn't want more damages weighing on my mind.

A few blocks east of my father's house in Freeburg, long rows of trailer homes begin to stretch out in every direction – a shit-stew of budding saggy-pants hustlers of every ethnicity, ex-cons, pedophiles, day-laborers, prostitutes, drug dealers, migrant workers, junkies and those who'd fit into several of those categories. The addicts are always the easiest to pin, sharing any or all of the following traits: a graying and powdery tone to the skin, mashed-up attire, jittery movements, lack of momentum or sense of direction, track marks, jacked-up teeth, unsure steps, lack of standards, and similarly frazzled acquaintances nearby. These zombies were everywhere as I neared the heart of this plagued anthill, Pearl's Laundrymat, with the queen, Pearl, swallowing a stool with her ass at the register, right where she'd always sit. It would have been déjà vu if I hadn't recalled coming here as a boy to play Galaga.

I started throwing clothes into a washer in the corner, where the least amount of people seemed to be congregating, and still I couldn't avoid the seated round man with the Jabba the Hut face and wispy white hair sticking out in every direction, except on top, where there was none. His cheap oxford shirt couldn't reach his blue polyester pants, so I was treated to his naked pink belly hanging over his belt and his scratchy tenor voice talking about himself into the cheapest of flip-phones. He stared expressionlessly across the aisle into his single washer of clothes spinning around in their own filth, the bubbly water a grayish-green goop. I stared at him staring there, his voice a sharp knife in my ear.

"No, not tilapia, salmon. Best sashimi in the ...

"Yeah, Connecticut, four seasons there, not just February and the rest of the year....

"No doubt about it, my friend! It *is* so important to visit a few times before you just jump in and ...

"Oh, yeah. Uh-huh. ... Best hunting and fishing anywhere. No, not boar. Black bears. No, *bears*. No comparison."

I listened. Where could this mystical menagerie be, this hunter's paradise? Somewhere close? I've never hunted, couldn't fathom the taking of such free-roaming life, but still I wanted to know where I could if I ever changed my mind. He didn't say. I wondered if my mother would just know by hearing his side of the conversation. Recent polls show that about 4.5 trillion worldwide don't believe in the nether realms my mother claims to access so fluidly with her brain. But I don't care about public opinion. She had my whole childhood to prove to me that she wasn't full of shit, and she failed. Lucky for her, that still leaves many millions reaching out faithfully for hobgoblins.

I was staring more invasively by then, but he didn't seem to notice. He'd become a Weeble-Wobble, all bottom and no head. A tiny phone pressed to The Blob's face. Soporific as it was, his banter had me eavesdropping keenly.

"Yep. Six years ago. Took me the early pension and said, 'Adios, Kunta Kinte' ...

"Then, 'course, the mill goes kaput, and ... yep ... kaput goes the friggin' pension...

"No, Alaska. That's me boy! Big-wig ranger now. Got his own park or some shit..."

"Hell, no. The whore even took my Barcalounger. My *Barca*lounger. Not that it matters, anyhoo. TV's gone, too... I know, I know: Off to drain the next sad sack..."

Our clothes were going into the dryer, him doing it seated by scooting his chair with the help of the tennis balls on each leg, and still jabbering on. He took his time, shaking out each tiny clump before loading it up.

Threadbare briefs, yellowed. "This is when you vote Democrat, even if it hurts inside..."

A torn white undershirt, armpit ripped, "Prose Before Hos" on the front over the bust of Shakespeare. "You know it. Eagles, baby. Fuck Pittsburgh..."

A brown holey sock, then another. "Fuck. The. Cowboys."

And a laugh, finally. His pink turns red and a little blue here and there. Still seated, he grunts and leans down to snag a T-shirt printed up for a black family reunion in Georgia that he had to have gotten at the Goodwill. This made me question not only his taste but also his coherence.

Still, I felt like the conversation was going somewhere, as he folded each item meticulously and loaded them calmly into a red *Dora the Explorer* backpack. For obvious reasons, I'd always pined to have little me's to play with. I guessed the bag was his granddaughter's. He must be staying with one of his kids nearby, I thought, helping out during the day while his son or his daughter toiled at the Widget factory, watching by turns the little ones and Regis Philbin. I kept listening for the point.

"This lady over here," he points to a dryer, "she thinks it's all that and a bag of chips...

"No fucking way. One stepping stone to the next, the sloot...

Another laugh as he's zipping up the bag.

"When you can, Paulie. When you can."

And then he hung up. In another half-minute he'd left. The place seemed empty then, though it was just as crowded; everyone seemed to be talking to someone but me. Talking and listening, hearing and laughing. Mocking surprise. Retorting in kind.

In a few more minutes, I was done, too. I spotted the man's

phone in the chair as I passed with my clothes bundled in my dad's sheets, which now smelled like everybody else's. I grabbed it and rushed for the door. He was gone.

I flipped it open, *come in Scotty.* "NO SERVICE," the screen read. I pushed all the buttons. "NO SERVICE." That's all it said.

* * *

I walked back to the box looking down at my shoes, realizing to most I must look like a packrat hobo, lugging my life's possessions to the nearest train yard. My appearance got me back fast. I locked up, closed the blinds, tossed the laundry on the couch and grabbed the cigar box from the coffee table. It felt light as I jiggled it on the way to the backyard, stopping only at the dining room table, where I dug out the white pebble from what was left of Deb Diamond's green. I trudged outside.

I was going to light it all up in the burn pit but decided instead to throw the box and the rock, in one hurl, as far into the woods as my father ever taught me to throw anything. The throw felt professional. The contents spilled out in the air. I waited to see where each little piece landed. I don't know why that mattered.

On the porch I lit up a half-bowl from the table, placed it back in cache deep inside a dead fern, tried to forget about it a long while, see how that worked. I listened to the cacophony of crickets, just rubbing and waiting for help to relieve their primordial itches.

I couldn't stand it. I spritzed on my father's Canoe in the bathroom, changed into a button-up shirt suitable for work or play, and checked my fading and receding orange mane in the mirror. I flexed my still-jutting jaw, tried to ignore the anteater's nose. As good as it would get. I headed to Gus's on foot, not a mile into town. In fact, everything was just a mile or two into town. The bar held a small place in my heart since I knew that my parents had gone there to drink back when they still had things to say to each other. I still wondered which table or bar stools they'd used, which drinks they'd ordered, which songs were playing, how happy they must have been to still have some questions stored up. I hoped Deb wouldn't be there, since I wanted to be.

I was glad I couldn't drive; I might have gotten pulled over for a DUI on the way back, since I planned to drink enough to lower my standards as far as needed to find a woman with whom to get naked. Not wanting to sweat, I passed through the omnipresent heat casually from low-rent neighborhood to trailer park to industrial park with just one factory left, a peroxide plant, still churning out something that some people needed, its lone smokestack puffing full-bore into the gray dusk. Barely distinguishable on the darkening horizon, near the back of the park, was the hulking steel mill, which used to keep some of Freeburg's youngest working at home but had been vacated a decade before by investors looking for cheaper labor in Mexico. It's the way of our places these days. The rest of the park's charred-looking buildings had doors left ajar, broken glass in the windows, seas of empty parking lots. They all seemed to be yawning. Inside each, I imagined tent cities of homeless, with unspoken rules and all rent paid in food stamps to a crack dealer landlord bent on industrial park dominance. On Sundays, perhaps, they played stickball or Spades or just prayed for forgiveness. Who knows? The buildings could have been empty for all I knew. In their place, near the entrance, a new gas station's fluorescents hummed like an orchestra of electric typewriters and cast too stark a light on strewn trash and cracked asphalt. From the front window, a cashier who looked to be from India watched me pass in the suspicious manner of a concentration camp guard.

I approached Gus's Bar in timid steps, checking for Diamond Deb's K-car in the parking lot. If she was there I planned to continue another mile into downtown. She wasn't. Everything was different now but somehow all the same. Formerly one among several storefronts, Gus's was the only building left now, surrounded by sandy, butt-strewn vacant lots that glittered with broken glass, which used to be a dry cleaner, florist, and video store. I had to wonder: Who used those types of places anymore anyway?

A budding domestic dispute frothed from the open windows of the apartment above Gus's. Its sign was the same straightforward declaration from my youth: green paint on brick, a few neon signs from a distributor in the thin, barred-up windows at head's height. I paused to listen – "Shut your fucking hole, you..." "You zip *your* fucking hole, you..." – then decided I'd heard that line already a million times.

Inside, the air was cool and bitter with generations of beer in all the cracks and every night's mop water. A cacophony of reassuring sounds filled the ear: the flat-screen over the bar blaring a pennant race implausibly featuring the Cleveland Indians; the jukebox singing, "Craaazy. Crazy for feeeeliin' so loooooneleeeey..."; a cue ball thwacking the rack apart. No one even looked up when the door slapped the jam behind me, not one of the 20 patrons, and that's how I liked it. Not one voice dipped. The outside disappeared. Seconds later, I was ordering a pint of whatever was on the first tap handle I read. I scanned the half-empty bar like I was picking out a lobster.

I came here for just a little while, on the prowl for some local company, in a time just before my new wife, my new ex, started yanking me out of dank bars and diners like this to drag me back into the lounges and bistros for which college educations provided. I'd come to visit my mother over a summer after my junior year, with a fake ID and no plans to even think about my father, and could only stay a week before I started pining for Tallahassee again. And Rebecca. I released her memory like a puff of smoke from a cancer patient's mouth. Half-guilty, half-gracious.

Only then could I count with a conscience: Three women, two single, one worth it.

I waited a few minutes at my side of the nicked-apart bar. As I measured the nation's recession by the holes in what used to be a solid wallpaper of scribbled-on bills, I waited for a boyfriend to emerge from the bathroom or sidle over from the pool table with a look of ownership for my benefit. I finished my beer in a gulp and walked over to her with my second. I told her my name before asking if she wanted the company. I'd never done that in my life, always thought it sounded pretentious and corny at once.

She looked down at the stool next to hers.

"What's your poison?" I asked the ice in her drink. Strike two, I thought, cursing the cowboy cliché. *I can't do this!* Luckily, she didn't hear or was pretending not to. I asked her name louder, so she'd hear.

I could barely make out "Red," so I looked at her hair.

"Red?" She was watching my lips.

"Right."

"Pretty."

She leaned closer, smiled and shrugged. She smelled astringent like the blue water that barbers put combs in. My confidence surged to equal par with her apparent inebriation.

"I said, Aren't you pretty."

"Like a doll pretty?"

I looked into her face. "Like a doll."

She rolled her eyes and smiled thank you in an exhale of blue cigarette smoke. Green eyes, my favorite. They matched the pool table light. But the eyes themselves were too cramped for my taste, her weak nose just a nubbin, her head a bit small for those big wings for ears. Her mouth was a lipless slit, in which she kept biting at stray strands of her flat-ironed, shoulder-length, red hair. She wasn't attractive or ugly, like me on confident days. I stole a glance down to a fat set of breasts that tucked confidently into an orange summer dress, orange sandals to match. Her legs were pale, freckled and strong. Her fingernails were red, like her toenails and her hair ... and her name. Overall: still out of my league, but perhaps buzzed enough not to notice. I wanted her.

She was smiling still when my gaze came back up to a face that looked instantly prettier with the silent invitation.

One woman in what had felt like forever, remember. None in a year.

"I'm Saul," I said to the bartender's ass walking away, during a quiet lull in the music. "Hello, Paul." I could barely even hear her say that. "Saul!" "Oh, Saul! Saul? That your nickname? You galoshing me?"

My face was a question mark. "It's so loud in here," I screamed over the pre-thespian Jon Bon Jovi, the bar banter. "Do you like this song?" She shrugged, stared at the TV. "He's a cowboy. From Jersey. And the tour bus is a steel horse. Wow, right? Leonard Cohen has his rightful heir." I think she thought I liked the song. "I like it," she agreed.

Spinning our glasses on napkins. It was loud. The Tribe were losing, defending against loaded bases, and I hoped for my dead father and dead grandmother's sake it would stay that way. I chomped a toothpick down to splinters, then some peanuts from a salt-slicked wooden bowl. She looked over and said, "I like Dr. Suess, but they aren't songs. Maybe some day." I had to agree: "a damn shame."

I like to hear and be heard while employing sarcasm, call me greedy for nuance, so I made another uncharacteristic move. "Wanna go someplace else? My car just conked out, but we can walk. Or take your car or something." The night was full of intrigue with all this boozy confidence: "Sure," she said, she wanted to leave, and "no," she added, "I can't drive." I knew that much.

I tipped the bartender three bucks, even though we only got two rounds. My head was swimming already in just two pints, a bathroom bowl rip and the increasing potential for a final nightcap. I hoped my generosity would reflect something dignified about me, more attractive than what could merely be seen, since all she really knew was my name and that I had a thing for making fun of hair-metal songs and ogling bartenders' asses.

We were out the door and I stuck carefully to pleasantries and compliments, bunting. Though we walked side-by-side, she seemed to be leading me somewhere. I let her.

"Nice night. For walking. For summer." "I like summer. That's when it's hot." "Really hot, though. A little too..." "I like it. When it's not ice cubes outside." "Oh, me too. Without question. Don't get me wrong."

It wasn't going anywhere, from my view. I must have sounded like a middle-school kid making conversation with a too-hot teacher. Another few minutes passed with just some distant sirens in the air and some talk about growing up in Freeburg. "Remember that candy shop over there? Where that half-way house is? Used to make chocolate-covered strawberries every season." "My Dad liked strawberries. My Mom hated them." The past tense made me change the subject.

"Oh, I'm sorry. So where you work?" "I don't work. I have school. School forever and ever." "*Tell* me about it. What you going to school for?" "I don't know. I hate school." I walked a little closer to her. "Me, too. I'm a teacher. Up north. In Ohio. At least I have been. I don't know. Who knows?" "Who?" "Sounds like we're in the same boat maybe." "Boat," she said. "We're on the *sidewalk*, goofnuts." "Right." "Right." She giggled at something, so I did too.

I couldn't place the accent. Nothing from the western hemisphere. I accepted it silently with the rest, something I might learn soon enough. She was warm and sure of herself. She smiled at the ground, making sure to miss all the cracks, a bounce to every step. I tried to mark her every step with mine, a cadence I hoped she'd come to want more of.

"How old are you? Not that it matters or anything." "I'm twenty-three-years-old, twenty-three-and-a-half next month." "Well, that's not old. I'm not." "You're not twenty-three." Not a question. Just a statement. "No. I'm not." She didn't ask, didn't seem curious. I answered with a lie anyway, a little one. "But I'm close. I'm twenty-seven." "That's only..." A long pause. "Four years difference," I answered. "Well, four-and-a-half." "Math is hard," she said, and I laughed because that was my kind of humor right there.

She tapped her temple on my shoulder but didn't stop walking. Like a dance move. Ginger and Fred, Danny and Sandy. I felt strong and full of the future like her for more than a second, not weak and empty at all. We passed three empty bars with boarded windows, some used car dealerships, one with what appeared to be a small controlled campfire somewhere deep inside, and the beginning of an alley fight between two skinny tweakers with no shirts and long chains on their saggy bell-bottoms. They seemed to be dueling for a skinny woman standing nearby with her hands cupped over her mouth, who didn't intervene but just screamed

"Stop it! Stop it!" in muffled commands. So they didn't. I sped up and Red followed this time. I didn't want to see who'd lose.

I asked if I could walk her home. "I want to get to know you better, that's all." "I know you do." I didn't think anyone would sleep with me in my father's dented bed. "Is that okay, doll?" "You are, sillyteacherman!" "Oh, I thought we were just walking." "We are." We giggled again. "Home."

I held her hand the rest of the way. She held mine back, laced-up-style. It was hot, and our hands were sweating, but our thumbs kept stroking upward to show how much we liked it. There was enough of a breeze, our breaths deep and calming.

At a clean Tudor two-story, in a long row of others just like it, she mounted the steps to a tidy wrap-around porch that was immaculately swept with freshly painted rocking chairs and hanging flowers at every cornice. I waited on the sidewalk. She turned to look at me at the top of the steps. She wore a bigger smile than all those before, a real unembarrassed smile.

"You won see my dollhouse?" "This isn't it?"

"This is a human house, sillycrazyman. Now shhhhh." Index finger on mouth, I repeated, "Shhhh," then crept like a cartoon burglar in exaggerated steps.

She walked sloppily up the steps, leaving the first floor dark. I followed like a shadow, connected and silent. She wasn't quiet at all. I imagined cranky roommates somewhere debating in whispers whether to come and confront her poor choices. At the end of a long, creaky upstairs hall, she shut her door behind me.

Just the dim help of a nightlight was all I needed to see that I was surrounded. A thousand sets of long-lashed eyes, some big, some tiny, some shelved, others lounging against pillows or the windowsills. Everywhere, everything was red and lace and little doll dresses and unblinking, judgmental eyes.

"Where's the dollhouse?" "Duh. *We're in it.* Don't they teach you anything in teacher school?" "Oh aren't you fucking precious. My little Buddha or some shit." "You shush it, pottymouth. Sillyteacherfuck."

I was harder than I thought I would ever be again. She couldn't wait to kiss me and smother it with her stomach. We fell into a bed so fluffy and narrow that we almost rolled off. More giggles. More kissing. Nothing frantic. As slow as the first time, we undressed each other. Never before had so few words gotten me here. She'd said even less. I fell in with no thought of protection, pulled out long before any real harm could be done, I thought. I put out of my mind the eternally unanswered question of how many had come before me.

"Thank you," she said, a few minutes – or hours? – later. "Thank *you*, doll." And we meant it.

The birds were still quiet in the gray when I shot up awake to an old woman calling me "Rapist!" from the door. The whole room stared toward the bed, every eye on the arena. She was telling me not to move. "Oh the police are gonna *hear* about the sickness you're spreading. In my home? Sick! (Mucus-y hacking) Just sick!"

"Red! What is...? You..." She was gone.

"Gramma STOP!" she demanded from under the red comforter, which was starting to show darker where her hot breaths were coming through. "I'm a *woman*. You know it! A WHOA-MAN! I LOVE him! He's MINE!"

I stared frozen a bit at the long lump in the bed. "You what? You love me? I'm what? I'm *yours*?"

"(Cough.) You got a whole lot to learn before calling yourself that, little Debbie." This shut her up. Too easily, I thought.

"Deb?" I was still staring at the lump. "*Deb!?*"

"*My* house, gramma. I'm 23-year-*woman*, gramma!"

"Red? Deb? But..." Some relief. "You're 23." Then I looked at this old hag in the door with a weak expression of exoneration. It was too weak. The old woman turned her rage back to me, whaling away at my back as I pulled on my clothes. I searched for my shoes as she swung at my head.

"Taking." Dodge. "Advantage." Duck. "Of a poor." Slap. "Disabled." Slap. "Girl." Block. "What kind of a." Block. "Pervert." Slap. "Rapist." Block. Slap. Block. "Freak." Slap. "Who." Slap. "Does this?" Slap. Slap. Block.

Out of breath, she regrouped with both hands on the bed. "So ashamed you must be."

And for the first time, I was.

"So alone."

I was.

I pushed past her bent frame without looking for answers. What could the fool say to the fool? She screamed, "Caaaall me!" at my back when I'd made it to the sidewalk, so rehearsed like she'd heard it on screen or coming out of a sister's window years ago.

"Rape!" I yelled. To the sky. To the dolls.

"Rape!" wailed the old woman back.

*   *   *

"...It's getting hot down here, McGinty! Come in! Over..."

Tapping at the hollow aluminum door. "Wha?"

"Come in, McGinty," came the cartoonish whisper insistent at the door. Yosemite Sam? "This is Checkpoint Charlie. Come in, break. Repeat: Shit. Splat. Fan. Over..."

It was dusk, the next day. I was sleeping off more somnolent shame on the couch. The voice was in my dream for longer than was safe. More tapping. More disbelief.

"Repeat: Come in, McGinty. What's going *on* over there? Over...."

This opened my eyes to stare agape at the popcorn ceiling, ringed around the fan with soot and shadowed in nightfall. Another round of tapping, this one staccato and urgent, a pre-raid formality, a prelude to concussion grenades and screams like "Get down!" or "Gas! Gas! Gas!"

"Come in, McGinty," came the voice now quieter, more weary, almost pleading. "This is Major Fuckup on behalf of General Stupidity. Please. Over..."

I sat up and fumbled for balance with one socked foot on the floor, the other tingly and dead in the clutches of a cushiony vise. I tried to raise the leg but had to use my hands to yank it free of the couch. The blood gushed back with an invasion of needles from an over-eager student of acupuncture. I stifled a moan and bolted for the peephole: a blur of olive drab and ratty hair, his hands shoved deep in a camouflage coat, despite the heat. He looked like the Predator.

"Not funny. Go away." I strained at the hole to identify who, for a moment, I suspected could have been the now-round Arredondo. I shifted to the blinds and peered through crusty sleep to see a much older man than my old nightmare awake, more spent and sullied with lines drawn deeply into the parts of his face not coated in fur, prematurely aged and spent. I looked past him up the street. Arredondo's house was as dark as the sky. The lone streetlight hadn't worked since I'd arrived, four days earlier, so almost everything was buried under a blanket of humidity and apprehension, everything but this man glowing orange in the dim doorstep lamp. A glaze of uncertainty marked his expression. This told me nothing; Serge could have new minions now, even more madcap and devious than Renaldo, who I'd hoped had escaped the family curse and perhaps taken to heart all those pleas from the men in uniform that had passed straight through the other males in his family like stale wind through a screen.

"Saul. McGinty. I hear you in there, shuffling around like some whore between shifts. Open up or you're dead to me, you hear?" The voice was clearly baffled, nowhere close to the misspent theatrics of a seasoned hustler.

I yanked open the door. "Can I *help* you?"

The hand not on the doorknob was on my hip. I stood there almost naked in yesterday's cargo shorts and my moon-glow chest, confronting scornfully not a stranger but the scruffy man selling steaks from his trunk, the satellite TV salesman with a deal I couldn't refuse and the would-be shepherd for Jesus, just in the "neighborhood" rounding up some particularly rebellious stragglers, just to give them "the good news," of course, about their salvation … if only, if only. He just stared at me in silence, from the face down to the fly that I noticed too late had been gaping wide.

No thanks, my body language said, waiting for his lack of understanding to give way to acceptance and an apologetic exit.

The man's jaw gaped open to a meth-mangled interior, then he raised dirt-caked fingers from his pockets to the sky, like his trusted mule had just flashed a badge and sent the whole racket spiraling. He was staring at the ghost of my father, I figured, shaking his head as slowly as he backed into the yard. I could barely see his legs in motion behind the Army-issued fatigues. His back was to the oak tree, halfway to the potholed cul-de-sac, when a breeze of understanding finally wafted across his booze-yellowed eyes, with the aid of my give-me-a-break expression. He floated back to the mat in the same vampire style and squinted at my father's nose, the overturned canoe of a mouth, his hairless torso and half-mooned hairline in basketball orange. He stood up straight then, man to man.

"Either I'm back with the sand niggers," said the Predator, making me wince and look around, "and this whole shit-stained life was just another bad trip or you're the spitting ..."

"He's not here," I interrupted in a nonchalant voice that was betrayed by averting my eyes. I tried to play poker in college a few times but gave it up for a reason: My words can lie but my face always tries to set the record straight. This is costly in poker. And life. Luckily, a history teacher is geared toward passing on at least the official version of the truth. In fact, my father *wasn't* there, nor would he ever be again.

"Uh-huh," said the Predator, forcing me to look back into his eyes, which were even more yellow now but also a little hazel and gleaming in the middle. He started stroking a silvery beard, stained around the mouth to tan with coffee and poor table manners, and clumped into mistreated dreadlocks at the ends to match the bolts of sandy hair darting out from a greasy Redskins ski cap, the logo half-peeled from his forehead. "You're clearly not here, Saul McGinty." A quick glance around the dim room behind me and he added, "Must be a big scoop or something to get a lump like that off the log."

"Right?" I looked down. *A friend?* I wondered. My feet were dancing from side to side, arms swinging front to back. By contrast, he was a totem of stoic disbelief. *What is this?* I kept from saying with anything but an eyebrow, tried to still my feet and regain the high ground this stranger had no right to occupy. Not here. Not now. But I'd made such a paltry dent in the clutter that the house looked much the same as when I'd arrived. It was still my father's house and he knew it.

The corner I'd piled waist-high with trash bags and boxes was out of view. The shelves I'd cleared (from the As to the Is so far, from floor to the ceiling, even into the bathroom) couldn't be seen from where they began behind the front door and wrapped around the next corner into the hallway where my father, just the left foot left for balance, had fallen from the bathroom and bled out his last obituary. The curb, however, was a bank of garbage he couldn't have mistaken for spring cleaning. *Get a fucking clue,* I thought.

"I really need to talk with your..." His eyes flickered left and right. "Sh."

A rustling in the vines draping over the tree line beside the Arbuckle's place, then another, louder, out back, no louder than a newspaper being scanned for just the headlines, shifted the man's focus to each side, to the outside corners of the house, and then his whole torso seemed to spin free of his legs, action-figure-style, so just his knees and feet still faced the house. His longest dreads flung lazily to the opposite shoulder as he turned in a nervous jerk toward some other suspected apparition; I leaned back to keep them from hitting my face. A humid breeze carried one of the distinctive smells or rotten egg yolks and/or funked-up well water. I imagined this man taking a whore's bath in somebody's sprinkler system before dawn. He was untamed to be sure, but still fragile somehow, afraid of all the things he'd never wholly comprehend. Like a resting bird with strange sounds at its back, his head and eyes surveyed every possible approach, while the rest of his body still waited for an invitation inside.

"My father, he isn't..." I started to divulge, finally ready to work this jittery bum toward the truth and out of my life, but all it took to keep me silent was his left hand, shooting up flat to flash the palm forward at the shoulder. He must have been a soldier once, I knew that, but something held him back there to keep him fearing who, to me, had merely joined the losing column in another war era's lesson plan. The frenetic twitching of his eyes through every shadow, the agitation at all things unseen and unknown, the raised hand, made me think of how a witness pledges credibility in court, but on a book full of rules to which he may or may not subscribe. He was a mystery. I marveled at some other more far-flung possibilities: He was about to lead a team of middle-of-nowhere militia members into my dead father's house, from where they lay hidden in wait like camouflaged Easter eggs. Or he was a sick, dangerous man in need of a fresh victim and another day's worth of fixes. Or he was my father's actual friend and he'd come to do what actual friends do: talk about the old days and how the new days didn't compare. I couldn't fathom what scared a man to such soldierly lengths, a man so obviously unafraid of other things like failure, dying alone or swallowing his pride to the point of suffocation.

"Is there something I can do for you? I'm kind of in the middle of ..."

"Sleeping? Your life away? Sh!" His whispers were perfectly enunciated. Only I would have been able to hear them. "Just watch."

He stayed frozen, perfectly postured. I thought of the sad Technicolor facsimiles of the wide-chested, pony-tailed Injun who stared dejectedly at all the settlers outside the clapboard dry goods store in every Spaghetti Western ever made. But the chipped pair of jail-issued flip-flops still pointing at the door, the soiled fingernails that could only have looked blacker if his skin weren't so leathery brown, the poorly attended dreadlocks that only college students in Oberlin or Berkeley can pull off as white people, pulled my attention back to his hapless state. His patience was magnetic, though. Finally acquiescing, I felt his eyes pulling mine toward unseen forces that only dogs, wild-eyed vagabonds, invisible cricket armies and Cassadagans could sense in order to properly gauge their potential for malevolence.

I don't know why, but I played along with the stranger, moving my head and then my eyes to mirror his. I even started feeling worried just because this other person felt there was a need. After a few fruitless minutes, I reached over and flipped off the outside light and started sifting through my own dread, the shadows that only I could see, my own dark inside. The Predator flashed me a thumbs-up in thanks.

It felt safer this way, putting us on equal footing with whatever demons this street was cultivating next. He thought his thoughts, and I thought mine: my mother in the little town made just for her; my father and the world that swallowed him piece by piece, until he'd finally had enough; Rebecca.

These musings led me back to scanning the street again with a fresher intensity, something closer to mirror the dread of this middle-aged man who still could feel something was wrong but hadn't figured out yet what. I found myself standing beside him. Our heads flicked around as one, our eyes peeled for the same mysterious clues.

Then I closed my eyes and stopped looking for anything at all, not giving up but surrendering to my other senses, like how the blind math teacher I'd worked with for at least a decade could sometimes just smell when a rule was being broken in his presence or could write legibly on the chalkboard just by feeling and listening to where the chalk was. I thought of what scared me about this place, this street, its history and my place within it, a meditation on darkness I hoped could illuminate those troubles that still weighed heavy on my heart that I couldn't name, make them less burdensome to bear; instead of thinking of life's torpedoes that were sure to be angling at any second to sink me, I relegated them, like the patterns of color that flashed against my eyelids, to harmless blips on a radar screen, warnings that could be spotted long before they could cause any fundamental damage.

It's hard to explain how or why, but when I opened my eyes, I could hear where to look and see where to listen. At the sharp bend in the cul-de-sac: Was that a rabid dog or a rabid Serge pacing nervously behind his wooden fence, weather-beaten to gray? Closer to the ground, dwarfed by a waist-high heap of bulging trash bags and the gutted rusty motorcycle that had been brought there years ago to die: Was that an eye, Serge's eye, in the oval hole that used to be a sappy knot in the fence, affording my former nemesis a sniper-like aim with a BB gun? A raspy cough flicked our heads to the left, seared our sights to the landlord's box across the street: Was that a fan or Mrs. Arbuckle jostling the blinds in the front bedroom? Did she still lure zit-deranged teens to that shrine, as she once and never again did to me, with a groan about heavy groceries, then ease like an aunt spilling old family secrets into tearless testimony about how the one true God's will and merciful love was all one would need to accept with grace something as terrible as her late husband's untimely end or my parents' sad but inevitable milieu? Did she take their hands in hers and wonder aloud how anyone would ever fill life's lonely holes without joyful praise for God's miracle child named Jesus? Did she grasp the tarnished gold charm between her breasts then to relive his barbaric execution or point instead to one of the others nailed up around the room? Did she run a lazy hand along the same-seeming spines of all the books her husband once used in his personal quest to prove the worth of faith, finding all his questions answered, she attested, in a field of study called "Christian Science"? Did she ask if they'd kneel at her side at a table crammed tight with more idols of saints that stared down to their sheep through the flickering candles, just to pray with a believer who'd actually felt the touch of this God's hand on her heart? Did she say they shared something special, her and them? Did she call them sinners who could sin to the end, just as long as their last words were uttered with noble faith? Did she turn then and ask for a hug that turned into a kiss? Did she get it?

"The eyes are dead at night," the man observed in my ear, apparently on to misjudging other things. "Give it time." I heard him but didn't stop staring at the room across the street. I imagined her there in the dark, on her knees, all alone, as her God, his son Jesus and all those saints must have wanted. I turned to him standing there, craning his neck at the door. From there, he could see the shelves I'd emptied. He looked back at me with the look of a child seeking answers.

"I'm sorry, but there's no one here but me." I stepped back through the door, gently nudging past to block his path inside again. Everything was calmer now, at least for me, as if the thorough searching had unearthed a less-ominous view of the world.

"I used to live here," he explained. "For a little while. With your..."

"I'm his son," I finally offered, all my fear of him vanished. "And you're...?"

"Go fuck a dick!" he said with a smile that was both hideous and sincere. He was loud for the first time, with no mind for the din of tropical sounds and distant arguments that slowly returned, any one of which could have been the lurking danger he so avidly feared not seconds ago. This time it was me who was scanning for danger. "I saw when you opened the door, that what-the-fuck-you-want? look that your dad used when he couldn't think of what to say. Not always easy to be spontaneous after leaving some of your brain on the concrete back in Saudi, you know? Guess you're finally come to rescue his sore ass from all this paradise, huh? Don't say I blame..."

"He's not with us anymore," I said, feeling somehow relaxed by not being the very last one to know. "It's been a few weeks now. I'm sorry."

He looked so grizzled I didn't think he could or had shed any tears for anything, ever, but he did shoot the most docile look of confusion that pleaded in sad empty silence for me to give him a moment. His left hand pinched at the inside of his eyes, trailing greasy marks behind. He didn't say he was sorry. He only stood there, staring a hole through my stomach.

"He hadn't been doing so hot," I said at the stoop, searching patiently for a clean path to the truth. I turned the front light on again. "The police said he'd finally gone batty, and..."

"And?" His hands were down deep in his jacket again, looking cold and alone and a little bit peeved, despite the overbearing heat. "And *what?!*"

"Guess he just couldn't adjust to the truth, that he wasn't the star of some reality show or something."

"So he thought somebody was watching him? 'Course that never happens, right?"

"Taping him, watching him, looking around, bugging his computer to control his emotions. Believe me: It was nuts. They didn't find anything. And I haven't either. I saw the reports. I read all his journals. I'm still trying to figure out what he was thinking."

"Soo...?"

"...soo the landlord came over for rent and found him dead in the hallway."

"Dead of what?" he was booming, "How's he dead?"

"Please." I held out my hand and stepped to the side. "Please come in."

"I said how?" he repeated on his way to the hall, where he gawked at the floor then back at me with scorn. "He was nothing like crazy."

"He cut his wrists, okay? Both of them. He was drugged up. He was bat fucking crazy and, believe me, I know better than anybody. I'm his son." I dropped into his dent on the couch facing the front of the house. He stayed frozen in thought as his eyes started bouncing a scared, searching dance through the room. I even caught him shoot a glance up to where the "I" books used to be, then back at the ground looking even more disheartened.

"Listen," said The Predator, showing me both grimy palms before sitting down on the couch across from me. "I'm sorry. I'm a dick. I had no idea. This is... I'm his friend, since Desert Shield then the Storm, and I'll tell you what: This stinks like a Cleveland Steamer you just left on my chest, okay? But you know what? No! I'm not a dick! Them's the dicks!"

The same creeping pity, as that which came from thoughts of *him*, lurked up my spine like a serpent. "Who's the dicks?"

"*Theeeemm's* the dicks!" He was pointing at anyone, everyone, several directions worth. "All them rat bastard cops, fer ones, don't know jack about jack. You think somebody's gonna just come up in here and shoot him like in the movies, maybe screw on the silencer and shit? Think they's gonna beat him with a bat just so he's got a few more lines left before he's dead. No, who done this don't want no hound dogs on the trail. KnowI'msayin'?"

"What's to know?"

"They say nothing, so I s'pose that's all us nothings will ever know. Am I right?"

"I don't know. And you are?"

"I said Hawk."

"No, I ... Wait. Hawk?"

"That's the nickname I got in the war, from your Dad."

I thought I'd dreamed it, that name, some residue left from the other side. I bounced off the couch and started tearing through the trash piled up in the corner of the room. "That's a proud nickname you got there. So why did my Dad start calling you that?"

"Well..." He stood up and made for the door.

"Hold on, Hawk." He stood by the door, looking at the floor. "I hear war makes a man do weird things, like throw batteries in fires just to hear them explode? Am I right? Just to see his friends jump for cover, thinking that was the one that would do them in for good, huh? Weird things like that?"

Hawk was glaring into me with laser beams. "So. Hawk, huh? You must have been the eyes and ears of your team or something."

"Something like that. That's besides the point, here, little Saul. They're saying he killed himself. Just because someone was watching him?"

"That's the word."

"That's whose word?"

"The police, the coroner. That's the facts. What's your take, *Hawk*?" I kept looking through the garbage.

"*What's your take*?" Hawk repeated then opened the door. He looked over and gave a sad shake of his head.

"Who's going to sit around watching my father, Hawk? Who's idea of primetime is that?"

I found the right bag, made sure to get it all, at least what mad Mad Libs and misguided porn I'd seen thus far. "I believe these are yours." I set the tall stack in his arms like a detective handing to forensics the most damning artifacts of evidence. My eyes threw shame and disgrace into his: The look said, "Nucking futs!"

"Guess you'd have to be this crazy to count my father as a friend. Please go, Hitch. I mean, *Hawk*." He kept standing there, man to man. "Go."

"I been gone since I got back, but ain't nobody noticed," he said with a turn of his dreads that left marks I could see from the couch on the door, greasy marks I was glad someone else had to clean. His camouflaged back faded into the street as I tried against reason to grasp what he'd meant, then I gave up when the words triggered something long dead in my mind. My dead father would say this same half-empty phrase all the time – "... I've been gone since I got back..." – whenever he needed an excuse for leaving so much lying bullshit behind him. No excuse, I thought.

"Caaaw!" I shrieked for Hawk to hear, then closed the door and watched him fade like a ghost.

Through the window I could hear, still can hear, that crescendo of dubious hate, of Hitch being Hawk: "Hawk's the crazy dumb fucker he's always been, *right*? Just like your old man, *right*? Just go, dummy fuckface! And keep your trap shut 'bout what you know! I got's the debriefing, don't you worry none..."

Stoop lights started coming on, blinds shoved aside, a garage door opened with three teens staring through smoke from a ratted-out couch, one with a cellphone held out for a video recording. I knew they'd all seen him come to and from here, not just this time but how many times before? I turned the light off again, bolted the door and went back to the window. That voice, sure enough: a downed hawk's shrill cry.

"...Step. Riiight up! Ogle the freakshow! Perhaps ya'll is wondering, why should I dole over my hard-earned ticket dollar for this bastardization of American nature. I hear you sir. You too madam, 'Just wait 'em out! Them crazy vets is brave enough to kill themselves. Jesgive'emtime.' But ain't time left, see? Not with all these niggers, spics and Jews done taking all the jobs and money, them sand niggers selling us all our gas and candy. Bygones is all? Well maybe a few wars on it's your kid walking by out here screaming shit and can't get no one a listen 'cause you're still too busy doing nothing but watching the whole freakshow from the sidelines. Huh? How's that gonna feel like? S'pose next president get put in ain't no nigger but a bitch, huh? How about some reality TV shmuck takes the reins? How far the world gotta turn before that soap opera you watching come to life...?"

He wasn't just leaving; he was the understudy, finally with his audience, exiting upstage and taking them with him: "...like them faggots all stuffed to the rim like cum dumpsters, them dike mouths so full of pussy 'cause they cain't get dick for nothing, that's..."

When I saw a man, next door to Serge's, step onto his stoop with a nine-iron and yell out, "Enough!," I actually plugged my ears, just like my father did for the cop, only I kept mine in until the street was silent.

This confirmed it. My father, though addled by war, drugs and an infamous gator, had been mining the depths for a friend, any friend, and it wasn't important how utterly racist and stupid and unkempt this friend was, as long as they both knew where the other was coming from. He was lonely and Hawk, He Who Hears Things That Aren't, probably had a hovel nearby and the same kinds of cravings for the drugs that could make each new day seem sort of worth living, the same horrid wrinkles to try and crease out. This marriage of dunces might seem quaint to the dunces, but to everyone else it's a waste of a joke. If it weren't so tragic, I would have been laughing, not crying for someone who never was there. I wouldn't be balling, know *that*. And I wouldn't have put hole number fourteen right above number thirteen.

Chapter 8

WHEREAS, Freeburg intends for this action to grow through the townships and villages, cities and counties and states, to awaken the Nation in adopting this path, that one voice will be heard as a sign to the world that America seeks not reward but respect. We accept that all those now entrenched in their riches will rebel in due haste to return us to silence. We welcome their votes on Election Day, too.

I was up at dawn with aims to make my father nuts again in my own mind. Before encountering Hawk, in light of official facts, my father already was surreally insane in my estimation, certifiably worthy of zombie-making meds and perhaps a revival of shock therapy treatments and lobotomy experiments. Post-Hawk, he'd been reduced to just a sad sick ugly man with a lame Purple Heart that he'd swapped for the real one. Compared to Hawk, my father deserved a higher place of honor.

I kept riffling through the books, though, inspecting the paper stock – *The Judas Goat, Killing Critics, The Lamplighter*.... I threw out some, but was surprised at my inclination to keep most of them now. I stopped inspecting them alphabetically after a while, moved more by the colors or the designer's whimsy. My mother always suspected that my father just pretended to read all these books, like a role he rehearsed but never performed. She just couldn't fathom how all of that knowledge could go in but so rarely come back out. She equated it once to eating food after taking a laxative, so the nutrients all just end up as shit in the toilet.

I knew better. I could tell that he'd read every one of these yarns – silly and serious, wholesome and vapid – by the notes that he'd left for the ages in the margins, by the bloating of pages and the splitting of spines. The few that looked unused had less grime on top than others, so I guessed they were in line for a spanking like the rest. Most comments were too scribbled for translation or involved some witty truism that my father just had to share for whomever came along next. A taste: On a particularly dense page of *Ulysses*, he added, *"What kind of English literature is written so that most English speakers can't even understand it? Fail!"* At other times, I thought I'd caught him pretending to be something other than himself: In *The Secret of Divine Civilization*, a Baha'i text exalting unity of all religions, he'd wisely underlined a crucial cornerstone: *"It is clear that life in this fast-fading world is as fleeting and inconstant as the morning wind, and this being so, how fortunate are the great who leave a good name behind them?"* Then, at the bottom of the page, he wrote, *"If a father gives his name and gifts of knowledge to a child, cannot both then be rewarded with some credit for greatness?"*

An idiot doesn't write those kinds of words. But still, when I read them, I cursed his name, my name, for tacking his far-from-venial delusions onto something meant to conjure inspiration for world peace. *What gifts did you ever give to anyone?* I wanted to know. This loathing pulled my interest from packing books toward the paint-peeled door of my old room, standing open a crack for a glimpse back in time I'd been avoiding like a trip to the dentist. I pushed open the door. Expecting a flood of grim reverie, I felt surprisingly ready instead. I took in all those things I deemed unimportant for adulthood, all the remnants of that fey boy who was all my father would ever know of me.

I thought of him kneeling here, a la Arbuckle, with sad, boxed-up action figures instead of saints to judge his worth, just as stern with their reproachful stares but much more imposing muscle tone. It was a consolation to think of him coming in here, perhaps when seized by life's regrets. He'd grab a piece of this or that, then pretend the boy me was just about to burst through the door to give him one more chance to be the father he never was. The vision proved illusory in seconds, of course, when I thought of him just too lazy-lame to be bothered with clearing out my long-ago left-behinds. It was much easier to leave everything in place, the door shut tight.

So I did what his one foot and half a brain had given him the excuses not to do: After pulling the shaky twin bed to the curb, along with the dresser and desk with no knobs, all in black, I carried in trash bags and put my childhood inside them with a cleansing joy I hadn't felt for years. The black sheets, black blanket/cape, black clothes and books on dark arts, magic tricks and war craft were all going to Goodwill, and then on to new children of darkness. Old report cards exhibiting standard improvement piled on top of old pictures of girls I once knew piled on top of *Cracked* magazines, cassette tapes and Sex Wax piled on top of the rest of the trash I once prized. Only the emptiest-hearted of hoarders, like my father, had use for mementoes like these. I left the posters on the ceiling for the next tenants to find.

The closet held more relics. Some were stale and others fresh. In the corner leaned the battered surfboard that I'd stolen with no guilt from a boy whose name I'd never learn, who'd made off with my girlfriend, whose name I can't recall. It was just for show; I'd never learned to ride it. Other keepers were the magic set that mystified new friends in middle school, only to make them think me nerdy when my freshman year began; the Monopoly game that I'd play with my sister some Saturday nights until dawn would declare the winner and lull us to our beds; the tiny cardboard box that still held my paltry collection of damaged and cut-rate comic books, the value of which will never amount to anything beyond the sentimental. I shook my old BB gun and found it still loaded, so I took it to the backyard, pumped it tight and lined the sights up with one of two jittery cardinals perched high in a maple tree. Just before the little balls flew, my breath held and trigger easing back, I pulled up and aimed high to fire way above their heads, the pop enough to startle them back to flight.

By then, I guess, I'd grown like most of Us to loathe the wrecking, the wasting, of any more lives.

All that remained in my childhood nest were useless curiosities. A bulky home stereo I'd bought sophomore year just stopped working in the middle of playing *Boston's Greatest Hits* for the first time. The boomerang my father bought me at the state fair outside Tampa, instead of looping to return, would always sail off and nearly kill someone. It was one of the few gifts my father gave me when it wasn't just my birthday or from Santa. Of course it didn't work. The yellowed computer still used MS-DOS. That wouldn't do. No one ever taught me how to swing either one of the tennis racquets I found behind the surfboard, though both sported scuffed-to-hell frames and snapped strings – my sister's fault, I guessed. The marble chess board had half the pieces missing. The Hungry Hungry Hippos game had only three balls left to feed their plastic mouths. All our trash.

The last thing out was a tubular Army duffel bag, my dad's name and Social Security number barely legible in stencil, that I'd hastily stuffed taut with all my stuffed animals in fifth grade. It was the only statement I could make to move us all past the day when my mother flashed all of my birthday party guests not just one but three aging photos that she'd taken of me smiling proudly in a bubble bath just a few years before, a tiny hairless penis unabashedly exposed. I threw the duffel bag in the keep pile that slowly grew out in the living room. Much of the rest was at the curb, as good as gone.

I was trying to hold each thing as if they were talismans, searching for some memory to make my father more useful or kind or consoling, but then my mother was knocking at the door and I'd come up with nothing.

"Coming!" I screamed, but stayed peering out the window. As usual, she wore the standard pagan uniform – the mauve hippie skirt fluttered over tattooed ankles, as thick around as healthy saplings, a loose flowered blouse flashing free-falling boobs that hung down to a belly more bloated than ever. As a boy, I would use all that for a pillow on the couch. She'd worn the same style of Birkenstocks ever since high school, but the fleshy folds between the buckles were no longer hills and more like small mountains now. "C'mon!" she yelled. Bang, bang, bang.

"Coming!" I skied through the living room on my socks.

"It's so good to see you," I said, as I hugged her as much as my arms would allow. "You look great."

"I'm so lucky my baby can lie like he loves me."

It was the truth.

I was worried. It'd been a few years since I'd seen her. She'd flown up at the first inkling of marital trouble, then left a few days later with instructions to move down with her if things kept spiraling out of control. Just the eyes were the same, blue and bright as a beach day, and maybe her hair, though dull gray now and wrapped in a top-knot with ribbon, which fell in split ends to an ass that seemed bigger with every new meal. Her demeanor was appropriate; she wouldn't smile, stayed on the mat, but gregarious yammering shaved off a few years and still put me at ease like a mother's voice should. "Coming in?"

"I'm not coming in and you know it," she said. "Are you doing okay? Aren't you done yet? No calls, well, just the one. No visit. You don't answer your messages...."

"I..."

"Do you eat? You're so skinny *and pale*. I got goulash for days, big loaf of pumpkin bread. Let's go. I been worried about you, all cooped up in here when you know what just, it's..." Back and forth, she was looking at me and then past me.

"Don't you have all these answers?" I said in the line that she'd learned to ignore long ago. "Mom, I'm fine. I'm so sorry, but this place is in shambles. And you know? It's not easy with everything, all the, well... It's just sad."

"He was sad. Crazy sad. Always was. But he loved you, I guess. In his way. From the clouds."

"I know that. It's the what, where and how that's a little distracting. There's enough going on and then this?" I leaned down to the left and locked eyes with a smile. She looked back from the room to return it. "Stop looking for something to float by in a sheet. Nothing at all to report."

"I'm just wondering why you're taking so long. It's just trash."

"It's more than just that," and then I scanned the room. It was all that she needed to be standing beside me. "Mom, get out. Now. You'll have nightmares or something. He's gone. It's all right."

"Son, my whole life is nightmares, one ghoul after the next. I'm just lucky they're everyone else's and not mine. It's fine. It was there?" She was facing the hall, squinting through black rectangular glasses that would have been fashionable if not for the old lady chain connected at the temples.

"You can tell?"

"From the blood. And that old bat Arbuckle. What, the cleaning crew can't afford some bleach? I mean, shit."

"It isn't hard to remember to step over that spot. I don't even look but it's there. I remember every time: he was there, you know? But it's okay. He can't hurt us or even the walls anymore."

"Looks like he left a few new ones as going-away presents." She rubbed the holes across from the front door, shook her head disapprovingly at the hole in the TV. "Still raging right up to the end. Probably didn't like the way a *Full House* episode ended or something. Can't say I blame him. Show pisses me off."

"Yeah." I looked out the door and then closed it. "He was always tilting at the fucking windmills. How *dare* they? Bastard windmills." My sarcasm seemed too forced. She studied my face in the silence.

"He's all over this place. I can still smell his farts. But you're right, baby. No more pain. He saved his own hole for last. I just wish I couldn't smell him."

"Try his sheets. I did laundry and still..."

"A brave soul, me boy. It wasn't always that way, though. You remember that time...?"

"In the attic. I've looked. Now that story can be put out of its misery just like the penis pictures."

"You went up there? My baby's a man now, official. And you're taking this well, all these changes. You can laugh, and that's good. I still got them Polaroids somewhere, you know. Gonna send 'em to my grandchildren someday. If I ever get any."

"If I'd known what was up there," I said, pointing up, "all the roaches and shit, I might have given the inspection a little more thought. It's the same shit as when Katie went up there."

"Down here, too. Just more of it. All these books for show, these newspapers. You know he read the *Eagle* every day but only to make sure his obits didn't have mistakes? Not a single headline. Probably thought we was still fighting the Iraqis right up to the bitter end. The loon."

She stepped well past where he'd died, her eyes on the ceiling instead of the tile. She traced every space from the corners on down, but always returned to the top and then paused. The master bedroom, if it's called that in houses this small, stopped her dead in her tracks, like the temperature changed or a poltergeist stirred. I watched with a grin. She stayed glued up above, moved her head, then her eyes, just like Hawk but not scary and ready to blow.

To me: "Wipe that smirk off your face. What do you believe, with that half-empty cup?" Then to "him": "Are you here, you big dufus-y fuck-lick? It's the family you sucked at. If you hear me, say something, like 'Der, I'm retarded,' you one-footed ginger."

"Some beautiful genes you two passed down." She wasn't listening.

"I can tell you haven't dug shit out of this room. You been sleeping all day?" I said nothing so she looked where I stood by the door. I didn't have time to stop rolling my eyes. "Well get moving. I'll be fine. I'm just curious. He's here. I know it."

"He's not here. Jesus. He can't see you. He's ash now that nobody went to collect."

"And you know this because...? You born special like me? I don't have the patience to get into this right now."

"I am special like you. I just can't talk with ghosts."

"When you die, you'll see. I'll go right there and find you."

"It's a deal. And if you croak first, I'll come and find you, too."

"Sure you will. Now zip!"

She moved through each room craning in careful sweeps, paying special attention to his favorite spots. She sat in his dent in the bed, then the one on the couch, his favorite creaky chair on the back porch.

"Any clues?" I asked flatly.

"Sh." She zigzagged across the house like a weekend Realtor. She paused outside my sister's old room, across the tiny hall from the master bedroom. In a flash of hot pink and doily yellow, she opened then closed the door, gulping deep the stale air from inside. "Nothing but vanity and boy crushes in there."

"Smells like success to me."

"Where'd the freak put that chair?"

"*The* Chair? In my trunk."

"In your car?"

"Got a problem with that?"

"My baby got the 'rrhoids? They run on your Daddy's side. Know *that*. Pro'lly what made him such a dickwad half the time. Still up inside, I hope, and not sticking out like your Daddy's nasty-ass tentacles."

"Ugh. Please." I skulked out to the trunk like my former goth self, grabbed The Chair and started setting it back up in his spot at the dining room table. She came out of my old bedroom, adjusting her eyes to the light.

"Least you got one room done. When did anger monkey leave?"

"You should have seen it before I emptied it out. The posters were the brightest things in there."

"Who's the ghoul?"

Assuredly, she buckled herself into The Chair. The metal stand groaned and bowed, the straps creaked ominously, but it easily withstood the weight. She seemed to know it would. She shivered and frowned, sending waves down her chins, then morphed into a smile to inspire some calm. "No denyin': This is one cozy fucking chair."

"That's why it's mine."

She closed her eyes. "Sh." I could see them rolling back in the sockets, totally free of each other's parallel pull. Breathing deep, she exhaled and opened her eyes with the whites still showing, then dropped the blue pupils down to stare directly at me across the table.

"And...?"

"He's a pussy. He's gone."

"That I know. Are you done? Can I get back to all this?" I rolled my head around but kept my eyes locked on her. "It's sucking me in."

"You'll be fine. Come and see me tonight, sevenish. K? Eat some food. Got a surprise for you, too. You gonna shit."

"Surprise, huh? You holding a demon hostage against his will?" I didn't mention the car troubles, thinking this a good excuse for getting out of dinner.

"You'll see. Seven. Just make sure you call if anything happens." She pressed her left foot to the floor, unbuckled that leg, then the other side. The stand relaxed to its original height.

"I will. I mean, I won't. What's gonna happen?"

"And don't be bringing any of that sad mojo with you. I got a reputation to uphold. Them's my peeps over there. So cheer up, see?" She brushed her skirt down her thighs.

"Love you, Mama."

She propped a hand against the dining room table, closed one eye but kept the other on me. "That's why I don't see you for years. Sure you love me."

"I've been working my ass off. And Rebecca, you know? I'm not used to being alone for this long."

"She's an evil temptress is what. A whore or a bitch, hon. Or both. You decide."

"I don't know. Probably neither, Mom. Just different, than before." I patted her back and she finally weebled off toward the door. I watched her squeeze into the Escort. She'd been leasing a different one for decades, ever since she could rightfully call herself "just a little big," just before growing "fat," which preceded "obese and diabetic." Somewhere looming up the road, we both knew, was worse.

"Be safe!" I yelled out.

"You be safe. You're the one still stuck in Disney's Haunted Mansion there." A weak laugh left her gut, which was pinned by the steering wheel, her boobs and the seatbelt. I laughed back something even weaker, full of worry I couldn't mask. She noticed and frowned.

Back inside, packing books with the front door open, it amused me to think of my father still here, looking down from the ether and ignoring her as always. Though I love her, I also delighted in knowing that she still hadn't been able to show me her superpowers, even in the aftermath of a suicide, an event she'd always sworn would leave "purgatorial paranormal residue." I looked toward the dim hallway, from the floor to the ceiling, and pretended belief.

I screamed into the empty chasm, "Run away, you pussy!" I laughed.

I listened for longer than felt comfortable, then added calmly, "Or stay. What's the difference?"

I heard an echo of my laughter.

For him to have heard that would have been a true godsend.

Chapter 9

WHEREAS, one cloistered God no longer speaks for all American ideals, "In God We Trust" an empty phrase we use to hedge our bets upon our money. The Founding Fathers framed the Constitution not to be myopically excluding; they stood for those who fled that sort of proselytizing in the land of the Crusades. But generations on, the offspring of progenitors had borne a double-headed monster – with one mouth yelling, "God and Country!" and the other whispering, "and all Ours, too." Freeburg seeks to be another sort of place, where every prophet's words are hailed to bring all gods to be as One.

On a fluke, I tried to start my car and I swear it rattled to life. I couldn't decide: be relieved or put out? I kept it running at the gas station and again at the Winn-Dixie, where I bought filterless Pall Malls (my grandfather's brand from when they stuffed them in his sea-rations), two cans of whipped cream, a bottle of Puerto Rican rum and a carton of pineapple juice. In the car, before leaving the lot, I uncapped a whipped cream and sucked all the nitrous oxide from the can, exhaling when I couldn't hold my breath a moment more. Repeat. Then, with full-spectrum swirling peripheral vision, I swigged a shot of rum, chased down by some juice, and took some calming rips off my father's old bowl that I'd crammed into the crack of the passenger seat, and only then could I proceed to my mother's house for Hungarian goulash and pumpkin bread. I felt strangely familial.

Sad mojo, as per mother's orders, was left to lag in my wake but always threatened to catch up. I cashed the bowl to keep it back there. Leading out of Freeburg, rainbow clusters of campaign placards littered the roadsides, jostling for dominant positions, optimum name recognition. Pallid strip malls or ho-hum houses served as backdrops for promises that no one had credentials to disprove: "HENDERSON MEANS INTEGRITY" (so he says), "SHERIFF OLIPHANT IS LEADERSHIP" (of one kind or another), "VOTE PEREZ FOR A CHANGE" (of scenery) and "MCGINTY IS RETARDED" (for reading all these signs). At least they gave the town sporadic bursts of needed color; at most, to me at least, they spoke to how most power, even here, went to those with the heftiest accounts. How much easier all that is now to fund and tolerate.

Then the blighted air, in a single bound over the gridlocked interstate, cleared into pastoral visions of what could at least pretend to be more easygoing times. On one of two roundabout ways into Cassadaga, the dying sun cast a paltry glow through wisps of cirrus clouds, across cow pastures and open sloping meadows subsidized into switch grass, clover and dandelions. A mounting storm in the Atlantic, just 30 miles to the east, brought a stout breeze that swirled the tops of slash pines and scrub oaks, launching birds into the graying sky or down into palmetto and bougainvillea shrubs. To my left, a coal sky flashing heat lightning sparks; to my right, violet-pink-orange, cotton-candied clouds. Above, at any moment, a sun shower could start. These are things that you learn here and never forget.

On the outskirts of town, ranches and plantation-style homes of the business class gave way to a valley of well-kempt cottages and bungalows, no two painted or plotted exactly the same. This was the downtown where I'd spent the bulk of my upperclassman years, rolling my eye-linered eyes and tossing aside a red mop of teased hair. "There's not even a fucking convenience store," I'd be caught remarking, justifiably. "Can a nigga get some Wendy's, for crying out loud?" It was that much of a bubble. Still was. Still is.

Along Cassadaga Road, two landmarks stand out for the polemic divide they've always produced in my head – the yin and yang of my spiritual compass: On one side of Stevens Street, now pedestrians-only, was the two-story, white-sided Cassadaga Hotel, which was imposing not from size but for ghost tour potential, its front porch abuzz with seekers and seers, the mourners and maladroit, all fretting and fussing over this card or that. And, in the hotel's long shadows, on the other side of Stevens Street, and in my thinking too, sat the New Age book shop, run by Emily Alcoe, a stout old believer who showed me who she thought our God was and came closer than anyone I've ever met, up until then or since.

"He/she" isn't "*their* God," she'd told me one day after she'd visited with my mother, in conspiratorial tones with a wave to the sky, but "the good deeds of my making," my "life's work of blessings," the "heart on my sleeve" or "my hand out to help." She had a comforting way of making "all good spiritual paths meet," as she'd say, "in the middle." In the same breath, Miss Emmy could quote Confucius – "Heaven means to be one with God." – then Romans – "Follow after the things that make for peace and build each other up." A real sage, she never would own up to being a certified medium, not like her husband, who'd taken an online exam and everything; what she claimed was an ear for hearing "the water under the rocks" – the Seneca phrase that gave Cassadaga its alluring name.

It all made sense to this kid. I can't say just how, but her words sent me seeking with a buoyant regard, from the darkest of goths to science-geek atheist in Professor Joseph Campbell's camp to an agnostic procurer of secular truths, then a student of Buddhism, secular humanist, to finally, at least for now like many of us, Baha'i-loving Wayne Dyer fanatics with a thing for teasing their chakras and Googling our brains bigger.

The shop Miss Emmy managed served, and still serves, as the town's de facto wishing well for all the hapless visitors to the

Cassadaga Spiritualist Camp, filled with every kind of New Age trinket and treatise, though the town's widely divergent and free-roaming resident flock really thought of their spiritual home as the Colby Memorial Temple, which was further up Stevens Street. (Mum's the word.)

On four tightly packed blocks surrounding the temple lived the seers, in more homes than not, most with shingles out front tacking off their great powers like Old West tradesmiths tackling New Age dilemmas. Literally a garden gnome's throw to the south from the temple a small plant-choked pond filled with feisty, curious gators writhes with snakes and turtles and lizards and mosquitoes. Some audacious believer once named it Lake Colby.

Perhaps it goes without saying that it was a New Yorker named George Colby who was inspired by a séance to found this serious camp of ghoul bait back in 1894, as a Spiritualist sanctuary for America's mediums, who faced only moderately less scrutiny as they had a few centuries before in places like, say, Salem. It was still a long haul before *Bewitched* would make all these witches pert and fulsome housewife types or bookish men with professorial airs and elbow patches on tweed coats. It was a welcome place from the beginning.

Within just a few decades, 55 homes had sprung up here, so tightly packed and close to the roads as to give one the impression of a big psychic hug, a communality rare for any hamlet so deeply Deep South. The ages would be kind to New Age ways of doing business, but they would still progress to wedge the commune right between a modern Sodom and Gomorrah: The Spring Break Capital of the World, Daytona Beach, just a sitcom's-worth of driving to the northeast, and the Plastic-Concrete Mecca for Material Consumption, Walt Disney World, the same alluring distance to the southwest. The highway leading back and forth passes just a few miles east of here, with rowdy, bo-hunk Freeburg lurking on the other side. But from my mother's home, at Marion Street and Cassadaga Road, this little town was still, in my ebbing buzz, a tiny plug of Pursley turf left on its own to grow into a verdant lawn, a guarded commune touched but never fondled by secular devotions, largely unfazed by fundamentalists or basic-cable dreams.

This thought was sadly fleeting as I pulled my hoary Regal into the driveway and stopped just inches shy of my sister's chromed-out Mercedes. I read her only bumper sticker carefully and couldn't help my head from shaking: "LIFE'S A WITCH AND THEN YOU FLY!"

"Fuck it all," I said, as my car coughed out the key and sizzled like frying bacon. I got out and felt the sun shower start to sprinkle my face. I couldn't help but think, when dropping back my head to gauge the clouds, that those birds of prey up there I guessed were hawks, inviolably high, were turning astral hoops directly over me. *Arrogant fucker,* said a thought that blipped into my head.

"How's my baby brother?" Katie asked with a tentative hug at the top of the porch steps. It was her standard greeting.

"Still trying to catch up, I guess," I said by way of a laugh, hugging her back with a snug right arm, hugging the cocktail supplies in the left. "I missed you."

"You okay?" she asked.

"Yeah, you?"

"Ptht," I blurted out, then wised up, "Oh, sure. How EVER does unemployment compensation cover all of that?" I pointed to the car but also to the sky like Miss Emmy always had.

"That old thing?" She couldn't hide her love for it, the actress. "Mechanic's dream. Always something."

"I'm surprised you even drove. Didn't you just hail a jet last time and take a limo from the airport? When was the...?"

"Two years ago, doof. I was shooting *Misappropriated Fun.* Der. And I didn't have the drive time in the shooting schedule, *sooo....* Are you holding up with the whole Rebecca thing and the Daddy thing and the..."

"Yeah, everything's clean and serene over here." I hugged the bag to my chest. She didn't need to investigate.

"Drive safe," she said, about-facing into the house.

Inside, my mother hadn't made many changes. It looked like an IKEA showroom. Her home isn't the stereotypical coven. No beaded entryways, no crystal balls on big round tables, no dragon kitsch, crystal shrines or percolating potions. She kept these things put away, preferring to exude a more up-tempo Feng Shui, as she was wont to point out, in case any potential suitors stopped by the parlor after-hours.

"Not all lovers are comfortable with my magic," she'd say.

There were more cats than usual, enough to call her a "cat lady" now. But the effect was that of just a few at any given time in any one room.

"I think we got an even dozen now," she yelled out from her cauldron in the kitchen. All but one, she said – a black Maine coon named Boss, with those yellow, blaming eyes – were cloned puffs of cotton balls with nothing but blue eyes to match the family pool.

"What do you call the rest?" I asked. "How do you call them anything?"

She poked her head into where we mulled around in the living room, her pink face turning redder with the stifled glee. "Those are Boss's slaves. Right, Boss?" She started laughing then tamped it down so she could explain the rest, for what was probably the thousandth time. "Boss names them. They're his, not mine. They're probably all just numbers, anyway. Right, Boss?" She ran a hand down Boss's back, where he sat, as enormous as a lynx, along the banister, then ducked back into the kitchen. "Don't worry: They all get food, baths and Mama love."

I lost a stare down with Boss, then looked at Katie, sitting on a leather armoire beside the matching sofa, and saw nothing but acceptance in her face for my mother's peculiar brand of irony, just smiling away and looking at old pictures on the walls. I hoped she hadn't seen Boss make me his bitch. I switched my expression to match hers before she looked back at me, where I was leaning on the breezeway from the foyer, trying to look at home. I couldn't help swirling my finger around my ear, but Katie just gave me a look like it was me she couldn't understand or even stomach all that much.

"Hi Boss!" she called and it made him hop down and slide up

under her arm, something only self-assured cats are capable of doing. "Did you see Mom's new sign over the door? 'Guru Ann.' Isn't that amazing? She doesn't even need to advertise her fields. Everyone just knows."

I came and sat on the edge of the couch. "Everybody's healed who wants to be. When's my turn?"

Katie shot me the same disapproving look as always when I shied from the family line. Insult even my father and you got a lesser version of the same.

"You do have to want it," she said, bugging out her eyes. Her lashes were so well-coiffed I thought they would reach the middle of her forehead. "Why is that so hard to believe? Why is it so hard for you to believe anything anymore?"

I couldn't answer that. Her magical power has always been shaping things in such ways as to give even unfathomable notions an air of glib truth and brilliance. That's not saying she'd given any Oscar-worthy performances by this point in her life. I still say she'll have to play an ugly serial killer or improve her British accent to gain those kinds of accolades, six daytime Emmys notwithstanding.

She glided into the dining room to look at pictures in there, poke her nose in drawers, then was back in hushed tones. "She helps a lot of people, Saul. More than you know. Did you know La Toya Jackson just called the other night? Yes, La Toya Fucking Jackson – to tell Mom she's seen Michael appearing behind the curtains in her house at night, that he was wearing the same pearls he had on in his coffin and that he keeps turning the lights on and off to let her know that he's still there watching over her. Did you know *that*?"

"So where did Mom fit into all that? Did she..."

"Keep your booze quiet," Katie said through clenched teeth. "I can smell it all over what you're about to say."

I dropped to a whisper. I've never been good at drinking sociably. "Was it all, 'Oh, that's perfectly normal, La Toya, baby. He just wants you to know he's all right, that's all it was. You know how he always was such a giving and caring and glad-handed man.' Then, that's it? Where in all that is she asking for credit card numbers?"

"It's not like that. She senses things, Saul. I've seen it. Matthew McConaughey didn't even know where fucking Cassadaga even *was* until he made an appointment to see her to sort out his feelings about the ghost his whole family used to see when he was growing up."

"What have you seen?" I departed deeper into the far living room corner.

"I've seen how she cares, Saul. How she tries, really listens, to hear what these people don't have ears to hear."

"Hm," I said, like the gym teacher who used to punctuate my sad tries at climbing a knotted rope to the ceiling. I pretended to scan through a scrapbook on the coffee table. Katie pretended to scan through a bookshelf.

There was a time when my mother's mythic ways had enchanted even me, her talk of reaching through a wall and pulling back some of the other side, but then a lie about an Easter Bunny became a lie about a Santa Claus became, at age eleven, me asking her if Jesus was even real, before I added, "What other lies you got in that sack, Santa Mommy?"

Then, in the summer before my freshman year, right after Mom high-tailed it to Cassadaga, I was rounding the bend at the center of town on my vintage, banana-seater Huffy and nearly vomited when I ran over what appeared to be a crushed and bloodied black cat, dented through by a car and left there to die. I didn't stop or turn around. I rushed home and returned with Katie, who jumped off the handlebars before I could fully stop and went immediately to lift up the animal's tail.

"It's a trick," Katie'd said before taking a small bite of a leg without flinching. This time I did vomit, on my shoe, on my shirt. Then she added, "It's latex, you stoop. Dumb like Daddy is what."

"Jesus! Why?" I asked in echo, first to the town, then to the world before scanning for suspects or at least a few witnesses. I didn't mean it. "Who would do such a thing?!"

The fake cat returned in what few nightmares I could ever

recall, scattered randomly enough to keep scaring me. In one dream, it's real, still alive; in another, it's real and in Katie's mouth anyway or telling me helpfully, "Your dumb father did it." My incredulity only hardened under this kind of duress, especially when some clues started to mount as to their source. I soon came to learn that these tricks were often the brainchildren not of know-nothing kids, but of some of the town's most high-minded of thinkers, just to "yank at the screens we can't see," Miss Emmy would say, "that are always there clouding up things that are clear." I was shocked.

My sort-of friend, Mort Huggins, confirmed this later that fall; he'd told me about seeing, from his dining room window, Miss Olivia Bishop, an old elfish docent, put another fake black dead cat over on Lincoln Street, this one just a few weeks before Halloween. This from the woman who had once told the both of us that black cats were a symbol of the dark arts. I raked my brain clean just to fathom her motive. Maybe some passersby would notice the dead cat as just that, a reverse omen that served to cancel out the bad luck that might have been experienced were it black and alive, and the rest would just laugh at the dead latex cat. All around town, I passed my theories about, until one day Miss Olivia stopped me by the arm from behind and said, "So we're all just that now, huh? Just a bunch of witches casting spells, with black cat armies sent to do our bidding?"

"Oh, no," I told her. "Not all of you."

"No, not all of us is right," she said, which I'm not sure I took the way she'd meant it. "Run along, little boy," which I did.

My mother always insisted the fake cats came from "prankster ne'er-do-wells" from Freeburg, which would be hard to discredit. My father, after I told him about the gossip, retorted from over in Freeburg that Cassadaga was "full of prankster goblin spawn," and you can't argue with that either. It's still hard to tell who was right.

"So you really haven't named these cats, Mom?"

"They're numbers, remember?" Katie answered, then laughed,

then screamed toward the kitchen, "Only Boss knows which number is which, right?"

"That's right!" And both laughed.

"You kill me," Katie said, then drifted off into reverie, which after a few seconds turned her grin to a grim upturned boat of loathing. *So rich,* I thought cheaply. *Should I take my shirt off so you can better lock into your motivation?*

"Mom, where's the, um..." Katie fumbled for words, which wasn't like her at all.

"Where's the what, honey? Oh! Look on the mantle. Is it there?"

Katie and I looked to a cardboard box that might have fit one cantaloupe inside. Or a head. I knew by her expression that my father was inside the box. My mother came into the room, wiping her hands on a tie-died scarf, a pinky-sized joint hanging out of her fat lips.

"You kids wanna smoke or is this shit gonna get too serious?" The joint went around three times before we stopped and stared back at the mantle.

I hadn't forgotten to ask what had become of my father's remains. I'd just forgone the question until presented with the answer. Honestly, I'd half-presumed some military officer, assigned to this part of the country, was tasked with collecting deceased war veterans and dispatching them to this cemetery or that. I was half-correct. The police had asked my mother, in the absence of a will or any knowledge of the whereabouts of kin like me or Katie, if she'd like to have my father buried by the Department of Defense or have his ashes sent by FedEx to an address of her choosing.

"I almost had them send the box to the White House, but then I thought about the aftermath of something like that."

My mother had pulled the biggest set of knitting scissors I'd ever seen from a high table in the hall to the kitchen and handed them to Katie, who floated ceremonially to the box, then sat back down in the chair and set him on her lap. Of course she would be the one; just like she was the one who always squashed the roaches at my father's house and tamed the house lion here. But something inside me wanted to do it, to relinquish her from these types of things, now and forever. My mother had prepared her, I could tell, because she had all her marks rehearsed. I let it slide.

After peeling the tape back from the top of the box, she opened the flaps and cut the baggie inside straight across the top seal. A small poof of his dust alighted and made me wince, but not her. She grabbed a pair of bobbles that hung from her neck, uncapped each and placed some of my father's ashes inside, then capped them back closed with a resolute breath. The rest she poured into a brass urn on the end table beside her, which had left a deep dent on a stack of *Psychic News Now!* trade journals.

"This one's yours," Katie said, handing over a miniature urn on a chain. "I got them in Cannes. Solid platinum. Bulgari." I tucked mine in my pocket.

"Fancy that," I said.

"Goulash?" asked my mother.

*   *   *

After dinner, drinks, another joint, and still no one claiming ownership of the balance of my father's ashes, my mother decided to pour them into a hole in the backyard and plant an orange sapling there to see "if something sweet could ever come out of it."

She had the tree in a plastic pot on the back deck, already sporting little nubbins of green fruit. She obviously was doing this whether we agreed or not. Katie and I watched her shift that carriage around adroitly with the shovel from two Adirondack chairs in the already tree-shrouded and vine-wrapped backyard, which by early afternoon was completely under the shade of her Victorian's deeply Seussian gables. I sipped on my second cocktail, red-eyed and enjoying the change of scenery. Numb, basically. Unfeeling. I looked over as Katie updated her status on Facebook with a photo of my father's final resting place: "Feeling ... Zen," she said as her thumbs tapped away.

A graying couple slugged by on Marion Street, holding hands and prying over the hedge.

"Hello, Guru Ann," said the man to my mother.

221

"My ex-husband!" my mother yelled out to them, pointing at the hole. "Ha-HA!"

"Saw that coming," said the woman coyly. "You'll have a great night now."

"You'll, too," said my mother and Katie in singsong unison. Notice: It had become over many generations the custom of some locals to assign the near-future's fortunes in passing salutations like this. A transplant like my mother found it charming. I'd always found it presumptive, even arrogant. While still in my teens, I'd purposely mope for the rest of the day just for spite; there in my forties, it had become comforting, though I still caught myself rolling my eyes.

"You gonna eat that fruit, Mom?" I asked, looking like I'd just squeezed a lime into a wound. "Ugh."

Katie answered for her: "I think it's meaningful, Goob. She's sending some to some of my friends in the Hamptons and L.A., too. Dad can nurture things now, fortify shit. Finally."

"*Zackly*, honey," my mother said, tamping down the dirt and calling over the hose that Katie had at the ready, then looked pityingly at me. "No, Saul. I'm gonna doll 'em all up like little pumpkins and throw 'em at the trick-or-treaters. 'Course we're eating 'em. We're not watering the thing with his piss or some shit, which, believe me, I've thought about. What's left of your Dad was already in the dirt here anyway."

"Der," Katie added.

This didn't feel like the time either. When would it ever be? I'd been rolling his suicide note into a ball in my pocket for at least a half-hour. It was softer than a tissue now, every fiber wrinkled tight then ironed out. I didn't know how to breach the subject, so I finally decided to just walk over to the tree and hock it like a wad of phlegm into the dirt. "Y'all wanna read his suicide note? I got part of it with me."

"You got part of it," said my mother in monotone, letting the shovel fall against the sapling and instantly uproot it.

Before I could retrieve it, Katie's hands were digging in my pockets and reemerging with the note from one side and my father's browned-out glass bowl from the other. She hastily threw the bowl into the mud and started reading the note out loud, as my mother managed to bend at the waist and yank the tree back upright, her eyes staying peeled to Katie's hands. I played cool by leaving the bowl half-buried in the freshly tilled earth and reassuming my perch on the Adirondack. By the end of their reading, they were both ogling me, their jaws slackened, like they half-suspected a dark practical joke or were at last welcoming one of my flippant rebukes to fill in the gap of their uncharacteristic lack of comprehension. Really: They were as dumbfounded as I had been for days.

The pregnant pause delivered into a flurry of questions, the answers for which I demanded a retreat back indoors to a smokier climate and a refill on my drink. It was dark and we were drunk by the time I could fully share the garbled gist of my father's journalizing, the war diary, the paranoid narcissism that ebbed and flowed through his whole solitary life. After the interrogation came another fleeting pause before the dubious theorizing ensued.

"It's like he wanted to fucking kill himself," said Katie, slumped in the chair where she'd dipped into my father's ashes, "but he was too much a pussy to own up to it." Not a trace of regret in her searching gaze. I love Katie the Wench. She rarely emerged back then. This was an early glimmer. It was the sister I'd wished for growing up and not the one who would bounce gleefully from soap operas to feminine hygiene commercials to *Lifetime* movie supporting roles. But then again, what had become of me up until then? "Or maybe he was just drugged out of his fucking gourd. Or all of the above, of course."

My mother was almost asleep on the couch but still searching with her pupils under closed lids. "Sounds like the holy trinity right there, K. You missed your calling. You know I still got room here for an apprentice." She smiled lazily.

"Adrienne Hughes *did* used to be a private dick before her cosmetics business started taking up all her time," Katie said with the same level of serious that she'd been coaxed to harness for her Emmys.

I was at my mother's feet at the end of the couch, my feet on the coffee table.

"One of our writers was a fucking ex-prosecutor, okay?" Katie deadpanned, then broke character to join along. "So, I mean. You can't get more realistic than that."

That was the last comment that any of us can remember. The phone rang in the middle of the night and I thought I could hear Rebecca's voice on the answering machine but then remembered that I was only dreaming.

The most uncomfortably situated, I was first to awaken on Saturday with the sun boring into my forehead through the picture window, my socked heels sore on the table and my mother's heavy heels boring into my crotch.

I didn't wake them up. Katie would be over in hours, I knew, to inspect the journals herself and maybe help me pack. I savored the idea of having a few hours alone before more questions started coming. Outside, I was alone in the early morning stew. I took my time in the driveway, putting the boy me here and there in every view in sight.

"*You'll* hang in there," I said to myself or the town or both, presumptive-tense. "Or *you'll* all die in your sleep." *Doesn't anyone here know what happened to him?* I was thinking of screaming.

I wished Miss Emmy hadn't died of a heart attack when I was in college. Not only would I have loved to ask her what happened when you added an "O" to God and took the "D" from Devil," but I'll bet she would have just known why my father killed himself. She could have made some sense of all this, even though nothing did anymore.

"Ya'll'll fuck off now, y'all hea?"

Chapter 10

WHEREAS, for too long Freeburg's future has been harnessed by a pious bunch, exalting God and patriotic zeal while greed and lust for power filled their pockets and their minds. That's why respected thinker/scribe Sinclair Lewis wrote in "peace" time, 1935, that "when fascism comes to America, it will be wrapped in the flag and carrying a cross." No doubt that menace lurked here long before he wrote those knowing words. Just when will these Crusades end?

A phalange of pricey cars clustered around the Arbuckle's when I got back to Walnut Circle. A few little girls in Sunday dresses slurped at juice boxes and hung from the legs of a tall, stooped man with a crew cut poking through tool cabinets in the plank-strewn garage, where Mr. Arbuckle used to play at being a carpenter like his lone prophet.

A blond, bowl-cutted teenager in a button-up and khakis sat on the praying bench Mr. Arbuckle'd built under the front yard maple, playing a game on his smartphone and swatting at bugs. His clone of a twin cut a severe profile rolling down the driveway on Heelies as if his reputation as an athlete depended on his every strident move. I sat in the car gawking, pretending not to gawk. Two women my mother's age, both in the same brand of formal brunch attire, came out the front door with drawn, sullen faces, their downturned eyes dragging liner-blotted circles. One of them was balancing a tall stack of photo albums; the other had framed photos in one hand, watercolor paintings of a too-white Jesus in the other. They were followed by a suited man with a too-black comb-over and briefcase. He laid a been-there-done-that hand on one of their backs, while directing some muted words at the other. I didn't need to hear what he was saying. She was gone.

I parked at the curb and climbed over the bags at the tree lawn with two steps reflecting a new steadfastness that nevertheless led to a third step through the back of a bookcase and me face-first in a hill of red carpenter ants. Flailing about, I half-anticipated a prayerful Arbuckle intervention, but they'd apparently been prayed out by that point in their lives. The man in the garage did take a few steps down the driveway, but even he was shaking his head in disgrace, no doubt confusing me for the garbage from which I'd just been launched.

I hurried inside, snapping at my shirt and fleetingly thinking about one of my own personal prophets, Krishnamurti, whose words I shot like paraphrased darts across the road: *Your particular belief in God, Arbuckles, is just an escape from your monotonous, stupid and cruel-as-fuck lives.* I couldn't wait to finish then. No more hapless seeking. No more saving trash. I was so close to leaving this sad-sack neighborhood behind for good, though I'd saved the worst for last.

I started in Katie's room and was done in an hour. She'd told me there was nothing in there worth saving, and she was almost right. Two things survived this particular purging: a blue, glitter-bedecked tackle box that I thought might finally inspire me to learn how to fish and an octagon-shaped desktop aquarium that I thought might inspire me to learn how to keep them alive and inspiring.

The aquarium safe behind a seatbelt in the Regal's backseat, I thought of delivering condolences to those who remained at the Arbuckles, then, remembering that they hadn't offered me any, thought better. I figured I'd express my deepest sympathies upon my final exit. I was going to tear though the master with the same resoluteness, but shifted course after peering into the abyss at the door. I stepped over his body and started in on what remained of the books, papers and candles in the living room. An hour later, Katie was lunging through the door.

"Aaaaargh!" the thespian yelled, gesticulating like a shaken ragdoll. "Thought I'd get that out up front."

Then she wilted and cried in the crook of my shoulder. I let her finish. She looked up and beamed a cleansing smile.

She didn't have anywhere near my level of dread about the place. Visits back to Walnut Circle would remain for her like a trip to a Ripley's museum, forays into memories of the few close friends she'd left behind here; for me, the memories would remain dreaded reminders of the world's darkest features. Katie did remember the puttied-up holes, though. By her arrival, most were exposed through the board-on-block shelves.

"At least he never laid a hand on any of us," she said while I taped up another box. She looked at me questioningly. "You think he ever even got in a fight? Like an octagon fight?"

"I think he pretty much broke even," I told her.

I slipped his second journal off the dining room table, flipped through to the middle and pointed at a page I pretended to know would include her answer. "Somewhere around there."

A few pages more and she'd found the passage, glancing up only briefly to shoot me a look of concern. This was my way of revealing the journals to her. Predictably, she was mesmerized:

"...All arguments aside, I've been in two scraps in my life. I won one I thought I'd lose and lost one I thought I'd win. Who needs more than that?

Growing up on a farm gets your hands tough and your head ready to deal with nonsense and gross smells and all that. But raising sheep doesn't get you ready for the ring. My father seemed the type who could have but he never railed all that hard at anyone but me. One summer day in junior high after he railed me especially hard for my lackadaisical job at shoveling his shit, I took off for town on my bike and hit a bump that made me fly into a ditch and twist my back out of place. It must have pulled the pin out of me, too, because I stared down hard the Lorrie brothers, whose laughs I could hear from across their pasture. I didn't just stare, either. I hopped the wire fence and squashed through patties to get close enough for them to elect the younger of the two, a boy everybody called Scratch who was a running back on the JV football squad. He comes out to escort me off their property. "You think it's fucking funny, Scratch? I fucking hurt myself, you cunt." I could have cried, almost did, but when he balled his fists and turned them about his eyes, my tears soured into poisonous rage. I summoned all the memories I had of watching Sugar Ray Leonard's comeback ass-kicking of Roberto Duran, the only fight I'd ever watched on television up until then, and set about landing blow after blow on Scratch. He couldn't touch me. I cut his lip and kicked him so hard in the stomach that he doubled over and started walking away, just like Duran did in round eight. I even threw my hands up in the air to an imaginary crowd. I stood there like that until Seth Lorrie, varsity linebacker, started heading over, which made me rush back to my bike. My luck wouldn't have been that good.

I managed to get out of Ohio without a scratch from any kind of licking, but in basic training, this thick kid from Boston named MacAteer balanced out my karma. He was my battle buddy on account of the bunks we shared in alphabetical order. A runty black drill sergeant named Brown told us on Day One that, if his experience "as Nostril-fucking-damus" had taught him anything, it was that our bunk had at least a 50-percent chance of producing a lunatic drunkard and a 100-percent chance of producing some angry killing machines. All we could do was agree, me loudly and MacAteer softly, that, "Yes, drill sergeant!" that was some time-honored math right there. Me, I was worried enough about what everybody had to go through to stir up any problems only I would have to suffer, but MacAteer was always looking for somebody to set him off. It must have been a family ritual he missed from back home. He was always trashing this scrawny Italian named Moretti about how he smelled like rotten fish, which was true. Moretti would say he didn't see the point in taking a shower, "not when no girls'd be around no ways." About a month in, late at night, I hear MacAteer slide off his bed above me and start whispering with some others in the dark. The night's CQ came up and started laughing real low. Then, all you hear is a struggle near Moretti's bed and him getting dragged off to the latrine. After some thumping around, Moretti was pleading to take his shower in a voice that can't be mistaken for anything other than a crying man. I saw the wet pillow case in MacAteer's hand when he came back to bed. I could smell the bar of soap inside it. The next morning when everybody was dragging ass out to PT, Moretti charged at me, a much smaller man than my battle buddy, and started whaling away at the air, landing shots. I knew I had to take him out, despite the pity I felt for him. This was downright irresponsible for Moretti to attach this attack to me, wishful thinking. I had neither the size nor the temperament, but I put up my fists like the Celtics mascot and started rolling them around and bouncing forward and back on my feet in a way that said, "What the fuck is this?" and "Who can be afraid of this punk-ass bitch?" But no matter how hard I tried to deny my involvement, or duck his blows and return fire with something worthy of a highlight reel, Moretti kicked my ass in front of everybody, even the drill sergeants from their office. He broke my nose, bloodied my ear, and swelled my eye up shut, before MacAteer finally pulled him off with "Smelling much better now, Moretti. Easy now. Why you think McGinty did it? It was you who done it to yourself..." I thought he could have gotten there much faster, for a battle buddy.

I'm still 1-1 today, though this new neighbor in his fucking jalopy looks like he's asking for it with his music all up in everybody's ears all day and night..."

"Wow," Katie said, running a hand through her hair from the couch. "It's all like this?"

"The war stuff's in that diary on the top, but yeah – the whole truth and nothing but the truth, I'm sure. Guess writing obits every day made him want to write his own."

"Can I take these back to Mom's?"

"It's your time. Far be it from me to stop you from wasting it. The other journal's worth skipping, believe me. It's the rest of the suicide note, which reads pretty much like that Unabomber Kaczynski's manifesto without the observations from Walden Pond."

She grabbed the stack off the dining room table and started reading them in the order that I had. I feared for her mental health, but welcomed the company. I kept stuffing newspapers, value menu wrappers and meaningless knickknacks like Happy Meal toys into bags; most of the books and candles were making their way into boxes by then. It took her an hour to get to the end of the first journal, then through the police reports and article about his supposed ailment that were tucked in the front cover of the second, which she started to read but then stopped and stood up.

"Jesus, Fuck!" she said. "Where did he come up with this shit? Study your history. The arrogant fuck. Silly to think is right."

"My words exactly. Well, almost..." I looked around at some of the holes.

"Where's the note?" It was still in my jeans. "I can't believe I want to see it again."

She read the note again, but with her fingers stroking the paper as if it were braille. "Study your history. Study your history. Start today. Start *today*. The newspaper. Which one did he tear it from?"

"A newspaper," I said, savoring the word like a mint. I punched my jaw enough to jar some cobwebs loose. I hadn't really read one of those for a year, at least, had lost track of the feel of the stock in my hands. "It could be any of them. I've thrown some out but..."

"Start today, or..." she said. "The day he died."

I bopped my jaw again. "What are we doing?" I asked her.

"Obeying thy father and mother is what."

"Mom said to just throw all this shit away and get the hell out."

"When have you ever listened to her?"

"It is the most he's ever even talked to me," I said, as much to myself as to her. "It's much more compelling conversation this way."

She flipped through papers on the coffee table, while I rifled through two bags by my bedroom door, but all those were flat tan and months or more old, not the sandy, less-dated hue of the note. She floated around his bedroom, then came back out to where I was riveted to the front page of the paper, found halfway through a stack on the dining room table.

"That's it?" She skipped in excitement over where his body had been.

"August 3," I said, matching up the edge of the note to its twin on the newspaper page. Katie read the lead news headline.

"*Rainbow Coalition Urges Freeburg Open Marriages.* Is this it?"

"Yikes," I said. I scanned the rest of the page. *Serial Rapist Found Hiding in Freeburg Trailer Park. County Republicans Seek 'New-World Diversity'. Libya Balks at Forced Weapons Inspection. School Board: Charter School Students Come Back.* I closed my eyes.

"Look inside, stoops. It's insiiiiide the rainbow. You're still at the treasure." She giggled. "You're right. We're retarded." Still, it looked to be more of the same inside. A police blotter was full of names we couldn't recognize. A boiler accident killed an ex-Freeburg councilwoman. An editorial urged Daytona leaders to take down red-light cameras. The dog of the day was a good-as-dead pit bull.

Before we could flip through any more, a knock on the door pushed it open to reveal a middle-age woman with a giant ram on a leash, its thick collar studded but pink. In the distance, I could see Serge milling around in his driveway, pretending to sweep it with weak swipes of a broom while glancing over at the livestock.

"Can we help you?" Katie asked, really meaning it.

"God bless us both," said the woman, whose dirty blond hair and saffron kimono made her skin even more sallow than it was. "Seems we're both going through some trying times. Seems your father passed just weeks before my mother, Ursula."

Katie shot me a look. I'd forgotten to tell her. Was there a need until now?

"We're so sorry," she said, looking over at my apologetic face then back at the door, at the sheep then its shepherd. "We weren't aware."

"Well, we're sorry for your loss," the woman said.

"And us for yours," I said, staring just at the sheep and its broad display of horns. Ramboillet is what my father called this breed that once was the McGinty lifeblood. "So..."

"Seems we'll be needing the key for the Realtor tomorrow. You can put it there under the mat when you go. And, of course, there's the matter of little Paul. He's been fixed, so you won't have to worry: relaxed as can be. Called a wether now, without the need to sire. Might even be a good guard ram besides the steady wool. That would be up to you to decide, of course."

"I'm sorry," I said, "but..."

"Yeah," said Katie. "Who's Paul?"

"Oh, we thought you knew. Guess your father was keeping him and a ewe name of Ann on his back porch for a while, but he couldn't let them out to graze since there isn't a fence here. That gator, you know..."

"So..." I felt where this was going and didn't like it.

"My mother," said the woman. "She thought her backyard would be the only way, the fence and all. They been back there a few years. At least. Never had to mow once, just spread some forb and fescue seed and the like after the last spring frost. They loved it. Made us all scarves and beanies and booties. 'Course we never had a use for any of it unless were going skiing or on some Alaskan cruise or something." She laughed, pointed to a tall painter's bucket, added, "They got lazy, though. Sometimes they'd just sit on the porch for days eating feed store silage and cereals and just watch the wind in the trees like old folks. Paul didn't move for a week after my mother found Ann lying there next to him – the sweetest thing you ever seen. We couldn't bring ourselves to take her to the butcher. My brother Aaron buried her in the yard under the grapefruit tree. Guess that was a few months back."

"So precious," said Katie, advancing on Paul with a stroke down his snout. He didn't flinch but actually stepped a hoof into the room and released a powerful stream of urine to mark his old home anew. "Well, we're more than happy to make sure he finds a new home now, someplace safe from the butcher. There's gotta be a flock in Ocala or something we can find him, right?" She took hold of the leash and guided him the rest of the way amongst the stacks of boxes, flashed me a pleading gaze. The woman set the bucket on the mat, let her downturned eyes plead around the room.

I shot Katie a fierce look of disapproval, which was my father's, then concealed it with something more flabbergasted. "We really don't know the first thing," I said, knowing full well that we'd just passed Sheep 101 in the matter of a few minutes.

"Well, bless you for trying," said the woman, already halfway into the yard. "We really don't have the takers on this side of the street, so we appreciate your understanding. He's got all his shots and just had his checkup."

Feigning intrigue, Katie closed the door. I was shocked. "She didn't want to hold hands for a parting prayer?" I wondered aloud, but Katie didn't follow. She was looking at Paul like he was peering out from a cramped cage at a Third World zoo. "You miss your sweetie-pie Ann, don't you Pauly Shore? Why do those names sound so familiar? Paul? Ann?"

"They're your grandparents, nimrod. Seems Mom's not the only one who likes to name her pets after people from the past. Can you get him on the porch, please? It smells enough like shit in here as it is." I raised a palm to Paul and turned histrionically away. "I resist the urge to consider Paul's cuteness and noble struggle for meaning and true love. Away with him."

"That's right," Katie said on the way to the porch. "Paul and Ann."

"Don't worry: They're fleshed out in Journal Two, a real barn-burner. You think Dad was King Dick…"

"No, I don't," she said, guiding Paul and his shrieking bleats through the dining room. "More like Prince of Pain." She made sure the screen door on the porch was locked, set the bucket of food beside Paul, then closed the sliding-glass door behind her.

Paul turned to stare at them, his dime-sized nostrils snorting snot down the window. I added dismissively, "Earl of Emptiness, Lord of the Lost. The man was a prick and you know it. Won't he just ram his way out of there or something? Isn't that what rams do? Ram into shit?"

"Apparently not. Just don't piss him off until I can ask Mom if she wants him."

"For chops, maybe."

She couldn't pin that smile down.

* * *

Katie was done with sleuthing. "You keep reading that boring-ass paper if you want," she said, a weary rasp I'd never heard, before chirping away with the second journal back to Mom's house. "I can't imagine finding anything inside that rainbow but the color black."

"Where are you going with that journal then?" A coy smile came out of her. I appreciated her reshaped view of reality, the emerging cynic, though I knew it would be fleeting, lasting just until she'd had a chance to smoke the day's first joint and finish her reading. I centered the remaining copy of the *Eagle* on the coffee table so as not to forget it. I knew she'd ask for it later tonight.

This left Paul tapping his horns dangerously against the glass. He seemed imperiled with just us left there alone. I was afraid to leave him but had to take the Regal up to the U-Haul and have a tow bar installed to rent a trailer, which cleaned out my checking account. I hadn't planned on bringing all this back. I actually welcomed the vision of buying new bookshelves and piling all these books up around my new apartment. Two steps forward. I had some cash and maybe $100 in savings for gas home, food and cigarettes until school started in a week. One step back.

I emptied out the rest of the house, leaving the dining room table and couches for the next tenant to remove. My arms were weak, shaking from the work. Then, by 4 o'clock, I stood staring down his bedroom, the nest within the nest. The last of his trash.

The books were easy to start with, then his dresser drawers, which revealed nothing anyone would ever want. The nightstand drawer housed a bedraggled array, an incomplete-yet-telling glimpse into an unkempt bachelor addict's nightly routine: hardened gummy worms, frozen in place like fossils; shards of Pringles; some condom wrappers; unwrapped sticks of gum, barbed with pot shake; playing cards; UNO cards; unsent and unsigned birthday cards for "Son" and "Daughter"; several pens stripped to the casings, presumably for snorting things; a handful of paper scraps with addresses, phone numbers and, on one of them, a lip-sticked kiss; and, most fuddling, two identical keys that didn't fit any locks here, on a ring that was cluttered up with a mass of NA keychains in every color of the spectrum. It was like finding a bunny in a chicken coop. I felt the word "harrumph" forming in my mind.

I was down to his closet when, entering the living room, I spotted Serge peering in through the window. It made me fall over the "coffee table" and spill open the box of books in my arms. I opened the door slowly, flushed and out of breath.

"Hi, um, Magumfrey," he said. He was wearing the same Mt. Dew shirt under baggy denim overalls that looked too clean to be his. His enormous boots were spit-shined like a soldier's. His hair and beard were combed and cinched in blue rubber bands. A big hand reached out for a shake, and, since he didn't look capable of being menacing this way, I gave it to him. "We're all grown up now, huh?"

His mitt still holding mine, I couldn't contain the quaking that shuddered from my spine out to my fingertips. I feared the worst, of course. That's what people do. But I spoke in a way to ignore it. "Speak for yourself," I said. "Comin' in?"

"Sure," Serge said, looking in my eyes incredulously. "I thought you was gonna hit me or some shit."

"Bygones."

"Huh?"

"I'm past it."

"I seen you over here, Saul..."

"Uh-huh..." I swallowed hard but my mouth was dry, despite not having smoked any weed that day.

"...but I couldn't think of what I was supposed to come and say," he said, sitting down on the couch like he'd been there before. "I got enough to be embarrassed about, and then you seeing me scrounging for cigarette butts before payday? All the helium just came right out of my sails. But I didn't want you gone without telling you sorry about what happened to your Pa."

"Well that's nice, Sergio," I said, knowing he hated his proper name. "I really appreciate it. He wasn't doing too well."

"Always real nice to me, especially after my Dad killed my Mom and stupid Renaldo went and killed my Dad. Should be rotting in prison, not Renaldo." Serge stared off into the ceiling and I couldn't help my jaw from slackening. "I'm sorry for a lot. Like how me and Renaldo was such big dicksticks to everybody, especially you. You was always shitting your pants, and I don't know why we liked that."

"I'm so sorry too," I said. "I didn't know. About..."

"He had it coming, but the rest of us..." He was staring out the back door. I heard the ram knocking his hooves on the glass ominously and bleating in staccato bursts. I looked over my shoulder. "Think something's wrong with Paul."

We rushed to the porch and saw an alligator, the alligator, in the backyard, slinking closer to the porch. It was bigger than Serge, who was a head taller and twice as big around as the 6-foot, 170-pound me, top-mop notwithstanding. The gator saw us but didn't stop approaching the porch in a slinking primordial rite. When it reached the door, its rounded toothy snout dented the flimsy aluminum kick plate. I shuddered and moved to stand behind Serge without realizing how ridiculous it looked. Paul bleated furiously now. Another lunge from the gator buckled the plate and popped two of four screws loose. Then the gator burst halfway through the door. It bent its open mouth in a hiss to show us its throat, its utter lack of dread. It was trapped, wedged in the door, at least for the moment. Switching to a low panicked growl, its little T-Rex legs could only kick off its instinctual death spin. Still stuck and hissing.

Before I could think of 9-1-1, I was in my father's closet and pumping his shotgun on the way back to the porch, where I slid the door open and took quick aim at the gator's head. I thought of my father's foot and Dharma inside it – way too much sustenance from one family for just one dinosaur. I blasted its head all over the porch screens. The hot shell hit Serge in the face, but he didn't flinch.

"Bad. Fucking. Ass, Magumfrey!"

"McGinty!" I started to laugh to suspend the tear that almost fell from my eye.

"McGinty! Right! That's the gator ate your Dad's foot, man! Holy shit!"

"And my cat," I reported, then added for the record, "Maybe."

I was spent. I felt like the shot had come out of my gut, up the barrel of my esophagus, through my mouth and into any dread I had left. "*Fuck*, right?"

"Fuck is right," Serge agreed.

After the police had come and gone, at the behest of an unnamed neighbor who'd reported the shot, Serge helped me try to yank the gator out of the door, which ended up off the hinges instead. The cops suggested we sell the meat, but we dragged the door and gator as one back down the slope into the woods, which should be called a jungle there. Slithery sounds receding from every step, I steered to make sure we pulled it back down the abbreviated stone path my father had made. It was overgrown with vines but still there. When we got to the pond, Serge picked the gator up like a mannequin and hurled it into the water.

"Your Dad said that gator was gonna end up eating me and my brother if I kept fucking with you all the time, and I believed that crazy fucker," Serge said. "Don't think a crazy fucker ain't telling the truth, right?"

Our laughter filled the jungle with humanity.

A few minutes later, I was hosing the bloody brain matter off the screens and concrete when Serge volunteered, without request, to take Paul off my hands. "We're buds," he assured me, clarifying, "Me and Paul. Buds. But he should be ashamed of that little ball-less sack back there. No more pussy for Paul, ain't that right? Ann was it. Can't do no better than that." He was cooing like Paul was a Pomeranian or a newborn baby.

"Sure you're not just stocking up a freezer full of meat for the winter?" I asked, keeping a smile planted as I wound up the hose outside. "You do work at a butcher shop. Wouldn't be the weirdest thing."

"Your Dad said the rams don't even taste good, not like the lambs and ewes. But I think Paul would want to be food. What's he gonna do with all that muscle when he's dead? He's got a few good years left in him, though."

"Send me some? Maybe some jerky, a roast?"

"I'll send you his fucking head on a stick, how's that?" A long pause. I stepped back like he'd punched me. "Relax, Junior. 'Course I will. He's still got some kick, though, don't you Paul? And look at that coat. How's about that? Maybe learn to make knitting or some shit. Make knitting? Wait..."

"I feel you," I said.

A pink sun was halved by the tops of the trees and screened by a tall pile of clouds by the time Serge headed back up Walnut Circle with his new pet, which at one point butted his new shepherd with a gratefully gentle tap of the horns. Aghast was my smile – and a little victorious. Fleetingly sentimental, I saw their backs cut a silhouette that was no less sweet than cute. It might not have been enough to keep me from thinking later of Paul hanging, gutted, by a hind leg from Serge's garage door opener. But it was enough.

*   *   *

I had my father's as-yet-uncharged laptop and death-day paper on the front seat, all his junk in the trailer or kicked to the curb; the whole length of tree lawn was a scavenger's anti-climax. I kept smiling, on pace to conquer the sunset. A '50s-era vacuum, spewing decades of dour scents, preceded my last pass through the bedrooms. A matted shop broom got the tile clean enough. A hard, shrunken sponge glazed the counters with scouring soot. By magical make-believe, they pulled me along. *Be our guest! Be our...*

"Ha-HA!" I announced to no one in particular, standing on the stoop. Two doors down, a teen girl in spandex and tube top glanced over from getting the mail. My face darkened. I smiled. So did she, in a way. "Just got done," I explained. "Couldn't tell," she replied then moved on.

Two cars were in the Arbuckle driveway when I went across to drop off the key a day early. "I'm the auctioneer," said the silver-haired man with the red bulbous nose at the door – a little too slowly, I thought. "My partner," he added, motioning to the silver-haired woman with the red bulbous nose behind him, also with clipboard. Concise, though.

I gave him the key and asked if he could deliver it to the family. He took it and asked if I wanted an advance poke through Faithland. "Make us an offer," he said. "Early bird discount." I had $20 in my wallet. As awkward as ever, I slipped inside.

With the couple back to marking merchandise with little tabs of masking tape, I passed quickly and unbothered through the rooms, a mirror version of my father's house, only this one was crammed tight with religious icons and Bible study books. Nothing but a few random pictures and mementoes had been claimed so far. The garage was still an organized heap of tools I'd never use. The family apparently didn't even fancy the cuckoo clock with a toddler, cloth-diapered Jesus poking his head out every hour to clang his kettle of frankincense. I avoided the shrine room like a smallpox incubator, but the other rooms held at least a passing fancy. Still, nothing of interest struck my eye until I poked my head in the closet in Mrs. Arbuckle's room and reemerged with a shoebox containing a clunky, shoulder-mounted video camera and a few VHS tapes, one labeled cryptically: "U.S."

"Ten bucks for the camcorder," the man said at the open front door. "Think that's what those are called." A theatrical laugh. "Tapes are free. Don't even sell those anymore do they?" I gave him my $20 and he gave me back change in seconds from a wad of bills in his front pocket.

"How much for the cuckoo?" I asked.

"Oh, that's not for sale," the woman said in a mad garbled dash from one of the bedrooms. "That's just priceless. We had dibs on that from the get. Not to brag, but we're putting it up in the dining room, maybe the parlor. Who knows? Maybe we take it on *Antiques Roadshow*. I can't imagine it's worth anything less than..."

The man shrugged his shoulders and smiled, shut the door.

I felt utterly insouciant all the way to the car, which started on the first turn of the key. Thought of the security deposit and then promptly forgot about it. I didn't even need to pull out my bowl before I put the car in drive. I took one last look, hit the brakes with both feet. The front light was on, the front blinds closed. I'd left the light off, the blinds open.

My mind flittered about for reasoning and came back with: somehow the man or his wife wanted dibs on whatever might be left inside, so they sealed things up under my nose to keep out prying eyes. Or an Arbuckle asked them to do that when they got the key back and I hadn't seen them do it. Or ... Silly, to think.

Chapter 11

WHEREAS, the Freeburg way of life is now reflective of the Nation's, its stark divide between haves and have-nots a deep valley to bury its people alive. This valley runs crooked along yet another that's deeper and darker but fully disguised: on either side, Mount Freedom of Republicans and Mount Equality of Democrats. Long heralded as glue to keep cemented this winding river that directs Us, these craggy peaks instead have served to keep at bay all those who would upset the norm, with every problem that floats its way downstream to wash upon this shore or that. Freeburg voters know these peaks shade only camps with equal aims – to keep their wealth and buy more power to make more.

I entered my mother's house around dinnertime feeling tranquil, the camcorder box in one hand, the *Eagle* outstretched in the other, just in time for Katie to crash like a wave from the kitchen onto my shore in the foyer.

"Give me that...oh," she said, her face inside the paper folds, her hand, also outstretched, pinching at my beard.

"Mom here?" I asked. "Her mind-reader son needs a shingle of his own."

"You're right," said Katie, heading to the couch with no patience for games. "Grandpa Paul was a dick. Poor Grammy. Poor Daddy."

"Poor's right. At least we know who to blame now for all our demons. Where's Mom?"

"Watering Dad. I wish we could have read all that when he was still alive. I might have sent a Christmas present every once in a while."

"Why? He never did. Was that Grandpa Paul's fault, too?"

"Guess not. Where *is* Paul?"

We both stopped to laugh a little. That sheep could have had no better name.

"At his new house," I said. "A neighbor wanted him." I set the box on the high-backed settee across from the couch then started packing a bowl. "You want a drink?" I asked. Katie was leering at me. "...'cause I want a drink. You making a drink?"

I didn't know how to reveal all of what had happened to me that day. I suspected that more terrible things were yet to be seen. I lit the bowl as Katie went to the kitchen to play bartender. "Rollin' down the street, smokin' indo, sippin' on gin and juice..." she sang in the kitchen.

"Laid baaaaaack...." I added from my cloud of despair.

Was I honor-bound to reveal the details right away? Only nestled in the context of the day's events could my decision ever be viewed as responsible. I was proud to recount the story, perhaps cross-legged from the chaise, channeling the diction of James Lipton, omniscient posture of a swami. I waited from that perch for my mother to shimmy back inside. Maybe I wouldn't mention Serge at all.

"You and Serge killed a fucking alligator?" Mom started in, with Katie finishing, "You shot it on the fucking porch?!"

"Easy sailors," I admonished, one regal palm aloft to face the scrutiny. "That's right. It was the least I could do to avenge us all."

"You ever hear of the animal warden?" asked Katie, stomping her foot to let me know that her question held the answer.

"The fucker was picking us off one at a time," I said, uncrossing my legs. "He had it coming. He ate my cat. He ate Dad's foot, and he already was a cripple. Paul was next. Who then?"

"Who's Paul?" my mother stammered.

She'd get her answer in due time. "All that separated that monster from us was a thin pane of glass. This thin." I squeezed a thumb and index finger together. "It was him or us. He had to go. You know I'm no killer, but I will kill if kill I must!"

"Who *are* you, 'tard?" Katie was red-faced. "Did they have you surrounded? It was stuck in the door. He could have been a her, stoop. She could have had starving babies waiting for her back in the pond. Hawk-bait babies now."

"She could have been pregnant," added my mom.

Katie pointed at my mom while keeping her eyes on me. "It could have been any alligator," said Katie, "which, as I'm sure even history teachers have to learn at some point, have to eat to live."

"How could you shoot anything out of anger, Saul?" asked my mother. Katie pointed at her again. "It's just not like you. Like you were with Rebecca."

"You weren't there," I said, my shoulders sagging now, my eyes averted, words garbled. "Ask Serge. That fucker had it coming."

"Oh, it's Serge and Saul now, sitting in a tree," singsonged my mother. "Those Arredondos made you cry almost every weekend of fifth grade, son. Serge probably killed your Dharma with a BB to the eyeball. Why didn't you shoot his ass? Couldn't figure out how to reload?"

Serge's apologies, news of his father's final spin on self-destruct, only added more consonance to their scorn.

"Made *you* feel like a big man," said my mom, "but all it did was add another scar to that man's heart. Got a problem? Grab the gun! Problem solved. He's probably back there right now, taking it all out on that poor ball-less sheep."

"I cleaned up the mess," I said, staring at my toes. My poise was utterly vaporized. "This is ridiculous. I'm not ashamed. Drop it." Maybe I was a little ashamed; definitely not proud of myself like before.

Katie took the *Eagle*, journals and suicide note out to the front porch swing. *Slam.* My mother made to leave for the store out the back door, so I asked if she still had a VCR. "Guestroom closet, upstairs," she said without looking over. "Tough guy." *Slam.*

After plying Katie with some of my mother's stash, luring her inside to the couch, she softened visibly but stayed glued to the paper. "You're reading everything?" "Yep." "That's brave." "Not like taking out a dinosaur for sport or anything." She managed a sliver of a smile, which was enough. "Least you gave its meat back to the jungle."

"I'm whipped," I said. "Think I'll turn in early." A lie preceded by a truth is easiest concealed.

"With the VCR?" asked Katie. "Can't unload that kind of guilt with Dad's porn, Saul. I guarantee that."

"Laugh," I said.

I'd take this one for the team. One tape turned out to be Arbuckle family gatherings in fast-forward. The prevailing expressions of the younger generations were unimpressed, exasperated, Christmas to Easter, miracle birth to resurrection. I don't know how, but I'd guessed correctly that the other tape would hit much closer to home, that "U.S." stood for Ursula and Saul.

At least they seemed to have made something like love. At least they were a little younger. At least my father was sometimes right. At least I could fast forward.

*   *   *

I felt so crestfallen, disgusted, bewitched and bemused that falling asleep seemed the only way out. I'd just called Escondido at home on a whim, imagining that, even though it was only primetime, I'd woken up a bare-assed Andy Sipowicz of *NYPD Blue* in the middle of the night. ME: *"Are you sitting down?"* HIM: *"I'm sleeping, John. This better be good."*

"No doubt, son, this points to some kind of weird doings," the real detective said, before hushing a child he referred to as "baby doll," "but not necessarily that a crime was committed. See? This could have been made with all parties' full knowledge. Just throw it away. It'll eat a hole through your heart and the drawer that it's in. It's gross, but there's people who do this out there, just swinging and swinging, one tree to the next. But say this guy or his wife, what's their names? ... yeah, Arbuckle, say they *were* taping his comings and goings, him or her. Well, the interested parties are no longer, well, interested. See? ... Son? See?"

I saw. I said, "Sorry," hung up and rolled over. So my father was a spectator sport for a dirty old man and his dirty old wife? So what?

The curtain was lace and open to stars and, below, the second floor windows of Cassadaga Hotel. Just one set of curtains were open. Inside, a young couple embraced, kissing curtly. Overloaded and dry with puritanical scorn, my eyes shut themselves against my brain's better wishes, and though I rarely remember my dreams, even nightmares, that time I did, every rote scrap of detail. As my mother insists, I was "touched by one of my angels," to which Katie still adds, "Molested maybe."

As I'm told nightmares will go, it all started serenely, with me driving the Regal at night and humming along to my pre-broken stereo. "On a steeeel horse Iii riiide..." I marveled at how the exhaust pipe was quiet, how my voice could actually carry along the melody. Then, as I've also been warned that dreams can shift and transfigure in a second, I was fleeing from something and nervous. It was them – the Arbuckles, the creeps – on my tail in a sports car, one headlight apiece. I sped up. They sped up. I braked, but I couldn't. The Regal was revving but not from my foot. The rattling exhaust took the radio's place. A yank on the emergency brake, a turn of my father's NA keychain: nothing worked. From desolate country into a packed city, my city of Freeburg, I braced for the end of my life and the lives of my victims. The woebegone houses were a blur on each side, as, ahead in the distance, a stooped figure hobbled into the road and froze like a dumbstruck deer. It was him, as you've guessed, but somehow also me. He got bigger and bigger, his face dumber and dumber, his foot planted deeper and deeper in place. I panicked: *Here goes.* Since dreams can reportedly also seem real and make stupid decisions seem entirely wise, I screamed through the windshield, "NOOOO!" then climbed to the backseat and buckled into the seatbelt. Why? Serge had taken the wheel, with Rebecca beside him demanding to drive, but Serge flicked her the finger and she threw herself out. We swerved just in time to miss Saul McGinty, then my eyes cinched tight for the oncoming crash. Instead, when they'd opened, Serge had vanished, the brakes worked, the radio wailed *"Aaaaaall ... riiiiight ... now..."* and the sun had come up to something like Freeburg, if Freeburg was something like somewhere else better. A reprieve, true relief, for a short jaunt through town from my road in the sky, floating free – random pealing of church bells, the trees in spring bloom, people actually walking, from this shop to that, a horizon of smokestacks all billowing money. It was even in the realm of real to see my mother alight into view amongst a flock of gulls, just waving and smiling from her push-broom ride, but then the sun, sharpening to a frigid white, was a spotlight revealing old Arbuckle, staring up with the shakes from my lap, dribbling drool. "Bless the Lord, how you've *grown*," she purred. Real panic erupted to curses and pleading for sleep, then I awakened to Katie standing over me and asking if I needed my binkie.

"Wha...?"

"Alcoe," is what she was really saying. "Grace Alcoe. Why's that name sound familiar?"

"Miss Emily's last name was Alcoe," I said, pressing my fists into my eyes. "I don't know Grace Alcoe. Maybe a relative?"

"Moooom!" she yelled with the bombast of Broadway.

"Kaaaatie!" she yelled back from her room up the hall. "Yaok?"

"Mokay," she said. I wasn't. It would be years before I'd be able to think lightly about any of this.

"Who's Grace Alcoe?"

"Hold on." She turned down the volume on the television, from a deep middle dent in her four-poster bed, and Katie's *Luck Struck* character stopped talking. "Can't tell if it's you or that bitch Madeline Brit talking. Grace is Miss Emily's youngest."

"Was," Katie said.

"Well, yeah. We all miss Miss Emmy. What a sensitive empath that one."

"No, Grace. She died in a fire, the day before Dad. A gas water heater exploded in her laundry room. She was sleeping on the couch in the next room and she was still there when they found her ... says she was on Freeburg Council for a term, but lost to some Republican in the last election. But," she checked the *Eagle*, "she was up for a comeback this year, running citywide, for an at-large chair ... Council President.... says the primary was too close to call a winner so they were set for the general in November ... fire marshall said it was a faulty gas line or faulty water heater or some ... couldn't be sure, since both blew...."

I was standing there now, behind Katie at my mother's door. Katie turned back and said apologetically, "That's all I could come up with. Sorry. It's nothing, right?"

"Poor, Wiley," said my mother. "That girl's all he had left. I didn't even know." She tossed back and forth like a rocking chair before she could swing her legs over and slide off the tall bed.

"Don't get burned?" I asked Katie.

"Don't get burned," answered my mother knowingly, slipping on her Birkenstocks and looking at the ceiling. "Curse you, Saul Sr. You old creep. Curse. You."

* * *

Wiley took down their shingle after Emily's second heart attack, the one that had finally made him what Emily called "a yin-less yang." He couldn't see replacing it with one that only had his name. Ten years her senior, at eighty-six, Wiley was supposed to be the first to go. He'd always joked that he should go ahead to see if it was safe. She'd always said, "That won't be needed, love. It is as it is."

As it was, at least a generation had gone by since anyone came calling just for Wiley Alcoe's counsel; they'd always wanted Emily or, more rarely, them as one. Widowed eleven years, he didn't have the eyes, ears or heart left to really listen and be of service to the seekers anyway, so he'd just sit around their Cracker cottage on Seneca Street and wait for the guidance that, any day now, unexpected, she might try to bring back from their long-shared beyond. *Ah, l'amour, si triste.*

Soon, his days would be measured in fossilized memories,

every change a new threat to the past they had shared. Like a cat, he'd stare out the front window and scowl at the throngs of new tourists; time to time, on blue days, he'd wheel through the new county park on Lake Colby and leer at all the "gawker Freeburgers" who'd be leering right back with, he knew, "faithless pity." He'd stayed free of the Temple from the night of her wake. He'd take most of his meals in his chair at the front window, factory microwaveables from a Lake Mary grocer, who still found it profitable to deliver to the elderly, rich and otherwise infirm. With Emily gone, he'd even stopped waving to neighbors and children, so, years later, no one ever tried waving or smiling at Wiley.

This had been his lot as a widower *with* Grace around, then his youngest of three girls was dead in a fire. His fate as a recluse was quietly sealed. Who else openly cared? His other kids were nearly old with tony empty nests themselves – in Amsterdam and San Diego – so maybe he'd see them at Christmas or funerals, get a call or one of those Skype messages now and then, here or there, but Grace had for three years been a widow herself and had never had kids but the ones that she'd teach to love words and their music. To Wiley's delight, she'd visit each Sunday to push him through the park and read Thoreau or Amichai on the lake shore. After retiring as an English teacher for the county school district, she'd started teaching poetry at New Smyrna Community College. She'd relay madcap stories about her new students or her new colleagues on Council, a job that she'd lost in a bitter campaign. From Grace, he had learned not all Freeburgers (sometimes "Freevillains") were awful. With her gone, they all were. He just *knew*. Every one.

For two weeks since her death, the curtain in the front window had been closed for the first time in decades. Wiley's whole life had become a death. He stayed on the couch crying, barely ate, slept or moved. "Die," he told the quiet. "Die." So, of course, he was startled to standing when our rapping echoed through the house; his hearing aid turned them to slaps against his skull.

"Holdonholdonholdon...!" he bellowed, interrupting the next more insistent round of knocks. "Can't have just anybody walking on in." He finally got to his wheelchair and navigated through the cramped parlor. "Who the hell is it?"

"Deacon Wiley, it's Ann. Guru Ann, over Marion Street? Got my kids out here, too – Saul and Katie, remember? Can we have a quick word?" Hiding the door, my mother took up the entire width of the porch. Katie and I stood in line on the wheelchair ramp. "We was just wondering..."

The faded red door creaked open. Mr. Alcoe rolled his chair back from beside the opening and peered up squinting into the noon glare, as if witnessing a landing spaceship. It would have been scary if it weren't so sad. What strands remained of too-white hair danced free with static in all directions from a greasy-pink and liver-spotted dome. His tall, lank frame was a POW's, evident in how the elbows and single knee stuck out inordinately far from the chair; the other leg, my mother says, had been claimed by gout that he'd ignored after Emily died. Food crusted the corners of his mouth and stained parts of his plain white V-neck, which was really yellow and several sizes too big. He had on black dress slacks, with the left leg hemmed into a pouch and both thighs stained to lighter shades from being used for days as a napkin. It was obvious he hadn't showered in maybe a week or even since the funeral. I thought of my father. Wearing a clown's frown that I couldn't have pretended, I looked far east toward the lake as a way to offer my respects. "Sorry," I whispered about everything to everyone.

"Hope y'all ain't looking for a reading. These damn cataracts – can't find my glasses much less the old astral body around here nowheres." This seemed to be his stock excuse for anything a visitor might be wondering these days, like whether Alzheimer's was sinking in, if he was still in the business or even perhaps on the cusp of a raging nervous breakdown. "C'mon back, Miss Anderson. Emily just loves your work. So how's the hunt?"

"Fine, fine," my mother said, inhaling deep and turning sideways to fit through the door. "We just couldn't help but think you might be needing some company, Wiley, what with all..." She trailed off in her way, following his chair into the kitchen, the dining room. We gaggled behind like her ducklings.

"What with what?" Wiley asked, coming to a stop at the table and turning just far enough for the hearing aid in his droopy left ear to pick up the signal. Before my mother could answer, his hands fell from the wheel tops. His arms swung like thin pendulums of loose skin. For a fleeting minute, he'd forgotten why he was supposed to be sad.

"What with everything you've been going through," my mother said. "Such an untethered soul that Grace, just like Miss Emily. And Grace: how well-prepared she was to grow into that name. What joy I'll bet it's been to have such love so long to warm you." She rolled it around her tongue then added, "What grace."

Transfixed by the delivery, I looked at my mother's mouth, then away into several glass cabinets of dried-up herbs and gypsy philters, not wanting her to see the admiration in my eyes.

"Emily named the girls," he said out of nowhere. "Old coot mechanic medicine man like me ain't qualified to think of naming his baby girls Hope, Faith and Grace. I'd have to say Grace was the only one to live up to the name, though. Hope and Faith lost theirs before they'd even had any. Oh they got hope and faith, sure, but in all the wrong things. There's always tomorrow, a-guess."

"Well now..." my mother added to shush her elder. The words seemed incongruously pure coming out of Wiley's muddied gourd. He'd even stumped the guru, at least for the few moments it took for her to add, "No doubt they've got more of both than most. Hard-chargers, those two: Lawyer and a vet, right? Big families?"

"Ach." He erased the words with his left hand thrown across his chest. It hit his right shoulder and fell limp to his lap.

Warily, as if approaching an open casket, we circled a dining room table cluttered with unopened bills, spent cans of Ensure and a few stacks of TV dinners that should have been in the freezer. Two cats stroked along the sliding glass door outside. Their bowls sat empty by the kitchen counter. We sat down and stared at him intently from every side.

"Mr. Alcoe," my mother said. "Katie said she could make you a sandwich or something while we talk. Is that all right?"

Katie, protesting with just her eyes, went into the kitchen and started rummaging through the fridge. My leg bounced impatiently.

"I know this..."

"We know," I said, "that this is a hard time for you, Mr. Alcoe. How couldn't it be? We recently lost our father, and he was nowhere near the person that your Grace or Emily were. My mother's right" – I looked at her and smiled – "untethered souls. But we're really interested, sir, in what you have to say about, well, you know, how Grace died."

"What you mean *what I think?*" he demanded, looking at me. "What *is* this? Grace was my life! She..."

"Nonosir, no, of course," I clarified, the alpha women fidgeting with exasperation. "What I mean, what we all mean is, is *how*, the *how* and *why* of *how* your daughter died. The fire, sir. The *why* and *how*."

"You lost me, boy," he said. "Cruel is what, to bring this type of talk in here. Inspector said it wasn't set, a gas line blew, heater blew. That's your *how* and your *why* right there."

Katie sat back at the table empty-handed, signaling that the fridge and cupboards were bare. She'd filled the empty bowls with cat food and water, though. I spied her expectant expression, the same as my mother's. They seemed to be bracing for my next volley. They wanted me to serve it.

"Mr. Alcoe, maybe all this is for nothing, and it very well could be just that. For that, we apologize. *So. Much.* But for some reason, my father, who died the very day after Grace, my Dad expressed more than a little, I guess, suspicion, fear. He was afraid of something strange, something evil, some evil tinkering in Freeburg. Of late."

"Evildoing, Wiley," my mother corrected. "Something bad. Witches tinker, Saul. Gypsies tinker. They *don't*, well.... Wiley, my ex, he thought – and, mind you, he was wrong more than right on more days than not – but he had pretty good reason to think,

251

reason to fear that maybe Grace's accident, that Grace's fire wasn't just a fluke like how it looked."

"Evil afoot. In Freeburg, you say?" He twisted up a dimple, closed an eye and stared out through the other at each of us like the butler in Frankenstein's manor. Some blessed calming wave, perhaps dementia, washed over him then and let him creak his red mouth open in a weak try at a smile. "Roll a bowling ball down Main Street and watch the freaks fly."

"Well, more specifically, sir, he seemed to suspect that the fire was..."

"No," Wiley said, his gray eyes back to marbles. "Not my Grace. Even the students she failed'd come back to visit. Enemies – those is something she didn't have. Well, no kind of enemies'd..."

"What was she up to these days?" asked my sister, tossing out the sort of line I should have cast first. Of course: She'd played an ace reporter, too, that one time on Fox. "*Eagle* says she'd gotten on the campaign trail again. Poll worker in the story says she used to walk the ward and knock on every door. She must have loved it. That's a tall order for somebody half her age, especially in downtown Freeburg. I can't imagine anybody, not even Grace, making those poor people happy. She ever talk about those times?"

"What times? So what?" Something surged through Wiley. He had ants in the pants, raging 'rhoids or both. He turned his wheelchair to face the table and seemed, for the first time, capable of self-sufficiency. "She had that whole ward singing praises, up one crummy block and down the next. Stepping on all the cracks. Don't ask me why. I know she hated being at home since Aaron died. Those two did everything together. I don't know: I don't think it was the politics; it was how she got to keep touching people, hand to hand. She told everybody, 'Call me Grace,' and everybody did, everywhere that old girl went. She was always bringing me cakes and casseroles they'd make her. It was too much for one mouth to ever eat. She was too busy to ever eat with me, always just snacked behind the wheel. I rode with her a few times when she had things to do, but I could never stand that place, all the concrete and boarded-up stores that Wal-Mart made. You ever spot any happy people, you know, just there? Didn't think so. But she was gonna make things better all by herself, right where the wounds were the deepest. I'd tell her all the time, sometimes in a breath, how proud I was to have such a sorry judge of character as my last daughter. That always made her beam that little girl smile of hers like nothing else. I always said that when I couldn't think of things to say, so, figure the odds, I think it ended up being the very last thing I said to her. Course, it could have been something else."

"I wish I could have met her," I said, staring into his eyes to show him that I meant it but also that this detour, though surely therapeutic for him, wasn't getting us anywhere. "She sounds like the kind of politician we need out there – you know? – inspired people with a way with words...."

"But not bullshit," Wiley added. "That's one thing that always got that red pen of hers flying. People would ask her all the time when the city planned to start boarding up all the vacancies or cracking the whip on all them thugs, and she'd tell 'em, flat-out, 'Maybe when some of you folks show up with me at the mayor's office to demand it. Think they listen to *me* up there? You get organized, though, and I'll be with you every step of the way.' She had such a teacher's way of being stern and sweet in the same sentence, she could get away with saying goodbye with things like, 'A good ante up would be to pick up all this trash in your yard. They might think you got a hand.' They'd go and do it right then, too. And keep doing it. Don't get me wrong now: She never had no more than maybe four people at any of her ward meetings, but she didn't run into people in the ward giving her any sour looks either. It was all, 'Miss Grace, give me a job!' or 'Amaaaaaazin' Graaaace...' They could tell she cared enough to tell it to 'em straight."

Being neither a poet nor a politician, I was still of the mind that, talent or pluck notwithstanding, both were at the core highly specialized and glorified bullshit artists. *It's in their job descriptions*, I thought then. *And hadn't Grace Alcoe tried to fit herself into both of those molds?* I scrunched my eyes at the old man, sizing up *his* hand. I would choose my words respectfully, but I would also find a way to fill in all the shadows and blemishes on this grieving father's caricature of his favorite child. As I'd already told this over-done and dried-up medium, I really wish I could have met her, but since I hadn't, she was too good to be true to the man I was then. Just as I didn't feel the need to actually be a poet or politician to spot one, not being trained as a detective would not prevent me from discovering Grace Alcoe's weaknesses, thereby revealing her truest sworn enemies.

"Takes courage to speak the truth like that to strangers," I said, dipping a toe in at the edge. "Especially when the truth hurts or when the strangers probably will just end up taking it for more lies. She must not have been afraid of anybody. Hard to believe that kind of idealism didn't ruffle at least a few feathers. I'm willing to bet at least a few of the hands she shook were too cold to ever warm up, you know? She had heart, but some of the best bullshiters seem to have 'em too. Wiley, isn't it likely that at least a few of those constituents were distrustful enough to put on some happy masks to cover up some hateful feelings?"

His face was a statue. Nothing was getting through. I felt awkward at first, especially with a regular Emmy winner in the room, but I decided to put my all behind the best Hispanic grandmother impression I could muster. " 'G'dace? Oh, tank ju G'dace for taking dee time out of djour beezy daze spending djour penchun dolling up dat beeg house of djours by dee spreeng, and jes to rye all dee trubbles in owr huarts in djur leetle cleepbuard? Por su puesto, dju weel haff my vote. Ai, dios mio, dju don turn G'dace away, doo dju? Dju jez puromise deez, G'dace, dat dju wheel go to Ceetee 'all and dju wheel tell it on zee mountain der – jus az we say eet ees. Do jew puromise us, G'dace'?"

I tilted my head an inch to the side, waiting for Wiley to either launch into my face or into something helpful. His eyes narrowed to see the look I was wearing. I wasn't wearing one, but Katie and my mother were: they were red with contempt for what today I can clearly recognize as a stereotypically white-bread stab at Spanglish. Gallantly, or at least curious, Wiley let me off the hook with a grin so slight that I'd almost missed it.

"Maybe at City Hall she had a few foes, who don't? But even the worst of 'em, they knew deep down she was right or at least she wanted to be. She had a way of finding the truth in things and pointing it out, even when everybody else was just shoveling lies on top of it to keep things in order. She had a way with things like that, of showing you her heart, and not just with the cameras rolling. Know why the worst students kept coming back, even more than her best ones? Her favorites were the worst. She'd get to yank them furthest from the dark. The light, course, is scary for your average politi-*coe*. Not my Grace. That girl was hell-bent on teaching that gas-bag Henderson a lesson. Know him? In the last race, that cad got on the radio and tells the town how she's a witch just like her folks, that we was in cahoots to ruin Freeburg, to make it communist like it is here in Cassadaga. The low-life acne scar. Like we don't like our money over here as much as the next."

"Silly, to think," said my mother, looking at me, who looked at Katie, who was looking straight at Wiley, looking lost. "So," Katie said, taking over from a new cornerstone, "this Henderson. What's he do nowadays, besides, of course, the people's business?"

"Question is: What don't he do? He's Captain America, for crissakes!" Wiley pounded the table with his fist. Finally. "Got that magical shield that's also a weapon, wouldn't you know? The man's everywhere 'cept his own damn ward: selling them big jim-dandy loans at the bank, leading his Boy Scout troop of clones, coaching Little League – who can watch that sport? – even ushers the old widows to their graves over at St. Bernadette's. (Times like these, see, you can't just network any-old-place.) He's not like Grace, like Grace was, eyeball to eyeball, word for word. He'd rather hang with the goobersnootchers over there at the country club and tell his people through the tube how much he cares. And don't go thinking I hate the bastard just because he turned us down for a refinance back in '86. That's beside the point; fact, that might be the only good thing he's done in life; that bill would have jacked us up real good."

"How far you think a guy like Henderson would be willing to go, Wiley, to keep Grace from getting back on Council?" pushed

Katie, in the fastidious character of a grad student. "I mean, why did he even run?"

Wiley shrugged. I rolled my eyes despairingly. *How the hell does this centenarian know about the underhanded machinations at the Freeburg Masonic Lodge, Katie?* Wiley saw the look in my face, but I couldn't remove it.

That foolish feeling kept churning in the place that calls itself my brain. Here we were – Dad's sheep, feeling our way through his darkness. I stumbled upon the thought that, somewhere out there in the nether-regions of purgatorial bliss, my father could see us all sitting here, at last as one and fully enveloped in what was still very likely to be his farewell Amish ambush. *If he could shepherd us this close to the cliff,* I thought, *it wasn't a stretch to think he could probably lead us right off the edge.*

"I'll bet he lives in one of those McMansions on the other side of the spring," I added. "Probably could care less whether he won or not. Just trying to drum up some more exposure, get the wife to give it up again."

"Close, son. He's out a few miles past where Grace lived, in one of them gated communities they just plunked down out there. He's in the same ward, but not by much. If he lived another block from downtown, he wouldn't just be over that line, he'd be in the next county. Not sure about the wife situation. We're not close, as you can tell. I sure as hell wouldn't let that asshole inside me, I'll tell you that. But one thing's sure: He wants that Council chair and now he's gonna get it without a fight. Banker man's got all the right folks fooled. Just once I thought this talk show host was getting ready to nail him to the wall, and it was only just a slow pitch. Daddy Warbucks just hands every bit of the housing crisis blame to his own customers, with this jolly giggle to make like none of it's as big a deal as everybody's making things out to be. The host is just givin' him the old reach-around while he's spewing the party line. Says buyers had their heads so far up in the welfare clouds for so long that they couldn't recognize rain, much less an adjustable rate mortgage. Says, 'It's right there in the bottom line, but they just want to know where to sign.' Says, 'We was only doing what the laws says we could'."

We all gasped when Wiley got out of his chair and let the cats in, then padded over to a kitchen cabinet and popped a few pills from a bottle at the sink. He sat back down and looked up. "Get on with it now."

"Wiley, how's a grubstaker like that get elected to a liberal town like Freeburg?" my mother asks Wiley, as if he were James Carville. "There's more soup kitchens than nice streets in that ward."

I braced for nonsense, stammering, silence or some of all; he wasn't even leaving the house at this point, much less reading the paper. Turned out, he'd been having more conversations with Grace about her political life than he'd earlier led on. He sounded like he hated Damon Henderson for more than just being an asshole, too. The man could die any minute of any number of ailments, from crotch rot to walking corpse syndrome, and it seemed as though he'd be content to do it while cursing Damon Henderson's name. He appeared to be answering my mother's questions in his head first, jotting them all down with his eyes on some scrap of imaginary paper, before reciting his scornful tally, top to bottom. I still wouldn't be surprised to learn that those pills were amphetamines.

"Well, don't you know, Miss Ann, the soup kitchen vote ain't all that much reliable for one. The vote in Grace's ward ain't all that reliable either. Then, a course, you have to figure in the *Eagle* endorsement. That's a sure shot. All them ads he buys? All his friends' ads from the car dealerships and the real estate agencies and the chamber? Sure, maybe the newsroom over there's filled to the gills with liberals crying about the plight of the poor, but not in the rest of the building. That's where they're more likely to be bawling their eyes out over the plight of the ad department. The man..."

"Ain't that the truth, Wiley?" I added without thinking, just two old curmudgeons slugging back Guinness at the chip shop and cursing the Church of England. "Sorry."

"The man didn't just get endorsed," Wiley continued, right where I'd interrupted, "he got done abetted. Same day, top of the fold, front page, here's this story, Freddie Mac, Fannie Mae owning up to their little sliver of the swindle, and who's the quote they got all pulled out and repeated there in bold letters? Why, wouldn't you know, it's Captain American Express, the local angle, Damon Henderson hisself, all woe is him. Says, 'How were we supposed to know that all these seemingly upstanding people were getting set to renege on all their promises?' A real swindle, that one, a hustler's hustler. I tell you..."

Wiley started wheezing. He grabbed a bill off the table and hacked up a few coughs onto it before throwing it weakly toward the overflowing garbage can by the stove. "That town's got no more than – what? – a few thousand Republicans? But, watch, this operator's got the salesmanship to land himself the job of Council chair. All locked up now. All locked up them. What were the odds of an honest, level campaign anyway? Not with odds like that for Grace to overcome. Worst kind of Freevillain there is, that one. The rest is just Brownies and Cub Scouts. Nearly gave Grace a stroke, out there walking the whole city, asking for every vote one by one, with that ... what that P.T. Barnum say? He says, he says..."

His eyes fell to slits, the indignant tirade darkening to match the bruised lids now on display. He put a shaking hand over his heart, bowed his head. I braced myself to hear the first refrains of the National Anthem billow manically from some subconscious place he couldn't control, having just expended what remained of his brain cells to stave off the Alzheimer's just long enough for him to rail against the only enemy his dead daughter ever had.

"Wiley?" I asked. "You in there?" His eyes were open but they were looking at memories.

He looked petrified, but not from what we'd initially suspected: not a carotid embolism or oxygen starvation or insufficiency of recall or even unwelcome flashbacks to Grace or Emily when they were still alive, but from a glare of disquieting awareness that pushed the sun back into crannies that so long ago had shunned the light. He looked at me and frowned: "Never thought I'd have to set my foot in Freedom Spring again. You got gloves?"

*   *   *

The following is an unedited excerpt from a *Good Evening, Sunshine!* broadcast reluctantly provided by *Action News 1*, which, ignoring three requests and as many formal threats of litigation, was able to stall its release until three months after a November election, at which point Damon Henderson was able to secure yet another at-large post on Freeburg Council:

KIP KNIGHTLY [reciting largely from index cards off-camera]: *"...Mr. Henderson, as you're no doubt aware, this campaign season finds our democracy healthy and secure with all the mudslinging and fiery accusations the voters've come to rely on to help them navigate this vibrant super-marketplace of ideas. As with all debates, probably since caveman times, some of the allegations flying around are bound to be viewed as doubtful, but others have been quite pointed and revealing. For instance, you've directed a substantial portion of your campaign fund toward print, radio and television spots that question the fundamental patriotism of your opponent, Ms. Alcoe, alluding to a darker, treasonous side to this, and I quote, "poetess indoctrinator."* Do you remain convinced, Mr., Mr....* [moment of silence while Knightly finds his place in the cards] *...Mr. Henderson, that your opponent is indeed a communist or is just perhaps a little 'too lost in the clouds,' to borrow from one of your more 'bewitching' ads this season* [shared laugh], *that Councilwoman Alcoe is, shall we say, too grounded in fiction to serve with tangible results a constituency already beset with its fair share of hardships* [holds hand up to silence Henderson]. *The thing is, we here at Action News 1 have yet to hear from the opposition on this, perhaps we never will, but just for the sake of the viewers out there who may be jumping to conclusions and calling these characterizations alarmist or even litigious, would you help them understand. I mean, it's pretty clear isn't it? I guess what some viewers may be wondering, sir, is despite America's unquestioned dominance in* this post-Cold-War, free-market world, is Ms. Alcoe's position a threat to business as usual, the bottom line, and, in fact, even an act of subversive oppression against her very own neighbors? ... Go ahead...

HENDERSON: Nice hand-off, Kip. You sure know your history. Me, I lived a lot of mine, my history that is. Never was much for sitting around in a chair and wondering what life might be like if everybody threw all their money in a pot and let the government decide how much of it we get back. My buddies and me, we were knee-deep in Cambodian muck for two years trying to keep that kind of Stalin-scape on the other side of the planet. My opponent has repeatedly balked at responding to this fundamental question about her political agenda that, I can only suppose, must speak to some [looks at cards] underlying lack of civic morality [to camera]: Grace Alcoe, are you or are you not trying to turn my beloved Freeburg into a welfare state on ration cards that tells its citizens how many children they can have or limit how much money they get to save for Little Sue and Sammy's education? [To cards for long pause, then back to camera:] Is your aim, Ms. Alcoe, to drain our city coffers by driving out what business interests still remain here as job creators, just to exact some long-dead Marxist grudge against society that's only gonna harm the neighbors you pretend to care so much about, all those moms and pops who work their fingers dry just to find some meager slice of American pie at the end of the day? How dare you, madam. Whose pursuit of happiness are you really working for?

KNIGHTLEY [to camera]: Meaningful words there from a man who's clearly spent some time down in the trenches, important questions that, three weeks shy of Election Day, remain unanswered across the aisle. [To Henderson:] Thank you for your service, by the way. We don't hear that enough. We owe our freedom to men like you – men and women like you, I guess.

HENDERSON: No regrets, Kip. These colors don't run.

KNIGHTLEY: Sir, moving beyond this passionate rhetoric, which is clearly coming from the heart and not some rehearsed *script written by party advisors,* [back to the index cards] *are you prepared to cite specific instances in which Ms. Alcoe's suspected socialist bent has been reflected in her day-to-day duties as city councilwoman?*

[Edited out of final broadcast:]

KNIGHTLEY [raising the football signal for time-out]: *I mean, we know what they are, we're right there with you, but you should really be the one to say. Is there some other stuff you got to...?*

HENDERSON: *You think the broomstick stuff and street thing's gonna be enough of a kill shot? I mean, I got some other shit to fill the space, but I don't wanna bog things down and look too mean, you know? Or maybe y'all got shit the lawyers say you can't say but I can...?*

KNIGHTLEY: *We don't have anything but what people tell us. It should be fine. You know, just keep it simple, um, señor.*

HENDERSON [laughing]: *It's stupid. Keep it simple, stupid.*

KNIGHTLEY: *In this ward, sir, it's either/or.* [Both men laugh and cannot stop through three aborted tries to pick things up, during which Knightley calls for a tissue to blot the tears of joy both men have shed, then nods for Henderson to start as soon as he can force his face back into a frown.]

HENDERSON [several minutes later]: *These aren't unfounded worries, Kip. A'course I got specifics. Let's see, which one, eenie-meenie...* [respectful laughing, this bout retained for broadcast] ... *No, well, yes Kip, there is one specific example I've repeated to astounded Freeburg citizens all along the trail this year, from pancake breakfasts to spaghetti dinners, and many have been kind enough to share their belief that it comes so close to perfectly illustrating Ms. Alcoe's wealth-robbing motives that it basically eliminates having to cite any other examples. I mean, you be the judge and jury, Kip. See if you agree. Well, first off, some of Freeburg's most drug-addled hermits would be lying if they said they hadn't heard of Mrs. Alcoe's well-publicized family history of witchcraft and psychic tomfoolery. This way of life actually forms what I can only assume to be a huge section of the foundation of daily governance for our dear-but-clearly-deluded-and-out-of-touch-with-time neighbor to the east, Cassadaga. I don't know if you know this, Kip, but the mayor over there gives psychic readings at the county fair every year. My wife had one and he was dead wrong about everything. But not just that. He told Peggy, that's my wife, that they try to see the future before voting on any new ordinances and such over there. So that'll tell you something right there. Who can see the future, Kip? But, hey, lookee here, wouldn't you know – and this is what I'm getting at here, Kip – that way of doing the people's business has finally crept its way over into Freeburg: in the clutch of one of Cassadaga's most well-educated exports. We're talking about Ms. Alcoe now, of course. Well, maybe you're thinking: Here's a former teacher, smart as a whip, right? So she says. And so what? Karl Marx, you may recall, Kip, was well-educated too, and that didn't keep him from coming up with the philosophy of socialism and defending it to the death. Albert Einstein? Great physicist, sure. But also a socialist. Emma Goldman? Clearly a Goldberg. So you see, Kip, we need to leave the governing up to those folks capable of doing it without ruining everything we've worked so hard to achieve here in this great nation, the freedom we've won through hard work and sacrifice, you know? First it's socialized hospitals and pretty soon they're socializing my branch of First United Trust. What then? The Wal-Mart? C'mon.* [Knightley shakes head morosely:] *Now, a lot of you're probably asking how this type of stuff could ever wreak any havoc here in Freeburg. We're not talking foreign policy or nothing. Well, I'll tell you how: Not a half-year ago, Freeburg Councilmen – and Councilwoman, can't forget her – they're fighting their yearly duel to dole out the people's quickly sinking revenues for some street resurfacing projects, okay? This here is when Ms. Alcoe's gypsy-socialist roots could no longer be denied. Over here, her colleagues are lobbying for this or that repair of the worst streets in their own wards or maybe, and this takes some selflessness here, maybe they're pushing for this street over here in somebody else's wards that's got some good prospects for a little bit of* economic development or community redevelopment and so forth. So what's Ms. Alcoe's stance? I'll tell you, Kip [facing camera]: She could think of no other way but to draw straws, fellow citizens, and, hey, just let all these contracts get rewarded on chance. Mojo, Kip. [Facing Knightley, whose head is wagging:] And, I can't lie; that makes me wonder why we didn't spend more time putting all this red flag waving to rest when we were over there, on the ground. [Facing camera:] It doesn't belong here. Not in my country. Not in Freeburg. [Facing Knightley, whose head is nodding and squinting thoughtfully:] It needs to be stopped. Ms. Alcoe [facing camera] needs to be stopped. Are we choosing our next city treasurer or police chief with the same divining rod? Maybe you can consult the I, Ching to figure out which neighborhood gets the next pocket park. Why not? [Facing Knightley to share in his snicker, then camera again:] And, what's even more worryful for a lot of the voters I've been talking with, Ms. Alcoe, is this: How often will you be tapping into those deep, dark roots of yours back home for help steering the biggest slice of the pie back to your ward, the poorest one in the city? Council chair's gotta look out for the whole city, Ms. Alcoe, not her own little f-ee-fdom.

KNIGHTLEY [facing Henderson]: Sir, wow. As you predicted, that was a crystal clear and pure distillation of what I must say is one solidly built platform – [facing camera] brought to you exclusively by Action News 1 – [facing Henderson] with no room or a second more to squeeze any more planks in there. [Facing camera, reading monitor underneath:] One would expect such biting criticism to prompt an immediate and vehement counter-offensive from an opponent who wants to represent all of Freeburg and hold the Council gavel; and yet, Ms. Alcoe continues to decline repeated invitations to attend her own taping of Good Evening, Sunshine! to air her defense. During an abbreviated phone interview this afternoon, in fact, Ms. Alcoe's only remark was something to the effect of, 'Why don't you just go [BLEEP] Henderson's [BLEEP], Kip.' [To Henderson, whose eyes are bugging:] Hardly the essence of civilized debate *there.* [To camera:] *Our guest tonight, conservative opponent Pat Henderson – war hero, Freeburg native, civic-minded community banker – points to this reluctance as proof that his allegations are not only well-founded but proof of his superior credentials as a leader for Freeburg. As the founders intended, though, it's the volunteer voters that get the privilege of letting Mr. Henderson know soon enough just how right they think he is – not to mention what they feel about Ms. Alcoe's medium-minded methods.* [Oooo, mouths Henderson off screen] *As always, Freeburg, this is Kip Knightley, Action News 1, and that was another sunset.* [Knightley slashes his throat with a hand and wink at Henderson.]

HENDERSON [patting Knightley's knee]: *Nice job, Kip. I got you.*

KNIGHTLEY [blushing]: *My pleasure, sir. Hey, thanks again for your service."*

* * *

Just west of Main Street in downtown Freeburg, a prototypically deflowered, denuded, devalued, deserted and defamed business corridor, Katie's black-and-tan Mercedes lost all anonymity and became, for every pedestrian and porch dweller we passed, an object of wildly divergent assumptions. Some rolled their eyes and smirked: *Show-offs.* Some tugged their children closer or averted their eyes: *Drug dealers.* Some raised their brows and lifted their chins in two, quick-but-distinct escalations: *Shoppers.* Many ogled lustfully like a tenderloin was rolling past on a cart or the trunk was an actual ass: *Mm-mmm.* I could swear that a few even looked tearfully envious: *Please, God.* The cops, on the clock for making these types of assumptions, were the best at it and seemed to pass through each of these options in studied succession before checking their work by running the plates. I could only assume myself why Katie wanted to roll her window down with the air conditioning on. *Celebrity.*

"You can take Michigan all the way out to the spring," said Wiley, slumped beside me in the backseat. At least he'd showered and changed into some shorts and an Izod polo, his one foot wearing a flip-flop. *How many footless men roamed the earth?* I felt guilty for wondering. He smelled like Irish Spring and syrup from the waffles Katie'd found in the freezer and insisted he finish before we'd left. He'd looked fragile chewing, like his teeth were always on the verge of crumbling or snapping off at the gums, and he still looked fragile in the car: His thin, drawn face was the stem for a dwindling head of dandelion seeds, each threatening flight with the subtlest of breezes. He strained his stringy arms to put a veiny hand on my mother's shoulder in the front passenger seat.

"You're ready for this," he predicted with no hint of a question mark. She said, "We're ready for this," in the same tone of affirmation. He leaned back in the seat. Something unspoken seemed to pass between them, and their eyes closed in unison, as if by remote. He'd just summarized the *Good Evening, Sunshine!* interview to us – with striking accuracy, the record shows – and seemed exhausted by the effort. I fantasized for a spell about what it would have been like to have had a father such as Wiley Alcoe.

This old neighborhood of brownstones, Tudors and bungalows immediately surrounding downtown used to be where many of its most affluent residents wanted to live with their forward mobility. Doctors and merchants, young lawyers and loan officers. As their descendants evolved and sprawled out to the country, it became where they'd wanted their tenants to live. So the once-grand houses had been segmented into smaller spaces, with government subsidies paying to keep most of them filled, many well above the occupancy limits. Some were demolished after fires or disuse; in their places came rowhouses, ramshackle chattels, homeless camps or tiny fields of waist-high weeds. Boards became the windows on every other house you'd pass, rats and squatters the new occupants. By and by, the place came to be populated by an uneasy mixture of ethnicities with the same pluck to escape as their forebears but insufficient work at living wages to provide the necessary hope for doing it. This particular brand of malaise has been proven to digress, time and again, into a stupor of neglect, desperation and despair, from which many inhabitants will begin to view activities such as slinging drugs in public, flicking off police cruisers or littering the landscape as perfectly acceptable displays of cultural rebellion, something you do to say, "Fuck this place and fuck you, too."

Grace Alcoe didn't live in this part of her ward, but she passed through it almost every day, on her way to and from work, the store, the hair dresser. She walked up and down its streets, too, got to know who lived there and what they hated about doing so. She tried to relate. She rode along with shift commanders, watched gangs use their youngest members to take the greatest risks, held community juntas that no one attended. Many have reported sensing in Grace what one jobless former constituent described as "a heart." With a mother like Emily Alcoe, it had been an inevitable development.

On the far western edge of this existential crater, the homes became single-family again, most proudly manicured. Another mile on and you found Grace Alcoe's charred, brick husk of a two-story prairie box, another mile shy of Freedom Spring and the county park that enrobed it. Grace liked to walk there, in the winters especially, to feel the pull of time; for countless millennia, the spring has drawn manatees to bask in its steady gush of 79 degrees Fahrenheit, and this would make her feel both enjoined with and detached from the chaotic universe. She liked to think of how Ponce de Leon had once passed through here on his conquest that had as its guise a quixotic hunt for a mystical fountain of youth. *How savage and stupid the civilized*, she'd once written at this spot. Sometimes, she brought her students' poems to grade along the spring run shore; usually, though, only good poems would suit the surroundings, so she'd have a book with her in her bag. After her husband of 32 years, a fellow English teacher named Aaron Bridge, died of a stroke one night in bed, right after they'd made love, quiet times at home with a book had lost every glint of their charm. In mere months, she came across a way to stave off the loneliness. Wearing through shoes, going door-to-door through some of her city's worst neighborhoods, hadn't seemed like a chore at all; being alone like her father – that would have been hell.

"She won with five-hunnert bucks," bragged Wiley as we approached her road, Elm Lane. "She bought signs with it, put one on the corner of every street she went to. Four candidates in the primary, she gets 66 percent of the vote. A slaughter. Don't even need a general for a win like that. Now, the competition wasn't what you'd call stiff – well, the high school kid was, but the barmaid going to phlebotomy school wasn't. And the other guy, some used car salesman, he was just bitter that he got turned down for some variance he needed to expand his car lot a block in every direction."

Katie pulled into the driveway without being told which one it was. Black wisps of smoke damage wrapped from the back around the left side of the house. Half the roof had caved in onto the second floor, the section surrounding the chimney. The shin-high lawn was still littered with sodden mattresses and scorched remnants of curtains and bedspreads. Wiley stared at all of it but somehow none of it, too – through it.

"It's okay," he said, handing me a set of keys. "You go on ahead. Just be careful. Can't get up the stairs so don't try. Just leave my wheelchair beside the car."

The front door was jammed, the paint glued to a warped frame. I shouldered it open and froze as plaster fell from cracks in the ceiling. I went in first, but, once inside, they pushed to point position.

"Scoot," said my mother. "You looking for the boogie man?"

"Roaches, probably," said Katie. "Don't worry: We'll get 'em, baby brother!"

We all seemed to be looking for different things.

Katie scanned family photos on the built-in shelves crammed with books, the framed expressionist paintings, penciled portraits and charcoal sketches of Key West landscapes that cluttered the first floor walls that weren't stained amber or stripped by fire to the frames.

"They're her husband's," she announced. "Some good shit,

right?" My mother ignored her. "Shush," she said, as she went about listening with her eyes, watching with her ears. "Your voice is a sledgehammer."

I believed it. The streams of plaster dust kept falling in places, usually when any of us stepped on a particularly creaky board. The whole house groaned in protest when a wind picked up outside or someone leaned against a door jamb. On the burnt side of the living room, one panel of leather-bound books formed a wall of wasted bacon above the couch where firefighters reportedly had found Grace's remains. It had been reduced to a frail skeleton encasing the metal, fold-out bed inside. I averted my eyes to the smoke-filmed window by the fireplace and nearly left my feet when I saw Wiley's figure trying to see through it.

"Want help getting in Mr. Alcoe?" I yelled out to another river of dust falling on my forehead. "You okay?"

"Can't get around in there," he said. "But you're on the right track."

"You think?" I asked. I was looking for just one thing, though I hadn't told anyone what it was, and I actually appreciated the blind encouragement that held within it a faith that didn't seem the least bit foolish.

"There's definitely something here we're supposed to find," added my mother, staring at the top corners of the dining room. "Hope the firemen got here in time."

I checked the kitchen cabinets, even the fridge and freezer. I poked my head into the laundry room and saw where the gas line and boiler had once met. Their remnants were shrapnel stuck into the burnt and splintered wood of the walls and even the front and one side of the washer and dryer. I opened those, too. In the living room, I fingered at the artwork. The dining room china cabinet had no china but instead a scattershot collection of worldly souvenirs like miniature pygmy masks, Russian nesting dolls and Faberge eggs tucked in amongst at least two dozen pickling jars and corked bottles of apothecary herbs, dried flowers, strips of bark and oils. Some were labeled with exotic-sounding names and helpful parenthetical reminders: "FOXGLOVE (heart)," "NIGHT PRIMROSE (arthritis/eczema/menopause)," "CINCHONA BARK (headache/sciatica/cramps)," "LEOPARD'S BANE (coldness/diuretic/night sweat)," "CARAWAY (memory)," "ANISE (nightmares)" ... Anything sounding vaguely familiar was being used for unfamiliar remedies. I wondered how much of this the pharmaceutical giants already knew.

"Looks like Grace was cooking up the magic potions," I said. "Can't find my dried toad or baby's blood anywhere, though."

"It's right there behind your brain, stoop," said Katie from the tiny downstairs bathroom under the stairs.

"So what?" added Wiley from somewhere outside. "She studied Ayurveda. It's older than dirt, you know. Older than you, that's for sure." I tried to find him in the windows. How he could hear anything, much less through the walls, confounded me.

My mother came into the dining room from the kitchen. She propped a hand against the dining room table, closed her eyes and swooned as if about to pass out. A small patch of plaster fell onto her head, leaving her hair and one side of her face dusted with powder, but she didn't startle.

"Mom?" "Shush. Grace?"

She opened her eyes and perked up a brow.

"What?" I asked.

"I don't know," she said, eyes closed again. "Why don't you ask your Dad? Something, though. Keep looking."

"Look for what?" I wanted to know. I stomped my foot and more dust fell from a crack in the corner. I whispered, "I give up. It's my fault, but this is starting to feel ridiculous. Let's just get Wiley out of here. I'm sor..."

"Shut," said Katie.

"Let her be," Wiley added from the window.

I stomped my foot like a toddler. "Mom!" More plaster, miserable groaning.

Spell-bound, temples sweating, she traced with her eyes the banister up the stairs, back down along the wall beside it with the haphazardly arranged photos, knocked to odd angles by the firemen or splayed and smashed about the steps. Her blue eyes clouded over, then narrowed to focus. She jiggled her face to erase something there, sewed her eyes up again, lifted her branches for arms straight out like a crucified Jesus and let her head fall back in exaltation: "Hello, Grace," she said, starting to spin in big circles, again and again, her sagging arms like wings, her balance top-heavy and precarious.

"Mom," I said. "Mom?"

She was making a mess, even more of a mess, knocking over a heat-wilted bonsai tree here, the mummified skull of a saber-tooth tiger there, a book on a stand sculpted into a handgun, a seared-to-brown blob of a cross-legged Buddha, the crispy skeleton of a Japanese fan, the grayed bust of some writer who looked like my father, a Cherokee earthenware pot smashed to crumbs, a wobbly tower of black Shaker baskets, Shiva and Vishnu embracing in death, a corroded menorah – "Mom!" – the tall, preserved candle of Lisbon's St. Anthony, patron saint, say the books, of lost things and lost souls.

Her eyes were still sealed when she slowed to a stop and stomped her foot to bring her heels together at attention, the dining room floor all around her in shambles. Just before her eyes opened, her smile was agape, her head pointed upstairs, where the candle of St. Anthony had just toppled over and rolled with a thud from a waist-high chest onto the second-floor landing. We all stared in shock.

On the right was a bathroom, untouched by the flames; on the left, a foot shy of the stairs, the spilled roof was a water-soaked pile of timber, insulation and plaster.

"Shit," she said. Her eyes shined like topaz against the bruised walls behind her. Her teeth gleamed with the smile she couldn't disguise.

"Shit is right," Katie said, drifting away.

Katie moved toward the door, taking artwork off the walls to give to Wiley. My mother was examining the crash of culture she'd left on the floor in her wake. "Quite the thinker," she said. "Freeburg's loss. Well, and Wiley's..."

Before they could notice I'd floated to the foyer and mounted the stairs. "Honey, please," said my mother. Then I stepped on my father.

The glass had already been webbed through with cracks, the frame splintered and broken at two corners, but you could easily make out the inhabitants of the photo. I shook the shards to my feet and peeled the paper from its cardboard backing.

"C'mon, Saul," Katie said, "Get the lead out, you goon. This place is a ticking time-bomb."

It made sense, at least a lot more than before. At a table, in what looked like a meeting hall, my father's arm wrapped snug around her to grab her bare shoulder. They looked far too at ease to be getting old. The kiss was too soft, too unmannered, to be friendly. Behind them, I knew from sporadic experience, scrolled those time-tested strictures, the twelve steps to Serenity. In their eyes: comfort. In their pupils: lucidity. I peeled out the picture and looked at the back:

"My Saul," the poetess-teacher had written in red. "Not my first love, my last love. Two years clear."

At first I felt shock that a woman of Grace's pedigree could find anything like inspiration from my scar-headed father and his lackluster life, then I remembered where we were and then why and for whom. My eyes filled with tears. I tossed the picture over my shoulder and, as they charged like dung beetles to feast on the picture, I kept toeing upstairs toward St. Anthony's loot. In seconds, they were climbing, too. "Holy shit, Mom!" I screamed. "You'll kill us all!" I put a hand over my head and ducked down, as if that shielded me from harm. A pile of rubble shifted somewhere to our left, then another even closer. A joint moaned overhead. Unfazed, Katie went into the bathroom, opened a medicine cabinet, let out some bored air through her pursed lips, then she was peeing. "Katie, are you kidding me?"

"You don't pee?" asked my mother, snatching the candle off the floor in front of the cabinet and dropping it into a sagging pocket of her neon-green mumu. She tugged at the cabinet doors. "Locked. Bring it down. We'll take an ax to this bitch."

Katie and I each took a side and followed her bumpily down

the stairs. Well-indoctrinated by the Hollywood establishment, I braced for the ceiling, at any moment, to cascade to the floor directly behind us and erupt in a roar of flames that would require, for our lives to be spared, a perilous dive from the front porch to the safety of the lawn below. But nothing like that happened.

On the front sidewalk, Wiley scratched his scalp and left a scribble of red lines behind. The cabinet, of cherry wood with Asian gardens etched into the doors, gleamed like its own fruit in the sun. None of her old keys fit. We stood around, hands on the hips, frowny-faced. Then, in a daze that turned divinely reflective, I became, for a time, a real Captain America.

I yanked a fat keychain from my pocket, the old man's and mine linked together, and every color in the rainbow alighted in our eyes. I looked inside it, clean and serene.

The cabinet could have been stacked with cash inside or a cache of more journals. That would have been all right, I guess. But it wasn't. All we found was our future. There, on top of it all, was a statue of the Bab, Persia's first great hippie, looking as we all seem to look these days – annoyingly overjoyed.

Under him was Our future.

Chapter 12

WHEREAS, for centuries this Nation has discredited its humblest servants, the lot of whom have grown too disinclined to feel their words have any weight. Election Day should bring a time for (almost; see Addendum A) all to say how freedom rings. True democracy, in fact, demands that those who have a voice to speak, have ears to hear and hearts to hold should take their place among their neighbors and cast their will upon the record.

A hard rain was indeed a-falling that historic night in late May. No one took it as a bad omen, not even Katie or my mother. It was the first May as an adult I can remember so vividly, since it was my first May without having to medicate myself into servitude. I have only my father to thank for that.

Those with deep institutional memory at Freeburg City Hall have confirmed that, by far, no other cause had ever filled Council chambers even close to overflowing; in fact, the only other time more than a dozen people had shown up was when a rowdy klatch of RV park retirees had come to protest all the bees landing in their clubhouse pool from a farmer's hives next door. Democracy at work. Most often, as was the norm for most pre-democratic burgs, the lone attendees were near-deaf elders drawn to voice their mind on each new piece of legislation. Council members would put on their most engaged expressions as these old men and women recited their speeches from rote letters to the editor that, after thorough editing, they wouldn't even recognize in the

273

paper until they read their names. And then they'd read them to their kids over the phone.

In Freeburg's case, that near-deaf elder's name was Wittgenstein "Witt" Carroll III, a steel mill pensioner who lost three fingers in a rebar roll up in one of the old Cleveland mills. Witt was agape with bugged-out eyes that squally night in May, perhaps speechless for the first time ever. I shook his hand. He shook mine back. He tried to ask about the crowd, all furrowed brow and war vet cap, but I just smiled and walked away. An ambush, dear old-timer, doesn't call for any trumpets.

The chamber was a din of furtive whispers from some hundred mouths. More were wet outside, some running late. It felt like 1932 and people needed things called a weekend and a minimum wage. Every face offered encouragement in widely varied ways, but shared a fevered look of doubt – as if good things in this great land could only come in tiny waves that won't upset the bottom line. Back and forth, I stared into each set of skeptic eyes, forced every mouth into a smile like mine to prove my grit, thanking them all if only just for being there, just as they were, all lined in rows to make me feel alive again, with things to share. For that I owe much gratitude to Grace.

A gavel pounded on the dais. Damon Henderson, Council chair, would start the show. "Call to order," he announced. He tapped the microphone and shot a look to the side at the city clerk, who was adjusting the knob on a dusty console. "Sorry, folks," he said after a scream of interference. "Haven't used this thing in I don't know..."

The pledge, the roll call, just like school. A prayer. With pride, I watched my students' faces register alarm. "Separation of church and state, my ass," one of my more vocal charges couldn't help but say above a whisper. The old minutes: approved.

My hands were clammy. I wiped them down my pants and rocked, the ordinance we came with underneath my feet like flyers I was keeping from flying off into the wind.

The Council chair gave a quizzical look to the clerk, who nodded at his silent question, which forced him to ask, "Is there anyone who'd like to speak?" I grabbed the papers, stood and swept the room with my eyes before I stared at Henderson alone for my walk to the podium.

"Name and address, please."

"McGinty, Saul. 4910 Elm Lane," my new refurbished prairie box.

"I'm sorry, sir. You'll have to use the microphone."

"He said it's McGinty," yelled Serge from behind me.

"Saul McGinty," I leaned down and said. "Elm Lane. I teach history."

"And this is..." Henderson motions with his eyes to the papoose at my belly, slung comfortably around my shoulders. She'd been sleeping. I'd forgotten she was there.

"This is Ingrid, sir." I bounced in place.

"Red," said Red. Her orange hair hit the light in ways that mine and her mother's never had.

"And her mother is...?"

"Well, it's pretty much just me and her, I guess. Mr. Council President. If that's okay with you."

"Well, you both may speak, sir, three minutes," Henderson said, then he leaned back in his chair a little too comfortably. Didn't he know what was coming? I scooped a bottle out of my pocket and guided it to Ingrid's waiting mouth without looking, then I locked eyes with Henderson in a way that would tell him I'd come to speak these words to him and him alone.

"Sir, tonight, I am here, we are here, to begin a long walk. But how else to get where we're headed than by starting, right?" Henderson huffed while I took a deep breath and the whispers died down. "I should start at the start, the beginning, of this."

I looked all around me then back in his eyes.

"1783. The British were leaving, right? Dejected. They'd lost their new colonies to some rowdy rag-tags. So then what? Well, I'll tell you. They looked to the east, to another New World, and they staked their new claim to Australia's riches, in Botany Bay, 1788, with a boat-load of convicts behind barbed-wire walls. Who would care if they died when the natives got restless? Pretty soon there were thousands, tens of thousands of Great Britain's supposedly seditious worst. They spread out to new jails, then, by turns, they were released into the wild. They founded a country across a whole continent. They had babies and funerals, just like us. A hundred years passed, just a century's all, and, by 1915, they were firmly behind a new law that was passed, a requirement that every man was required to vote on referendums and, by 1924, all these Australian voters, the woman as well, had to vote or face fines in all federal races. Now, I ask you, what reason did..."

"I'm sorry, sir, really, this has been a truly riveting lesson in another country's history, but your time has expired. Please take your seat." Henderson's pink fleshy face had turned red with the strain of his thoughts, but still he eked out a smile of dominion.

"That's all right," I said, turning around with a smile.

"Is there anyone else? We've got work here tonight."

My mother was already standing behind me, assuming the podium, turning the page. "Annabelle Anderson," she said, then garbled an address like that teacher, Miss Othmar, in *Peanuts*. "... Well, I'll tell you – we'll tell you – the reason they did it, all these kids and grandkids of these felons and gunslingers. They were scared of things turning out something like this." She swept a big hand, underlining the dais. "What's that, you might say? Nothing there but the floor? Well, that star-gazer Carl Sagan called it one of the saddest lessons of history." She looked at the page. "If we been bamboozled enough, we tend to reject any evidence of the bamboozle, or something like that. We're no longer interested in finding out the truth, see? The bamboozle's done captured us. Like it's just too damn painful to accept, even to ourselves, that we been taken. 'Once you give a charlatan power over you,' the man said, 'you almost never get it back.'" She stared hard into Henderson's eyes, scanned the others to his left and right. "Let's see what the Aussies got right..."

"Ma'am, this is all fine and good, but we've got business to take care of tonight," Henderson said, looking at his colleagues to see if they agreed.

She checked her watch and looked up. "Seems I got more than

a minute to go, sir, so I'll tell it like this: Are the Aussies alone in this backward old outback, making everybody vote like a bunch of heathens? No, they're not, sir. They're not. You got Bolivia, Egpyt, Greece, Singapore, Italy, Peru – we're talking 30 in all. Need the list? Here!" She threw it forward and the sheets fanned out into a collage on the floor. "Maybe more, when the time comes." She paused for effect. *C'mon, Mom*, I was thinking.

"Hadn't heard a man can't get rich in those places, neither. Now let's look at the numbers, which, my son says, don't lie. In Australia, they got 95 percent on board, every election. Every. Election. How's about here? Well, lemme see here... There it is: 54! 54 lousy percent." She stopped, shook her head in shame, as if Freeburg Council assumed all the blame. "You see what all this gerrymuckering, this elitist Electoral College, these, these special interest love-ins all up and down the..."

Henderson jumped forward to fill the silence with something. "Ma'am, with all due respect, this is all starting to head in a very utopian direction here. And I'm not sure this talk is what's going to get the right potholes filled tonight, see? I'm sorry, really, but your time has expired. Now please take your seat."

Katie was standing there, taking the podium, taking her time, a well-studied monologist finally getting the grade she deserves. I was thinking about what could go wrong, then about how thinking gets you nowhere, that it always moves on to something else, like my mother thinking aloud in my ear – "...would you stop thinking about...!" – but also somewhere else entirely: for instance, how we all are former monkeys, former amoebas in the gunk, then how nice it would have been for my father to have seen this ... this *thing* he helped us do at last ... and then, everything that could go wrong was just outside the door, not just in here and now, this door, but anywhere and always, all doors, out every window, I saw the rain, and I saw Hawk, dreadlocks dripping, breath on the glass, and there behind him, Mr. Arbuckle, laying cable in the signal corps, back to HQ to radio more deadly artillery coordinates in; another window, Deb Diamond holding a phlegm-strangled baby screaming, and behind them, it's goiter man, gripping a penny and scratching and scratching and scratching the itch at his neck, at his throat, at my throat, at our throats. Then I squeezed my eyes shut, looked again. And they were gone. All of them. Just my heart thundered on. And the cleansing rain....

The room had hushed for the Emmy-winner's words. *My sis*, I thought. My home-run hitter, center stage. My blood surged into hers. Her presence, I presume, wasn't enough to pull the broadcast hacks away from other bits, stories with 1) murder; 2) mayhem; 3) malfeasance; 4) more than one of the above, but at least the *Eagle* was there, one man-boy in the back scribbling notes that would try but fail miserably to paint anything like a good picture of this, but at least a try, a heart for something heartfelt, something 101, but still: Katie received a card from that reporter, and he hadn't even tried to talk to me, chief organizer.

No worries – history was made: Four dozen YouTube videos collectively received some seventeen-million hits worldwide in just the coming week. It wouldn't matter that the *Eagle* ran the story on B6 the next day, below the weather. Another day, another quick rebuke.

"... and if ignorance is the greatest tool for oppressors," I heard Katie say,

"this is the greatest tool for empowerment and evolution, see?" I beamed and beamed. That's my sister, my smile said, not the eager DA or the eager grad student. Just Katie. Believing. "Silly to THINK, huh? Will we vote with a dart to the wall?" She turned to her left. "Will you, sir?" To her right. "Will you, ma'am?" Every head in the front row was shaking and mouthing their no. "Will you, sir?" she asked the Council President.

Henderson glared. A few of his colleagues were shaking their heads right along with the people. Katie, front and center, held her hold on Henderson's eyes at the center of the elevated stage: "No sir, not the dumbest KKKlansman, *I'd* think, would cast a vote for Master Obama, not on his wisest day." The audience laughed, every face relieved, a few Councilmen too. Smart as a whip, this tall glass of water, this. All of this was in the script, of course, but who would have noticed with this kind of performance? Laughter filled the room.

"Order," ordered Henderson, his gavel limp above the block. "This isn't soap opera time now, folks." Knock-knock. "It's business time. Ma'am, if you'd..."

"Forty-five seconds, sir," Katie said to shut him up. His colleagues shrugged. At least they seemed to have their wards in line. "We've come today with signatures, more than enough for this petition to ask the voters if they'd like to see this kind of thing in Freeburg next election day, in these voting districts anyway, maybe enough to get the whole county on board, see? Perhaps you know the author of this new law that we stand behind. No?" She glided up and slammed down a copy of the referendum before each Council member, then returned to the podium, carrying with her every set of eyes in every sort of frenzied stare. Even the asexual had to have been focused on the hips. She picked the stack of papers up and started reading, right on cue: "*WHEREAS...*"

"Madam, your time is up. Can we move on?" Henderson mouthed a question to the law director, who, nonplused if not enthralled by the proceedings, gave him a shrug to serve as legal tender. The gavel pounded to silence the crowd, half of whom were then standing and holding their phones out, recording. "I said your time's up, Miss, Mrs. Hollywood, there..."

Henderson looked at his colleagues, who seemed resigned, shamed, even curious enough to hear things out. No one would second his motion to move on to the agenda. He had to speak louder than the woman and her stage voice before him: "You would think, madam, that a federal, maybe a state referendum would be more, well, appropriate, for this, this, kind of magical mystery brand of fix-it-up glue you're proposing here. This here, this political venue of Freeburg, well, this is hardly the place to start these utopian kind of pipe dreams like you're imagining. I mean, maybe we do all own a part of this, in spirit, but ain't it true we ought to pick our representatives by virtue of the stock we own? I mean, I mean, stake we have in the fight, well ... um, like stockholders elect their boards, in proportion to each level of the stock they hold? The ownership they have in...? I mean..."

The *Eagle* reporter had given up trying to transcribe a complete quote from this dissenting voice. Like everyone else, he started recording the melee with his phone, it being history and all, which demanded a proper transcription. The paper would run the whole clip on its website, which soon enough, as we all know, would pretty much become the paper itself anyway. Half the audience was hissing and booing, the other half in shock. "Ladies and gentlemen, a vote ain't a right, *it's a privilege, ain't it?* Tell me I'm wrong. Can you tell me I'm wrong?"

"You're damn wrong, fool, now shut your trap!" yelled Serge. It was his turn. Our muscle. A knot of nerves, Serge stood there at the lectern in his black baggy suit to round his shoulders down and give him harmless lines. (I'd bought it for him.) He was visibly shaking but spoke with as much conviction as the rest of us: "I can't thank with all your banker talk. Serge Arredondo, Walnut Circle. *WHEREAS...*"

I screamed it with him in my head: *WHEREAS!*

The room was spinning, in a good way, like a ride. Most had left their chairs to stand to give their phones a better view. I turned to see, two rows behind, if the gaggle of my most determined students knew their time had come. Already, they were filing up the aisle. They took their place, but kept their phones recording.

In unison: "Freeburg *Manatees! WHEREAS...!*"

My Uncle Floyd, wife No. Four beaming from the audience: "(...deep coughing...) *WHEREAS...!*"

The mayor of Daytona Beach: "*WHEREAS...!*"

A local Baha'i leader: "*WHEREAS...!*"

Elder Wiley Alcoe, around his neck an ankh of eternal peace: "*WHEREAS...!*"

Student body president of Stetson University: "*WHEREAS...!*"

Volusia League of Citizens: "*WHEREAS...!*"

My garbage man: "*WHEREAS...!*"

The gavel was below the roar, ignored, disgraced. Chairman Henderson was on his feet, his fleshy face a jumbled mess of words no one could hear, not even him. Witt Carroll couldn't figure out that his little flip-phone didn't have a camera. I raised my hands and all was hushed. "Now listen here!" the chairman yelled. "I hope you've brought along a sack of money to pay for all of this, this *crap!* 'Cause..."

"You listen *here!*" Serge yelled, looking back at me. I nodded and Serge pressed play on the tiny hand recorder that we'd found in that beautiful cabinet in Emily Alcoe's house, my house today. I smiled. Almost the whole room did.

The tape-recorded voice of Miss Emmy's little girl all grown up ascended to the water-damaged ceiling tiles, the speakers crackling, even Henderson a flub of quiet, dazed by death: "... You'd think that big old ball'd be getting pretty hard to push uphill by now, you *trough-sloppin' pig.* How 'bout you step aside and let us give a little push? ... *BE IT ORDAINED*, in Section I., Freeburg declares that all those who must register their vehicles, identities, their guns and dogs, who pay taxes and serve at their country's demand to pay the ultimate sacrifice, who must work to earn their keep or suffer under the shackles of physical and/or mental duress, should also be subject to cursory voting [see exceptions, Addendum A], by which it is hoped that the great majority of its populace will ultimately evolve to one more acquainted and attuned with the system set forth to guide them in their own individual pursuits of happiness and harmony. And then of course there's Section II.

(Now watch this shush them greedophilic mouths up like a perfiderole:) "To cultivate a budget that's both fair and cost-effective, this bold new plan must find some fault in all those clinging to their lazy freedom. When any voter made to register is absent from the virtual polling place, a fine commensurate to speeding through a school zone shall be levied, with driver's license revocation until all fines are paid in full. With this new fund we'll build a well of eager, educated voters with all the stolid bricks of those electing carelessness instead. And feel free to muddy all this up with your Addendum this and Addendum that,

Henderson and Company. We'll understand. And with that, I'll just say God bless, the one God of every one of the prophets, see?"

Wiley's whimpering was the only sound I could hear by the time Grace's voice was gone. That, and a little cooing from below in the Red department. I looked down and a long string of drool reached from her mouth to the floor, her eyes, like all of ours, fixed in a trance on Henderson, who was gathering his papers and leaving the chambers in a huff, staring at his feet a little too forcefully. Det. Escondido left behind him, two patrolmen in tow. We all know what happened to Henderson. No use going into all that again.

Then it was nothing but applause and tears. An elderly woman passed out into the outside aisle, knocking down a picture of the mayor. Pretty much no one even knew his name anyway. I turned to leave, smiling, and that's when the clapping and cheering escalated to a din. I joined in. I'd never really clapped for everybody before. None of us ever had.

The rest of the agenda was abandoned by the audience. By then, the rain had stopped outside. It was dark and wet but clear. I could see my mother winding her way through the throngs of people, handing out oranges and lining up appointments. Everyone was smiling. And then, there ahead of me, I saw Rebecca in the mist of a sewer grate, her red hair shining almost as brightly as her eyes. My knees turned to jelly. She was looking at Ingrid. Ingrid was looking at her. The applause rolled outside into the night and was just as loud or seemed that way. I blushed because that's what men like me do. Red beamed. That reporter with the phone camera was standing there, turning in circles to capture it all. It felt like everyone was watching.

Addendum A
[REDACTED]